Midnight Rambler

Third book in The Psychological Thrillers series

CHRIS SIMMS

Other novels by Chris Simms:

The Psychological Thrillers
Outside the White Lines
Pecking Order
Midnight Rambler

The Supernatural Thrillers
Sing Me To Sleep
Dead Gorgeous

Jon Spicer Series
Killing the Beasts
Shifting Skin
Savage Moon
Hell's Fire
The Edge
Cut Adrift
Sleeping Dogs
Death Games
Dark Angel

DC Iona Khan Series
Scratch Deeper
A Price To Pay

DC Sean Blake Series
Loose Tongues
Marked Men

Copyright © 2024 Chris Simms

The right of Chris Simms to be identified as the author of this work has been asserted by him in accordance with the Copyright, Designs and Patents Act 1988.

All rights reserved.

ISBN: 9798324342081

To Dan.

Thanks for all the fascinating insights (and gruesome details!).

PART 1

CHRIS SIMMS

CHAPTER 1

Come on, come on, where the hell are you? Ryan Lamb slung the camera's strap over his shoulder and began patting the various pockets of his ski coat. 'La-la, it's me,' he said into the phone wedged against the side of his face. 'I just got...you know. Another. It's just pinged up.'

His mind settled briefly on the code that had appeared on his phone less than two minutes before. He'd immediately opened the what3words app, fed the code in, and retrieved the location. Pinnington Street, Salford. Just outside a building at the end of the road. From his and Carla's place, a five-minute walk, maximum. But this message also had a time. 10.20 pm. Normally, he'd just receive a location and get there as fast as possible. There'd never been a time as well. He frowned: how was it even possible for there to be a time? It didn't make sense.

The fingers of his free hand were now ferreting at the thigh pockets of his black cargo trousers. A tiny clink of metal. What the hell were they doing there? 'Anyway, there's pizza on the side and I left you a little something in the fridge.' The thought of her face when she discovered the chocolate dessert made him smile as he produced his keys and deadlocked the door. 'See you in a bit. Bye!'

Out on the street, he checked the time: 10.04 pm. Sixteen minutes to get there. Easy. Maybe the person who'd been sending him the messages finally wanted to meet? Could that be it? But why the rush? And why this time of night? And what was even at the top of Pinnington Street? Striding fast, he brought up the app once more, switched to satellite view and zoomed in.

A typical urban road. The roofs of the buildings that lined it didn't look big. So, a residential terrace, probably. There were certainly a fair number of parked cars clogging the road. A bus stop. A pelican crossing. Didn't look like the type of place where there'd be a pub or bar or any kind of place to meet. He homed in on the exact three-metre square denoted by the code. Left hand-side of the road, directly before the doorway of a building near the junction.

He glanced up from his screen, saw Spear Street was on his left. He could cut down it and then turn onto Hilton. It would add a couple of minutes, but the route would take him past the Sussman Gallery. He couldn't resist. This time of night, it would be shut. No chance of being spotted by Ivan, the owner. Ryan couldn't think of anything more cringe-worthy than being caught hovering outside, peering in at the poster for his own exhibition.

He thought about the show opening in just three days' time. My own photography exhibition. He shook his head and managed to twist the burst of incredulous laughter into a stupid little cough. Mine! Just considering it powered him forward. Long legs scissoring, he skirted round a dawdling couple, one hand clamped on his CanonEOS 850D to stop it thudding against his hip. In his head, he was floating through the gallery's side room that had been allocated for his images. Yeah, it was only a side room. But every journey starts with a single step, right? Ivan had already said *Vulpine Plunderer* needed to be up front. Hero of the show. It was, after all, the shot that had kick-started everything. The flood of reactions on Instagram and Pinterest. The sudden surge of traffic to his website.

Interviews with photography bloggers.

And then, of course, the anonymous codes arriving on his phone.

How many of the mysterious alerts had resulted in shots that formed part of the forthcoming exhibition? The massive brawl outside The Sawyer's Arms on Deansgate. The office building ablaze beside the Oldham Road. The multi-car pile-up on the Mancunian Way. He'd taken his shots of that particular accident from a flyover, looking straight down onto the tableau of wrecked vehicles. How had Ivan described the resulting triptych of images? As if captured by the eye of God.

And tonight: what sort of image would result from tonight's alert? Pinnington didn't look like the type of street for a car crash. Maybe a house fire? A burglary? Or something else. Something new. He felt a twinge of excitement before a new thought almost froze him mid-stride.

What if the person wanted money? Christ, was that what the latest message was about? To demand a cut of his earnings? But the gallery owner didn't pay upfront. It was commission only, and that's if anything even sold. Did the person not realise that's how it worked?

Directly ahead, he could make out a small sign that cast a tapering shadow down exposed brickwork. The Sussman Gallery. The lettering Ivan had chosen was understated. Refined. He drew alongside the large window and risked a sideways glance. For a fleeting moment, his own image filled the glass. The ones who used to pick on him at school called him Lanky Lamb. The figure before him was tall and, yes, still thin. A beany cap jammed down over dark straggly hair. A pair of black-framed glasses. The thick lenses flashed silver as he stepped through the pool of light. Reflections within reflections.

Inside the gallery, a few strategic spotlights had been left on. They picked out the larger works on the walls. Manchester cityscapes. Paintings and photos. Some a blend of the two. Work by artists he'd long held in awe. The poster about his coming exhibition was mounted on an easel directly behind the glass. Ryan checked no one else was on the narrow street before feasting on the words.

Opening this Monday: *Urban Trauma*. Ryan Lamb.

He let his gaze rest on the final two words. Ryan Lamb. Just seeing his name like that, as part of a proper poster. Tears of pride caused the words to shimmer. It didn't matter, he could have recited them out loud.

Unflinching in nature, the images captured by Ryan Lamb on his midnight ramblings force the viewer to witness the struggles – often brutal – that play out in the heart of the city. "More than a street photographer, Lamb is a contemporary chronicler extraordinaire." Julian Templeforth.

Ryan Lamb, aged 25, is a graduate of The University of Salford. This is his inaugural exhibition.

Ryan blinked his eyes so he could focus on the Julian Templeforth quote. OK, the man was a good friend of Ivan's and he was always happy to plug newcomers to Manchester's art scene. Nevertheless, the bloke was a genuine, certified icon of the city.

The lower half of the poster was devoted to three images. Largest was *Vulpine Plunderer*. The fox had taken Ryan by surprise, not that he'd ever admitted it. Well, only to Carla. It was the man who'd eventually keeled over on the bus shelter's bench that had been his actual target.

Sensing an opportunity, Ryan had tracked him as he'd staggered away from the food place on Portland Street. The bloke hadn't made it past that first bus shelter. For a bit, he'd sat there staring dumbly at the carton balanced on his lap. Ryan had loitered on the other side of the road, using the opportunity to work out his shot. He'd gone out with a fast lens on his Canon, knowing levels of light would be poor. Here, away from Portland Street, they were dimmer still. He'd increased his ISO setting to 800, widened the aperture and slowed the shutter speed, hoping the camera's IS feature would compensate for any movement of his hands. The man got the carton lid open, but then his chin had slowly begun to sag. Soon after, the snores started and, inch by inch, he'd toppled to the side.

Ryan had moved forward to the middle of the street and crouched down, not caring if a cab beeped him. And that was when the fox must have ghosted out of an alley. First Ryan knew, it had slid into the shelter where it began to delicately tease the burger from the bun. Had the meat been too hot? Ryan would never know. But the animal had drawn its lips back, and that's what his shot had captured: a grinning fox relieving a snoring man of his food.

His phone vibrated. Carla, home already? No: it was from him. If it was a him. This new message consisted of a single word. *Hurry.*

CHAPTER 2

The turning into Pinnington Street was just ahead. No echoing sirens or pulsing blue lights. So unlikely to be a car crash or similar type of accident. No surprise there; the message had a specific time. 10.20 pm. So, this wasn't about an incident for Ryan to capture on film. Not unless whoever was sending the messages could now see into the future. He checked his phone. Three minutes early. What else could it be but a meeting?

He and Carla had often discussed where the person who sent the messages could be getting their information. Carla was convinced it was some kind of geek who'd hacked into the emergency services' communications network. An acne-ridden teenage boy, alone in his sad bedroom.

Ryan rounded the corner and surveyed the road ahead. It had been terraced houses, once. But the ground-floors of the buildings at the top end of the street had been converted into a little row of shops. All closed. A couple of offices, also shut. Only the convenience store called Pop-In still had its lights on. Everything was quiet. No one was in sight. He noticed a car had been double-parked right outside the late-night shop. He checked the app: the location appeared to be right on its front doorstep. He hesitated. This felt odd. Instead of crossing the road, Ryan checked behind him. A recessed doorway of an estate agents. He approached it slowly, unsure if anyone could be hiding in the deep shadows at the back. 'Hello?'

No reply. He used his phone's torch to take a better look. Nothing. He scanned the property notices filling the windows. Flat rentals in converted warehouses and mills; just like the one he and Carla lived in. Except these, being in Salford, were a notch cheaper than theirs.

A muffled shout sounded from somewhere. He turned, eyes immediately drawn to the convenience store. Enormous window stickers obscured any view inside. A plump loaf of bread. A tray of eggs. Three cartons of milk: skimmed, semi-skinned and full fat. Another shout, followed by a cry of anguish. Glass smashed and Ryan's heart was suddenly thudding. Maybe the sound was coming from a TV? But the first-floor windows above the shop were all closed, the rooms unlit. Another raised voice. Male, like the one before. The door opened suddenly and a figure wearing a balaclava stepped out and immediately looked left and right. Was that a hammer in his hand? Ryan moved further back into the doorway. The person twisted his head. 'Move! Come on, fam!'

Another crash of glass followed by a high-pitched cackle. A second figure appeared, face also obscured by a balaclava. This one a bit taller. Maybe six foot? He had a machete in one hand and a holdall in the other. As he let out a whoop, the first person to emerge reached the side of the double-parked vehicle. He pulled the driver's door open and jumped in. Glass clinked as the second figure placed the bag and machete in the boot. The engine started to rev as he jogged round to the passenger side.

Ryan realised he was clutching his phone. He raised it and pressed record as the vehicle's lights came on and it sped off up the street. Once it had turned the corner, Ryan pocketed his phone and approached the shop. What he was seeing felt like a recording. As if he was watching footage that someone else had shot. A hand-held camera, things bobbing and jerking with each step. Even his shallow breathing sounded like it was a sound effect.

The shop's door was half open and he peered through the gap. First thing was a broken CCTV camera. It lay among crisp packets and sweets scattered across the floor. And beyond them, in front of the counter...Christ, oh Christ. A middle-aged man lying on his face. A large pool of blood spreading out from beneath his head. Ryan realised there were also drips of blood running down the counter's front. The till had been turned sideways; its drawer fully open. He noticed a bent bracket and wires hanging from the wall above. Where the CCTV had been positioned.

He got several shots of the wrecked till, then a close-up of the blood streaks. Next, he took a couple of the man on the floor. A display stand lay across his lower legs, a few packets of Moams clinging to the wire hooks. The bright greens and yellows on the cellophane sat really well with the redness of the blood.

Ryan crouched down for a better angle and was lifting the camera to his face when he heard a whimper. The sound caused him to stop. He blinked with shock as the realisation of what he was doing hit home. If the camera hadn't been attached to the strap round his neck, it would have dropped to the floor. Another whimper. He stood. Do something, you twat!

Dreading what might be there, he looked behind the counter. Oh my God – it was a little old woman. She was propped against some shelving units, blood pouring from her nose. White hair was in a neat bun on top of her head. Hands shaking in her lap. He wanted to give her a hug. 'Hey, are you OK?'

Her head turned and she stared blankly past him.

'Don't worry. I'm getting help' Ryan said, taking his phone out and dialling 999.

A voice was on the other end of the line. 'Hello,' he said, 'there's been a robbery. Police and ambulance.' He glanced down at the stricken man. 'There's...there's a lot of blood. The late-night store at the top of Pinnington Street, Salford.'

#

Carla Bell tongued chocolate dessert from the upturned teaspoon in her mouth. She was sitting at the breakfast bar of the little apartment's galley kitchen, phone propped against a stubby pepper grinder.

'Oh my God, Carla,' said the woman on the screen. 'I think I just saw your come face.'

Carla's half-closed eyes snapped fully open as her cheeks flushed. 'Simone!' A dark fleck escaped onto her bottom lip and she scooped it back into her mouth with the tip of her little finger.

'Look at you. Such an English rose.'

She waved a V sign at the screen.

'Seriously, girl. That pudding and you should just get a room.'

She shook her head in despair and began scraping at the little pot once again.

'So,' Simone's voice had lost some of its light-hearted tone, 'you have told him?'

She slid the spoon from her mouth, put the now-empty pot down and sighed.

'Carla, what the fuck? Why not?'

'Well, he's not here for a start.'

'I mean in general. You said last week you were –'

Carla clamped her head between her palms and let out a strangled groan. 'You didn't see his face. That time when I...you know, the time with Marcus.'

'Marcus, honey, is gay.'

'I know that! But Ryan didn't. God, his face. He made me promise I'd never dance with another man like that again.'

'Carla, what's happening now is a whole world away from backing your peachy little arse into someone's –'

'Tonight, OK? I'll tell him tonight.'

'You better. What that creep did; Ryan needs to know. Where is he, anyway?'

She checked the dessert pot. Definitely empty. Bugger. 'Could eat another one of those.'

'Lucky bitch. I eat one and that's it. Water for the rest of the day.'

'Really?'

'Oh yeah.'

'But you're so tall. So slim.'

'Because I don't eat stuff like that. Plus, Fiona scares the living crap out of me.'

Carla pictured the fearsome owner of the Q2 agency. There wasn't a model who worked there that wasn't terrified of the woman.

'Hang on,' Simone chided. 'You changed the damned subject.'

Carla picked up her phone and sauntered towards the front window. The city sparkled beyond it. She peered at the side road below, watched a couple forlornly trying to flag a passing Uber. 'Out. One of his little late-night jaunts.'

CHAPTER 3

'Help's almost here,' Ryan said to the old lady. He suspected she was concussed. That or in shock. One of the men had punched her. She'd tried to mime the action, but with her thumb wrapped in her fist. 'Boof' was the sound she'd used. He'd torn open a pack of toilet rolls and formed two wedges of tissue, indicated that she should plug her nostrils and then tip her head back. A dark green fleece with a Pop-In badge was hanging from the door into a storeroom. He draped it over her shoulders.

The distant screech of sirens was growing in strength.

'OK, stay there.' He made a patting motion with both hands. 'Stay still. I'm just over here.'

The man was wearing the same type of fleece. So, another staff member, Ryan thought. Not a customer after all. Ryan knew enough about head injuries to not try moving him. Instead, he raided the shelves for more items.

One of the sirens was now directly outside. The noise abruptly cut and Ryan glanced towards the open door; powerful flashes of blue light made the figure standing there indistinct. Reflective bands on the jacket. Outside, more sirens were reaching a crescendo. He heard vehicle doors slamming. Another paramedic – this one female – was now beside the first.

'It's OK,' Ryan said to them both. 'You can come in. It's safe.'

The lead one stepped warily through, eyes flitting about as he picked his way through the debris on the floor.

'Two injured,' Ryan announced, nodding down at the man. 'Him and, behind the counter, an elderly lady who –'

'Stasiu!' A wavering voice called out. 'Stasiu?'

'I think she's talking about him,' Ryan whispered. The prone man he was kneeling beside was, he guessed, in his late forties. The old woman about sixty. Their resemblance was unmistakeable. 'Her son, I reckon.'

'How long has he been unconscious?' the paramedic asked. Outside, the other sirens were falling silent.

'Less than ten minutes.'

'OK. Becca, you want to check the other casualty?'

'Will do.'

The male paramedic placed his bag to the side of the blood-soaked mat of kitchen roll. 'What's your name, mate?'

'Me? Ryan. Ryan Lamb.'

'What's the nature of the wound?'

'A deep gash. Kind of from his hairline down to the bridge of his nose. And one across his right hand, too.'

'You applied this bandaging?'

Ryan nodded. He'd found it by the toiletries section. Rolls of white material. There were no plasters big enough. The paramedic was pulling on latex gloves. 'And the marigolds?'

'Sorry?'

'The gloves you're wearing. Your idea?'

Ryan looked down at his hands. The bright yellow rubber was now coated with dark blood. 'Oh. Yes.'

'Clever. Becca, scores on the doors?'

'Possible concussion.'

The man gave a nod. 'OK, let's take a peek here. Ryan,

you've done a great job. I can take over now. Ryan?'

He realised he was still holding the bandaging in place. 'Right.'

A new voice spoke out from behind them. 'What's the situation?'

Ryan looked round to see a uniformed police officer.

The paramedic's attention was on the injured man as he spoke. 'Two injured. This one,' he lifted the bandaging and winced, 'will need surgery.'

The police officer's eyes were on Ryan. 'Was it you who made the call?'

'Yes.' He sat back on his heels. 'I was outside when they came running out. Two blokes.' He turned to the paramedic. 'One had a machete thing in his hand. That's what probably...' He nodded at the unconscious man's head.

Another, older, police officer was now in the doorway. 'PC Scott, you'll be wanting to take this man outside, away from the crime scene.'

'Sir.' He beckoned to Ryan. 'This way, please.'

Ryan got to his feet. The paramedic had opened his bag and was removing foil-wrapped packets. Ryan wanted to ask if the injured man was going to survive.

'Quick as you can, please,' the older police officer said.

Ryan was half-way to the door when he paused. 'Erm, I should leave some money, shouldn't I? For all the stuff I opened?'

He registered the amused expression on the paramedic's face. 'I think they'll let you off.'

Outside, the younger officer guided him towards a patrol car parked across the pavement. An ambulance was beside it. A motorbike, with two more patrol cars, in the road. Another ambulance beyond that. Through the multitude of silent flashing lights, Ryan could make out an officer in a hi-vis jacket running police tape out from a lamp post. A few locals were gathered further along the pavement.

'You can pop those in here, thanks.'

It was the more senior officer. He was holding out a clear plastic bag. 'The gloves. Peel them off and drop them in, thanks. PC Scott? Take his account of what happened.'

'Sir.'

Ryan removed the marigolds then found himself being ushered into the back of the nearest police car. The door shut and, for a moment, he was alone. He had time to check the bulge of his camera wasn't showing beneath his ski coat. The strap was safely tucked beneath the collar, too. That was good. The front passenger door opened, and the constable climbed in and half-turned. 'So, I'm PC Matthew Scott. What I need to do is ask you about what happened here. Is that OK?'

The officer sounded slightly nervous. Ryan reckoned the bloke was a year or two younger than him. 'Fine.'

'Good.' He removed a pen and pad from the glove compartment. 'Right, let's see...you said you were passing by the shop. When was this?'

'Quarter past ten? Maybe a minute or two later.'

'And what did you observe?'

'Well — nothing, at first. I heard shouting. A bloke shouting. Then another sounding distressed. I wasn't sure if a window was open and it was a film playing. Then the door of the shop opened and the first one appeared.'

'A male?'

'Yes. Wearing dark clothes and a balaclava. Plus, he had a hammer.'

'OK.'

'He shouted "Move" back into the shop.'

'How old did he seem?'

'Mid-twenties, I guess.' Ryan clicked his fingers. 'And he said, "Fam" Actually, it was, "Hurry up, fam." So I reckon in his twenties.'

'What did he do?'

'They had a car double-parked directly before the shop's doors. The —'

'Sorry, they had a car?'

'Yes, a white Golf. The first one: he got in the driver's seat, the second one –'

'Any description?'

'A bit taller. Maybe six foot. And he was bulkier. He was carrying a hold-all and a machete.'

'You said a machete?'

'A big blade, anyway. Fat and curved. The bag looked heavy; bottles clinked when he put it in the boot. He then jogged round to the passenger's side and – ' Ryan's eyes widened. 'I got it on film! As they pulled away.'

'Sorry?'

'I filmed them driving off!'

'On your phone?'

'Yes.'

'Can I see?'

Ryan produced it from his pocket, brought the footage up and passed the device over.

PC Scott eagerly studied the clip. 'Can I borrow this for a minute?'

'Of course.'

The officer climbed swiftly out of the car. 'Sarge? We've got the car on – '

The door slammed shut and Ryan was alone again.

He realised his fingers were trembling. This was crazy. I need to mention the bloody photos! He thought about the images he'd taken. They were probably of no use to the police. Why bother?

The windows were starting to steam up; he cleared a circle to see through. PC Scott was showing the footage to several colleagues. The sergeant was already on his radio. I've given them the useful stuff, Ryan thought. Surely?

PC Scott was heading back towards the car. The door clicked open and he retook his seat. 'That's really useful, thanks.' He handed the phone back, along with a slip of paper. 'Can you WhatsApp that to the number written there?'

'Sure.' Ryan sent the file on its way.

'You got footage of them driving off. Then what?'

Ryan peered back towards the convenience store, gathering his thoughts. An image of the man stretched out on the floor filled his head. The glistening pool of blood. Tell him about the pictures. You have to. He rubbed at his forehead with the tips of his fingers. Two people in suits were now ducking beneath the police tape. One male, somewhere in his forties. Chunky, but not fat. The other was female, probably a decade younger. She had light brown hair tied back in a ponytail. They walked up to the uniformed officers outside the shop.

'I realise this must be hard,' the constable said. 'Take your time.'

'Erm, once the car was gone, I hurried across the road. The staff member was lying where you saw him. The elderly lady was sitting on the floor behind the counter. I rang 999 and then did what I could to help them.'

The police sergeant was talking to the pair in suits. The three of them looked across at the patrol car. Ryan imagined his face behind the glass. Do I look guilty? Can they tell I've been lying? He had to bow his head and study his hands.

After a second, he glanced up to find PC Scott studying him. 'Anything else, Sir?'

'Yes – the second one. When he came out of the shop, he let out a whoop. Like he was enjoying himself.'

There was a knock on the glass. Ryan raised his chin to see the male of the pair opening the door. About forty-five, flecks of grey in his short hair. Square features and eyes that were just slightly too close together.

'Evening,' he announced, squatting down and holding out a business card. 'My name's Graham Roebuck. You're Ryan Lamb?'

He took the card and saw the man's title. Detective Inspector. Christ. He had to clear his throat. 'Yes.'

'I hear you've been really useful, Ryan. Even got us

some video to work from.'

'Yeah – if it's any good.'

'Oh, don't worry, it's good.' He pointed a forefinger to the sky. 'You'll be hearing the helicopter very soon. These two men who came out. You heard them speak, correct?'

'Only the first one. He said "Move. Hurry up, fam."'

'Any kind of accent?'

Ryan thought about how the vowel in 'Move' had been stretched out. 'Yes, he sounded local.'

'Salford?'

'Not sure. Manchester, definitely.'

'And the other one. Did he say anything?'

'No. I mean, yes. But it was just a shout. Like of triumph.'

'And he's the one who had the weapon? The blade?'

'Yes.'

'And the bag he was carrying. Did you notice its colour?'

'I'd say it was green. Sort of a khaki.'

'And he was somewhere in his twenties, about six-foot in height?'

'He was.'

Roebuck's eyes drifted. Ryan could almost see the man mentally sifting through potential suspects. He got the feeling he was good at his job. Very good.

'OK, thanks,' the detective said. 'The officer here will finish his questions and then I reckon you've done plenty for one night.' His eyes dropped slightly lower.

Ryan's heart lurched in his chest like a frightened animal. *Has he seen the camera bulge beneath my coat?* He was sure he was hunched forward enough to keep it from showing. But the detective's eyes were narrowing. Ryan suddenly felt very hot. He became acutely aware that his coat was zipped all the way up to his chin.

'Napa – Napapa – ' The detective chuckled. 'I can never say that make. My lad wants one though. Cost a bit, don't they?'

Ryan dropped his chin, saw the Napapijri label on his chest. Relief, like a waft of cool air, ran through him. 'Oh, I got this on eBay. Hundred and twenty quid.'

'Yeah? Ebay?' Roebuck winced as he straightened up. 'The officer here will drive you home, Ryan.'

'Honestly, I'm fine,' he replied, trying to wave the offer away.

The detective stepped back. He was now looking across the top of the car. 'By the way, where were you when you started filming?'

'Where was I?' Ryan pointed across the back seats, even though the detective could no longer see into the vehicle. 'There. Outside that estate agents.'

'The estate agents? The one opposite?'

'Yeah – I was looking at the property ads. My girlfriend wants to move over here because the rents are cheaper in Salford. You know, for apartments and similar.' He was speaking too fast and forced himself to stop.

The detective leaned down and scrutinised him for a second. The lack of space between his eyes made his stare more piercing. 'But for how much longer, hey?' He pointed at the card in Ryan's hand. 'I'll probably be in touch at some point tomorrow, but call me straight away if anything else occurs, won't you?'

Ryan gave a nod. 'No problem.'

'The officer here will drive you home.'

'Honestly, I'm fine,' he repeated.

'Nonsense. It's the least we can do. What's your address?'

'Jethro Mill. It's on Loom Street, Ancoats.'

The detective patted the top of the vehicle. 'Constable? You heard the man.'

CHAPTER 4

From the pitch-black interior of the apartment directly opposite Flat 16, Jethro Mill, a motionless figure stared at Carla Bell. She slid off the bar stool and moved lazily towards the bright window, phone held delicately in one hand. His eyes tracked her every move. The sense of wonder at getting this close! The same feeling from his childhood when his mum took him to The Blue Planet aquarium. His first ever sight of a seahorse, the dainty creature's tail flexing slowly in the water, bringing it to within inches of the glass. Like a creature from another world.

'Carla.' He couldn't stop himself from whispering her name out loud. It didn't matter: no one could hear him in here. No one could see him. 'My precious Carla.'

She was still speaking into her phone, gaze flitting briefly to the street below. It seemed utterly bizarre to him that four full weeks had passed since he'd first looked properly into those eyes. From the moment he had, he'd known. He'd known that he loved her and that they would be perfect together. Her chin had been lifted slightly, as he'd requested, and her stare had been unwavering and trusting.

He'd felt a caress of warm air across his lips. Air that, a moment before, had been in her mouth and, before that, her lungs. Deep inside her body. He'd drawn it down his own throat and, if it had been possible, would have held it in his chest forever. Bringing his face a fraction closer to hers, he'd shone the beam of his pen torch first at one pupil, then the other. He'd realised that her irises weren't actually a uniform blue. The outer edges were fringed by intricate swirls of amber, some of which dissolved into miniscule flecks. Stromal melanin, if he remembered correctly. Safely sealed behind a layer of aqueous humour. The golden fragments seemed to swirl across the deep and distant shades of blue. It was like those photos taken by the telescope they'd sent far out into space. Billowing nebulas hundreds of light years away.

He blinked back to the present, wondering who she was speaking to. Not Ryan, that was for sure. He pictured the scene of carnage in the convenience store on Pinnington Street. Would Ryan even be alive? Not if Liam and Zack had lost control. A machete and a hammer? Those were deadly weapons. He imagined Ryan spread-eagled on the shop floor, his skull caved in. Flabby bits of brain in a pool of warm blood. Like dirty fragments of iceberg. Unblinking eyes fixed on the ceiling lights' cruel glare.

Even if he survived, he'd never be the same. Confined to a hospital bed, lungs only working because of a ventilator. Tubes for his food and shit. How could Carla ever love something like that? A dead weight. A useless lump. Soon, she'd see how pointless it was. In his mind, he conjured the moment when she finally accepted that. Tearfully turning from the hospital bed, legs giving way and him, stepping forward to catch her safely in his arms.

#

Carla turned her attention from the view of the street below back to her phone.

On the screen, Simone looked confused. 'One of his late-night jaunts? On a Friday night?' she asked. 'When will he be back?'

She gave a shrug of irritation. 'Since he was offered this exhibition, it's all about the shot. He cannot stand coming home empty-handed.'

Simone looked bemused. 'Strange hobby he has there. Anyway, back to this weirdo. If you don't mention it tonight, then first thing tomorrow. The longer you leave this, honey, the –'

'Oh my God!'

'What's up?'

Carla watched Ryan closing the door of a patrol vehicle down on the street. 'It's Ryan. He just got out of a bloody police car!'

'Is he OK?'

'I don't know. The car's driving away. I'll call you tomorrow, babes.'

'And now he's back you can also tell him –'

She cut the call and hurried out of the apartment. Looking over the railings, she could see him coming into the lobby. 'Ryan, are you alright?'

He tipped his head back, face ghostly white. 'La-la, I need a drink.'

He disappeared from sight and she listened to him trotting up the stone steps. The moment he came into view, she asked, 'Why were you in a police car?'

'Tell you inside.' He gave her a tight smile, headed straight to the cupboard in the corner of the kitchen and surveyed the meagre selection of bottles. Gin, Baileys, half a bottle of tequila and some port. 'Can I pinch some of your gin?' He'd bought it for her birthday; a posh Manchester variety that she dipped into on special occasions.

''Course,' she replied, closing the door. 'Where's your camera? It hasn't been stolen, has it?'

He poured what he thought might be a double into a

small glass and whacked it straight back. The urge to cough was strong as he shook his head. 'Under here.' He touched his fingers to the front of his coat.

Carla perched on the closer of the two bar stools and lifted an immaculate eyebrow. Tousles of shoulder-length blond hair framed her oval face. Her questioning expression involved a slight pout of her small lips. As usual, he just wanted to kiss them. Instead, he gestured with the bottle. 'Want some?'

'No. I'm back in at eight tomorrow morning.'

Of course, he thought. The big shoot for the ex-Manchester City player's new brand of leisurewear. He'd seen the bloke's ridiculous Bentley in the VIP area of Q2's car park earlier that day.

'Don't forget, you are, too.'

'Yeah, but not til midday.' He poured another generous splash, eyes cutting to the counter where the empty dessert pot and teaspoon lay beside her phone. 'Hey, you found your treat, then?'

She smiled her thanks. 'Ryan, what happened? Why's your camera under your coat?'

He undid the zip and shrugged it off. Then he looped the camera strap over his head and carefully placed the device on the breakfast bar. 'So, I got another message earlier on.'

'You said in the voicemail you left me.'

'Right. The location was the top of Pinnington Street, just over the river in Salford.'

'And?'

He took a sip, placed both elbows on the granite surface and took her through what had taken place: the two men running out, the injured staff, the arrival of the emergency services. The only thing he skirted over was the photos he'd taken.

Her expression had slowly turned from curiosity to shock. 'I don't get this. How...how did our spotty teenager know about a robbery before it had happened?'

He drained the rest of the gin and took his phone out. 'Here's the message: 10.20 PM. Which is almost exactly when they came out of that shop.'

She regarded the handset suspiciously. 'Tell the police. What did you say the detective was called?'

'Roebuck.'

'You have to tell him the truth. That you were only there because you got a message from an unknown number. When did it come through?'

'Not sure. About ten past?'

'No way. The message you left me was just after ten.'

Reluctantly, he checked his phone. 'Nine fifty-nine.'

'So he sent it to you over twenty minutes before they left that shop? This is serious, Ryan. Really serious. What if that injured man... what if he dies?'

'He won't die.'

'OK. He just has a machete slash down his face. That's not serious?'

'I'm not saying that.'

She cocked her head to one side. Feeling her stare, he busied himself with his phone.

'Ryan, why aren't you calling the detective right now?'

He glanced up. 'You know why! Without these messages I'm getting, there are no pictures...'

'Ryan!'

His gaze dropped again. 'Yeah, but it's true.'

She cupped a hand over his wrist. 'It's one thing to get the odd tip from a computer nerd who's listening in on the emergency services. It's another to be told about an armed robbery before it has even taken place.'

He let his head hang. 'We don't know that for sure. Maybe there was an alarm in the shop that was set off. Plenty of businesses have alarms that connect to police control rooms. The person could be tapped into that network.'

'And then sends you a specific time to be at the shop by? It just doesn't fit.'

'What I'm trying to say is that we don't know what's going on.'

'So that's exactly what you tell the police.'

He didn't reply. The silence was broken by someone on a nearby street bellowing a long and aggressive, Yeehaar! He couldn't help half glancing towards the window, picturing the scene. Thinking of the picture.

'I can't believe you're doing this.'

Anger prickled his face and neck. He flicked her hand off his wrist. 'If I call him, it's over for me. My career as a photographer.' He snapped his fingers. 'Gone.'

She looked at him incredulously. 'Gone? You are a photographer.'

'Taking pack shots of kitchen products and toiletries and fucking gardening equipment in a windowless studio?'

'Jesus, we're back to that? The worthiness thing? You earn money by taking pictures. The work at Q2 is just a steppingstone.'

'The work at Q2 bores me rigid. The shots in my exhibition, Carla. That's what being a photographer is about.'

'You'll find other subjects on your own, Ryan. You've got the talent.'

'*Vulpine plunderer*? Luck. You know, I had no clue that fox was about to appear.'

'Not just that one. You capture amazing images. Can you not just believe in yourself? The rough sleepers, the burned-out car in that park, the...' Her eyes roved the room. 'Loads of stuff.'

'The space the Sussman Gallery has given me fits about fifteen, maybe sixteen, images. You know how many of those came about because of those messages? Eleven. Ivan only took me on because of them. It's the only reason.'

She sent him a despairing look before jabbing a finger at his phone. 'So that's what you're building your career on? Anonymous tip offs? Including ones about armed robberies that are about to happen. What will the next message be about? Ryan, it will not end well. You must see that.'

He closed his eyes. 'I just need time to think things through.'

'Yeah, well, it's late and I've got work. So...you think it through. Don't wake me up once you have.' She marched across to the bedroom and swung the door shut.

CHAPTER 5

Four weeks earlier.

'Go on, pal. It'll be cracking.' Tony's ruined face wrinkled in a smile. Teeth like smashed tombstones. 'What if I sit like this? My head here. Like this.'

Ryan watched with a feeling of dismay. Down in the litter-strewn doorway, the man was letting his upper body keel over so a cheek came to rest on the hip of his comatose companion. Beneath them, a raft of flattened cardboard kept the coldness of concrete at bay. Tony and Rich. He'd photographed them too many times now. Besides, it was obviously staged. Tony was even rolling his eyes up. The pantomime pose of an asylum loon. A froth of spittle was being squeezed from the corner of his mouth.

'Take it,' he mumbled. 'We look proper fucked, don't we? Out of it, like.'

Ryan didn't raise his camera. Instead, he felt in his pocket. 'What's Rich had, anyway?'

Hearing the chink of coins, Tony struggled back to a sitting position. 'Prega,' he sniffed.

Pregablin, Ryan thought, dropping a palm-full of

change into their collecting cup. Some kind of nerve depressant. Ever since the city's main supplier of Spice had been chucked in prison, the pills were sweeping through Manchester's rough sleepers. £5 a strip on Bury New Road. 'You take care of yourselves, yeah?'

'Oh, aye. We're cached.' Tony was peering into the cup. Checking for quid coins and not bothered that Ryan could see. 'Bless you,' he said, spotting several. 'Where you heading now?'

Ryan looked along Mosley Street towards Central Library. Almost half-ten on a Saturday night. The bars along the edge of Albert Square would still be heaving. There could be a few skaters near the entrance of the library, the clatter of their boards echoing off the surrounding buildings. Or he could skirt by them and cut down Southmill Street towards the Great Northern. Catch the crowds coming out of the cinema's late screenings. 'Not sure. Wherever the wind blows me.'

'See you when I see you, then.'

'Yeah, cheers.' He drifted along the street and the pale dome of the library came into view. Off to his right was the cenotaph, damp poppy wreathes visible as red blotches at its base. His phone began to buzz and he fished it from the front pocket of his ski jacket. Carla. 'Hiya.'

'Hey, you.'

She was pissed. It was always 'Hey, you' when she was pissed.

'Everything OK?' There was music in the background. Was she still in the studio?

'It is. We're almost finished. I'm going for a quick couple with Simone. Been a long day.'

You've already had a couple, Ryan thought. And it's never just that with Simone. 'Right. Try not to stay out too late.' He said it light-heartedly, knowing full well it would be the early hours before Carla stumbled in. That's if she didn't end up crashing out at her friend's place.

'Where are you, anyway?'

'Oh, the city centre.'

'Any good shots?'

'Nah. We'll see what happens at closing time. Might get something then.'

'OK. Later, then.'

'Later.'

'Love you.'

'Love you.'

#

Carla slipped her phone back into her bag.

'Sorted?' Simone asked from the adjacent sofa.

She nodded. 'Sorted.'

'Well, see that off then.'

Carla took the half-full flute and drained it.

'I fancy Pasha's,' Simone stated, unfolding her impossibly long legs and feeling about on the rug for her shoes. 'You fancy Pasha's?'

'You know the clubs better than me. Any good this time on a Saturday?'

'It will be once we're there.' Simone let out one of her throaty laughs. In the main part of the studio, a couple of assistants were dismantling the lighting rigs. 'Besides, I know one of the bar staff working tonight. Free cocktails? Yes please.'

Carla shook her head. 'You are so naughty.'

Simone checked no one was watching, then slipped the half-finished bottle of Champagne beneath the fake pink fur of her jacket. 'For the cab ride,' she whispered.

Carla shook her head again.

The click of their heels carried across the near-empty car park of the photographic studios. In the security cabin at the main gate, a bored-looking man with a fuzz of grey hair lifted his chin.

'Night, Martin,' Simone called out.

Now smiling, he slid his little window open. 'Hitting the town, are we?'

'You bet,' Simone said, coming to a stop. The bottle appeared from beneath her coat.

'Simone,' Carla said, nodding at the nearby CCTV camera. 'Careful.'

Simone raised a middle finger in its direction before taking a swig. Bubbles surged from the neck as she passed it to Carla. 'No one ever checks them. When do you finish, Marty? Seven tomorrow morning?'

He nodded uncertainly.

'We might still be out then,' Simone replied. 'You could come and find us.'

'Give over!' He waved a hand. 'You young things. Wish I had your energy.'

Simone's finger wagged. 'You're only as young as you feel, Marty.'

He turned his eyes to Carla. 'You take care of this one. Wild, she is!'

'Don't I know it,' Carla replied, drips of champagne still pattering the ground at her feet.

Simone floated a little wave in the security guard's direction before turning to the stream of cars working their way along the nearby road. 'Oh! There's a cab!'

'Taxi,' Carla laughed. 'Not in New York now, babes.'

#

He shone his pen torch into her eyes for far longer than was strictly necessary. Anything to keep his face this close to hers. Anything to keep gazing at her. The seconds ticked slowly by as he directed the beam to her other eye yet again. He knew he'd have to speak, but breaking the silence between them – it felt like putting a brick through a window of stained glass. 'Are you sure there's no headache or nausea or dizziness?'

'None,' she replied, a hint of a smile now on those exquisite lips. 'Honestly.'

He replaced the pen torch in his medical case. Her heavily dilated pupils told him she was under the influence of alcohol. Possibly other substances, too. 'OK. But if you feel any of those things, you're to take yourself along to the Accident and Emergency. Immediately.' He turned to her friend, a freakishly tall black girl with hair like a giant dark halo. She was wearing silver hot pants and a furry pink jacket that ended well above her hips. A bottle of champagne dangled from the fingers of her left hand. It appeared almost empty. 'Can you keep an eye on her, too? Any slurring of speech or unsteadiness on her feet.'

The friend gave him a salute. 'Roger that! A and E and no hanging about.'

He looked back at her, then to the taxi they'd been travelling in. Its crumpled front panel. Fragments of plastic from the smashed headlight casing littering the tarmac. The van that had collided with it was sideways across the two lanes, front bumper hanging off. Police were now talking to both drivers. On the far side of the road, traffic was edging by at walking speed. 'What'll you do now?' he asked. 'Because your cab is going nowhere.'

The black girl sidled closer. 'Mmm...' she murmured suggestively. 'Any chance you can give us both a ride?'

'Simone!' she exclaimed. 'You are so filthy.'

The black girl sniggered at his obvious discomfort. Crass jokes like that were part of the job. But he didn't like them. Didn't like them at all. He made sure not to even look at the black girl. Simone. He could see it was a friendship that would have to be discouraged.

'I apologise for my friend. She's American.' Fingers trailed through her fine blonde hair. 'So are we done?'

'We're done.' He nodded at the sheet of paper in her hand. 'You've got your report form. I don't know if you'll want to contact your insurance.' Normally, he didn't actively encourage people to put in a claim. But she was different. She deserved only good things. Her soul was beautiful, he could tell. And this would only be the start of providing for her. Protecting her. Caring for her. 'My guess is you'll have some stiffness in your neck tomorrow.

Maybe a bit of trouble sleeping.' He shrugged. 'It'll probably be worth a bit of a payout.'

'Really? How much?'

He closed the clasps of his medical case. 'I don't know. A grand, maybe?'

'Bloody hell. Hey, Simone, the rest of the night's on me!'

He placed the case back in the side pannier of his motorbike. 'And drinking any more alcohol really isn't a good idea. Same goes for not wearing a seat belt when in a vehicle.'

'Right.' She was examining her reflection in a little round mirror. 'I'll stick to fruit juice.'

He didn't believe her. That would need to change, when they were together. He didn't like women who got drunk. It wasn't a nice thing to witness.

'Cab!' The black girl yelled, suddenly tottering towards the middle of the road in her high heels, bottle swinging at her side. She raised her other hand to her mouth and a piercing whistle rang out.

'Listen,' Carla said, putting her mirror away, 'you've been really, really sweet. And I meant what I said; you and me, we both make people look their best. I'm right, aren't I?'

He nodded. She was drunk. 'You're right.'

Her mouth broke into a smile and, without warning, she stepped up and placed a kiss on his cheek. 'Thank you, my guardian angel.'

Delicious jolts of electricity were firing out from where her lips had made contact. Guardian angel. He hoped she wasn't expecting an answer; his throat was too tight for his voice to work.

'See you!' she said, hurrying after her friend who was now striding towards a black cab at the far kerb, its hazards flashing. He looked on as she broke into a little trot, waving thanks to a car that let her cross. Next thing, they were both climbing into the rear of the taxi and it was pulling away.

He'd been with her for no more than ten minutes, but seeing her go left him feeling bereft. He undid the zip on his sleeve pocket and removed his copy of the incident report form. Large letters at the top spelled: North West Ambulance Service. In the top left-hand corner, below the fields for incident date and number, was a series of little boxes. Each one was now filled with his handwriting.

Gender: Female. Patient first name: Carla. Patient surname: Bell.

Patient address: Flat 16, Jethro Mill, Loom Street, Ancoats, Manchester.

Date of birth: 19 May 1996.

Did that make her Cancer? He laughed to himself. He didn't even believe in all that star sign stuff! And here he was, suddenly intrigued. He felt certain a Cancerian would be the ideal match for his star sign. Maybe he'd check that later, just to be certain.

She was twenty-five years old. Her estimated weight was 58 kg. Next was her telephone number and, below that, a name and number for her next of kin. Maggy Bell. She'd said that was her mum. Contact number was a landline. He wasn't sure which region the code was for, but he would find that out soon enough. Once his shift finished, he'd get started. Probably begin with where Carla lived. Jethro Mill. Had to be one of those places full of trendy flats. It would fit with what she'd told him about her job. A make-up artist. The sheet of paper in his hand gave him so much to go on. So much to discover. It was a new beginning. The start of the rest of his life. A life with Carla. Her guardian angel. A life where, finally, he was going to be happy.

CHAPTER 6

By the time he drove his BMW R1200RT back to the ambulance station, it was nearly one in the morning. After restocking his medical packs, he'd checked in his handset, helmet with integrated radio mic and mobile data terminal, then changed out of his paramedic's uniform. Before filing his incident reports, he'd photographed Carla's in the deserted locker room. Had to be careful, doing that. Paramedics had lost their jobs over less. Everything done, he was free to go home.

By ten-to-two, he'd locked up his Honda Fireblade in the rear shed of the small terraced house he'd inherited from his parents. Crash helmet hanging from one hand, he'd stifled a yawn while regarding the brightly lit kitchen windows. He shook his head. Bloody Liam.

He opened the kitchen door on his older brother and Zack Patten. Pungent smoke hung thick in the air. There was a bottle of Kraken rum on the kitchen table between them, less than a tenth of it left. Scattered about beside the bottle were empty McDonald's cartons and a few bags of Doritos. Nice, healthy food, as usual, he thought.

Liam puffed on a joint and held it across the table to

Zack. 'In you come, Our Kid. You'll be letting all this nice ganja out.'

He closed the door behind him. A large green hold-all was on the floor. He glimpsed more bottles of Kraken inside. Smirnoff vodka, Jack Daniels. Even Baileys.

Zack had angled his head. 'Hey, Jason, you done another evening shift?'

'Another evening shift,' he sighed, heading towards the fridge.

'Come on then, spill,' Zack said. 'What sort of grim shit did you deal with this time?'

'Pretty quiet, actually.'

'No way! Saturday night? It's never quiet. What was the best one?'

He half-turned. Part of him wanted to say he'd just met the girl who he wanted to spend the rest of his life with. 'Stabbing. Guy was squealing like a pig.'

Zack had sat up. 'Whereabouts?'

Even though Zack was a total fuckwit, Jason didn't mind him. The bloke always wanted to know about his work, for a start. Unlike Liam, who treated his job as a Motorcycle Response Unit Paramedic with either boredom or contempt. 'What, the stab wounds or the incident?'

'Both.'

'Just off Barbirolli Square, near Deansgate Locks.'

'And where'd he been stabbed?'

'Buttocks. Three times in each.'

'No!' Zack squirmed delightedly in his seat. 'Stabbed in the butt cheeks!'

Jason nodded. 'A punishment, I'm thinking.'

'Of course. Police there?'

'I was first. Police were on their way, though. He would have thrown any stuff he was carrying before I got there.'

'Or the other lot had taken it,' Liam announced, re-taking the spliff and gently blowing ash from its glowing tip.

'Much blood?' Zack asked.

'Not from a blade to the arse,' Liam stated. 'That right, Our Kid?'

Jason nodded, slightly concerned about his brother's knowledge. 'That's right. No major arteries or veins in your glutes.'

'Not like your thighs, hey?' Zack asked. 'What's that one that spurts?'

'Femoral artery,' Jason replied. 'Cut that and you don't have long.'

'Femoral artery.' Zack's eyes were sparkling as he glanced at Liam. 'Your little brother: he always was dead clever.'

CHAPTER 7

The flush of the toilet woke him. He turned over to see the door to their little ensuite was wide open. Light was spilling into the dim bedroom. Wearing only her knickers, Carla came into view. Head hanging forward, she placed a hand on the door frame.

'Oh God,' she announced. 'I feel like shit.'

'Good night, then?' he asked, watching her zombie-like shuffle back towards their bed.

She collapsed into a foetal position on the mattress, a hand blindly groping for the folded-back duvet. 'Make me a massive tea, will you? Please?'

He sat up. 'When did you get in?'

'No idea. Late.'

'I didn't hear you.'

Her eyes were closed. 'I was very quiet. Tippy-toes.'

'Right.' He climbed out of bed and went through into the living area of the one-bedroom apartment. Her clothes were strewn across the sofa, shoes lying on the floor, handbag and bra alongside them. That's why I didn't hear you, he thought. You got undressed in here.

Waiting for the water to boil, he studied his shots from the previous night on the camera's viewfinder. The one of the fox. It definitely had something.

'Here you go. Tea, two big sugars.' He placed the Sports Direct mug on her bedside table. 'And loads of milk.'

'Ready to drink?' she asked, struggling into a more upright position.

'Will be with your asbestos mouth.' He climbed back into bed and continued scrolling through the images. 'Where did you end up? I got in at half-one.'

She took a few sips before leaning her head back. 'A few in this place called Pasha's. Tucked in near Oxford Road train station.'

'Not heard of it.'

'It was all right. Bit of an older crowd, but Simone knew someone behind the bar. We did some tequila shots. Don't ask me why.'

'That's why your head's sore.'

She drank some more tea. 'Licking up all that salt. Mixed with the alcohol. I feel like a shrivelled raisin.'

He glanced at her. 'What did you do to your face?'

She opened one eye. 'Mmm?'

'Above your left eyebrow.' He eased some strands of blonde hair aside. 'Like a little bump. Did you bang it or something?'

Her eye re-closed as she walked her fingertips across her forehead. 'Oh yeah. I don't...no, hang on. Christ. The taxi we were in had a prang. Hit another vehicle. Bloody hell. We had to get out. The police showed up. When was that?'

He stared at her. 'You mean, you don't remember?'

'Well, yeah, obviously I do. Just not when it happened.' She hauled herself out of bed and walked across the room like a priceless vase was balanced on her head. A few seconds later, she was back with her phone. She went into her contacts screen and brought up a number. 'Simone,' she said. 'Oh my God, I'm not going out with you again. You are terrible.'

Ryan heard raucous laughter coming from the earpiece. Indistinct words.

'Did we?' Carla asked, sitting back on the bed. 'Ma Things? After Pasha's? Really? When did the taxi have that prang? I've got a bloody lump on my head.' She listened for a few seconds. 'Oh my days. I blame you, Simone Occleshaw. You bad person. OK, speak to you later. Love you, too.' She put her phone aside and retrieved the mug of tea. 'Thanks for this, Ry.'

'So?'

'So what?'

'So what happened with the taxi?'

'Oh, it was on the way to Pasha's. It wasn't anything serious. I just didn't have a seatbelt on.'

'It hit another vehicle?'

'Yeah, but it wasn't full on. I knocked my head on the window frame bit inside the car. But it was fine. An ambulance guy checked it over.'

'Hey, what do you reckon about this one?' He tilted the camera so she could see the little screen.

She twisted round, squinted for a moment, then gave up. 'What even is it?'

'You don't see the fox?'

'Sorry. Head's pounding here.' She finished her tea, lay back and closed her eyes. 'Describe it to me, sweetie.'

'It's the last thing I took. This guy had passed out in a bus shelter.' He smiled. 'Not as drunk as you, needless to say, but still pretty bad.'

'Don't,' she muttered. 'I feel bad enough.'

He lifted the screen closer for a better look. 'I was about to get a shot before his burger dropped on the floor, when this fox...' He shook his head in disbelief. 'It just came slinking out of the shadows and I captured it, the exact moment, as it stole the burger. It's, like, a thousand-to-one chance. In fact, better than that.'

'Sounds good. Really good. Those urban foxes, a lot of

people are interested in them. You see news stories all the time.'

'Yeah, I reckon I'll put it on my Instagram page. What's the word for anything to do with foxes? It's like the name for Spock in Star Trek.'

'Ry, do I look like a Trek geek?'

'Vulcan! That was Spock's...you know, planet. It's almost the same as that.' He grabbed his phone from the bedside table and Googled it. 'Vulpine. That's it. Vulpine Munchies, how does that sound?'

Carla said nothing for a moment. 'Not working for me. This fox, it stole his food, right?'

'Vulpine thief, then?'

'I don't know. What about plunderer? Then you get the 'p-p' thing. Vulpine Plunderer.'

Ryan smiled. 'I like it.'

'Not too much like a crossword clue or something?'

'No, it's good.'

It was another three hours before Carla felt well enough to go out.

'All Things Nice?' Ryan asked as they descended the stairs to the lobby. 'Pancakes and bacon and maple syrup?'

Carla slid a pair of dark glasses on. 'I reckon my stomach can handle that.'

As the doors to Jethro Mill slid open, they paused to let a man with a miniature dachshund on a bright pink lead saunter by. Sunlight was flooding the street. A Deliveroo rider was waiting beside the intercom. Seeing the two of them, he unzipped his case. 'McDonald's, yeah? Apartment eleven?'

'Not us,' Ryan replied, turning back to see a bearded man in his late twenties bounding down the stairs.

'Yo!' he called out. 'I'm the Maccy Ds!'

Carla linked her arm through Ryan's as they set off along the pavement. Music drifted down from an open window somewhere above them. A laid-back beat like something you'd hear on the beach in Ibiza. 'Lazy

Sundays,' she murmured, leaning her head against his shoulder. 'I bloody love living here.'

#

The engine of Jason's BMW made a languid hum as he turned into Ancoats. A gently warped grid of narrow streets made up this section of the city. A few years ago, it was all abandoned textile mills and industrial buildings. But the transformation of the Northern Quarter on the other side of Great Ancoats Street had created a ripple effect. Bars, restaurants and pubs had made the jump across the busy road. Empty buildings started getting snapped up by property developers and turned into apartments. A young crowd had soon started colonising the area.

Jason was well aware that, while on shift, his exact location was constantly visible in the control room back at base. A GPS tracker in his handset and on his bike ensured that. But at work, he didn't like to sit it out at base, waiting for a call like a lot of his colleagues did. Lounging in the rest area, playing cards or just chatting. Moving your mouth so idle comments came out like jokes and stuff. Banter, they called it. It didn't work when he tried. He thought that, maybe, he spoke for too long. He'd timed other people's comments. Hardly anyone spoke for more than five seconds. He found it hard to be that quick.

So, instead of sitting at base, stuck at the edge of things – there, but not quite there – he preferred to get on his bike, find a good tactical spot in the city centre and wait. His controllers liked it, too – especially Danny. Danny said it was a better spread of resources.

As the bike moved almost silently along the street, he noted how so many of the people he passed wore odd clothes. Men with jeans that clung to their legs and often ended above their ankles. No socks. Knitted tops or woollen coats. Some wore waistcoats or tweed caps, while others had their heads covered by things that resembled a tea cosy. And the tattoos. So many tattoos.

He took a left onto Cotton Street and then a right onto Loom Street. Jethro Mill was at the first junction. Dark, solid-looking stone. Five floors, each one with a row of imposing windows. On the higher floors, the developer had attached massive metal sunflowers to the sides of the building in an attempt to brighten what had once been a dim and dingy prison for the legions of mill workers slaving away inside.

He drew to a stop at the junction, raised his visor and got out his mobile data terminal. Made a show of studying the iPad-sized screen. The device linked into the system back at base, displaying all 999 calls coming in, including those yet to be dispatched. Categories told you the type of incident, with an address, sat-nav location and brief notes. Most of his colleagues had downloaded the system as a secure app on their phones. That way, they had one less item of tech to be carrying around. Jason had reluctantly done the same, but he wasn't sure. He didn't like the idea of work technology on his device. People spied, didn't they?

He glanced right and left, pretending to search for a building name. The main entrance into Jethro Mill was a metal-framed door set into runners. The sliding mechanism would be activated by the keypad beside it. He could see a dimly lit lobby through the glass and wide steps leading up. She was in Flat 16. That probably meant a first-floor apartment, possibly one facing onto the adjacent street.

He glanced at the building opposite. A similar affair. He'd been hoping for a street that was less exposed: perhaps a cafe or two with seating areas. Somewhere he could park up and keep an eye on things. This was frustrating. He checked the building across the little junction. A large sign was stuck to the entrance.

Coming soon: contemporary living in Manchester's most exciting quarter.

Oh, he thought. Provocative. Referring to Ancoats as a quarter. A challenge to the nearby Northern Quarter, no doubt. More writing beneath:

Another luxury development by Nail & Cable.

He made a note of the enquiry number in his phone. Of course, he wasn't going to actually move here to be closer to her. How weird would that be! But he might check out what the rents were. Perhaps even look round one of the apartments, especially if it happened to face Flat 16, Jethro Mill.

His MDT gave a loud beep. A job had come in and he was optimal position to respond. He'd just finished reading the text when his helmet mic came to life and the voice of the dispatcher filled his ears.

'Red base to MC02.'

'MC02, go ahead,' he replied.

'MC02, can you confirm you have received CAD number 4567, twenty-three-year-old male impaled on railings?'

'Red Base, yes, all received, edge of Whitworth Park, ETA three minutes.' He lowered his visor and checked the road behind. 'Are there any safety concerns, and do we have any other resources or police running, please?'

'Third-party caller is still on the phone to the call-taker and has no apparent safety concerns. We have a DCA assigned, ETA twelve minutes, and police are aware, but no ETA as yet. Can I chase them up for you?'

'Thank you, Red Base, I'll give you a report on arrival for critical care. Might be worth considering Fire, too – not sure how high these railings might be.'

'We'll request them now. Thank you MC02. Red Base out.'

He closed his eyes for a second to work out a route. There was a sat-nav on the dashboard of his bike, but he rarely relied on it; once en route, he was usually travelling too fast for the device to keep up.

CHAPTER 8

'La-la! Oh my God, La-la, you will not believe this!'

She turned from the bubbling pan of pasta and wiped her hands on a tea towel. 'What?'

Ryan got to his feet, eyes still locked on his phone. 'Holy shit.' He turned away from her to pace out into the middle of the living area, the fingers of his free hand clenching and unclenching at his thigh. 'I mean, it's genuine. It has to be genuine. Why wouldn't it be genuine?'

Carla's smile wavered between confusion and curiosity. 'What, Ryan, are you on about?'

He span round and half-lifted his phone. 'Julian Templeforth has just followed me on Instagram. Julian bloody Templeforth. He's even left a comment! "Beautiful shot." I mean, can you freaking believe it?' He stared at her in wonderment.

'Ryan, that is massive! Oh my God.' She raced across and squeezed him tight. 'Vulpine Plunderer, yeah?' she asked, stepping back.

He nodded, attention shifting back to his phone.

'How many likes has it got now?'

'It's gone bat-shit crazy, La-la. Three hundred and, no...

over four hundred. And my followers just keep going up.'

'Crazy. Start of the week, you had, what, a dozen?'

'Yup. And I've had another blogger get in touch.'

'Interview?'

'Yeah. People are messaging asking where to buy my stuff. One person asked if they have prints for sale in Kube. Kube! Me stocked in Kube. It's surreal.'

'I'm so happy for you. You've worked so fucking hard for this, you really have.' She moved back to the galley kitchen. 'Oh, and I forgot to say, I got an enquiry through on my website yesterday. Amongst all the spam and scams and random shit that's usually sitting there. It's only to do the make-up and nails at this kiddy party out at Alderley Edge. Princess theme. Still, two-hundred quid isn't bad.'

'Yeah?' Ryan briefly raised his eyes. 'Two hundred? Sounds good.'

'Well, if I add it to the shoot at MediaCity next week. The one for the TV show – it's looking like a decent month, money-wise.' She waited for a response, but all his attention was being sucked through the screen of his phone. 'Ryan?' Nothing. She raised her voice and tried again. 'Ryan?'

He regarded her. 'Sorry, what?'

'Don't forget your shifts at the studio, will you? We're both in on Thursday and Friday, but you're booked for two days next week, too. Is that right?'

He sighed, slipping his phone into his pocket. 'That place gets me down.'

'It's work, Ryan. Paid work.'

'I know that, but... every hour in that building. It feels like I'm in a gigantic tomb. Trapped with that living corpse, Ian.'

'Ian?'

'One of the full-time photographers.'

'Don't think I've met him.'

'You wouldn't have. He spends all day in that oversized shed, taking product shots of toiletries and kitchen utensils and cleaning products. It's sucked the life out of him.'

Carla shrugged. 'Because the work lacks, what's the word you used the other day? Gravity?'

'Gravitas.'

'Right. It isn't profound,' she said wearily, giving the pasta a quick stir.

'You don't know what it's like. You're up in the old mill with the music and lights and...energy.'

She put the spoon aside. 'It's work, Ryan. Yes, I happen to enjoy it most of the time. But is it what I wanted to do while I was at uni?'

He knew the answer to that. During her degree course, Carla had gone for theatrical and special effects options. But jobs in the industry were so scarce. He could still remember her final-year project. She'd turned him into Caliban from The Tempest and he'd ended up completely unrecognisable, encased in layers of latex which Carla had then painted in a dizzying swirl of greens. A row of stubby horns across his forehead, yellow contact lenses and a jagged hole for a mouth out of which peeped double rows of small fangs. The reason she didn't win a prize was, he suspected, because her work had scared the crap out of the judges.

'If you stopped to think about someone other than yourself, for once, you'd realise all I do is make pretty people even prettier. That, you could argue, also lacks gravitas.'

'Yeah, but I didn't do my degree to end up taking photos of air diffusers or whatever they're called.'

'I know. You have an urge to be out there,' her eyes cut to the window. 'And that's good, having that ambition.' She glanced at him.

His head was down.

'But in the real-world,' she continued, 'there's my mortgage for this place. Electricity bills, and food shopping.'

He didn't look up. 'I'll pay you my share. I've got that

cheque due for last month. As soon as –'

'I'm not worried about it. It's fine. But just tell me you're not about to jack it in at Q2.'

He didn't reply.

'Ryan?'

'No, I'm not jacking it in.' He tipped his head back and blew air at the ceiling. 'Don't worry.'

'Good. Because it was me who gave them your number, remember?'

'I'm not packing it in! Not yet, anyway.'

'Not yet?'

'If my photographs keep getting this attention, it could lead to all sorts of stuff. Paid stuff.'

'Ryan, you've added a few thousand Instagram followers.'

'And one of them is Julian Templeforth.'

'Let's not get carried away. That's all I'm saying.'

He dropped his phone on the sofa and drew himself up to his full height.

Carla started shaking her head. 'Ryan...' She pointed to the saucepan of pasta. 'I'm trying to cook here.'

He began shuffling toward her, shoulders raised and cheeks sucked in. 'We can all dream, Carla,' he rasped.

'No!' she half-shouted. 'Not Slender man. You know it totally freaks –'

'You wouldn't deny me that, Carla, would you?'

She grabbed the stirring spoon and raised it. 'Ryan, I mean it!' She failed to suppress a giggle. 'Keep away!'

His fingers started writhing back and forth as he closed in. 'Is it time for your tickling, Carla?'

She tried to race round the island and across the living area towards the bedroom. The tiny ensuite had a lock on the door. The only one within the apartment. With two stiff strides, he cut her off. Ducking under his outstretched arms, she veered round the sofa, but he hurdled the backrest. A strangled shriek escaped her as his hands clamped round her waist, fingertips furtling their way towards her ribs.

'No, stop. Please stop,' she laughed, trying to prise his fingers away as he dragged her down onto the thick rug.

#

Jason looked around his empty bedroom and sighed. He was missing Carla. He so wanted to see her. A hand reached for the computer mouse. Once he had her website on his screen, he read the paragraph on her 'About Me' screen yet again.

I am a freelance make-up artist and hair stylist with over four years of experience within the fashion and beauty industry.

Born in Cheshire, I attended The Chester College where I completed a Level 3 course in Media Make-up Artistry. I then successfully completed the BA (Hons) degree course in Make-up for Media and Performance at the University of Salford. I also have diplomas in fashion, fashion styling and media make-up.

My work is my passion and I only use the best products – Mac, Nars and Illamasqua. I like to work closely with my clients to understand the brief and ensure the results are exactly as they want.

The words were a disappointment; they didn't capture any of what made her so special. Looking at her face, you'd never guess those dull words were describing someone so unique. He noted that she'd been born in Cheshire and entered the area code for her mum's phone into Google. Chester. He thought there was a good chance it would be the house Carla had grown up in. He was sure it would have a garden. It would be a nice house with a chimney and a path lined with flowers leading up to a porch and the lawn probably had a swing, maybe hanging from the branches of an old oak tree. He'd like to visit the house and meet Carla's mum and sit in that garden and imagine Carla as a little girl, playing on that swing.

He clicked on testimonials, eager to hear what other people said of her. The page was disappointingly empty.

'I've used Carla for the last couple of years on set and I am constantly impressed at how professional she is.' Bernadette, Manchester Fashion Magazine.

'I booked Carla at short notice for a tricky shoot. She is so professional and great at what she does, plus she uses Nars which in my opinion is the best.' Patricia, Belladonna.

'You are super talented, Carla, and a really good laugh and one girl. Everyone is so relaxed with you! We are so lucky to have found you.' Fiona, Q2 Photography.

Jason nodded. That was better. That gave you an idea of her magic, how she must light up any room with her energy.

A different tab caught his eye. One for 'SFX and theatre'. He stared in shock at the panel of outlandish and disturbing images now filling the screen. A zombie or ghoul with rotted teeth and strips of flesh hanging from his face. A nymph with sparkling skin and frail antennae sticking out from the top of her head. An ogre or something: it had mottled green skin, horns bursting through the skin of its forehead, yellow eyes and fangs.

There were also close ups of an assortment of wounds: a forearm slashed open to the bone; a man with a gaping wound to his throat; the same man with the handle of a knife sticking from the side of his head. Blood coated his face and neck. Jason scrutinised it: the blood looked very real. Maybe it was an animal's. That of a pig, or something. He didn't like these pictures. Maybe there'd be some sort of explanation in the text.

As part of my degree course, I specialised in SFX and theatre. Halloween parties, drama productions or any other event – let's talk!

Why hadn't she mentioned this to him? She'd said she made people look their best. Not this. He examined the man's gaping throat more carefully. It was very good. She'd attempted to show the pretracheal fascia, and an exposed section of cricoid cartilage. The man was in his early twenties, tall, with straggly black hair and large brown eyes, like a Labrador dog's. Jason was pretty sure the zombie thing was him, too. And the monstrous creature with horns and green skin.

Was he just someone off her course or was this person her boyfriend? He suspected it was her boyfriend. Why else would she use the same person so often? They'd probably spent hours together in her room. She would have had to get really close to him to apply the layers of rubbery flesh. Probably as close as he'd got to her the night when they'd met. Maybe this person encouraged her to create such ugliness? Yes, it was probably his idea. Jason felt angry that the person had made her do it.

He leaned closer to the screen and examined the man's slightly sallow face. The small scar high on his forehead, the knife's handle embedded in his temple and the blood. The crimson river running down his neck. Jason gazed for a long time at the blood.

Finally, he closed the website down and turned his attention back to the Incident Report Form. Patient telephone number. He reasoned that, if she had a boyfriend, they'd talk on the phone. Leave each other messages. He wondered how old her telephone was. Could it be a make and model that still allowed you to dial in to the voicemail from a different number?

If she had an old phone on an old contract, it was possible. Of course, she'd have a newer version! But if she didn't, perhaps she was unaware of that vulnerability. That

– if anyone guessed the PIN – they could listen to any voicemails she had stored. And it was amazing how many people's PINs were simply the manufacturer's default code. Or permutations of the person's birth date. He checked the fields on the form. 19 May 1996.

It had been a while since he'd done this. And, of course, since then, most phone operators had updated their systems to prevent it. But perhaps he should see if it worked with hers. Not to listen in or anything. Just to make sure she hadn't left herself exposed to people with malicious intentions.

He made a list of the four likeliest PINs. The two most common manufacturer ones were 0000 and 1234. After those were birthdays. Carla's day and month of birth was 1905. Month and year were 0596. He knew he would only have four tries. Any more than that and it could lock him out and send her an alert. He checked the time. Almost three in the morning. Would she still be up to answer her phone? He doubted it. In which case, it would go to voicemail. He glanced at the list of PINs. What if she answered? To hear her voice speaking to him again! He felt giddy. Excitement caused a fizzing in his fingertips as he took an old pay-as-you-go handset from his drawer and plugged the charger in. He keyed the final digit of her phone number in, breath frozen in his throat. Each ring of her phone was amplified in his head. The repeating tones stretched for eternity. It was agony, but an exquisite agony. A voicemail message was the next thing he heard. Her phone was turned off! Perfect. He immediately pressed the star key, then 0000.

Nothing.

The lack of a message to say his PIN wasn't recognised meant carrying on was futile. Even so, he pressed star again and then tried 1234. Now the burr of a dead line. He cut the call and clamped the phone between his palms. That was good, he told himself. She was safe. No one could snoop on her. That was good. It was.

He put his phone aside. Of course, there was decryption software out there, if you knew where to get hold of it. Stuff that could get you into any phone, even the very latest handsets. It was the sort of thing Zack, with the amount of time he spent on the dark web, would know all about. He could always ask Zack about it. Maybe.

CHAPTER 9

'That was bloody delicious,' Carla announced, pushing the wooden board her pizza had arrived on to one side.

Ryan studied the crusts she'd left before plucking the largest one up and biting it in half. 'Got to be the best pizza place in Manchester,' he said, surveying the cramped interior. The large copper dome of the wood-fired oven filled the far corner, a staff member expertly exchanging cooked pizzas for fresh ones. Conversations around them rose and fell, punctuated by the clink of cutlery and staff calling out to each other in Italian. The shelves on the far wall were lined with products customers could buy: jars of olives, packets of unusual pasta, bottles of oil. Salamis and hams hung from the ceiling.

'And one minute from our pad,' Carla smiled, lifting her glass of wine. 'So, where are you taking me next?'

Ryan raised his glass of craft beer. 'Hey: to us.'

She grinned. 'To us. Where is it we're going, then?'

They chinked glasses and Ryan looked out the window. Beyond the plate glass, Finney Square was heaving with people. 'Somewhere new. Well, we haven't been there before. It's been around for a bit.'

'Walking distance?'

'Yeah, course. It's over towards the Rochdale Road.'

'What?' She feigned shock. 'Outside the Northern Quarter?'

'Edge of it, don't worry.' He caught the eye of a server and signalled for the bill.

They were approaching the top of a side road which led out onto Great Ancoats Street when the sound of siren started slicing through the air. What traffic they could see in their narrow view of the main road ahead began pulling over as the throb of blue flashes grew brighter. Moments later, a fire engine roared by. The sound of the siren subsided only to swell in volume once again. It seemed to be echoing more loudly, blue light growing stronger. For a moment, Ryan wondered if the vehicle was reversing back. Then a second fire engine sped past. Now the wail of sirens died down properly.

'So many of those things flying around,' Carla frowned. 'Does my head in.'

'So many?'

They emerged on to the main road and both looked to the pair of emergency vehicles as they moved swiftly in the direction of Ardwick.

'Yeah,' she said. 'Have you not noticed?'

He nodded. 'I had. But you do know the main fire station for the city is just over there?' He pointed off to their right. 'A few hundred metres up the Oldham Road?'

'Is it? Bloody hell. Really?'

Ryan tried to suppress his laughter. 'You've been living here all this time, and you didn't know? Oh, Christ. That's hilarious.'

She batted him lightly on the arm. 'Don't laugh. I just thought there must be... I don't know, loads of fires in this bit of the city or something. I don't know!'

His entire body was shaking. 'Sorry.' He waved a hand. 'Loads of fires in this bit of the city.'

She started to giggle, too. 'Well, how should I know there's a fire station up there? It's not like I ever go to

Oldham.'

Ryan wiped a tear from his eyes. 'Oh, Carla, I stinking love you.'

A couple of minutes later, he came to a stop. 'We have arrived at our destination.'

A few shops with their shutters rolled down were beside them. On the opposite side of the road was a decrepit work unit. There was a turning bay before its drive-in entrance. Carla could see a couple of semi-dismantled vehicles just inside the dimly lit interior. One of the ceiling lights was blinking on and off. She checked the road again. Further along was a Chinese supermarket, but it was also closed.

'I don't get it,' she said. 'Where?'

He nodded at the garage opposite. Faded lettering above a rusted sign said, Chop Shop.

'That?' Her eyebrows seemed to levitate. 'Seriously?'

'It's not what it seems,' he replied, leading her across the road with a smile. They stepped into the workshop area. The strip light above them continued to flicker. A door at the rear was marked "office". Beyond it came the faint thud of bass. Ryan pointed up at the faulty light. 'Notice how it's in time to the music?'

'Oh yeah.' Carla started to examine the interior more carefully.

'The stack of tyres over there?' Ryan pointed. 'They're all glued together and bolted to the floor. The vehicles are just shells and all the tools you see hanging up are attached to the wall with little brackets. You can't remove them. Not sure about the manky work overalls. You can probably help yourself to those.'

'This is weird,' Carla murmured. 'So it's a bar?'

'It is. But before that it was a real garage. Was both for a while, apparently. Come on.'

Specks of grit on the concrete floor added a faint crunch to their footsteps as they continued towards the far door. Ryan pulled it open and the sound levels instantly increased. Curtis Mayfield or Otis Reading. Ryan wasn't sure which. Carpet covered the floor beyond. A musky aroma filled the air. Sandalwood. Perhaps patchouli. A scattering of work benches served as narrow tables. Chairs were metal barrels or actual car seats on stubby little legs. A variety of weird objects dangled just below the ceiling. Hub caps, looping jump leads and spanners. The main light comprised dozens of cars' side mirrors clustered round a huge bulb. Beams shone out in all directions. A shower of sparks cascaded down from a tower-like installation in the far corner. Carla watched the dots of bright yellow skittering across the metallic base.

Ryan was beckoning her to a bar that seemed to consist of plywood. A staff member slouched over and dropped a couple of beer mats down. 'Evening. What'll it be?'

Ryan was scanning the blackboard above the bar man. A variety of real ales along with strengths and prices were listed there.

'Do you have wine?' Carla asked uncertainly.

'Sure we do. Red or white?'

'White?'

'French? Italian? New World?'

'Oh, just something that's dry. Pinot Grigio?'

'Large, medium, small?'

'Large.'

He nodded, eyes moving to Ryan.

'And a pint of the Blackjack IPA, cheers.'

'Coming up.'

Carla glanced over her shoulder. 'Kind of like it,' she whispered. 'Sort of industrial chic.' The people at the nearest tables seemed as eccentric as the setting. A couple of bearded biker types, well into their fifties, were chatting to a bald man in a high-visibility tabard. There were quite a few women. Harsh bobs or braids, piled high. A table of intellectual looking types in deep conversation. One or two solitary drinkers, faces illuminated by their MacBook screens. 'So, who even drinks in here? I didn't know it existed.'

'It's popular with the arty crowd, I think. Staff from galleries, the odd actor, that kind of thing. Oh, and musicians who've been playing at The Band On The Wall. They often head over.'

Carla was surveying the walls. Posters for upcoming gigs. A listing for coming acts at The Comedy Club. Performance schedule for the Royal Exchange. Another for The Lowry. 'How did you hear about it?'

'Just trawling twitter feeds. Saw it mentioned once or twice.'

'Whose twitter feed?' She turned to face him properly, eyes narrowing.

'What do you mean, whose?' He glanced back at the beer pumps. 'Must be changing the barrel.'

'Ryan.' She was leaning in now, forcing eye contact. 'I've said it many times. You're a shit liar.'

'What do you mean?' he asked, half-laughing. 'OK, I might have seen it on Julian Templeforth's.'

'He drinks in here?'

'Sometimes. Apparently.'

Carla's gaze swept the room. No sign of the famous designer. 'Now I get it.' She smirked. 'He followed you on Instagram and – pure chance, obviously – you just happen to fancy taking me out for a drink in this particular venue.'

'You're making me sound bad here.'

She threw him an amused glance. 'No, fair play to you. What'll you do if he comes in? Ask for his autograph?'

'Yeah,' he smiled. 'Like fuck, I will.'

'But seriously, what'll you do?'

'I wouldn't do anything. I just, you know, wanted to see what it's like in here.'

'You are funny, Ryan Lamb. Just wanted to see what it's like.'

'Yeah, but maybe he'd come over to us,' Ryan said quietly. 'He knows who I am.'

Carla gave a silent whistle. 'Now we really are getting cocky.'

#

Zack was sitting at the kitchen table, deep in conversation with a man Jason hadn't seen before. Both of their heads were down and neither seemed to notice him as he opened the back door.

He stood there for a moment. Empty cans and bottles cluttered the kitchen table. There was a bottle of whisky and vodka, both with the supermarket's security collars still attached to their necks. Their voices were raw and husky from booze. The man he didn't know was about to tap cigarette ash into a vase. It had been one of mum's favourites. A limited edition made by Royal Doulton and glazed in a flambé tradition that, the certificate that came with it had declared, was redolent of the style pioneered during China's Sung dynasty. Piece of tat, if the truth be known, but that wasn't the point.

Jason stepped over to the table and plucked the ornament clear. 'Use an empty fucking can.'

The man sat back, bleary eyes settling on Jason. He had a thick neck and bulging trapezoids. 'The fuck are you?'

Zack lifted a hand. 'Easy, Tolly. It's Liam's little brother. He lives here.'

Jason glared at the man. 'You're actually in my house.'

The man looked him up and down. 'Didn't know Liam had a brother.'

'Yeah,' Zack replied. 'I did tell you. He's the motorbike paramedic. Flies all over the city. Proper grisly: car crashes, stabbings, shootings, people falling off stuff. Jason, tell him about the Pikey fucker the other day.'

Ignoring the request, Jason looked towards the doorway through to the hall. 'Where is he?'

'Liam?'

'Yeah.'

'Upstairs, but I reckon he's about finished.' A smirk

was sent toward the other man, who smiled briefly in return. 'Come on, Jason. Tell Tolly about the Pikey. The one who tried to rob that restaurant.'

Jason shook his head. 'Another time. I need to sleep.'

Zack scowled briefly. 'Jason here's seen it all. Works his arse off all hours, don't you, Jason? Proper grafter.'

Jason placed the vase inside his crash helmet and carried on to the front room. A few more people were in there. Their outlines hazy with the amount of hash smoke floating in the air. Music thumped away. He heard footsteps on the stairs and looked up to see Liam making his way down, a girl who was barely twenty trailing behind. His brother wore no top. Crude tattoos were sprinkled about his torso and arms, no pattern or symmetry anywhere.

'This can't go on,' Jason announced.

Liam trailed his fingers along the banister. 'What's that, Our Kid?'

He gestured at the front room. 'This. All this shit. You said you'd be moving out.'

Liam sighed. 'You really want to do this now?'

'What, two-twenty in the morning on a Sunday night? Why not? Didn't think time really mattered to you.'

Liam got to the bottom step and moved aside. The girl slipped past without a word to join the rest of them in the front room. 'I will be. Soon.'

'You said that weeks ago.'

'I'm waiting on a couple more jobs. Once they're in, I'm out. You can go back to your sad little lonely life.' He stepped closer and tapped a forefinger against his brother's chest. 'Even if half of this house should be mine.'

Jason shook his head. Their parents had left nothing to Liam. 'Eight years you were gone for. They thought you were dead.'

Liam tipped his head. 'And here I am, live and kicking. Live and fucking kicking.' He danced his way into the kitchen, span round and booted the door shut.

Ryan pushed it open again. 'What jobs are they?'

Liam paused, hand on a bottle of vodka. 'You what?'

'The jobs you're waiting on. What are they?'

Liam's eyebrow lifted a little. 'Off to your bed now.'

'Wanker.' Jason stomped up the stairs and unlocked his bedroom door. He went to the place mum's vase on the windowsill then realised the thing now had that ashtray stink. He opened the window and shook out a cascade of cigarette butts, crumpled roaches and torn Rizlas. Bastards. Window closed, he flopped on to the bed, grateful for the relative quiet.

The knock on his door came a few seconds later. He lay still, happy to ignore it. A tiny creak as it opened. He lifted his head off the pillow. Shit. He realised he hadn't put the bolt across. A girl, this one in her mid-twenties, peeped round.

'Toilet's further down, on the right,' he announced wearily.

More of her came into view. She was wearing a white vest top and faded jeans with a high waist. A wide belt with a fat brass buckle. Nothing on her feet. 'You're Liam's brother, right? Saw you talking in the hall.'

'Yeah, I'm about to crash out. Been a long day.'

'They said you two look the same. Almost twins. Who's older?' Moving unsteadily, she slid properly into the room. Wavy brown hair hung loose over bare shoulders. She had a little paunch. A bottle of Jim Beam hung from one hand.

Seeing his eyes on it, she raised it towards him. 'A wee nip?'

'No. I need to sleep.'

She pushed out her lower lip. 'So, who's older?'

He sat up. 'He is. Year-and-a-half.'

'Right, I can see that a bit, now you've said. Sure you don't want any?'

As he shook his head, she took a decent slug for herself. 'They said he's the good-looking one, but I don't think he's any better-looking than you. You look sweet.

Sweeter than him.' She touched a finger below her nose. 'What happened here?'

He had to fight the temptation to cover his top lip with a hand. A reflex reaction born from years of questioning glances, often accompanied by expressions of mild distaste. Sometimes revulsion. 'Just a thing.'

She smiled. 'So bad-boy Liam has all the tattoos, but he doesn't have a scar like that, does he?'

He shrugged.

'Don't say much, do you?' With a rush of little steps, she was sitting beside him on the bed. Angling her head, she studied the deep grove that ran from his top lip up towards the underside of his nose.

'It's actually from surgery,' he murmured. 'You've never heard of a cleft-palate?'

'Cleft what?'

'Pal –' He sensed she wasn't capable of taking in anything too complicated. Booze. Lack of brains. Maybe both. 'They had to fix it when I was little. A big operation.'

'Right.'

Even as he was replying, she'd begun looking round the room. He thought about how Carla hadn't commented on it. Had hardly even looked at it. None of that usual thing where the person he was talking to continually broke eye contact to glance downward. As if he had a bogey poking out of a nostril. Or a bit of spinach stuck in his teeth.

'My name's Mia, by the way.'

He said nothing.

'So,' she drawled the word. With deliberation. 'What should we do now?'

'I said, I need to sleep.'

'I need somewhere to sleep, too.' She gave him a sideways glance.

'Actually, I've got a girlfriend.'

'You have?' She looked round the room again. 'Then where is she?'

'She's not here.'

'I can see that, stupid! I mean photos or something.'

She had a point, he thought. I should have a picture or two of her.

'You don't have much in here, do you?'

He considered bringing up Carla's website on his computer. He liked the idea of pointing to her image and saying, there. That's her. That's my girlfriend. We're a couple. Together. It would be a kind of rehearsal, to say those words. To say them out loud to someone. Practise for when they were real. This is Carla, she's my girlfriend.

But he immediately saw the danger. The person beside him on the bed might go straight downstairs and tell Liam and then his brother's laughter would rise through the floor. Big mocking bellyfuls of laughter. Followed by all the usual shit he liked to come out with. No. Can't risk that. 'I like to keep it tidy.'

She took another sip of bourbon. He thought about Carla's recent tweet. The fact she was 'stoked' to have this 'gig' out at MediaCity. Working on a TV programme called *Unsung Heroes*. It was going to be shown weekdays on Channel 5. Actual times to be confirmed. He'd sent her a message to say congratulations, but she hadn't replied. Hadn't yet replied to any of his emails, in fact.

Maybe he could just mention to Mia that his girlfriend was a make-up artist who worked in TV. He wondered where Zack and Liam had found Mia. Probably in a local pub, working behind the bar. Or wrapping up portions of chips in a kebab shop. What's she even doing in my room, anyway?

'So,' she said matter-of-factly. 'Are we going to fuck, or what?'

Looking from the corner of his eye, he could see the flutter of her external jugular vein beneath the smooth skin of her neck. To the front of that, nestled alongside her sternocleidomastoid muscle would be the external carotid artery. A sharp, well-aimed slash with even a relatively small blade would be enough to release a mini geyser of blood. His ceiling would be coated in seconds. Just a minute or so to unconsciousness, death resulting soon after. Unless, of course, he chose to save her by stemming the bleeding with a compress. Who did she think she was, this person? Tempting him to be unfaithful. 'No, I just want to sleep.'

She got back to her feet. ''K. See you about.'

As soon as the door closed behind her, he hurried over and slide the bolt across.

CHAPTER 10

After signing in and handing over their tickets, they all sat in the studio's lobby area for another half an hour. If Jason had realised getting audience tickets for live TV shows was this easy, he'd have done it before. When he'd looked at the website, he couldn't believe how many programs were filmed out at MediaCity these days. Kids' shows. Quiz shows. Comedy. Even Blue Peter, not that he recognised any of the presenters. When the online form had asked for an email, he'd typed in another one of his disposable addresses and used a pretend name. His older brother had shown him a trick or two for not leaving any trail when using the internet.

As he'd printed off the ticket, he had a nice feeling in his stomach. *Unsung Heroes*. He wondered if they might call on any audience members. That would be good: Carla seeing the guardian angel from her own accident trotting down the steps where the audience sat! In fact, she might have to do his make-up before he went on stage. Could you imagine? Their faces inches apart, only – this time – she would be treating him. It was just like she'd said; they both made people look their best. He smiled. That girl. She saw him for who he really was. Just like he saw her.

Looking at his fellow audience members, he thought he might be the youngest person out of everyone. Most appeared to be well over fifty. Eventually, a woman wearing headphones collected them all. The studio they were filming in was odd; the part beneath the massed spotlights occupied so little of the space. Beyond the flimsy, fake walls of the set were wide swathes of dark floor. A multitude of cable snaked across it.

They were herded to a load of cramped seats. Everyone found their own spots but, shortly after, they were all asked by the woman in headphones to stand up again and squash into the centre section directly before the stage. To create a better atmosphere, she said. He examined the railings bolted into the black ceiling above. So many spotlights attached to them. He counted forty-six before his neck ached too much for carrying on. Staff scurried around the set. Some sat behind giant cameras, which began to move silently about. A man in beige chinos and a white shirt came out and talked to them for ages about how things would work. When you were permitted to leave your seat. How much fun it was going to be! And don't forget to keep an eye on the man in the mauve T-shirt on the front row. When he claps, you clap.

#

Ryan thought she'd got the room set just right. Beautifully folded towels on a stone-cold heating rail, a roll of toilet paper hanging beside a toilet cistern which held no water. Trendy little hessian mat beside the unplumbed bath. Walls painted a dusty turquoise. Beyond the frosted window, a hanging backdrop of branches and natural-light lamps completed the impression of a first-floor bathroom in an impressively sized house, with a generous garden beyond. Victorian. Somewhere leafy, like one of those big houses in Didsbury. Off-road parking and separate garages. Aspirational.

Vicky, the room dresser, was sitting on the toilet rolling

a cigarette. 'Product's coming from Ian in a minute. He's still finishing pack-shots for the room freshener.'

Ryan looked round the fake wall and across to the far side of the hangar-like studio. Ian, one of only two salaried photographers at Q2, had fixed his camera to a frame that allowed him to raise and lower it above a curving sheet of non-reflective white Perspex. Positioned directly beneath the lens was a small bottle with a tapering neck. 'Christ, how many shots does he need to take?'

'He was in before eight,' Vicky said, before running the tip of her tongue along the cigarette paper. She stood up, turned round, and carefully brushed a few stray strands of tobacco off the toilet lid into her palm. 'I'm off outside to kick this in.'

'I'll sit with you,' sighed Ryan.

Once they got to the corner, she scooped aside the blackout curtain. Ryan shuffled in next to her. When she let go, the two of them were sandwiched for a moment in the dark narrow space between heavy fabric and door. It always made Ryan feel like a child. Games of hide and seek in a big house in the Peak District his mum and dad rented once when he was little. Musty wardrobes and dusty gaps beneath beds. His cousins' shrill voices as they searched for him. Then Vicky hit the release bar and daylight flooded in.

At the side of the building were a couple of plastic dining chairs that had gone unclaimed after a kitchen shoot. Next to them was a stack of wooden pallets. Vicky perched on them, slid a Zippo from the front pouch of her dungarees and flicked the wheel. 'Footballer lot are back,' she announced, looking across the car park. 'Turned up in a Porsche today.'

Ryan followed her gaze. 'Gold. That's disgusting. Who gets a Porsche and has it painted gold?'

She blew a stream of smoke in its direction. 'Same sort of twat who gets a Bentley and has that sprayed silver.'

Ryan turned to the main building and the series of

arched windows on the first floor. Q2 occupied what had once been a derelict cotton warehouse. When the agency owners had acquired it, they'd stripped the floors back to bare wood, torn off any plaster to reveal brick and exposed every beam and metal pillar they could. Industrial chic: so very Manchester.

Massed arc lights inside had turned the windows into beacons, even though it was daytime. Hazy figures moved through the dazzle and the thud of bass carried across to them. He knew there'd be unlimited drinks in the big glass-fronted fridges. Next to them, old-fashioned seafront vending machines salvaged from a faded coastal town. There were even pots of the old-style pound coins to release handfuls of the brightly coloured sweets inside. Racks on the walls with mini tubes of Pringles, every flavour you could think of. And, if the shoot dragged on until after dark, there'd be other stuff on offer, too.

He imagined Carla up there, flitting around the models, applying touches of make-up here and there, rearranging hair to perfection.

'Have you seen his range?' Vicky asked, using her thumb to wipe a speck of ash from her black Doctor Martens. 'Carla show you?'

'No. What's it like?'

'Pure shite. Think that crap will.i.am peddles, but worse. And everything plastered with his initials. EM, EM, EM. Even the soles of the trainers so you can leave a little trail in the snow, or sand, or dog shit, or whatever you step on.'

He liked Vicky. She had a healthy appreciation of how utterly superficial and meaningless most of what they marketed here was. Froth, clinging to the surface of society. Just as transient and insubstantial. Destined for landfill in a few months. 'Cheap, too, I bet?'

'Oh yeah.' She dropped the end of her cigarette down the neck of a waist-high vase. Another abandoned photo shoot item. 'Your weekly wage might get you a sniff of some hideous bandana. If Ian's still stretching things out, we can just start on the toiletries. No way I'm staying here after five.'

'Suits me.'

Back in the dark and silent studio, they could see Ian loitering by the room set. He'd stepped on to the lino floor to fiddle with a wicker basket.

'Out!' Vicky shouted.

He jumped back like the floor was red hot, then hastily re-adopted his slouch.

'You've not got overshoes on!' She half-turned her head and spoke from the corner of her mouth. 'If that dick's left any marks on my floor.'

'Calm down. These are my work shoes.' Ian's nasal drawl was strong. 'They never leave this building.'

'And what a favour to society that is,' muttered Ryan.

The older man was wearing the sort of thing you had to put on at bowling alleys. Beige, with blue and red trimmings. Ballroom dancing, if Ryan correctly remembered an earlier, tortuously dull conversation.

'So, it's all there,' Ian said, indicating the flat-bed trolley laden with the items that needed to be shot in situ.

Ryan regarded the wispy strands of dry hair that hung down the sides of Ian's pale face. The man reminded him of gloomy; what a career spent in this dingy cave did to a person. 'Cheers.'

'If you wouldn't mind signing, I'll be off for my rather late lunch.' He removed a clipboard hanging from the trolley's handle and held it out.

Like you sign for anything without meticulously checking each and every item, Ryan thought. But he refused to allow the other man's cynicism infect him. 'No worries, here you go.' He casually scrawled his name in the field near the bottom of the form and clipped the pen back in place.

'Obliged,' Ian nodded. 'Vicky, you were witness to that.'

Same joke every time, Ryan thought. Vicky wasn't smiling either.

'So,' Ian added, refusing to melt back into the shadows beyond the room set. 'I hear you've got an exhibition happening.'

'That's right,' Ryan replied cautiously. Word was really getting round Q2 if Ian had heard.

'A few of your own shots, I believe. Stuff you do on your days off.'

Ryan had to make an effort not to react to the other man's faintly mocking tone. 'Well, more night-time, actually.'

'I like a bit of weekend photography myself,' he continued. 'Beaches and seascapes. The dunes at Formby?'

Now he sounded vulnerable, as if he'd just shared a personal secret. Something he feared could open him up to ridicule. Ryan looked into the other man's eyes. There, he saw the faint glow of dying dreams. Shit, he thought. Please don't let me end up like you. 'Yeah? We looked at Lowry's paintings when I was a student. He loved to paint seascapes, didn't he?'

Ian's expression soured. 'Oh, I don't like Lowry. Those childish figures with their matchstick limbs.'

Ryan was about to point out the seascapes didn't contain people. But what was the point? The man wasn't listening. Had probably given up listening years ago.

#

Jason kept checking the poorly lit side areas of the TV studio, desperate to catch a glimpse of her. Finally, she appeared. A kind of apron with pockets at the front hung over her dungarees. As the two presenters took their places on the sofa, she crouched before them and started to check their faces and hair. Jason didn't like the way both seemed hardly aware of her. The female continued speaking to the man, even as Carla made adjustments to her hair. Rude. Rude. Rude. Jason felt like shouting it out.

The enormous screen behind them glowed with the words *Unsung Heroes*. A young man came on stage and spoke into a walky-talky as the program title was replaced by a new caption. Danielle, nursery nurse. The accompanying photo showed a rosy-cheeked woman in her late thirties. Next photo was Ted, litter picker. He was balding, sunken cheeks and scraggy neck. Then Ann, a hospital volunteer. She'd be needing medical attention herself soon, Jason thought, judging from the ripples of fat bulging out from beneath her chin.

The elderly lady beside him brought her face close to his ear. 'Who are you here for?' she whispered.

He angled his head away from her. 'Sorry?'

'We're here for Mariella.' She tapped her companion's knee. 'Aren't we, Betty?'

Betty turned her head. Smiled briefly. Little peg-like teeth, yellowed by smoking. 'Yes. We saw her first on *Bric-à-brac Facts*. Such a lovely way about her.'

'Who's Mariella?' Jason asked.

They looked at him suspiciously.

'The presenter,' Betty eventually said. 'Mariella Francis?'

The one who had treated Carla like dirt on her shoe, thought Jason. He turned away from them without replying.

A few minutes later, Carla and everyone else retreated from the set and filming began. It was the last he saw of her for over two hours. The guests each made an appearance. Daniella: same nursery for over thirty years. Produced a handmade birthday card for every child, even though she wasn't paid for them. Video messages from adults who still remembered her cuddles. What a comfort she'd been. Ted, who voluntarily cleared an average of three bin liners of rubbish a week from his local park. And tended to the flower beds. Ran a lost property forum for all the items he found. One time, he returned a purse with ninety pounds cash in it.

Jason shifted in his seat. Yes, Ted, you're a true hero. Where the hell had Carla gone? He began to realise there'd be no audience participation. If anyone in the place was an unsung hero, he thought, it's me. Did the guests so far actually save lives? Had they any idea what to do with a pedestrian with crush injuries from an over-turned car? Someone electrocuted by faulty wiring? Bludgeoned by a breeze block?

Last up was Ann. He sighed. Ann. Salt of the earth, she was. According to the nurse who appeared on the screen with a recorded message, anyway. Ann walked over six miles every week along her local hospital corridors, escorting patients to where they were supposed to be. Six miles, Jason thought. Maybe she should try carrying the patients on her back; at least then she might lose a bit of weight herself.

Another long round of applause and – thank Christ – all the lights came on. Camera men took off their headphones. The presenters leaned back on the sofa.

'Excuse me.'

Jason looked to his side. The two women were on their feet, desperate to get past. He stood up and watched as they shuffled down the steps to the barriers that prevented access to the set. One started calling out. 'Mariella! Lovely show, Mariella!'

The presenter flashed a false smile in their general direction.

Jason stood to the side as the rest of the audience filed past. A door opened to the rear of the set and Carla stepped through. Now! Now was his chance. At least the entire trip wouldn't have gone to waste. Heart suddenly thudding, he crabbed his way along the barrier, away from the rest of the audience. 'Carla! Excuse me, Carla!'

She didn't hear, but the man in the white shirt did. 'Hey, can I help?'

Jason's hand slid into his pocket, cupped the velvet case containing the silver pendant. It hadn't been easy finding a male angel. In the end, he'd ordered it from a church in America. Gabriel. He'd paid an extra thirty dollars for expedited shipping. 'Could you give Carla a shout? Carla Bell? She does the make-up. She's somewhere just over there.'

'You know Carla?'

'Yes. Well, kind of. We met recently.'

The man's smile was fading. 'Does she know you're here?'

'No. It's kind of a surprise.'

'Right. And what's your name?'

'Just say it's her guardian angel. She'll know.'

'OK.'

The word was unnecessarily drawn out. Jason wanted to order him to hurry. Before Carla left the studio completely. The person who'd led them all in from the reception area was now making her way along the narrow gap between the first row of seats and the barrier.

'Hi, there. We need to take you back to the —'

'It's OK. I'm here to see Carla.'

She looked across the waist-high railings to the man in the white shirt. 'Who's Carla?'

'Make up. Can you stay here with this gentleman? I'll not be long.' As he walked away, he started speaking quietly into a walky-talky. Let him be suspicious, Jason thought. Once he saw Carla's reaction, he'd know he owed Jason an apology. He pictured Carla's delighted smile. Everything would be all right.

'Did you enjoy it this morning?'

He didn't glance at the woman hovering by his side. Nerves were getting the better of him. Hand tight round the pendant's case, he kept looking at the set. He had to be facing Carla when she appeared. 'It was OK. Went on for ages, though.'

'Is...is this your first time being part of an audience?'

'Yes.' He could see shadows moving on the studio's back wall. The man in chinos and the white shirt came into view. And another man, also in a white shirt, but with dark trousers. He was black and very big. He had markings on the sleeves of his white shirt. Carla was beside him. The one in chinos lifted a hand, pointed in his direction. Jason could see that he wasn't smiling any more. Carla peered uncertainly. Jason tried to nod at her encouragingly. Remember me? From when the taxi you were in...

Carla stared for a moment longer and shook her head. Jason didn't know what she meant by that. Why would she shake her head? The one in the chinos said something from the side of his mouth and the black man continued forward on his own. Carla? I came to see you. I sat here all this time. She was turning away. Why had she looked at him like that? The man in the chinos placed a hand on her shoulder and guided her back out of sight.

'Sir, we need to clear the studio now.'

It was the security man speaking.

'Sir, if you can –'

Jason didn't want to hear what the fucking nigger had to say. Why would Carla do that? He rubbed at his forehead with his knuckles. The woman beside him had stepped back. She couldn't have recognised him, that was all. He looked up. These stupid lights! They shone straight down, so his face wasn't easy to see. And why did I use my code name? Guardian angel. She just hadn't worked it out. Yes, that's all it was.

'Sir?' It was the woman speaking this time. She had a similar expression to the one he'd seen on Carla's face. You think my intentions aren't honourable? That I'm here to hurt someone? He almost shoved her aside. Dumb fucking bitch.

'It's the far door, sir.' The security man had let himself through a gap in the barrier. 'Over there.'

'I know where it is,' Jason murmured. 'You don't have to treat me like some kind of freak.' The tears made it hard to see, and he almost fell over the lowermost step. Why had I thought about it? Why? He wanted to punch himself.

You always do this. Get carried away. They don't like it when you do this. They don't. A fire extinguisher was mounted on the wall beside the exit door. He saw himself lifting it off and smashing the base into his mouth. Snapped teeth falling from his bloodied lips. He could turn it round and ram the nozzle down his throat. Deep down his throat so that, when he turned it on, the foam would tear his lungs open. He would die right here, vomiting blood, right in her place of work. And she'd know. She'd know for evermore that it was her. That she'd killed him. Her. Her.

CHAPTER 11

'Fuck!' Ryan rubbed at his hair with the fingertips of both hands. He checked his reflection in the mirror again. 'It's just not sitting right. Today of all days. I look like a total bell end.'

Carla put her magazine aside and got to her feet. 'Come here.'

He glanced at her, then checked himself again. 'And I'm not sure about this top, either.'

Carla was placing her make-up case on the island. 'The top is fine. You need to stop stressing out, Ryan. Come on, over here.' She patted the seat of a barstool with her palm.

'Well, what are you going to do?'

'Get you looking fresh, of course. Come on. Sit.'

He walked over and perched uncertainly on the seat. 'Been ages since you've had a go at my hair.'

'Had a go? Charming.'

'You know what I mean.'

'That top needs to come off.'

He pulled the Penguin polo shirt over his head and lobbed it onto the sofa.

'I'm not making a habit of this,' she stated, taking a tea

towel off its hook and draping it over his shoulders. 'Women who cut their partners' hair is tragic, so don't expect a repeat, all right?'

'How much are you taking off? It's only the fringe, isn't it?'

She circled him slowly, head cocked to one side. 'Yeah, mostly. I'll tidy it up around your ears, too. Bit of liner to emphasise your eyes. Touch of concealer beneath them. Have you looking good enough for the telly, basically?'

'Eye liner? What if he notices?'

She started snipping tiny bits of hair away. 'It'll be subtle, stupid. Don't worry.'

'Still can't believe he rang me. Ivan Sussman. Shit! What the hell will I say?'

'You'll be brilliant, Ry. Just be yourself. Do that, and he'll be enchanted. Trust me.'

'You reckon?'

'Ryan, how many twenty-five-year-olds do what you do? Walk the streets at all hours to capture the side of a city no-one sees? And you do it night after night, whatever the weather. You know the people who live out there. Not only that, they like you and they trust you. Because you're trying to show things for what they are. Not the honey-coated crap of social media. That's why people are taking an interest in your stuff. You're genuine.'

He pushed himself further back on the seat. Straightened his shoulders. 'Might he want to buy something? Perhaps he saw something on Instagram. Or in my Facebook store.'

'You'll find out soon enough.'

Ryan swallowed back a mouthful of air. 'Can't believe I'm this nervous. Feel like a school kid.'

'Oh, did you get back to Trevor?'

'Trevor?'

She stepped away from him and lowered her scissors. 'Trevor Price. You know, the traffic manager at Q2? That place that pays you to take photographs.'

Ryan scowled. 'Right. Not yet, no.'

Carla put the scissors aside, leaned over her case and lifted up little pots, one after the other. 'You need to ring him, Ry. It's not fair to blank him and, besides, we need every shift going.'

He sighed. 'When was it again?'

'Wednesday and Thursday, I think.'

'Can you call him? Tell him I'll do it?'

She met his eyes. 'Ryan, do I look like your bloody secretary? Book your own work in.'

He stared back at her for a second, then looked away. 'Sorry. It's just all this stuff going down with the photographs. Hard to concentrate on anything else.'

'Yeah – well, you're not a superstar photographer. Yet. So don't be fucking it up with the only paid work you've got. Besides, it's me who put your name forward at that place, remember? You start acting up and it's me who looks like the twat.'

'I know. Sorry. I'll call him.'

'Good. Now, lift your chin.'

#

There was a woman waiting beside the entrance to Sunlight House. She was wearing a grey business suit with a white shirt beneath the jacket. Hair tied back in a neat bun. Not quite blonde. More a pale brown. One hand was holding a bunch of keys, the other a folder with the words 'Nail & Cable' on the front.

Jason propped his Honda beside a lamppost and considered his own clothing. Hiking shoes, jeans and a black Rohan sweatshirt beneath his black leather biker's jacket. He wondered if he should have worn something smarter.

She'd taken a couple of steps in his direction. 'Mr Kirby, is it?'

'Yes.'

'Oh, pleased to meet you. I'm Tabitha Ross. We spoke on the phone.'

'Pleased to meet you,' he replied, crouching down to loop the security chain about his bike and the lamppost.

'So, are you based here in Manchester?' she asked, eyes flitting for a moment towards his mouth as he straightened up. The place where they always looked.

'Yes, that's right. I work as a paramedic.'

She had half-turned to the door of Sunlight House, but looked back, eyebrows raised. 'In an ambulance?'

'No, MRU.'

Her smile faltered. 'M...?'

'Sorry, Motorbike Response Unit.'

'Wow!' Her eyes cut to his bike. 'Hence...'

He nodded. 'Although that's not my work one, obviously. I would have worn a suit, but I don't need one. Not in my job.'

She waved his comment away. 'Don't worry! I'm only dressed like this because I came straight from our office on Deansgate. Looks pretty fast, whatever it is.'

'Oh, it can shift, all right.' He removed his gloves and stuffed them into his crash helmet as she got the door open.

'Paramedic. You mentioned you sometimes worked nights when you called about viewing one of these apartments,' she said, as the door slid back.

'Part of the job.'

'I suppose so. After you.'

He stepped into a dusty lobby area that smelled of concrete. In various places, wires hung from the unpainted walls. Stainless steel ducts ran across the ceiling.

'I've never met a paramedic before. How do you even become one?'

'It's all degrees, nowadays. I'm among the last who came through the old-fashioned way. Volunteering for the St John's Ambulance service, then a job with the ambulance service.'

She was now relocking the door. 'Just so no one sneaks in while I'm showing you round.'

Amazing, he thought. Mention you're a paramedic and look at her. Happily locking herself into a building with a man she's only met seconds before. 'Once you're signed off as a PM,' he continued, 'you can start doing extra qualifications.'

'PM is paramedic?'

'Yeah, sorry. Acronyms: can't escape them. I wanted to work on the bikes, which pretty much means specialising in trauma. Not emotional trauma. Physical. Stabbings, shootings, that kind of stuff.' He realised she was staring at him. 'Sorry, once someone gets me started I tend to...'

'You must see some pretty shocking sights, if that's the right word.'

'Yeah.' He placed his helmet on a nearby box. 'Plenty of those.'

She shuddered. 'I can't even imagine. So, this entire area will be completed last. Carpeted, tiled, recessed ceiling lights. There'll be secure mailboxes along this wall.' She gestured to the area beside the door. 'And the lift will be functional, too. But, for now, we get to use the stairs.'

Her heels echoed slightly as she led the way up a wide flight of steps. 'You specified a first-floor apartment when we spoke.'

'That's right.'

'Just as well you didn't want anything at the top. I think the upper two floors have been entirely taken. Hong Kong investor. Each floor will have eight apartments, four each side of the connecting corridor. As you can see, the doors haven't gone on yet.' She stepped through the first doorway on her left. 'Floor space is –'

'No, not that side.'

She turned. Confusion had left her mouth partly open.

'I..I...' He scrabbled for something to say. 'That's not facing the side I want. For the sun. I don't like sun in the mornings, you know – with working shifts.'

'Oh, right. Well, I don't think the sun will be an issue. Not with the surrounding buildings. But if you prefer the ones on this side...' She stepped back out into the corridor. 'This first one?'

He had already worked out which apartment would be directly opposite Flat 16, Jethro Mill. 'Maybe the end one? So it's not near the stairs. People going up and down.'

'End one it is. As I was saying, floor space in all these units is over fifty square metres. Generous for a one bed apartment. The windows are all double-glazed with Argon gas filling the void. Here we are.'

He followed her into a wide, open area. As far as he could see, there was only one interior door, on the far side.

'That is the wet room,' she said, following the direction of his gaze. 'With integrated bath and toilet. If you'd got in touch a fortnight ago, you could have specified which tiles you wanted. Anyway, what I think you'll love is the mezzanine design for the sleeping area.'

She moved to the centre of the room and turned back. 'Up there. It's a cosy little area with enough room for a double bed. There's a recess for hanging clothes, too.'

He tried to show interest in the little balcony thing that ran across one wall. 'Looks great.'

'Doesn't it? This will be the kitchenette in the corner. Of course, by purchasing now, you can specify all your own units and decor. Even have your own trade people do the work; we like to be flexible on that count.'

He turned to the row of three large windows. 'You said these are double-glazed?'

'Yes. And filled with Argon, which is two-thirds better at trapping heat than ordinary air, so lower energy bills for you.'

He made a show of running a finger down the metal window frame then brought his face closer to the glass, as if trying to discern the gas itself. Carla's flat would be slightly to the right. The lights were on and he could see into the living area. Someone was standing with their back to him, fiddling about with something on a breakfast bar. Was it her? He thought it could be her. Blonde hair. His heart was racing. Another person came into view. A male. Whoever was at the breakfast bar turned their head. It was her! It was Carla and she was smiling. The male was touching his fringe, looking pleased. She nodded and turned back to what she'd been doing: placing items into a case. Jason knew he had to say something. That he couldn't just keep staring. The male was the same as the one on her website. In the photos. The one with the knife sticking out of his head. Jason felt ill. Do you live with him? I don't believe you actually love him, even if you do. Not proper love. He managed to clear his throat. 'The things they think up. Filling it with gas. So clever.'

'Yes.'

There was a hitch in the woman's voice. He glanced at her and saw the mildly disconcerted look on her face. Had he stared into Carla's apartment for too long? Had she seen through his act? Guessed what he was really here for? 'Of course, if I bought it, I'd put up curtains. Floor-to-ceiling, I should think.'

'Of course.' She lifted a hand. 'Would you like a closer look at the mezzanine floor?'

'No,' he said. 'I don't think so.' All he wanted to do was look back into Carla's apartment. See what the bloke was doing now. 'It seems like it might be what I'm after.'

'That's brilliant. In here, I've printed out a load of documents.'

Her attention went to the folder, and he used the opportunity to glance across the street once again. The male now had a camera in his hands. He was standing beside a breakfast bar, lifting a set of keys. He went to check what Tabitha was doing, only to find her staring at him. 'I'm just amazed at how you can hardly hear anything from the street. So quiet.'

'You'll find all the information the communal charges for –'

'I'll go over it all at home.' He stepped toward her, hand outstretched. 'Thanks.'

A hint of a frown. 'I was going to take you through the finances, too. If you do go ahead, we'd need an initial deposit of –'

'It's fine. I mean, I actually need to get going. Sorry.' The male could already be on his way down the stairs. 'I can call you with any questions.'

'OK.' She handed the folder across. 'If you're sure.'

'I am.' He smiled. 'Right, I'd better be off.'

'No problem. I'll show you out.' As she set off for the doorway, he risked a last glance back. Thank God: the male was still there. But he was now putting on a coat. Definitely leaving to go somewhere.

Down in the lobby, she swept a hand towards the counter on the far side. 'I forgot to say: there'll be a virtual concierge service, which is also covered by the monthly –'

'You'll need to let me out.' He nodded at the door, bike helmet already in his hands. 'You locked it earlier.'

She looked slightly irritated.

'Sorry,' he said. 'Just, it's later than I realised. If you could...'

She produced the keys and took far too long selecting the right one. Through the dusty glass, he could see the front door of Jethro Mill sliding open. The male emerged onto the street, an absurd beanie hat now on his head. He had long lanky legs and a stupid dumb face. And his eyes were big and scared looking. A door slamming would probably make him jump. She couldn't really love someone like that, he thought. Could she?

'There you are. Free to go.' Her laugh was uncertain.

He was out the door and on the pavement. 'Thanks so much.' He tapped the folder. 'I'll be in touch.'

'I look forward to it,' she replied. 'They're going fast though, these apartments.'

He set off after the male who was now striding toward Great Ancoats Street. 'I'll collect my bike soon.'

'Bye.'

'Yes, bye.' He turned away from her, his gaze immediately fixing on the back of the male's head.

#

'Hey, Carla – how's things?'

'Good, thanks. You?'

'Yeah, but damned, it's hot.'

Carla peered more closely at her phone's screen. The sky behind Simone had that leached-out blue of holiday photos. 'Where are you?'

'Cape Town. Flying back tomorrow.'

'Cool. Simone, you know that night we had? Pasha's and Ma Things.'

'Just about, babes. Why?'

'Did we…did anything happen? Maybe with a bloke. Anything with me?'

Simone looked bemused. 'What do you mean?'

'You know how it all got a bit crazy. Did I, maybe, flirt with anyone? Or…I don't know. Do you remember anyone trying it on, or anything?'

A spoke started speaking off camera and Simone waved them away. 'Carla, these are really weird questions. Has something happened?'

'Kind of. The other day, a strange man turned up at the studio where I was working. He'd been in the audience. Then he hung around after shooting, asking to speak with me.'

'Holy shit, Carla! How close did he get? Where the fuck were security?'

'Oh, it wasn't like I was in any danger. Security were right there. They asked him to leave. He just…I don't know. He gave me the heebie-jeebies.'

'Herb what?'

'Jee – he freaked me out a bit.'

'These fucking arseholes. What do they think gives them the right? Did you file a report?'

'A report? No! It was just some bloke asking after me. That's why I wondered, if we'd –'

Simone raised a finger. 'You need to get that studio on it. Freaks like that, believe me, you have to be careful. Has he tried contacting you any other way?'

'You what?'

'Have you got any unusual messages? Emails via your website, for example.'

'Not that I've noticed. You make it sound like a psycho-stalker or something.'

'Did you tell Ryan?'

'What?'

Someone spoke at Simone again and she nodded quickly. 'Ryan. He needs to know, sweetie. The person could show up where you live. Anything.'

Carla laughed weakly. 'I'm not sure Ryan needs –'

'Tell him, Carla. You did nothing wrong. And make a report. That's how to deal with things, just to be safe. Now, really sorry, but I've got to go.'

'OK. See you soon.' The call cut and Carla cradled the phone in her hands. Maybe it was an American thing. Or the sort of stuff models had to deal with. Either way, her friend had gone a bit overboard about it.

CHAPTER 12

Once on the other side of Great Ancoats Street, Ryan turned right as if heading towards Victoria. He then cut left onto Spear Street, old warehouses looming large on either side.

Things opened up a bit at the junction with Thomas Street, and he jinked through a couple more turns. An odd-looking building was now before him. The ground floor looked like a shop of some kind, with a line of straggly shrubs partly screening its front window. Above it seemed to be offices.

Ryan paused for a second. Be calm, he ordered himself. You have no idea what this is about, so why be nervous? You're absolutely fine. You have got this, pal. You're going to smash it. No doubt about it.

As he approached the building, he caught sight of his reflection in the front window. Looking good! And the touches of make-up Carla had applied made him appear somehow more alive. Intense. Not that he could really make anything out at this distance.

The door at the side led into a strange hybrid of coffee shop at the front and bookstore to the rear. Ivan Sussman was at a table in the corner. There was no mistaking him: a big bear of a man with a bushy beard and trademark fedora hat. He was already rising to his feet.

'Ryan!' he announced in a voice far too loud for the setting. 'So lovely to see you. Do take a seat, please.'

'Thanks,' he said, voice barely above a whisper.

'I've only just ordered. What'll you have? The coffee – and trust me on this – is bliss. They order their beans from the same place as me, so I should know.'

'Sounds good. Coffee it is, then.'

'Latte? Cappuccino? Flat-whatever-it-is?'

'Just black is fine, thanks.'

Sussman let out a deep chuckle. 'A man after my own heart. Ryan, we're going to get along.' He looked toward the counter. 'Leah, my dear? Another large black filter coffee for my guest.'

#

Jason stepped through the door and quickly spotted the man who'd been in Carla's flat. He was sitting down at a corner table with a large man in an attention-grabbing hat. Jason made his way through the cafe bit into the main room beyond. Place was weird. Free standing bookshelves were interspersed with an odd assortment of chest-high vases, quirky pieces of furniture and large armchairs. In the centre of the room was a fountain where water trickled down a series of slates into a pool. Below the rippling surface, orange fragments of fish floated above a bed of pale pebbles. Poser-hat-man's voice boomed out once more.

'I am so excited about your work, Ryan. It gives me goosebumps. Actual bloody goosebumps!'

So that's your name, Jason thought. In his opinion, Ryan seemed more than a bit nervous. He drifted to the far side of the shelf unit closest to their table and picked out the biggest book he could see.

Unforgettable locations to visit before you die.

Poser-hat-man was now asking Ryan how his day had been.

'All right, thanks. I was out last night 'til about four. Got a few good shots of these rough sleepers who've snuck into an empty building just a few streets from here.'

'What, you just walked in there? With your camera? Were they OK about that?'

'I know them. Sort of know them. We were chatting and they said that's where they were heading for the night, so I tagged along.'

'Gosh. I do respect your commitment to your craft. I don't suppose there's any chance that you'd like to show me?'

'The shots?'

'Why, yes.'

'They're not with me. I don't have my camera with me.'

'Of course! Sorry. You shoot with a...'

'Canon EOS 850D.'

'A nice bit of kit, I take it?'

'Very.'

'Let's talk Instagram followers, Ryan. How many do you have?'

'Well, currently, it's almost two-thousand-seven-hundred.'

'That's not so bad. Not for someone at your stage of their career.'

'Thanks.'

'And the important thing is they're growing, am I correct?'

'Yes. All since *Vulpine Plunderer*. Before then, it was only a few dozen.'

'You like the street photographer, Jamal Shabazz, don't you? You mentioned him in a recent interview.'

'I do. Wow, you've done your research.'

'Of course. He has over one-hundred-and-thirty-seven-thousand followers. Bruce Gilden? Over one-eighty thousand. Gordon Parks? A few thousand more than that.

Don't look embarrassed, Ryan! It'll be you, one day. Trust me.'

'That would be... a dream.'

'Obviously, you've got your own website. Facebook, too?'

'Yes, but I'm not that active. On Facebook.'

'I couldn't find your page. It's not under Ryan Lamb, is it?'

Jason took his phone out and typed: Ryan Lamb.

'No – it's a shop page because I use it to try and sell prints. Street Views, it's called. It's a bit corny, I know. Kind of a play on Google's Street View.'

'I see, I see. Clever. Perhaps you get clicks from people meaning to search for Street View?'

'Maybe, I suppose.'

'And how many visits does your site get a week?'

'Term, I'd need to check. But there's not that much traffic on it, if I'm honest.'

'Well, you're fast gaining a reputation here in Manchester. And that's – ah, Leah, you're an angel, thank you.'

Jason flicked to another page. An immense tongue of jagged ice cut a pine-carpeted slope in two. It plummeted into a lake whose shore was obscured by an armada of little bergs. Soaring above it all were distant snowy peaks. The tink-tink of a teaspoon.

'As I was saying, here in Manchester, your work is gaining a following. Just the other day, I was talking to Julian Templeforth. He is an admirer, you realise?'

'Well – he started following me on Instagram. You know Julian, then?'

'We go back years. What I'm saying Ryan, is that I think – I really do – that the timing is right for a show.'

'A show? You're serious?'

'Ryan, it's not just Julian who is talking about you. Important people in the city's art scene.'

'They are?'

'They are.'

'Well, where do you have in mind?'

'My gallery, of course! Not the main room. Not yet. But the smaller side room is perfect for someone with your profile. Ivan Sussman presenting Ryan Lamb's inaugural exhibition. Sounds good?'

'Jesus, yes, I just can't quite...it's amazing.'

'Just keep producing images, Ryan. Speaking to Julian, he thinks the ones that are concerned with trauma. Life and death struggles. Those mini dramas – they are where your talent shines brightest. And I agree.'

'Life and death?'

'You know, the people at the edge of things. Whether that's society or life itself. It's the rawness of those images.'

'Right.'

Jason glanced up from the image. Ryan's voice had gone very small.

'Don't look like that, Ryan!' Ivan laughed. 'I'd say we're only a handful short of what we need. And by that, I mean a show that will really get people's attention.'

'I really don't know what to say.'

'Is that realistic, Ryan? I'm only talking maybe a dozen more shots. But on a par with *Vulpine Plunderer*.'

'Probably. I mean, yes. I'll be out every night. Whatever it takes.'

'Don't give up the day job. Not just yet. But if that's viable, give me three weeks, a month tops, to set things up my end. They'll be queuing to get in Ryan. Queuing! Apologies this is only coffee, but cheers.'

Jason heard their cups clink. He found himself staring at a new page. This one was of a grinning old man sitting in a low-slung boat. A thick cane of bamboo was balanced across his shoulders. Perched on one end was what looked like a large seagull, except it was black. A loop of cord had been tightened about its neck, and a longer one ran from one of its webbed feet to the pole. Jason wasn't sure how, but he suspected the old man had somehow trained the bird to benefit himself.

Once he got back to his bedroom, he searched for 'Street Views' in Facebook. See what sort of crap the idiot was trying to flog. Black and white close ups. Craggy-faced rough sleepers and other city-centre dead beats. A crowd gathered round a tram that had come to a stop outside Selfridges. By the horrified expressions on their faces, someone had gone under it. A middle-aged man flat out in Piccadilly Gardens, blood-stained shirt pulled up over his face and one shoe missing. That lone shoe, fallen on its side by a bin. A seated man, body sagging to one side, in the shadows of a bus shelter. Jason realised the person wasn't alone: a fox had also crept in, neck extended, jaws delicately tugging the burger from the man's bun. That was quite cool, actually. But the rest of the pictures? Jason snorted with disgust.

A thought occurred to him. One strong enough to make him sit back in his seat. What if I help him with his photographs? The man who owned the art gallery said he wanted more, what was it...life and death ones. I see that every single shift. Every one. It's what I'm paid to deal with. I could tip this Ryan person off about stuff. So he could get there with his stupid camera.

Jason wasn't sure where he was going with this, other than to make some kind of connection with the photographer. And through that, be a touch closer to Carla. Maybe, one day, he could let Carla know it was him behind Ryan's success. That he was the person who really made things happen. Saved lives. Actual peoples' lives. And then she might love him instead.

He brought up the photographer's contact details: a mobile phone number was listed. Jason took a screenshot.

CHAPTER 13

'One more?' Ryan asked, his forearm draped over Carla's thigh, remote pointed towards the screen.

Carla twisted her torso so she could see the clock above the fridge. 'Better not. It's nearly midnight. I need to be out early tomorrow.'

He pressed a button before Netflix could start showing the next episode. 'Back in Q2?'

'Not until the afternoon. That production company wants me back out at MediaCity. She swung her legs off Ryan's lap and sat up straight, yawning as she did so. 'Some cutaways they want to do with the presenters. Three hours' work, tops.'

'Which production company?' Ryan asked, dropping the remote and reaching for his phone.

'Avalon. That show, *Unsung Heroes*.'

'Right.' He was now scrolling through screens, eyes constantly moving about.

'Actually,' Carla said, toying with a strand of hair. 'Something odd happened when I was over there the other day.'

He lifted his eyes for a second. 'Odd? How?'

'This weirdo bloke was asking for me. Or the girl who

did the make-up, anyway. Said he had a message.'

Ryan swiped across to a different feed. 'Holy shit! Vulpine Plunderer is topping a thousand likes on Instagram. That is crazy. Bat-shit crazy.'

She regarded his profile in silence. Eventually, he glanced across and his grin faded. 'Sorry. Some weirdo? What did he say to you?'

'Nothing. He didn't say anything to me. Dom came to find me after filming had ended. Said an audience member was asking for me. Said the bloke seemed a bit of an oddball.'

Ryan nodded slowly. 'Who's Dom?'

'The floor manager. He took me on set so I could have a quick look. Never seen him before in my life.'

'Does sound a bit strange,' Ryan muttered, attention straying to his phone once more. 'But he just left, I take it? You didn't actually speak to him or anything?'

'No, I just said that. Not a word.'

'Well, how old was he?'

'About our age. Maybe a bit older.'

Ryan started swiping at his screen again. 'Wouldn't worry. Those live TV audiences must be packed with all sorts. Especially if it's daytime TV. I mean, who in their right minds watches that shit, let alone applies to be in the audience?'

'True.' She stared at the rug for a few moments. 'But even so…'

No response. Carla's eyes slid to the side. He was fully engrossed in his phone, thumbs busily tapping out a reply to someone. She slipped through to the bedroom, where her own phone gave a muted beep. Message from Simone.

Carla selected Facetime, glad of the chance to see her friend on-screen. 'Hey sweetie, how are you?'

Simone looked like she was getting ready for bed. Pyjamas and face covered in a pale green cream. 'Absolutely knackered. Got a shootout near Prestbury tomorrow. How did it go with Ryan?'

'I just tried to mention it to him. Like, literally a minute ago.'

'Tried?'

'It's all about Ryan at the moment.'

'Meaning?'

'He was too busy getting back to his social media admirers. Probably adding up how many new followers he's got. Don't think he really heard a word I said.'

'Grab his phone out of his hands. Then he'll listen.'

'Yeah, right.'

'Seriously, you need to say something.'

'I will.'

'When?'

'Maybe after this exhibition he's got.'

'That's weeks away!'

'When some normality returns, then.'

Ryan's voice – high and excited – rang out from the main room. 'La-la, you in the bathroom?'

'Later,' she sighed, ending the call and placing her phone on her pillow. 'No, not yet.'

'Check this out. It's... fuck knows how to describe it.' He plonked himself down on the bed beside her. 'Right, twenty minutes ago – when we were watching telly – I got a message. See?'

She peered down at his screen. 'Is that one of those code things?'

'Yeah. what3words. It's for a precise location. Could be anywhere in the world down to within two metres or something.'

'Two metres?'

'Something like that. Mountain rescue teams use it. If the lost person can ping them a code, it's easy to find them.'

'How the hell does that work?'

'Absolutely not got a Scooby-doo.'

'OK. So, where's this one for?'

'Unknown number sent it. Remember that. So, I open

up the app and put the code in. Turns out, it's for Manchester. To be precise, directly in front of the Palace Theatre on Oxford Street.'

'I don't get it.'

'Neither did I. Until I checked a local newsfeed. There's been a traffic accident. Quite serious by the sound of it. Multiple vehicles. Car has gone off the road and hit some pedestrians. Fire crews, ambulances, the lot.'

'And you're saying that's where this code was for?'

'The exact same spot. Exact! Outside the Palace Theatre.'

'Someone who's there is letting you know about it?'

'What I thought. Except,' he tapped at the side of his phone in confusion, 'it's only just started to appear on newsfeeds in the last few minutes. The code was sent nearly half-an-hour ago. Must have been pretty much as soon as it happened.'

Carla had a frown on her face as she leaned away from him. 'That is plenty strange.'

'Isn't it?'

'Have you tried the number?'

'Yup: turned off. No answer phone, nothing.'

Both their heads turned. They regarded his phone in silence.

#

Once Jason sent the code, he immediately turned the old keyboard-operated Nokia off. Scooping up his smart phone, he checked the secure work app which displayed details of incoming calls to the ambulance service. Location of the incident and a brief description. The one outside the Palace Theatre was looking juicier and juicier. The dispatcher had now allocated six ambulance crews to it. Police and Fire were also in attendance. The Accident and Emergency Department at the MRI had been instructed to prepare for multiple arrivals.

Would the photographer work out the significance of

the code he'd just received? Jason propped his smart phone in its desk-top holder and looked to his PC. How long had he now spent on the internet trawling, digging, delving? Clicking through endless screens. Poring over threads, scanning through message boards, scrutinising banks of images. Picture after picture enlarged, each background scraped for clues. Everything carefully filed.

He now knew that Carla's mum lived in a nice-looking cottage, which formed part of a row in a tiny village just outside Chester. Wasn't sure about the dad. Seemed Maggy lived alone apart from a black and white cat that, according to a stray comment on Facebook, was called Domino. Maggy enjoyed eating in Florentino's in Chester. From a few of the photos she'd taken of her meals, she seemed to favour the pasta dishes, often with a side-order of young broccoli. She loved it when Carla came to stay, which wasn't often, except on her birthday, which was on the eleventh of March. Maggy was fifty-two. Certainly looked good for her age. On one of her friend's timelines, there was an old photo – admittedly from almost ten years ago – of Maggy on a beach in Portugal in her swimsuit. He'd printed that one off. Jason could imagine Carla would look similar to her mum as she grew older. How nice it would be to grow old with someone who ended up looking as fine as Maggy did.

Without taking his eyes off the screen, he reached out and turned the old Nokia back on. It took a while to boot up, but – once it had – a missed call icon appeared. Ryan's number. That was good. The message had been received and had piqued his interest. Had he spotted something on the news and realised what the what3words code corresponded to? If he hadn't, he would have done by the morning.

He turned the phone off, happy his first, tentative step at forming a link to the other man seemed to have worked. He turned back to his PC and resumed his research. By the time dawn was breaking, he knew a lot more. Carla had gone to school in Chester. St James'. She'd done her GCSEs there, but didn't stay for A levels. Instead, she went to Chester College to do a Level 3 in Media Make-up and Artistry. Jason wasn't sure about any boyfriends from her time at school. He'd found some old photos that included Carla on a college friend's Instagram page. But there wasn't any male that featured with worrying frequency. Not until the one called Ryan Lamb and, by then, Carla was studying for her degree here in Manchester.

Ryan was from Manchester, too. Well, south Manchester. Reddish. That was why their accents weren't all that different. His mum (Tessa) still lived in the little semi-detached house that Ryan had grown up in: 15, Melrose Crescent. The dad seemed to have disappeared quite some time ago. From a photo of the man sitting on the sofa in an absurdly tight top, Jason guessed it could well have been a heart attack. The bloke had obviously used steroids on a regular basis.

The friend Carla had been with on the night their cab collided with a van was called Simone Occleshaw. Odd name, but she was American. Born there, at least. In Atlanta. Had worked as a model in the UK for many years. Not catwalk, though. A little too large-boned for that. Lots of pictures of her out in Manchester. Flashy places that would cost a fortune. Not a problem, of course, if someone else had paid for the drinks in her hand. Jason didn't think she would have. Women like her didn't buy their own drinks. Some of the places were in London. Down there on work assignments, no doubt. She'd obviously been sensible with her earnings, though. Owned a little place that overlooked Heaton Mersey Common. Very pretty. On Google earth, he zoomed right in on it, saw that it was at the end of a narrow lane. Nice views, he guessed, from the back windows.

As the light grew stronger round the edges of his curtains, Jason was viewing Ryan's photos once again.

Vulpine Plunderer – that was the name of the photo of the thieving fox. He'd looked up vulpine.

Adj. 1. Of or resembling a fox. 2. Foxy; crafty.

How awfully clever. Arty. Couldn't just call it 'thieving fox'. Oh no. Jason toggled between a close-up of Ryan's face and the photos he was trying to flog. The guy's thin features. Eyes a fraction too large behind his glasses. Long hair. He looked permanently startled. Slightly on edge. Probably bullied at school.

Jason knew a bit about that, but he hadn't let it get to him. No, he'd believed in himself. Made something of himself. Left those cruel little shits way behind. He guessed Ryan was about five inches taller than him. But the bloke had bony shoulders. Slender arms and long fingers. He thought he weighed more than Ryan, despite the other man's superior height. He didn't want to, but he pictured Ryan naked. The bloke probably had one of those long saggy scrotums, balls swaying about, stubby penis shrouded by a black fuzz of pubes. That wiry hair trailing up his belly. Patchy across his sunken chest, clustering about his nipples.

He switched back to the gallery of photos Ryan had for sale. The images of drunks. Slumped figures in doorways. Four people crammed into a phone box, apparently asleep on their feet. A lone figure stretched out in an underpass, graffiti of crudely drawn knobs and carrot-shaped spliffs swirling above him.

What was so special about this shit? Did Carla think Ryan was cool because he took photos like this? Did she? Jason shook his head. I shall show your boyfriend better stuff than this. Way better. Street bloody Views. Jason wiggled his fingers at the screen. 'Woo! Big deal.' The photos he'll get because of me will make Carla realise who the genuine hero is in all this. The one who comes to the rescue, not the clown who turns up afterwards with a dumb fucking camera.

CHAPTER 14

Ryan's phone beeped. It had taken him just over a week to associate that sound with a tidal wave of emotion. Exhilaration. Anticipation. A small dose of apprehension. But, best of all, some of the finest photographs he could have hoped for. His hand shot into his pocket, spine writhing with excitement as he regarded the screen. Another code! This was unbelievable. He had to pause for a second with his head bowed. Get your voice under control, he said to himself, before looking up. 'Vicky, I'm really sorry about this. My mum – she's got some health issues going on. I'll be an hour, hour-and-a-half, tops. He retrieved his bag and started backing towards the blackout curtain. 'If you want to set the products up how you want, that's fine with me. I won't alter anything.'

She put a hand on her hip. 'I have to be gone by five. It's gone half-three now!'

Off to his side, Ryan could see Ian lurking. The bastard was enjoying this. 'I know. I'm so sorry. Honestly, I'll be back soon.' He pulled the curtain to the side. 'Promise.'

He managed to flag a cab almost straight away.

'Where to, pal?' the driver asked, regarding him in the rear-view mirror.

'Two seconds.' Ryan put the code into the app. The map which opened up was displaying the section of A56 that crossed over the Mancunian Way. He could be there in a few minutes. 'Chorlton Road. The very start of it. Where it joins that big roundabout above the motorway.'

'You mean the Mancunian Way?'

'Yeah – the roundabout there.'

'You want me to drop you off on that roundabout?'

'If you can.'

Shrugging, he pulled away from the kerb. As they turned down Moss Lane East, Ryan took his camera out of his bag. As he checked it, he tried to put together a mental tally of the messages he had now received. Was this the fifth or sixth? His mind skipped across the images he'd recently captured. There'd been the building fire. An office on the Oldham Road. Next tip had been better. Much better. A stabbing right outside the Crown Court on Gartside Street. That had been paramedics, not fire crews. He'd got there while the scene had still been taped off. An abandoned bike and splashes of blood on the white steps. Like someone had stumbled up them holding a bowl of tomato soup. Plate glass to the side of the court entrance providing a watery double of the carnage outside.

Then it had been an incident in Hulme; a police chase involving a lad on a scooter. The abandoned bike was lying at the end of an alleyway when he'd arrived. The kid driving it had got away. While officers were speaking to locals, Ryan moved slowly about, lifting his camera to his face every so often. At one point, he'd crouched down and taken a shot from pavement level towards a sign at the top of the alley. A circular sign with a thick red line running through the silhouette of a black moped. No bikes.

Ryan wasn't sure if the police officers were even aware of him. And if they had noticed him, what could they do? It wasn't a crime to take images of emergency services while they were working in the public domain.

There'd been the derelict car showroom on the A57 at

Belle Vue. That had been confusing when he turned up at the scene. No big commotion: just a private ambulance parked up and a uniformed police officer standing by. The constable had been happy to chat. The body of a homeless woman had been spotted inside. She was lying in a corner. Ryan had approached the windows, which were largely covered over with fly posters for things like club nights, concerts and passing funfairs. By quietly tearing a few corners from the glass, he got a ragged view in. The medics – if that's what they were – had the body in a bag and were in the process of lifting it onto a gurney. He didn't have time to plan the shot. More a case of point and hope. But the result had been striking. Blurred colours from the ripped posters in the foreground, then the grim tableau of people. And, behind them, out-of-focus wall hangings that showed gleaming Jaguars drenched orange by the setting sun.

The taxi was now on Chorlton Road. Ahead, the road began to rise where it joined the elevated roundabout above the Mancunian Way. A ripple of rear lights was surging back down the road towards them. Ryan lowered the window. Distant sirens were growing louder.

'Something's up,' the driver announced glumly as they eased to a halt.

Ryan checked the app. The spot he was being directed to was only two-hundred-and-thirty-six metres in front. 'You know what? I'll get out here. What do I owe?'

He shoved a tenner through the opening in the Perspex and jumped from the rear of the vehicle. Lots of sirens. Holding his camera against his chest, he raced along the pavement, weaving through pedestrians, swerving round bus shelters and benches. He soon realised it would be quicker on the edge of the road itself: the traffic wasn't moving, after all. As the road rose higher, the lanes of the M57 started coming into view. The sound of sirens was coming from down there. *Why am I heading for the flyover?* He ran on regardless, hoping for a better view of what was going on. Traffic on the far side of the motorway was creeping. On his side, it had stopped completely. Now he was on the roundabout itself, cars bumper to bumper. He sprinted to the place where the dot on his map was and peered over the railings. Oh, you beauty. This was stunning. He let his bag drop to the floor and lifted his camera up. Below him, crumpled cars formed a haphazard arrangement across the motorway lanes. Seen like this, from directly above, the angles were amazing.

A few people were gathered on the hard shoulder, most of them quietly chatting. A man was sitting on the metal barrier, pressing a cloth to his head. Apart from him, no one seemed injured. No fatalities. That was something. His attention returned to the jumble of vehicles. Like items on a conveyor belt that had gone wrong, he thought. Which was what motorways were, in an odd way. Conveyor belts. He started to take photos. A faint whir as the passenger window of the motionless car directly behind him was lowered. Man's voice, soured by a scouse twang.

'That's bang out of order, mate, taking piccies like that.'

Ryan kept clicking anyway.

CHAPTER 15

Footsteps on the front path outside. Someone slinking out of the house after Liam's gathering last night? No: the footsteps were approaching the house, not heading away. The letterbox gave its customary clang, and the footsteps grew fainter. Jason lifted the corner of the curtain to see a figure in a red top moving up the street. Seemed a bit early for the post. He checked his watch: 8:48 AM. Later than he realised. How long have I been at my computer? Ten, eleven hours? He realised he was hungry.

He'd lost count of the number of tips he'd now sent Ryan. Maybe five each week? Over the time since he'd started, that must have added up to almost twenty. The results were starting to show, but not in a good way.

He'd noticed the reactions to anything Ryan put online had shot up. The one of the car crash on the Mancunian Way had got him over three hundred likes on Instagram in less than twenty-four hours. The number of people following him was rocketing, too. Was he helping turn Ryan into a star? That wasn't his plan. Not at all.

He clicked on the Sussman Gallery's site. The forthcoming exhibition dominated the home page. Urban Trauma. Fuck's sake. Ryan glanced at his certificate for dealing with trauma. Real trauma. The results of a knife slicing through an artery, or a bullet through bone. He was the one who knew about bloody trauma, not Ryan! The paragraph below infuriated him even more.

Images that force the viewer to witness the struggles – often brutal – that play out in the heart of the city.

You mean the stuff I sort out every day? Every fucking day! Where's the applause for me? The big slap on my back? The people lining up to offer their thanks?

He kept checking Carla's social media feeds. Searching for anything that might indicate she knew where credit for Ryan's photographs really lay. Just a love heart for the NHS would do. An angel icon. Anything to hint she got what was going on. But all she'd tweeted was how proud she was of her boyfriend. That and a link to his exhibition, now less than a week away.

Jason shook his head. That decided it: no more codes to Ryan. The bloke was getting a big fat nothing from now on. Fuck all.

He opened his window and retrieved the carton of milk he'd placed on the sill the previous evening. In the silence of his house, sliding the bolt on his door back sounded like something in pain. Down in the hall, a single brown envelope lay at the base of the front door. He picked it up, picturing the cupboards as he trotted towards the kitchen in his socks. There'd better be cereals. And bread, too.

The envelope was official-looking. Words on the front said do not ignore. There'd better be bran flakes. Visible through the little window on the front was his name and address. Transferring the milk carton to his left hand, he tore the envelope open, barely registering that, for once, the front room had no one dossing in it.

The large letters at the top of the letter halted him in his tracks. Notice of Intended Prosecution. What the hell? He scanned the opening lines. A speeding offence? That wasn't possible. But the middle section had it all listed.

Vehicle: Honda Fireblade
Offence: Exceeding 30 mph speed limit
Speed: 37 mph
Location: A57, Hyde Road

Jason didn't understand. It was his bike's registration on the form. He checked the time and date of the offence. Twelve fourteen, Tuesday before last. Tuesday? He went to the calendar hanging from the wall in the corner. No way: he'd come off a late shift that day at ten in the morning. So he'd have been in bed, earplugs in, eye-mask on. Fast asleep.

Had someone cloned his registration? Stuck it on a stolen Fireblade? Stuff like that happened.

He put the carton on the table and flipped to the second sheet. A grainy image of a bike, flashed by the camera that was, he guessed, at the junction of Pottery Lane. This made no sense. He hadn't been that way on his bike in weeks. Months. The inner picture had a close-up of the bike, registration clearly visible. He scrutinised the person riding it. Was that his spare helmet? The one he kept in the cupboard beneath the stairs? He could make out the familiar Isle of Man TT sticker on its rear. A three-legged emblem at its centre. The leather jacket, though, wasn't his. Lighter coloured. Realisation like a kick in the balls: it was Liam's. He could see a foot, too. One of his brother's old Adidas trainers.

He was taking the stairs three-at-a-time before any conscious thought kicked in. The fucking arsehole! How had he unlocked it? How did he get it started? He brought his fist down on the door once before smashing it open and stepping into Liam's room. Not Liam's. Liam's proper room, with its single bed, was down the hallway. This was Mum and Dad's before they'd died. He hadn't even changed the mattress.

'You took my bike! You total fucking shit, you took my bike!'

His brother was turning over, raising himself up on one elbow, squinting at the bright doorway.

'I can't believe this. You took my – . This is it, you fucker. You are out. You are fucking out!'

Liam had lifted a hand. Beside him, some female was flipping herself over.

'The fuck?' Liam croaked. He ran fingertips down his throat. Coughed. 'What you pissing your pants about, now?'

That choice of words. Belittling him as usual. 'This! This, you prick. Can't believe you'd do it.' He waved the sheets of paper. 'You took my bike when I was asleep and fucking broke the speed limit. 37. My job – no, my career, my entire career – and you...you fucking dickhead, you take my bike and then break the speed limit.' He wanted to upend the bed. Send his brother sprawling to the floor. Drop it back down on his skull. 'I want you out of my house. Today. You're gone. I don't give a shit where, you're gone.'

'Shall I go?' the girl whispered to Liam, who was now propping himself against the head rest, a hand idly scratching at his bare stomach.

'Easy,' he murmured, before glancing at Jason. 'Don't know what you're on about, Our Kid.'

'Oh, get to fuck. It's you! It's fucking you.' He stabbed a finger against the image. 'My bike, with you riding it. How did you even do it? Have you taken copies of my fucking keys?'

Liam just shook his head. 'What are you on about?'

'It's all here. Try and deny it, I swear I'll come back here and slit your throat open in your sleep. I swear!'

'Whoah!' Liam said, beckoning with the fingers of one hand. 'No need, no need. Let me see it. Give.'

Ryan handed the sheets over and stood back, arms crossed, eyes glowing in the dimness of the bedroom.

The girl kept glancing between the two men. 'I'll think

I'd better go,' she whispered uncertainly, turning away and trying to scrape a t-shirt from the floor.

'Yeah,' Liam said quietly. 'Do one.' His eyes turned to Jason. 'Didn't realise the camera got me. It's a thirty zone, then?'

Jason was vaguely aware of the girl trying to pull her t-shirt over her head while keeping the sheet up around her chest. 'It doesn't fucking matter. You stole my bike —'

'Borrowed your bike.'

'Rode it... fuck knows where. Doesn't matter if it was thirty, forty or fifty. You were speeding. Speeding!'

Liam laid the printed sheets across his lap, reached for cigarettes on the bedside table. The girl was now on her feet, snatching clothes from the floor. 'Later, Liam.' She padded warily past Jason.

'Had to drop something off in Denton. Urgent, like. That was the quickest route, across to the Hyde Road. Didn't mean to get you a fine, bro'.'

'A fine? It's three points, you cunt. I'm an MRU paramedic. No bike, no fucking...you know what? Fuck this. I'm not taking points for you. No. This is on you. Your points, your fucking points, not mine.'

Liam placed his cigarette on the plate taking up most of the bedside table. 'That's not happening. I don't even live here.'

'Really? That's your —'

His brother's voice grew more menacing. 'I don't live here, right? And you never threaten to slice my throat open. Say shit like that, and you'll be waking up in a wheelchair. No more riding bikes for you. Ever.'

They stared at each other in silence. As the seconds ticked slowly by, Jason felt the power being sucked out of him. Bit by bit. Every time he exhaled breath, more left him. He could sense it flowing through the air, transferring itself across the room and into his older brother. Just like it always did. For as long as his memory went back. Well, not any longer. Now he finally had some control. Something he was in charge of. 'You're a fucking arsehole. I want you out of this house. I mean it.'

Liam retrieved his cigarette. 'Yeah, yeah. I said: couple more jobs, little bro, and I'm gone. You won't need to worry about me.'

Jason stepped forward to retrieve the penalty notice from the bed. 'I won't, you can be sure of that. Not one bit.'

'Not very brotherly.'

As he lifted the sheet of paper, he decided to play his trump card. Rip that infuriating look of victory off his brother's face. 'And you haven't time for any more of your jobs. I want you out now. You know why?' He waited a second.

Liam stared at him with a bored look.

'Because I'm selling this place. Buying somewhere else.' The surprise in Liam's eyes! Fucking ace. He genuinely looked lost for words. 'Be here, if you want, when the estate agent shows the new owners in. I'm sure he'll be wanting to know who the fuck you are.'

'Selling? Since when? Fuck off.'

Jason walked calmly to the door. 'Find yourself somewhere else,' he said over his shoulder. Back in his own room, he slid the bolt across then clenched both fists and raised them above his head. Yes! That felt so good. So, so good. He brought up the number for Tabitha Ross at Nail & Cable.

'Yeah, hi. You showed me round the first-floor apartment on Loom Street. Sunlight House. It was a couple of weeks ago now. I arrived on a motorbike?'

'Yes – Jason, is that right? The paramedic?'

'Yes. I don't suppose it's still free? The apartment?'

'I believe it is.'

'Oh – in which case, I wanted to tell you I'll take it. The one you showed me round. That one.'

'Great! Did you go over the information in the folder? The finance options we have available?'

He looked down at the folder, lying on the floor unopened. 'Not really. Look – can it just be a deposit? I'll pay the balance when the house I'm currently in sells.'

'That's certainly an option.'

'Good. How much do you need? For me to get the keys now. How much?'

'Well, it wouldn't really work like that. There are health and safety issues with access. I mentioned some contractors are still on site, I think.'

'Yeah. How much longer are they there for?'

'If it goes to schedule, about another four weeks and you can be in.'

Four weeks? He couldn't wait that long to see Carla again. 'What about having the keys for a weekend or evening? When the workmen have gone. Like when you showed me round? Just so I could go in and start planning stuff? Measuring up and things? I wouldn't be actually living there.'

'If a deposit has been paid and contracts signed... I'd need to check with my manager, but that could certainly be possible. If it's just for measuring up. But only at certain hours.'

He thought about his savings. The money he'd inherited after Mum and Dad died. He could do it. Easily. 'All right. Can you check, please? I want to get this moving.'

'Certainly.'

'And I'll get the deposit. Just tell me how much. It won't be a problem.'

He ended the call and immediately scrolled to the main station's number. He lowered the handset back down. Tilted his head to stare up at the ceiling. How do I say this? Which words should I use? He glanced forlornly at his collection of certificates. The years of effort. The hours he'd spent right here, in this chair, at this desk, studying.

Anatomy, physiology, protocols, doses, policy...so many skills.

The Notice of Intended Prosecution lay across his keyboard. It was like a bell ringing out. The death of his career. That shitty, useless brother. Why did he have to come back?

His eyes shifted to the images of Carla he'd printed off. In the centre photo, she was smiling at him. What would you say if in my position? You'd be so much better at this than me. The right words would come easy to you. He gazed at the pendant hanging from a small nail beneath his montage of images. The guardian angel he'd ordered from America. He was her guardian angel. She'd come to realise it, too. She just needed more time.

He pictured his line manager. Danny. Ex-army. They got on OK: Danny wasn't bothered that he didn't spend hours at base aimlessly chatting to the other PMs. He felt he and Danny had a kind of understanding. He pressed green, waited to be connected and then entered Danny's extension.

'Danny Hayes speaking.'

'Danny, it's Jason. Jason Kirby.'

'Jason, didn't expect to hear from you today.'

'Yeah, the thing is, something's happened.'

'Oh. What do you mean?'

'You've not heard, then? There's not been a call or anything?'

'A call? No. A call about what?'

'Well, I've had this letter through. A Notice of Intended Prosecution? My motorbike. It was on the A57. Tuesday afternoon, it was. Twelve fourteen in the afternoon. Not this Tuesday, the one before last –'

'Jason, you've been caught speeding? Is that what you're saying?'

'Well – there's a photo. It's my bike's registration and make.'

'Your bike's registration and make?'

'Yeah.'

'But it's not your bike? Is that what you're saying?'

'No, it is my bike.'

'OK, sorry mate, you're not... I'm struggling to understand. You were on your bike Tuesday before last and got flashed by a speed camera on the A57?'

I wasn't on it. It wasn't me. It was my bike, but my brother had taken it without asking. No insurance or nothing. He used it to ride drugs or something to someone over in Denton.

'Jason?'

'Yeah, that's right.'

'Shit. How fast?'

'37.'

'37?'

'Yeah.'

'So that's three points?'

'And sixty quid.'

Danny sighed heavily. 'What were you thinking? You know what this means, right? You'll be taken off driving duties. Jason, are you there?'

'I'm... I'm really sorry.'

'Jason, listen, there's no need to get upset.'

'I just... I really am sorry. Letting you down like –'

'Jason, it's not the end of the world, OK? And you're not letting me down. Are you listening?'

He wiped the tears from his eyes. Sniffed back snot. 'Yes.'

'OK. You were doing 37 in a 30?'

'Yes.'

'That's right on the edge. People get offered the speed awareness course for that, sometimes. Probably GMP already filled their quota for it or something. That's why you've been given a straight three points. Let me have a word with the operations manager here. See if we can get you on a course instead.'

Jason lifted his chin. 'You think that could happen?'

'I don't know. I really don't. But it's worth a try, isn't it?'

'Yes.'

'Too right. Don't beat yourself up over this, Jason. You're a good MRU Paramedic and I will vouch for that, you hear?'

'I hear.'

'OK, let me get back to you.'

'Should I come in tomorrow?'

'Assume not. Unless I call you before then. You've got holiday to take?'

'Loads.'

Danny laughed. 'Of course – you have to be told to take it. How could I forget? Take a day or two. I'll call you, OK?'

'Thanks, Danny.'

'Don't you worry. We'll sort something.'

'OK.'

'Speak to you soon.'

He kept the phone to his hear, listening to the dead air. Speed awareness course. The humiliation of that would be worth it. Circling a parking lot with a bunch of novices and mid-life crisis dickheads. Who cares? He'd not have the points. He could keep working; that's all that mattered.

His eyes were pulled to the largest photo of Carla. He'd been planning for a while to drive over to her mum's place in Chester. Well, now he had time to actually do it. See it in real life. The curtains, the colour of the front door. If it had a burglar alarm or security lights. Chester was a nice place. Even so, you had to be careful nowadays. He hoped she'd got proper precautions in place. He really did.

After that, he could swing by where Ryan Lamb's mum lived. The pokey little terrace in Reddish. Probably on a right crappy street. All sorts living there. He imagined the views into drab front rooms. The sorts of places with sheets in the bedroom windows, not curtains. He'd been in plenty, sorting out overdoses and attempted suicides.

Victims of domestic violence. Kids with no clothes on, kitchens with no food, parents off their tits. Carla didn't deserve all that in her life.

CHAPTER 16

Zack was downstairs at the kitchen table, flicking through his phone. Someone had broken one of the other chairs. A leg was missing and what was left had been shoved into the far corner. 'Yo, Jason. Not got any lives to be saving?'

'Day off. And you?'

Zack glanced up to spot Jason's wry smile. He grinned. 'Just checking in for work myself.'

Jason nodded towards the hallway. 'Where is he?'

'Said he was popping out. Getting milk and stuff.'

Turn up for the books, Jason thought. Him actually buying anything. Though if he thinks that's going to change anything, he's wrong. Crouching at the corner cupboard, he removed the half loaf of bread he'd hidden in a saucepan. There was a bit of coffee in the jar. He flicked the kettle on. 'So, this work you and him have been doing...'

Zack's eyes lifted from his screen. 'What about it?'

'How's it going?'

There was a pause. 'What's he said to you?'

'Not much. Just that he had a couple more jobs lined up.'

'Did he?'

'Yeah.'

'You know, it's one of those. Nothing's certain.'

He glanced across. Zack was back on his phone. Jason could tell he wouldn't get anything useful out of him. He put a couple of slices in the toaster, then filled the kettle up and switched it on. 'Hey, you know how it works with phone hacking nowadays?'

Zack didn't even look up. 'Yeah.'

'So go on, then.' He opened the fridge. The lower shelves were all empty. Up top was some margarine and an opened tin of baked beans.

'There's software that does it. You've got the person's phone number, right?'

'Yeah.'

Zack waggled his handset from side-to-side. 'Just go on the dark web. Shit's listed there. For an iPhone it might be, dunno, hundred quid or so?'

'Seriously?'

'You want me to show you?'

'Fucking hell.'

His brother's voice. Jason's head whipped round. Liam was standing in the hall doorway. Bastard must have let himself in through the front door.

'Which poor bitch is in your sights this time?' he asked.

Jason felt his face grow hot. Thistles prickled his armpits. 'No one.'

Liam was laughing as he dumped the shopping bag on the kitchen table. There was a smirk on Zack's face, too.

'Didn't you just say to Zack you've got her number?' asked Liam. 'Mia, right? She'll let you bang her. Just ask her like a normal person. No need for all your weird shit.'

Jason turned his back on them both. 'It's for someone at work, actually. Thinks his wife might be fooling around.'

''Course it is, little bro'. 'Course. I thought you were over that, anyway? All them sessions with the brain doctor –'

'Shut up!' He whirled round. Zack looked swiftly down at his phone.

Liam raised both hands. 'He's gonna pop! Fuck me, he's gonna pop!'

Jason pointed a finger. But he couldn't make any words happen. Nothing. Liam lifted his eyebrows, the familiar mocking expression contorting his face.

#

The next two days drifted by. Jason tried to sleep when it was night because he knew that was important. The circadian rhythm. Your internal clock that made you go to sleep when it got dark and wake up when it got light. It was important for people who worked shifts to try and let that cycle reassert itself whenever possible. It wasn't healthy to disrupt it by working at night, forcing yourself to stay awake through the small hours.

But he'd worked as a paramedic now for six years. On the bikes for three of them. His circadian rhythm was no longer in good shape. Often, he'd climb out of bed and go on the computer. Not good: he knew that. The blue light emitted from screens suppressed the production of melatonin, disrupting sleep patterns even more. He'd spend quite a lot of time on Carla's feeds, concerned to know how she was, what she'd been doing. Time felt like it was slipping by. Time they could have spent together. He had to remind himself he was still young. Twenty-seven. Carla was twenty-five. Average life expectancy was now about eighty. They'd have decades together. Plenty of time for children, too, if she wanted them. He wasn't bothered, but he'd happily do it for her.

Sometimes he'd go on her website. Nothing much changed on that. But if he sensed she was feeling lonely or was maybe worried about not getting any new messages from him, he'd send her one. Just something short. Sweet nothings. Things like, Believe in Yourself. My heart is yours. You are beautiful. UR the 1.

She never replied, which was a little disappointing. After all, he'd started signing each one, 'All my love, Gabriel'.

But maybe she still hadn't made the connection to the night they'd met. Just as long as they weren't ending up in a spam folder. That would be terrible.

One afternoon, he went into town. Walked along Loom Street, checked the building contractors were keeping busy in Sunlight House. The main doors were open and he saw into the foyer. The walls and ceiling had been done, but the floor was covered by a protective layer of plastic. All the men were gathered around, watching a video on one of their phones and laughing. At two-forty in the afternoon? He'd called Tabitha about that, and she'd sounded shocked. She wanted to know if he was actually there, outside the building. Yes, he'd said. I was happening to pass by. So she said she'd have a word and thanked him. He'd also asked when his keys would be ready for collection. They'd already taken his deposit, after all. Soon, she'd said.

He caught the train to Chester. Made his way to the outskirts where Carla's mum lived. Her cottage was on a quiet little road. Trees at regular intervals. Well-tended front gardens, as he'd expected. He wondered how much cottages like these were worth. One day, it would be Carla's. It was good to know they'd be financially stable. Was thinking in those terms a bit mercenary? No. It was practical. Planning for the future, that was all.

When he reached Maggy's cottage, it was lovely. No tree or swing. Maybe one in the back garden. He was a little concerned with the chimney. There were some traces of moss between the bricks; he could clearly see them, even from the pavement. That would need pointing. No car on the drive, which had been recently repaved with little amber bricks. So she did what she could to maintain the place. That was impressive, her being a woman living on her own.

And it had nice curtains, like he knew it would. He spotted Domino on the windowsill of the front room and almost waved. But then he realised he was being watched from the neighbouring house. A sour-faced old fart in a cardigan and tie. Blatantly staring down at him from an upstairs window and not caring that Jason knew. He wanted to raise two fingers up at him, but you had to be careful nowadays. CCTV cameras were everywhere. He took a last glance at the front of Maggy's. She didn't have a camera. Not mounted on the exterior of the house, anyway. No security lights that he could see. Or burglar alarm. That could be something he'd get her. When Carla and him were together. After she'd brought him here to meet Maggy. It was a practical present, yes. But one that showed consideration and, perhaps more importantly, concern. An eagerness to protect those that are near and dear. She would, he was certain, be touched.

When he got home, the house was deserted. The front room was a wreck. Empties everywhere. Something dark had been spilled on the carpet. Red wine, or maybe rum. He checked the time. Almost four. The kitchen wasn't much better: the broken chair was still in the corner; cigarettes had been stubbed out on side plates; food cartons lay on the floor beside the overflowing bin. Fucking pigs.

His phone started to ring and, when he checked the number, he saw it was work. 'Hello, Jason here.'

'Jason, it's Danny. How are you doing?'

'OK, I suppose. Bored.'

'Well, sorry for the delay. Listen, GMP are really dragging their feet. I spoke at length to the ops manager here, David Archer.'

Jason knew who he was talking about. A cadaverous-looking man of about six-foot-four who was rarely seen out of his office. 'What did he say?'

'I explained that you're an asset to the team. And God-knows we can't afford to be down an MRU. But whether we get you on the speed awareness course or not, it's a black mark on your record. So don't, for God's sake, do anything like this again.'

'I won't.'

'Honestly, Jason, you need to realise this. Archer is trying to pull strings, but it's a one-off. He was keen I stressed that.'

'Understood. Thank you, Danny. Really, thank you.'

'While we're waiting on the GMP's decision, I reckon you should just take it easy. You've got so much holiday allowance stored up, so why not –'

'Can I come in? It's not good being off like this.'

'You can't go out, Jason. No bikes until this has been resolved.'

'I don't care. I can do admin, restock kits. Anything.'

'You wouldn't mind the... attention? You know how people like to chitter-chatter. Especially in that rest area.'

'I don't care, Danny. I just want to keep busy.'

'Well... we might be able to get you the odd shift in the ambulances, too.'

'Don't mind going back to that.'

'OK, let me see when you were next due to be –'

'Tomorrow. A ten 'til seven.' He listened as his line manager tapped away on his computer.

'You're right. And then you're off until Tuesday. Sure you want to come in for just the one day?'

'I am. Been crawling up the walls here.'

'Tomorrow it is, then.'

'Thank you.' He sank down into the nearest seat and looked about. A can of Stella was on the edge of the table and he lifted it up, testing its weight. Full. He rarely drank, but – sod it – why not? Might help him sleep. As soon as the tepid liquid flooded his mouth, he spat it straight back out. Bloated cigarette butts skidded across the floor.

CHAPTER 17

'There's a few going for a drink, if you fancy it?' Vicky asked. 'Happy Hour in the White Lion.'

Ryan turned the last of the studio lights off and pulled the door shut. He had received no new codes for a few days now. The exhibition was almost here. He needed one more – just one – decent shot. 'Sounds good, but I've got other stuff planned. Sorry.'

'No worries,' she replied. 'When are you next in?'

'Nick mentioned a shoot next week. A range of bathroom fittings? Can't remember the name of the company. They also do sinks, shower units, towel rails...'

'World of Aqua. I'm down for that, too. I'll see you then!' She set off for the entrance into the main building.

Ryan hitched his bag over his shoulder as he strode across the half-full car park. No point going home. He needed to find something worth photographing. A bus was idling at the stop a little way along the road. Its sign said Piccadilly Gardens. Maybe head there? He sighed, knowing he'd covered every nook and cranny of the place already. The same old homeless people. The buskers and street preachers. Clusters of school kids and the men lurking at the edge selling drugs.

He jumped on anyway, took a seat, and immediately checked his phone for any new messages. This was getting to be a compulsion, he thought. Of course nothing's there. You'd have heard the notification alert. He wondered if it was worth sending another text to the number. Was the person even reading them? Ryan had no way of knowing.

The bus made its way down Oxford Road. What were they calling this stretch now? The Academic Corridor: was that it? He eyed the university buildings that lined either side of the road. Soon, he was passing his old School of Art. Harry Cooper – his photography tutor – had got in touch the other day. Asked if Ryan could come in and talk to the current crop of third years approaching their finals. Just a half-hour talk. Nothing formal. And he'd mentioned the End of Year show, wondering if Ryan would like to attend the opening night. Free drinks and canapés. Ryan felt like he should offer something in return, so had invited Cooper to the opening of his exhibition. Him and up to three others. He'd figured Sussman wouldn't mind.

They were now passing beneath the Mancunian Way. Stubby concrete pillars supported the motorway lanes above. It used to be a gathering place for the homeless. Somewhere relatively safe and dry. He'd taken some of his earliest portraits beneath that flyover. Most of the other people on his course had, too. He remembered the skate park that had been built beneath a similar flyover just a couple of streets across. It was also a favourite haunt of photography students. A few days ago, Ryan said to himself as he got out of his seat, you'd never even considered somewhere so clichéd. Not now, though. Not now you're desperate.

He got off where the old BBC building used to be. Towers of offices and apartment blocks now surrounded a central plaza. He cut across it and was climbing a flight of steps up to Princess Street when he heard the wail of a siren. His head instantly turned. Where was it coming from? He ran up the last of the steps. There! A solitary ambulance emerging from a side road. Was it heading to, or from, an incident? If there were two sitting in the front, it was on its way. Only one, and it was returning to hospital, with one of the medics in the rear tending to the casualty. He opened his bag and looped the camera strap round his neck. The vehicle was turning left, heading away from him. Shit. He started sprinting along the pavement but, within seconds, the vehicle was going too fast for him. He kept running all the same, reasoning that – as long as he could see the throb of blue lights – he could still catch it up when it stopped. It reached the junction at the end of Upper Brooke Street just as the lights changed to green. Accelerating through, it turned its lights off. You're returning to the hospital, Ryan realised, slowing to a walk. Fuck, fuck, fuck! Now breathing heavily, he looked around. He was part way across a wide verge of grass. He spotted a subway going beneath the junction. Walls plastered with graffiti. Worth a try, he reasoned, wandering into it. The thing stank of piss. No surprise there. The path at the far end branched in two directions. A few dilapidated blocks of flats were off to his left. This area was a lot quieter. Poorly lit, too. Trees and bushes formed a screen from the nearby road. Ryan was trying to work out the best way to get to the skate park when he heard footsteps behind him.

'Give us your bag.'

He turned round. Two lads. About seventeen. One white, one black. Both with their hoods up. The black one dropped his eyes. 'And that camera.'

The white one had moved behind Ryan to block the way back into the tunnel. 'Do it, you lanky fucking dickhead.'

Ryan retreated a step. His only chance was the pathway leading towards the cluster of flats. But that's where they probably lived. Probably knew every inch of the place. A hand grabbed at the strap of his bag. It was the black guy. He looked angry. Ryan suddenly thought about his dad.

He knew what the man's advice would have been. Start swinging. Don't back down. Never back down. Fight.

'Here, take it,' Ryan said, shrugging it off his shoulder. 'It's yours.'

The black guy beckoned with his fingers. 'The camera. And your jacket.'

The other one's voice sounded behind him. 'Trainers, too.'

'Come on,' Ryan said, attempting a smile. 'Really?'

The black guy stepped in closer. He moved like he was in a boxing ring. 'Now.'

'OK, OK.' Ryan started kicking off his Adidas trainers. 'Just not the camera. Please? You can have the rest. But I –'

A sharp impact into his kidneys cut his words off.

'Have it!'

Pain stabbed up into his ribcage and he felt himself stagger to the side. The black guy was up on his toes, both fists raised. Did he just punch me? He did.

Voices from further up the path. The reverberation of little wheels.

'We've got you, arseholes!'

'Smile for the camera!'

'Livestreaming, livestreaming, livestreaming!'

The black guy's head twisted to the side. 'Shit.'

The other one spoke. 'Let's go.'

They both sprinted in the opposite direction. Ryan turned to see at least six skateboarders gliding down the path towards him. Two at the front had their cameras pointing at him.

'You OK, bro?'

The lead one came to a halt and stepped off his board. 'Close one, hey?'

Ryan pressed a palm to his side and winced. His kidneys were pulsing red hot. 'Think so.'

The others were slowing up, crowding round him with

curious faces. One retrieved his bag and held it out. 'Here you go.'

'Thanks. They just appeared from out the shadows.'

'Yup, they often do.'

A girl turned in the direction the pair had fled. 'Cocksuckers!'

The word echoed momentarily in the tunnel.

'You gonna be OK?' someone else asked.

'Yeah,' Ryan replied. 'I think so.' He glanced at the group. Spotted Carhartt beanies over dreadlocks. Goatie beards and neck tattoos. The smell of spliff wafted into his nostrils. 'Hey, can I take your photo? Like, all of you?' He glanced back at the tunnel. The receding row of strip lights on the ceiling, each one encased in wire. The mass of graffiti forming an unruly mural on both walls. 'Perhaps gathered here, in the entrance?'

CHAPTER 18

'Have you got it?' Ryan asked, seated before his iMac, phone held to the side of his face.

'I have, Ryan, I have,' Ivan replied. 'I'm looking at it now. It's very striking. Undoubtedly.'

Ryan nodded, eyes on the image he'd just sent across to the gallery owner. The crew of skateboarders posing at the entrance to the tunnel. Considering the low levels of light, the shot had come out really well. The group was little more than a silhouette. Behind them, the clinical lines of the harshly lit tunnel contrasted with the more organic, crumpled outlines created by their baggy clothes. 'I so like the way you can just make out certain features. Like the strands of hair of the guy at the back, on the left. Or the glint of the skateboard's wheels the girl crouching at the front is holding. Their body language: it's got great energy.'

'It does, Ryan, it does. But is it not portraiture? Which is not what we're really after. The grit and the gore, Ryan! Blood and guts! Well, not actual blood and guts, but you know what I mean.'

Ryan felt like a sandbag had been laid across his shoulders. He'd persuaded himself that this shot was viable. But Ivan was right. He gave it another push, even though he could see it was no different to the shots you could see in any photography student's portfolio. 'It's still sub-culture stuff, though, isn't it? Plus, we've got the dusk setting and the underpass itself. It would sit quite nicely alongside some – '

'We don't want the underpass, Ryan. We want the underbelly. Nothing posed. Think of the wonderful quote Julian provided. The brutal struggle. That's what we want!'

Ryan closed his eyes. 'Right. The brutal struggle.'

'Just one more shot, Ryan. I think that will do it. The exhibition is this Monday. There's still time. Go out and work your magic, Ryan. Use that sixth sense of yours to find one more shot. I know you can do it!'

Not while the what3word codes have dried up, Ryan thought. Without those, I'm well and truly screwed.

'Ryan? Do you hear me?'

'One more, yes.'

'Do you think you can do it?'

'I'll do my best, Ivan. I really will.'

'That's what I like to hear. Right, I've got to go. Keep me posted!'

The line cut and Ryan lowered his hand to stare at the phone's screen. Come on, he thought. Whoever you are, get in touch again. For God's sake, get in touch.

#

'Jason.' Danny Hayes started to get up from behind his desk. 'How are –' The line manager's cautious smile disappeared. 'Are you OK, Jason? You look like you're just coming off a night shift.'

'I haven't been sleeping so well. Been feeling a bit stressed with all this, if I'm honest.'

'Yeah – I can see that. Please.'

Jason took the chair Danny was pointing to.

'Try not to worry about the speeding offence, Jason. David upstairs is fighting your corner. I asked him what was happening after I spoke to you yesterday. He's going to call his opposite number at the traffic unit again.'

'OK. Thanks.'

'In the meantime,' Danny clapped his hands together, 'have I got some choice tasks for you!'

Jason could hear the mock-cheer in his line manager's voice and tried to respond with a smile.

'I've got you a desk in the admin office. It's that lovely time when we need to get the CPI audit done; staff appraisals start next month.'

CPI, Jason thought. Core performance indicators. The percentage scores each person received against a range of pre-determined actions allowed management to gauge how everyone was doing. With the speeding offence, his appraisal was going to be truly shit. But for the audit to even happen, someone had to go through each crew member's paperwork and enter the data into the system. 'I don't mind a bit of key tapping,' he replied.

Danny smiled. 'You don't need to pretend data entry is fun. But someone has to do it. Maintenance of vehicle stock, general station duties; I'll get you other stuff, too. It won't be forever.'

'If it gets switched to a speed awareness course, do you know how long I'd have to wait until that happens?'

'I should imagine a fortnight. We'll get you a place on the first one possible, don't worry about that.'

'Right.' Two weeks. Two weeks of non-operational crap. He got to his feet. 'I'll head to admin, then.'

'Good lad. It's James Parker who runs the show. He's expecting you.'

Halfway up the stairs, his phone beeped with an incoming text. Another one from Ryan, asking if everything was OK. What he really meant was, will there be more codes? At least I have this small piece of pleasure, Jason thought. Making the arsehole suffer. Smiling, he returned the phone to his pocket.

#

Outside the admin office, he bought a packet of Extra Strong Mints from the vending machine. It was a trick he'd learned while revising for his more tedious paramedic exams; the sharpness of mint helped you from nodding off. The packet was half-gone when his phone rang. Fifteen minutes away from his lunch break. Unsure whether to take it, he checked the screen. Nail and Cable's number.

He grabbed his phone and headed for the door, hips and knees feeling stiff from too much sitting. 'Jason here.'

'Jason, it's Tabitha Ross, can you talk?'

'Yes.'

'Oh, good. Wasn't sure if you might be responding to a call. Sounds quiet wherever you are.'

He pushed through the doors into the corridor. 'Yes, I'm inside at the moment.'

'Not racing about on your bike?'

'No, not at the moment.'

'Anyway, it's all sorted for you.'

'Sorry?'

'The keys! You can collect a set and access the building this weekend.'

'This weekend?'

'Well, you can call by tomorrow evening to collect them. The security system for the main entrance is now live, so I'll give you a fob for that. But I'll need everything back by first thing on Monday morning. The contractors are finishing off a few things, so you won't be allowed in the building after Sunday.'

Jason felt like he could leap into the air, high-five the ceiling with his free hand. Three nights and two days! He could take food and a sleeping bag. Water bottles if the taps weren't working. An entire weekend to be close to Carla. Just the width of a narrow street and a few panes of glass separating them. He couldn't believe it was going to happen. 'When can I collect them on Friday?'

'We close at six. So, I suggest about a quarter to?'

'That's great. Quarter-to-six tomorrow. Thank you, Tabitha.'

'My pleasure. See you then.'

The afternoon slid slowly by. Each time he completed a sheet of paperwork, he allowed himself a look at the system. At least three calls would have made good tips for Ryan. That's if he was still prepared to help the bloke. It felt fantastic to just cut him off like this. Show him what can be given can also be taken away.

It had just gone half-six when another text pinged on his phone. A lot of the admin staff had finished at five. For the last hour, he'd been alone in the office. He leaned back in his seat, expecting to see something more from Ryan.

'Hi Jason, Eddie Mellor here. See you in twenty minutes.'

He frowned at the screen. Eddie...? Shit! He'd totally forgotten about arranging for the estate agent to visit his house for a valuation. He fired a text back. 'Running ten minutes late. I'll be there for ten-past, thanks.'

CHAPTER 19

He pulled his Fireblade up alongside the little red Audi parked outside his house. The man smiling at him through the windscreen had a bald head and pale blue eyes. Jason thought he looked hardly old enough to be out of college.

'Jason Kirby?'

'Yup,' Jason replied, climbing off his bike.

'Eddie Mellor. That looks like some machine. Does it go ridiculously fast?'

'It does. I'll get it locked away and we can go in the back.'

There was an iPad in the estate agent's hand and he was already looking up at the roof, eyes sliding down the exterior of the house. 'No problem. Looks like the tiles and guttering are in good nick.'

As Jason stepped out of the shed and put the padlock in place, the estate agent was pacing the perimeter of the back garden. Overgrown borders were littered with cans and bottles. Someone had chucked the broken chair out onto the unkempt patch of lawn.

'Listen,' Jason announced. 'It's in a bit of a state, I know. But I'm after a quick sale, so don't feel you've got to go for a top asking price, OK?'

'Let's have a look inside. I sold one identical to this on the next terrace last month. Got two hundred and twenty-five for it.'

'Sounds overpriced. Right, this leads straight into the kitchen.' He pulled the back door open to find Liam and Zack sitting at the table in a fug of hashish smoke. He stepped back to let the air clear a bit. The estate agent was peering in with an uncertain expression.

'So,' Jason said. 'The kitchen. Utility room through that door on the right. I'll take you through to the rest.' He glanced at Liam, who was drilling the estate agent with an aggressive stare.

'Who the fuck's this?'

'An estate agent,' Jason said matter-of-factly. 'He'll be seeing the sale through. That's right, isn't it, Eddie?'

The estate agent stepped gingerly inside. 'That's right.'

'Fucking dick,' Liam murmured, lifting a can of Red Stripe and taking a long pull.

Jason waved at the stain-covered carpet in the hallway. 'I'm guessing this will need to be properly cleaned. Or it can just be ripped out. Whatever. So, you've got two rooms –'

'Yes,' Eddie cut in. 'It's the same layout as the other one I mentioned.' He glanced quickly through the first door. 'When did the double-glazing go in?'

'I don't know. Six, seven years ago?'

The estate agent made a quick note on his iPad. 'Right.' He walked to the other door and looked through. 'Very good. There's broken glass in there, you realise? On the carpet?'

Jason sighed. 'Do you need to see upstairs?'

'Yes, please.'

'OK. So, you'll remember there are three bedrooms.' He tapped on the padlocked door at the top of the stairs. Number one. Main bedroom, is it called? That's at the far end. Other one is on the left, opposite the bathroom.' He watched the estate agent set off along the short corridor and look briefly in both rooms, then the bathroom. When he came out, he was wrinkling his nose. 'You might want to see about getting a plumber. There's quite a smell in there.'

Jason remembered the sink had been blocked that morning. He'd shaved in the shower instead.

'Can I see in this room?' The estate agent was nodding at his bedroom door.

Jason was thinking about the mass of Carla's photos that covered his wall. There were a few of Ryan, too. But he'd done stuff to those. Just for a bit of a laugh. Scribbled over his eyes and a few other things. 'No.'

'No?'

'It needs sorting out. I'll do that before anyone comes for a look.'

'OK. Is it in a similar condition to the other two bedrooms?'

'I suppose so.'

'And the loft. Can I take a quick look up there?'

'Be my guest. I'll get you the hook thing.' He went into what used to be Liam's room to retrieve the pole from its place beside the door. He hadn't checked in here for a few weeks. The covers had vanished from the bed. What looked like blood was peppered across the bare mattress. Spots of it dotted the wall above the headboard. In the far corner was a crumpled item of clothing. A skimpy t-shirt or perhaps a large pair of boxer shorts. An empty bottle of vodka and pile of scrunched-up tissues were on the bedside table. Jesus Christ.

The estate agent completed the rest of the inspection in near silence. Less than twenty minutes after he'd shown the other man out the front door, Jason's phone went off. He'd kicked off his shoes and was lying on his bed, gazing at Carla's pictures.

'Jason, it's Rachel Sanders here. I run the local branch of Ridgeford Estate Agents.'

'Hi.'

'Hi. Er... I just wanted to check back with you about your property. The one my colleague, Eddie, just looked round.'

'I said to him, I'm not bothered with a top price. I just want to get rid. Two hundred grand will do.'

'Well, I don't think it will be possible to find you a buyer. Not in its current condition. As Eddie mentioned, he got a considerable amount more for a house with an identical –'

'What needs doing? To get it sold?'

'Well, the way to sell a property – you may know this – buyers want to imagine how they'd have the house. To make that easier, you want to reduce visual distractions to a minimum. I'm talking about clearing away clutter so you have plain, simple rooms. Neutral colours on the walls. Magnolia paint throughout wouldn't be a bad thing. Carpets a simple grey or beige – or none, if the floorboards are in good condition.'

'I'm not redecorating the place. It's take it as it is, and the price can reflect that.'

'Then my advice is that you get the property deep cleaned. By a professional company. I can recommend you an outfit we've used –'

'Deep cleaned?'

'Yes. It really needs a good refresh.'

'How about just asking for less money? I've seen places where it says refurbishment is needed.'

'That could be an option. But that doesn't address the other major problem.'

'What other problem?'

'Who were the other people in the property?'

'No one. They're...no one. Why?'

'Do they live there?'

'No, not really.'

'Eddie found it quite...you know, he hesitated coming in, if I'm honest. I wouldn't be comfortable arranging viewings while they were in the property. The whole drug thing; it's just not good.'

Jason closed his eyes. Liam. I can't escape. While he's here, I'm trapped. He dragged a palm down the side of his face in despair.

'Mr Kirby?'

'Yes?'

'Will you be able to say that those two people were just visiting? That, for the purposes of any viewings, the only person present in the property would be you?'

'I'll call you back.'

'Pardon?'

'Just... leave it with me. I'll call you back.'

'OK. Sorry if this –'

He ended the call and got to his feet. Fucking Liam. This was the last straw. The bastard was leaving. Jason didn't care where he went to. He opened his door and was about to storm down the stairs in his socks when he heard the murmur of voices in the kitchen.

The door was slightly ajar. Normally, Liam kept it shut if the two of them were having one of their discussions. He leaned over the wooden railing, head turned slightly. What were they talking about? The way they were keeping their voices down, Jason knew it was dodgy.

He caught a couple of Zack's words. Do-able. Cashing up. He looked at the stairs. Can I creep down? They'd hear me; every damned step creaks. There was only one way he'd get close enough to listen in – and he hadn't done it since being a child. He swung one leg over the banister and lowered his torso, pressing his chest and stomach against the smooth wood. Then, lifting his other foot from the top step, he loosened his grip enough to start sliding slowly down.

Halfway, he stopped and tried listening again. Zack was still speaking.

'... fucking right. Toddy was thinking about it for himself. Before he got caught for that garage thing. He already checked it out. There's only two on at that time of night. Piece of piss.'

Jason's eyes narrowed. Two on. That sounded like they were talking about a petrol station or something similar. Liam asked something, but his words were indistinct. Jason let himself slide down a bit further. Now he was five steps from the bottom. His face was level with the top of the kitchen door. Through the crack, he could see Zack's elbow resting on the table's edge. He tipped his head to the side, hardly daring to breathe.

'... about seventy,' Zack said. 'Old fucking dear, she is. And her son, well into his forties. What's he going to do? We hold a blade to her throat, he'll do exactly as we fucking tell him.'

'How do we know they won't have cashed-up earlier?' Liam asked.

'Toddy said. His cousin worked there, but they were too tight to keep her on. Polish, they are. That's why it's only them two. And they put the money in the back once they close.'

'Which is ten thirty?'

'On Fridays, yes. To avoid the piss-heads after closing time.'

'The Pop-In on Pinnington Street?'

'Yup.'

'So we go in ballied-up at, what, ten fifteen and clean them out?'

'Easy.'

'And you want to do this tomorrow?'

'Why not?'

'Problem: we'll need a car. If it's Salford way, we'll need a car.'

'I've got a car. A Golf. Took it the other day, down in Sheffield.'

Jason's mind was racing. They were robbing shops! Putting on balaclavas and robbing shops! Zack had mentioned a blade. He thought about the hold-all he'd seen on the kitchen floor. And all the bottles of spirits lying about.

'Security?' Liam asked.

'Shite. One camera above the front door. I go in with the hammer, like last time, and take that out. You've got the blade. We get the granny and the son's not going to do a thing.'

Jason pictured the two of them charging in through the door. Threatening an old lady. He imagined them emptying the till. Sweeping bottles of booze and cigarettes off the shelves. Suddenly, it was all so bloody obvious. Then, in his head, another person appeared. Just as the two of them were about to get away, someone else comes through the door. And that person had a stupid camera in his hands.

Ryan.

He knew Zack had been done in the past for GBH. And Liam? God knew what he was capable of. Next to arrive, Jason thought, will be the police. Because I'll ring them. Soon as Ryan is through the doors, I'll ring 999 and tell them an armed robbery is in progress. Response time for an incident like that on a Friday night? Four minutes, maybe less. Jesus! This could be it. Ryan maimed, maybe killed. And Liam gone, out of his life. At long last.

There was no way he could climb off the banister and make it back up the stairs without them hearing. Which left him with only one option. So what if there was a creak as he swung his leg back over? He made sure his feet connected heavily with the last few steps. Jumped off the bottom one so he landed in the hallway with a thud. The kitchen had gone quiet well before he pushed his way angrily through the door. 'I told you to leave! So what are you doing still fucking sitting here when I'm trying to show an estate agent round?'

Liam exhaled smoke up at the ceiling. 'You're really starting to piss me off, Our Kid. Seriously.'

'Really? Sorry about that. There's going to be viewings

from Monday. So, unless you want the estate agent asking awkward questions, you need to pack your stuff and go.'

Liam's head shook. 'There aren't going to be any viewings next week.'

'No? Why's that, then?'

Liam stood up so fast, his chair toppled over. Two strides got him round the table. Jason felt a hand clamp his windpipe and he then he was up against the door frame with the glowing tip of a cigarette so close to his eye, he could feel its heat. 'Because I fucking say. I told you, couple more jobs and I'm gone. Get that in your skull.'

When Jason tried to speak, his voice sounded comical. Like Donald Duck. 'Get. Off. Me.'

Liam moved the tip of the cigarette slowly across to Jason's other eye. He was desperate to blink, but sensed that was what his brother wanted. Liam's fingers unclenched and Jason felt the pressure in his temples dissipate. Rubbing at his windpipe, he backed out the door. 'You are such a cunt.'

'People keep telling me.'

As Jason jogged back up the stairs, he fought to keep the laughter inside. He'd heard everything. Everything! And they had absolutely no idea he had. So that was it; just after ten-fifteen tomorrow night, there was going to be fireworks on Pinnington Street.

PART 2

CHAPTER 20

Jason couldn't stop fiddling with the set of keys he'd collected from Tabitha the previous day. The Nail and Cable lanyard had two keys attached to it by a chunky ring. He'd need both for gaining access to the apartment. Last item was a small black fob. This was for touching against the reader at the front entrance. He'd been so desperate to drive across to Sunlight House and take up his position at the window. But he knew he had to wait. He needed to be in his house, monitoring Liam and Zack. The two of them had been lurking in the kitchen during the early part of the evening. When he'd gone in to put the kettle on at about eight thirty, they had a few lines of coke arranged on an upturned dinner plate. He could sense the tension in the air. Liam had reverted to his old-school punk groups, which was always his choice of music when psyching himself up for something bad.

Back up in his room, Jason could feel the thud of music coming up through the floor. An urgent military beat. The lead singer, sounding like his vocal cords were starting to fray and snap as he shouted the same words over and over.

Johnny, Johnny, Johnny, Johnny was a good man.

At nine thirty-seven, Zack left the house. Jason knew he was currently living less than a ten-minute walk away. Stay calm, he told himself. He'll be back soon. Downstairs, the music switched. Ryan recognised this one. Was it The Clash? The chorus kicked in. *Death or glory. Becomes just another story.* His brother was joining in, yelling the words out. A glass smashed. No, a glass exploded. Liam must have thrown it against the wall.

At nine fifty-seven, a white Golf pulled up outside the house. Jason had all his lights off with just the crack of curtain open. He could see Zack at the steering wheel, glow of his phone lighting his face.

The music cut. A second later, the front door slammed and Liam came into view, walking like a prize fighter who'd just achieved a knock-out. He had the empty green canvas hold-all slung over his shoulder. At the broken front gate, he gulped back the last of a bottle. The empty was slung into the hedge. As soon as they set off, Jason picked up his phone. He'd already prepared the what3words code in a draft text to Ryan's phone. On impulse, he added something else: 10:20PM. He pressed send at nine fifty-nine and closed his eyes, willing the message through the air, across the rooftops of Beswick, over the curving rim of the Etihad and then onto Ancoats, swooping down to Loom Street and into Ryan's phone.

#

Ryan kept his pace up. Maybe whoever was sending the codes had been off sick. Or away on holiday. That's why they'd abruptly stopped. Whatever. The important thing was, they'd started to arrive once more. Thank Christ! He glanced at his phone again. 10.06 PM. He still had fourteen minutes to reach Pinnington Street. He'd easily get there for twenty past ten.

He reached the intersection with Hilton Street. Tables arranged on the pavements outside allowed drinkers to enjoy the mild night. Myriad glints of light dancing in their glasses and bottles. A billowing vape cloud emerging from a guy's mouth, the nose of the woman next to him wrinkling with distaste. That would have been nice to catch on film. A black caravan of idling taxis in Stevenson Square. The white walls of a takeaway across the road bleaching the faces of the staff inside. His eyes never stopped roving.

It felt like the city was his again. A giant scene constantly unfolding before him. His to record and document. Odd how, the day before, he'd been stalking these same streets with a sense of mounting dread. Now a new code had appeared, all his enthusiasm had come flooding back. Like a tap had been turned. He wondered again what the incident might be. If the street was residential, burglary seemed a likely option. Except it wasn't the early hours of the morning, which was when he thought burglars usually struck. Perhaps it was some kind of domestic incident. A house siege? An ex-partner who'd tracked down the woman who'd left him? A hostage situation would certainly be interesting; he'd never photographed one of those before.

#

Jason stood and started pacing his room. 'He just goes down to Great Ancoats Street, follows that to Victoria,' he said to himself. 'Cuts through the station and across Trinity Way. Yeah, no sweat.'

By ten-past ten, he was tapping his phone against his thigh. What if he gets side-tracked? Steps for the toilet in Victoria Station? Doesn't even go through Victoria Station, but tries walking round it?

He brought Ryan's number up and sent another text: Hurry.

That was it. Short of ringing to ask what was happening, he could do no more. Except, of course, call the police. He slid the old pay-as-you-go handset from his pocket, counted the seconds until ten-seventeen, and dialled 999. 'There's a shop being robbed. Two men carrying weapons. It's the Pop-In on Pinnington Street, Salford. They're in there now. Right now!'

He ended the call and turned the phone off. Then he opened the case, pulled the SIM card out, and flexed it back and forth until it splintered.

It felt like the oxygen had been sucked from his room. He had to lie down on the floor and regulate his breathing. In for two, hold for two, out for two. Repeat. When he felt a little better, he turned his head to look at the print-out of Carla. If only you knew how much I've done so we can be together! Not that I mind. I don't, I really don't. I'd do anything for us. For our future.

He got onto his hands and knees, crawled across to the wall and brought himself up to a kneeling position. Her face was right before his eyes. She was smiling. He leaned in closer, remembering how it had been when he'd treated her. Her soft breath on his face. He stayed like that for a bit then, quickly, guiltily, stole a kiss. Right on her mouth. The paper stuck to his lips as he brought his face away. He lay back down and lifted his smart phone and looked up at the screen.

Ten nineteen. By now, the robbery would be well underway. Ryan should be arriving, too. He flicked across to his work app and signed in.

There was his call, second one down, logged at ten seventeen. Report of an armed robbery in progress at the Pop-In convenience store, Pinnington Street, Salford. Single patrol car despatched.

Above it was a call that had come in one minute ago. An incident outside the Wetherspoons pub in Piccadilly gardens. Female of about thirty with a glass injury to her face. He lay the phone on his chest and made himself count to fifty. When he checked the app again, a new incident had been reported. A middle-aged man who'd climbed over the railings of a footbridge across the M60, just past junction five. Jason banged his hand against the floor. Had something gone wrong? Why weren't they sending more units across to Salford? He started counting again, but this time only got to thirty before having to check the screen again. At last, an update for the incident at the convenience store on Pinnington Street.

Jason felt a jolt of adrenaline go through his system. One male unconscious with serious lacerations to the head. They'd attacked Ryan! Police would be swarming at the scene. Armed robbery, slashing a witness, stealing a car. He wouldn't be seeing his brother for a long time.

He turned his head to look at Carla's montage and smiled.

The dispatcher had allocated two ambulance crews. Jason sat up. He felt queasy. Maybe Ryan would die. Imagine that! Liam on a murder charge. Carla suddenly alone. He sent a concerned glance at the pictures. Maybe he should visit his apartment? It would be good to see what happened when the police called. How she reacted to the unfortunate news about Ryan. Especially if the injuries were fatal. There'd be shock and disbelief. But, perhaps, a hint of relief? To know she had, at last, been released from a relationship that was already dead. Jason didn't expect it would be easy to spot that particular emotion among her inevitable tears, but he was pretty sure if anyone could, it was him.

CHAPTER 21

Jason inserted the key in the lock of his apartment on Loom Street. But rather than open it, he stood still, waiting for the corridor lights to click off. He couldn't afford for the windows of his apartment to be lit by even the faintest glow. To do so risked giving his presence there away.

There was a click further down the corridor and everything went dark. He turned the key slowly and opened the door a crack. A small amount of light from the street outside was spilling across the bare concrete of the floor. That didn't matter: anyone outside the building would only see black panes of glass. He clicked the door shut, dropped to all fours, and began crawling across the cold floor.

The ride from his house had only taken seven minutes, and one of those had been spent waiting for the traffic lights at road works on the A635 to go green. Once at the building, he'd been struck by the irrational fear that the key fob wouldn't work. But the door had slid smoothly back, and he'd wheeled his bike onto the pristine carpet of the deserted lobby.

He didn't care that his hands and knees were getting covered in a fine white dust; the windows of Carla's apartment were now bobbing into view. When he reached the far side of the bare room, the cosy interior of her home was before him. He froze. There she was! Right there. If there were no windows between us, I could say her name and she'd hear. He stared, utterly transfixed at the dainty way she was working a teaspoon round the inside of a little purple pot. Was she also singing to herself? Her lips were moving. The spoon went into her mouth and her eyelids lowered with pleasure. It was, well, it was almost sexual. Jason felt himself blush and almost had to look away. She gestured at something propped up on the breakfast bar. Her phone. Of course, she was on a video call with someone. Someone she was friendly enough with to stick two fingers up at. Whatever the person had said, Carla now looked sad. Distracted. She even briefly raised both hands to the sides of her head in despair. What's bothering you, my sweet?

She climbed off the stool. Phone in hand, she started wandering straight towards the window. Straight towards him. He kept absolutely still. After what felt like a lifetime, she turned her head. She had been looking right at me! Had she seen? Oh God, did she? No. Think of her eyes. They weren't focused on anything. Just staring. Or were they?

He remembered when he was little. When he believed that women on the telly were able to see him. That they were speaking to him. The one from Blue Peter, who he thought was so lovely. How, when she said goodbye at the end of the programme, it was really just to him. Mum and Liam had found it so funny when he'd whispered goodbye back. Of course, she couldn't see him. He'd accepted that, eventually. But when he'd gone to see Rihanna when he was fifteen, that was different. Even though he was too far away to properly see where she was looking, there were times in the performance – he knew this with all his heart – that she was singing directly for him. That she'd spotted him there among all the other faces and something had clicked between them. He'd waited for ages after the concert, jostling among the stupid autograph hunters, but she hadn't come out looking for him. He'd been so upset.

Now he fixed his eyes on Carla. It might have been impossible for her to have seen him consciously. For him to register in her vision as a physical object. But he knew something had passed between them. On a spiritual level. On a level you couldn't measure by ordinary means.

Her body language had now changed. He craned his head to see where she was looking. Oh, they were here! A police car had pulled up on the street below. News of Ryan. News, perhaps, of his death. He checked Carla. You need to be strong, my darling. This next bit will soon be over. It's only your old life being left behind. She said two words and it didn't matter that he couldn't hear her voice. He could read her lips: *It's him*.

Jason's gaze dropped. No, no, no. It said serious lacerations. They'd sent two units. How could Ryan be climbing out of a car, head not even bandaged? Saying thank you and then walking across the pavement...

Carla had already cut the call and was rushing to the door. Jason wanted to check the app on his phone, see what the latest report was saying. But he couldn't risk the screen's glow. This didn't make any sense. It just didn't. He felt like he might be sick. Seconds later, Ryan was in the apartment and they were talking. The two of them were moving stiffly. Carla was frowning. Ryan looked scared as he drank back glugs of a white spirit.

Jason glanced over his shoulder to the door. I need to get back to Beswick, find out what's happened to Liam. Across the street, Ryan was showing Carla his phone. My message. Are you showing her my message? Carla looked cross. In fact, she looked furious. She had lifted a hand, kept chopping it down as she spoke. Keeping low, he scuttled back across the dusty floor. At the door to the apartment, he turned for one last look. Ryan was avoiding her eyes, looking miserable. Jason wanted to shout out.

Oh, Carla, look at him! Look at how weak and miserable he is. He edged back out into the pitch-black corridor.

#

As soon as she'd closed the bedroom door, Carla leaned against it. This whole thing with the photographs was getting out of control. And Ryan couldn't see it. Or was totally in denial. She wanted to sink to the floor and cry when she considered how much he'd changed. How he was so determined to bet everything on making it as a photographer. Risk his only paid work. Race after anonymous tip offs about the most horrific things. Events that involved people being injured, maimed, traumatised. Even killed. Although he was careful never to show any victim's face, they were still people's family members. Sons, daughters, sisters, brothers. Ryan just couldn't see that. All he sensed was opportunity.

She slumped down on the bed. But, she asked herself, wasn't that the kind of mindset you needed? To make it in this type of industry. To succeed. Ruthless ambition. Single-minded focus. An obsession for your art. Where would it stop? How far was he prepared to go? To sacrifice? She studied the backs of her hands. And what about me? Am I also something to be discarded, if he had to choose?

She didn't want to think about it. Not here. Alone. She thought about Simone. Chatting things through with her was always worthwhile. She checked for her phone. Shit. Her eyes cut towards the door. It's out there. On the island where I left it. Silly cow. Now you've got to go back out there. She shook the thought from her head. Go back out where? To the living room of my flat. My flat, not his. He doesn't own the place, I do.

He was hovering by the sink. Even though he was only filling the kettle, he looked faintly guilty. Or was it contrite? Crossing to the breakfast bar, she hoped desperately he'd turn and look at her. Say he was sorry. But he didn't. Are you really going to pretend to not realise I'm even here? Jesus, how pathetic. 'Forgot my phone.'

His head turned and he feigned surprise. 'Say again?'

She picked it off the work surface and held it up.

He gave a nod. 'Oh.'

'Night.'

'Night.'

Back in the bedroom, she pushed the door shut once more. Missed message from Simone! She immediately went into the tiny ensuite and turned on a tap. Once water was gurgling down the plughole, she called her friend. 'Hi, you. Just saw your message.'

'Carla! How's it going? You sound... are you on the toilet?'

'Not quite. But I am in the bathroom.'

'OK. You're not sounding happy.'

She sighed. 'Yeah, it's not good.'

'Because you told him? He reacted badly?'

'I've not told him.'

'You've... why not?'

'I don't know.'

'Carla, speak to me. Why haven't you let him know?'

She could feel tears welling up. 'I don't know if we'll even be together.'

'Why?'

'He's acting like such a twat.'

'About what?'

'This exhibition. His photography. Instagram followers. Everything. I'm getting sick of it, Simone, I really am.'

#

Ryan waited until he heard the bedroom door click shut. Feeling lightheaded from the booze, he slid the camera across and turned it on. The shots from the convenience store were all there. He scrolled through them on the tiny screen. Bloody hell! The shop's fluorescent strip lights gave the pictures a harsh, clinical look. The sort of lighting a crime-scene photographer would use. But the way he'd framed them, zooming in on the skewed till with its money tray protruding out. The single drip of blood making its way down the glass counter, blurred jars of sweets on the other side. Less is more, he said to himself. Little details that hinted at so much. And the man on the –

Carla's screen coming to life broke his chain of thought. He only just had time to see the incoming message before it faded.

I hope he took it OK? Simone xxx

He'd been still peering at the blank screen when he'd heard movement beyond the bedroom door. Not wanting to be caught snooping, he sprang off the stool and was filling the kettle at the sink when the door opened.

'Forgot my phone.'

He half-turned his head. 'Say again?'

She lifted it towards him.

'Oh.'

'Night,' she said guardedly.

'Night.'

She vanished back into the bedroom and he continued staring at the door for a second. I hope he took it OK? Who was Simone talking about, he wondered. Me? The shots from the late-night shop jostled the question from his head. He lifted the camera again and squinted at the screen. So much blood! Drips running down the counter. Spreading out from beneath the man's head. Slick and dark. Like cooling gravy.

The boiler kicked into life. That meant she was in the little ensuite, filling a sink with water. The presence of the images in his camera's memory made him feel uncomfortable. What if Carla stumbled across them? That would be bad. So bad. He crossed the room to his little workstation in the corner. A spare memory stick was lying beside the iMac; something he'd probably used to transfer a few images to at some point, even though he backed up everything to the cloud. He plugged it into the camera's USB. Once the images were saved across, he removed the stick and deleted them from the camera itself. He looked around. The second drawer down contained all the stuff Carla never touched. Screwdrivers and Allen keys. A can of WD40. A tangle of old mobile phone chargers. He took the lid off a plastic takeaway carton where he dumped used batteries and hid the stick beneath them.

#

As his house in Beswick came into view, Jason spotted Zack's little black Renault. It was parked right outside the front gate. Nothing made sense. Jason dropped the bike's revs and glided the last thirty metres. He didn't want anyone in the house to hear him.

After wheeling the bike down the side of the house and leaving it in the shadows, he crept towards the back garden. He could hear music thumping from the kitchen. Someone was in there. Next came a roar of triumph. Liam's voice. A whooping immediately followed it. Zack. How could this be? Jason peeped round the corner. Light from the windows lit the overgrown patch of lawn. Glass clinked. He edged out into the middle of the grass and turned to the window. They were both in there. Liam was on his feet, jumping up and down on the spot like a football supporter celebrating a goal. He could see Zack hunched over the kitchen table, head nodding away. The Clash was back on, playing loud. Liam was singing along.

You been drinking brew for breakfast,
Rudie can't fail

Jason stared in disbelief. He'd seen the call come in. Ambulances and the police had been there... He walked up the back steps and pushed the door open. Zack glanced up from the enormous joint he was building. Liam stopped dancing long enough to swig from a bottle of Kraken rum. The hold-all was on the floor. Its zip was open and Jason could see it was stuffed with more bottles of spirits. Cartons of cigarettes. A machete, stained with blood. Liam had followed Jason's gaze. He nudged the bag beneath the table. 'Little bro', how's it going?'

Jason focused on his brother's face. Tiny dark flecks dotted it. He didn't need to look any closer to know it was blood. More of it stained the edges of the fingernails on his right hand. The hand he was using to hold the bottle. The hand he would have used to hold a blade.

Zack spoke up. 'Have a drink, Jason. Come on mate, everything's better with a little drink in you.'

Jason's stare was still fixed on his brother. Liam was grinning back, but a wariness was now showing in his eyes.

'So, what's going on?' Jason asked.

Liam tipped his head back like he was about to yawn. Instead, he roared up at the ceiling. 'Fuck off! Just fuck off!' He turned to Zack. 'Can't believe this little twat is my brother sometimes.' He pulled a chair out and sat.

Jason didn't move. 'What's in that bag under the table?'

'Knock off booze. You want some? What do you drink, Jason, when you're having some? Tia Maria? Fucking Malibu?'

'Don't,' Zack muttered to Liam. 'Leave it.'

Liam shook his head. 'Well, are you just going to stand there like a retard? Shouldn't you be fucking off to your room?'

'Knock-off booze,' Jason said. 'Course it is. Bought it in a pub, did you? The Wheatsheaf, maybe?'

Liam just shot him a scathing look.

Zack glanced up at Jason again. 'As I said, get yourself a drink, Jason. Looks like you've had a tough one.'

Jason moved closer to the table. 'You're in my house. And whatever you're doing, I don't like it.'

Liam slid a cigarette out and lit it. 'You don't like it?' he asked, smoke trickling from his lips with each word. 'Know what? I don't like what you're up to either.'

'And what's that supposed to mean?'

Liam gestured with his cigarette hand. 'You're forgetting, but I've seen that look in your eyes before, bro'. Your shifty little cunt look. Do I need to warn Mia? Tell her to start locking her door at night? Should I?'

Jason felt his lower eyelids tingle. It wasn't fair that Liam used what had happened with Rebecca as a way to get at him. It had been years ago, for a start. He knew that it had been bad. But it had been an accident. And he wouldn't do it again.

'Look!' Liam's grin was back. He nudged Zack. 'Am I fucking right, or what?'

Zack kept his head down.

'Get some help, Our Kid. If you're heading down that road again, get some fucking help!'

When it mattered, why would the words never come? Just getting his mouth to unlock took so much effort! 'You...you don't know anything about me, you little fucking bastard.'

Liam took another slug of drink. 'Don't want to, mate,' he breathed. 'Not nice in that skull of yours, I bet.'

If Jason had a weapon, he'd have used it. An axe to split his brother's head in two. That would be good, seeing his brain exposed to the light. Or a baseball bat. Yes! He'd seen what happened when you used one of those on someone's face. The way it went like a puffed-out lumpy potato once the maxilla, nasal and lacrimal bones had all been shattered. Nodding happily at the thought of it, he turned round and stormed back out of the house.

CHAPTER 22

Carla's side of the bed was cool beneath his outstretched fingers. Vague recollections of her moving quietly about the room at what had felt like the early hours of the morning. Head throbbing from the gin, he turned over and reached for his phone on the bedside table. Gone nine o'clock. Oops. He was due at the Sussman Gallery in less than an hour.

This would be his third visit. First time was for being shown round while they discussed the exhibition in general terms. They'd also given him some documents to sign. Ivan had taken him out to lunch afterwards. The flashy Spanish place on Thomas Street. Ordered two bottles of wine with the meal. The gallery owner seemed to know the name of every server. Second time was to discuss actual details of the exhibition. Dates and times. Number of photographs Ivan wanted for it. As he was leaving, Izabella Lefteri had turned up to take Ivan through her latest paintings. Ryan had done his best to act nonchalant. His life suddenly seemed surreal.

Ten minutes after getting out of bed, Ryan was showered and dressed. Sitting at the breakfast bar with a bowl of granola and oat milk, he studied the police officer's card. Detective Inspector Graham Roebuck, Major Incident Team, Greater Manchester Police. There was both a landline and mobile phone number. Ryan spun through what he would happen if he called.

Hi, Detective Roebuck. I'm ringing because I didn't mention something from last night. I'm sorry. But, you see, the reason I was on Pinnington Street was because I received a message instructing me to be there. I've been receiving quite a few. Yes, it was stupid of me. I wasn't thinking straight. About a dozen. Probably more. No, I don't know who is sending them. Until last night, it's always been just a location. For similar incidents to last night's, yes. But the one from yesterday also included a time. 10.20: when the two people came out of that convenience store.

He shook his head; his phone would be the first thing they took. He'd probably never see his SIM card again. Interviews, statements, questions, questions, questions. What a ball-ache. How fast would they track the owner of the phone number down? Work out the person's address? Hours? Days? What did it matter? He'd never receive any more messages. Game over.

He pushed his bowl aside and rubbed his hands over the thighs of his jeans. It was Carla's reaction from the previous night that decided it for him. The look of disappointment on her face. He needed to call the detective and admit to everything. I'll try his landline first, Ryan decided. Hopefully, the detective would have been on a night shift and not taking calls.

His fingers were inches from the screen when the phone began to ring. He read the name he'd allocated to that number: *Posh Annabelle*. Ivan's assistant at The Sussman. He really needed to change the phone's entry to just *Annabelle*. She would not be happy if she saw it. 'Hi, Annabelle. You OK?'

'I'm fine, Ryan, thanks. You?'

As usual, she sounded like she was clenching a pencil

between her arse cheeks. 'Yeah, good.'

'Lovely. You're due here at ten, but Ivan was wondering if he can bring it forward by twenty minutes?'

'Oh. Of course, no problem. I'll set off.'

'Wonderful. See you shortly.'

#

The Northern Quarter was strewn with the usual detritus from the night before. His eyes settled briefly on the silver canisters of laughing gas that dotted the pavements. Spent torpedoes that had hit their target. Giant white refuse sacks, their sides bulging like sales in the wind. Abandoned pint glasses precariously balanced on low walls or abandoned on shop doorsteps. Murky, flat beer lurking inside. There was a time, he reflected, when I meticulously photographed stuff like this. Now? Compared to what he'd captured last night, it all seemed so amateur.

Motionless at the front desk, Annabelle looked almost like a piece of artwork herself. Light brown hair arranged in an elaborate plait, ochre wedge-shaped earrings, a white turtleneck top providing a clean backdrop for a necklace of – what was it?

'Morning,' he announced a little uncertainly. Each time he came through the door, he felt like they were going to ask him to leave. That it all had been a mistake.

'Ryan, hello.' Her lips adjusted into a temporary smile.

'Hi.' He moved across the polished wooden floor. 'That's a great necklace. What is it?'

Her eyelashes fluttered and her features softened a touch. That was the secret to Annabelle, he thought. Pay her a compliment. Beneath the brittle exterior, she was really a bubbling mess of insecurities.

'Polished coconut shell,' she replied, fingertips of one hand brushing over the jagged pieces. 'I got it on holiday a few years back. St Lucia?'

'It's really striking.'

'Thank you. Ivan's just parking. Would you like some coffee?'

That was a no-brainer; the gallery's coffee was incredible. Ivan had confided in him that he bought it from a place on Great Bridgewater Street that roasted its own beans. 'Please.'

'White and one sugar, isn't it?'

She was good, he thought, watching her glide gracefully across to the machine in the corner.

'Did you see the poster?' she asked. 'We put it up a few days ago now.'

'What's that?'

'Have a look at the easel in the front window. I think you'll like it.'

Feigning puzzlement, he stepped back to peer round it. 'Wow! And you've included the amazing Julian Templeforth quote.'

'Of course. Ivan was categorical about that,' she replied, heading back with a white cup and saucer. 'It's such an incredible endorsement to have.'

He was taking the drink from her when the door opened behind him.

'Ryan, you bugger! Beat me by a whisker!'

Hurriedly, he put the cup and saucer down on the front desk.

Ivan was in his trademark black fedora, bushy great beard hanging like a fuzzy bib over the lapels of a herringbone coat. His warm eyes were alive with what Ryan always concluded was a touch of mischief. 'Hello.'

'Looking well,' Ivan beamed, clasping Ryan in an embrace before moving straight to Annabelle and doing the same to her.

Ryan looked on with a smile: it was such an endearing trait of the man that, no matter how recently you'd seen him, he greeted you like a long-lost friend.

Freed from his grasp, Annabelle was already heading straight back to the percolator. 'Medium or large?'

'Large, for God's sake,' Ivan gasped, unbuttoning his overcoat. 'The traffic coming in from Didsbury. I really should start cycling, if I wasn't such a fat old bastard.' A chuckle rumbled up from somewhere beneath his beard. 'Tickets, Ryan, are going very well. Very well, indeed. Approaching fifty, is it, Annabelle?'

'Forty-six, I think.'

'And that doesn't include the media lot. Saskia from *Cheshire Life* will be here, and the Arts correspondent from the new online magazine for Manchester, *Gristle*?'

'*Grit*,' Annabelle chided. 'You'll say that to the wrong person one of these days.'

Ivan's eyes twinkled as he straightened a tweed waistcoat over the swell of his belly. The paisley handkerchief poking from its chest pocket had been folded immaculately into two points. 'And, and, I may have even lured the chap *The Guardian* use for cultural events in the north. Lucas Pelling?'

Ryan shook his head. It was like he'd been swept up in a tornado.

'Well, he's heard of you, Ryan. He took the cup from Annabelle. 'Thank you.'

Everything came to a stop as he closed his eyes and took a long sip. Ryan found himself staring and quickly retrieved his own drink.

'Aaah,' Ivan breathed. 'I am human once again. Now, come, come, come. We have a dilemma.'

Ryan followed him into the side room and looked about. Still can't believe this. All three walls were adorned with his photographs.

'Annabelle and I have been playing about,' Ivan announced. 'I hope you don't mind. But this arrangement serves us best, wouldn't you agree?'

Ryan took a long, slow look. He realised the first wall was almost entirely filled with his earlier stuff. Shots he'd taken before the tip offs had started arriving on his phone. Best of those was the old woman who'd stepped in front of the tram outside Selfridges. You couldn't actually see her: it was the faces of the people surrounding where she lay beneath the front bumper that made the shot. The contorting effect anguish had on a face.

The back wall was, as they'd agreed, dominated by *Vulpine Plunderer*. Either side of it were images from the last few weeks: every one the result of rushing to a location he'd been sent in the form of a what3words code.

The third wall had the triptych of the pile-up he'd taken from the flyover across the Mancunian Way. Below it was a space.

'Here,' Ivan said, pointing at it. 'We've still got this blasted gap. It's the last thing the viewer will see. I always like that image to be something recent, but also something that serves as a full stop. Assuming you've not managed to have any luck since we last spoke...' He glanced at Ryan.

'Sorry, no.'

'OK,' he sighed. 'Annabelle and I have been looking at what we could use, but we're torn. Annabelle likes the shot you took of the moon shining through the tower of that spooky church on Oxford Road.'

'The Holy Name?' I snapped that as a student, Ryan thought. Waiting for the Withington bus back to my shitty flat above the mobile phone repair shop.

'But for me, it's not really saying urban trauma.' Ivan took a sip of his coffee. 'Granted, it's at night when most of your images are taken. But it lacks that human element. I was considering the crashed scooter.'

It had been a police chase. Two lads emulating what they'd seen happening down in London. The passenger had been snatching phones and handbags in Hulme and jumping back on the pillion seat before the pair of them raced away. But they'd targeted the same few streets too often. A plain-clothes policewoman had been given a charity shop overcoat and grey wig, then sent to walk the area, handbag draped temptingly over her shoulder. The pair had struck and found themselves immediately pursued by several police vehicles. They'd made for a ginnel, misjudged how narrow it was and smashed into a side wall. Ryan had made it to the scene in time to get the mangled bike lying at the base of the 'no entry to bikes' sign.

'Kind of a concluding image, wouldn't you say?' Ivan asked.

Ryan hesitated, Ivan's words reverberating in his head. A full stop. He could see the glass cabinet from the night before. The faint trail leading down to a single fat drop of blood. Could we use that?

'Ryan?' Ivan prompted. 'What are you thinking?'

Ryan cleared his throat. 'I'm not sure... there might be something.'

'Oh. What's that?'

'I haven't actually shown it to you before.'

Ivan turned to face him. 'Really?' His eyes shone with anticipation. 'You're a dark horse, Ryan. Why ever not?'

He hunched a shoulder. 'I don't know, but I think it…maybe it could work.'

'Care to give me a little –'

The ring tone of Ryan's phone caused Ivan to pause. Irritation showed on his face; something Ryan had never seen before. Normally, he'd let it go to voicemail and judge whether it was worth calling back from any message left. But with the thing from the previous night... 'Sorry,' he said, reaching for his pocket. 'Just need to check who it is.'

'Of course,' Ivan said a little sharply, stepping past him and moving back into the gallery's main room.

Ryan examined the screen. Unknown number. 'Hello?'

'Is that Ryan Lamb?' a female voice asked.

He was expecting it to be a sales call, but there was no background noise from other people speaking on phones. And her tone was somehow kind. 'Yes?'

'Hello, my name's Pamela Harris. I work with the Victim Support Unit at GMP.'

'Greater Manchester Police?'

'Yes. I'm at the hospital where Mrs Witas was taken last night.'

The old lady from the shop, Ryan thought. 'How is she?'

'Well, that's why I'm calling, actually. She's asking to see you.'

'Me?'

'Yes. I wouldn't normally do this, but she's become, well, a little agitated. She wants to thank you for what you did. She feels she didn't show her gratitude properly.'

He shook his head. 'Honestly, there's no need. It's not like I did that much.'

'Not in her eyes. And from what I can gather from the police officer who popped in, she's right. I realise I'm asking a lot here, but could you possibly swing by? It would only be to sit by her bed for a minute. Her son's in surgery and everything has left her shaken. I think this would help her a great deal.'

'Is he OK, the son?'

'I believe so. They've done some scans and are looking at those. You're in Manchester, is that correct?'

'Yes.'

'So could you? Come by? We're in the Manchester Royal Infirmary.'

'When?'

'Are you free now? She's really very keen to thank you.'

He glanced up at the ceiling. Recessed halogen lights hurt his eyeballs. He tried to blink away the pain. This is bloody awkward, he thought. Ten o'clock now. Not due in at Q2 until noon. I do have enough time. 'OK.'

'Thank you, Ryan.'

'How do I find you?'

'If you come to the main entrance, just look for the big noticeboard in the foyer area. We're on Ward One. It's easy to find. Just let the nurses' station know you've arrived and I'll come and find you.'

'Ward One?'

'That's right.'

'I'll be half an hour.'

Ivan had sidled back through the doorway. 'Everything alright? Did I hear you say that was the police?'

Ryan realised he hadn't exactly been whispering. 'Yes. Well, victim support. There was an incident last night. I was walking past this late-night shop in Salford and two guys came bursting out. They'd just robbed it.'

Ivan's hand was over his mouth. 'You're a witness?'

'Kind of.'

'Kind of?'

'Well, yes. I suppose.'

'What were you doing over in Salford?'

'Just, you know, wandering.'

'Midnight ramble?'

Another expression on Ivan's face Ryan had never seen before: the man looked faintly incredulous.

'Go on, you're passing this shop...'

Jesus, Ryan thought. He reckons I'm being shady. 'Yeah... I went in and ended up helping the two members of staff. This old woman, Polish maybe, and her son. Just until the ambulances arrived.'

Ivan now looked intrigued. 'You mean first-aid? They were injured?'

'He was. She had been punched.'

'My God, Ryan. That must have been an adrenaline rush.'

He nodded. 'She wants to thank me.'

'The old lady?'

'Yes. She's at the MRI. In a bit of a state.'

'Now? She wants to see you now?'

'I'm really sorry, Ivan. I couldn't really –'

'Jump in a cab.' He produced a clip of notes from his trouser pocket and peeled off a twenty.

'What? No, honestly –'

'Take it!' He pressed the note into Ryan's breast pocket and took the cup and saucer from his hand. 'Go, go, go. All this? Mere frippery. Go and see the poor woman!'

#

Jason came to with a start. During the night, the cold of the concrete floor had seeped deeper and deeper into his body. He remembered waking up at some point, climbing to his feet and padding down to the front lobby. He'd found several off cuts of carpet thrown behind the front counter and carried the largest pieces back up to the apartment.

Now he found himself stretched across them in a room lit grey by the pre-dawn light that was filtering through the windows beside him. He couldn't be here. Not now that he'd be visible to anyone looking in from outside. He crawled across to the bathroom and, only once the door was closed, stood. The rims of his eyes were red and his teeth felt fuzzy. There was nothing in the bathroom, not even a roll of toilet paper or a towel. At least the water was connected. He filled the sink and submerged his face for several seconds.

The thought of going home made him feel ill. His plan had failed. Liam was still there. And he'd mentioned the thing with Rebecca. Brought all those memories back. The bastard. There was only one thing Jason could think of doing to make himself feel better. He set off for the foyer.

Once the A57 had merged into the M67, he didn't feel quite so bad. He let the Fireblade's speed pick up, leaving cars far behind as he raced past Hyde and on until the motorway ended. Soon he had sped through Glossop and was carving his way along the Snake Pass. Out here, in the wilds of the Peak District, the only speed deterrents were the roadside posters announcing how many bikers had died in the previous twelve months. Who cared? The sensation of hitting blind corners at over seventy, the shocked faces of oncoming drivers, the rush of air and the feel of the bike beneath him. He burned along little B roads, sometimes sending startled sheep careering down gorse-strewn slopes. Once or twice, he spotted an animal stumble and fall. In a secluded lay by, he saw a couple perched on camping chairs by their car. The boot was open and they had a little picnic arranged there. He lifted the visor of his helmet and let out a howl as he flashed past them at over eighty.

CHAPTER 23

'Ryan, thank you so much.'

He turned from the mass of thank you cards adorning the notice board beside the nurses' station. A silver-haired woman of about fifty was walking along the corridor toward him. She was wearing an olive-green shirt and grey trousers. The ID card round her neck shifted from side to side with each step.

'I'm Pamela Harris, in case you weren't sure,' she added, coming to a stop before him and lifting the card up. He glimpsed the words Victim Support before she lowered it. 'I didn't think you'd be here so quick.'

A light shake of hands. Her skin felt very cool and dry. Or was his clammy from the journey across town? 'I got a cab.'

'You did? If you have the receipt, I can see if –'

'Don't worry. Call it a business expense.'

'Are you sure?'

'Yes. Positive.'

She stepped back. 'That's very good of you. Shall we?'

'Is she still flustered?' he asked as Pamela started leading the way.

'Better, knowing you were coming. She doesn't

remember everything. And her English isn't brilliant. But she understands it was you who called for help and attended to her and Stanisłow, her son.'

'She was calling him something else.'

'Stasiu?'

'I think so.'

'Pet name.' She smiled.

'Any more news on him?'

'Not as yet. She doesn't know about his head wound, by the way, so best keep that quiet.'

He started to slow. 'I'm feeling a bit nervous. What should I say to her?'

'Don't be,' she replied, glancing at him with a smile. 'You're a good person, Ryan – so say whatever you like. I'm sure she'll do most of the talking. And I'll be there, too. It will be fine, don't worry.'

She came to a stop by the door to a private room. Another quick smile and then she opened it. 'Renata? The person you wanted to see is here.' She stepped to the side.

The old lady was propped up by at least three pillows. Her hair was tied back in a neat bun. Ugly smears of purple sat below both eyes and her nose looked puffy and swollen. For a moment, she seemed confused, and a touch alarmed.

'It's Ryan,' Pamela prompted from beside him.

She smiled. 'Ryan! Please, come here.'

All he could think of was the cute granny in Little Red Riding Red, eyesight not strong enough for her to realise she was letting a wolf into the cottage. She patted the arm of the chair beside the bed.

He hadn't even sat down before she grabbed his hand to smother it in kisses. When she pressed it against her cheek, the skin felt impossibly soft. What sort of animal, he thought, could punch you in the face?

'You help,' she said in a husky voice. 'Stasiu and me, you help. Thank you, thank you.' His hand was still in her grip.

'That's OK,' he said, sitting forward to place his other hand over hers. He could see her left eye was badly bloodshot. 'How are you?'

'You help. Nice man, you help.' She gazed adoringly at his face for what felt like ages. He had to break eye contact to look at Pamela with a smile that bordered on embarrassed.

'Stasiu, you help him. He is with doctors now.'

All Ryan could think about was the photos he'd taken. Her son, blood pouring from his head and I took photos! His smile felt as grotesque as a clown's as he turned to her. 'It's good to know you're both safe.'

'Yes, yes, safe.' She rubbed and squeezed his hand.

He kept smiling, even though his fingers felt trapped by her grip. You're a bloody fake. He wanted to flee from the room. There was a crucifix hanging round her neck and a joke popped unbidden into his head. Mary and the others falling to the ground at the foot of the cross. Looking up at Jesus, one of them controlled her wailing long enough to ask, 'Does it hurt?'

Jesus considers the question, ribs straining with each breath. 'Only if I laugh.'

A sob-like giggle broke free of his lips and he had to turn it into an overly dramatic sigh. 'I'm so glad.' He felt lightheaded, as if he might float towards the ceiling. Only the old woman's grip was anchoring him to the seat. Fuck, I have to get out of here.

'Well, Renata, maybe it's time we let Ryan get back to work.'

'Yes, work.' She nodded, lifting his hand for a last few kisses. 'You come to shop. When we open, you come to shop and see Stasiu, too. Yes?'

'That would be great, thanks.' As gently as he could, he extricated his hand from her fingers. 'Both of you, get well soon.'

'Yes, yes.' She nodded delightedly. 'Thank you.'

He paused in the doorway to lift a hand. 'Bye.'

'Bye-bye, Ryan. Bye.' She kissed the tips of her fingers and flicked them in his direction.

'Thank you for doing that,' Pamela said quietly, leading him back down the corridor.

'That's fine,' he said, eyes on the double doors at the end. Let me bloody out.

'Are you OK, Ryan? I realise she was a bit intense.'

'No, I'm fine. Just...it was a bit overwhelming in there, wasn't it? And hot.'

'That's hospitals for you. Ryan, have you been offered any support?'

'Me?'

'Yes, what you saw in that shop must have been a shock.'

Yeah, he thought. Such a shock I photographed it. 'No, I'm fine. It all seemed to be over in a...' He wanted to say 'flash'. Of what? A camera? 'Over really quickly.'

'You may well find your mind starts to unpack those memories in a bit more detail.'

'Right.'

'You can always call me if you'd like to talk.'

'Thanks.' They'd reached the doors.

'Well, thanks again,' Pamela said. 'It meant a lot to her. And, well done, you. It was a very brave thing you did to go in there.'

'Why?'

She blinked. 'Before the police or anyone had arrived.'

'Oh.' The same stupid giggle got out. 'The shop. Right. I thought you meant...' He waved vaguely toward Renata's room. Why would have going in there been brave? Only if you were a complete fake. 'I'd better be off.' He pushed a little too eagerly at the exit doors, but the damned things were stuck. He tried pushing again, harder. Why the hell wouldn't they open?

Pamela stepped forward and pressed the green knob on the wall beside it. 'There you go.'

By now, he was certain his face was scarlet. 'Cheers.'

When he reached the main foyer, he looked at the arching atrium high above him with a sense of relief. Space. Light. Someone was playing a piano in the corner and the pleasant melody immediately began to have a soothing effect.

He started making his way between the rows of seating toward the glass doors leading outside. About twenty metres from them, an attractive woman of about thirty stepped out. Almost apologising for the near collision, he tried to step round. She moved the same way. He shifted to his other foot just as she did. He raised both palms, trying to think of something witty.

'Excuse me, are you Ryan Lamb?'

Now wrong-footed by her hopeful tone, he almost glanced over his shoulder. As if another man who happened to share his name was positioned behind him.

'The photographer?' she asked.

'Well... I take photographs, yes.'

She actually bobbed up and down with excitement. 'I thought so! I really, really, like what you do. Would it be OK to get a quick photo?'

He wanted to ask if she was being serious. 'A photo? Yeah, of course. Here?'

She glanced about. 'How about here?' She gestured to a towering rubber plant beside the notice board that listed all the wards.

He felt slightly ridiculous, but also delighted. This is what happens to celebrities! Don't forget this feeling, he said to himself. And, however tedious these requests might eventually become, always be polite. 'No problem.'

She had what looked like the latest iPhone. 'Just a little to your left.'

He'd assumed she'd be after a selfie with him.

'There, yes.' She took several photos, even going onto one knee for a couple. 'Perfect, thanks.'

'That's fine,' he replied, slightly embarrassed at how people were beginning to stare.

'So,' she said, quickly checking through the images. 'Must have been quite frightening last night?'

He frowned. 'Last night?'

'Being first at the scene.' She looked up from her screen. 'The robbery at that convenience store?'

'What?' He cocked his head to one side. 'How…?'

'Will the lady you helped be alright? What about her son?'

He realised her phone was partly raised up. Was she recording this? 'I'm sorry – do you work with Pamela?'

'Pamela?'

'The Victim Support Ser –' His words died away. Stupid.

'I work for the *Manchester Evening Chronicle*, Ryan. Pretty sure this will be a feature in the next edition.'

'I don't understand. How do you know about this?'

'Are you excited about your forthcoming exhibition at the Sussman Gallery?'

Ivan! The bastard must have called them.

#

When Jason neared the outskirts of Sheffield, he doubled back on the A625, then the A623, roadside reduced to a blur. Signs rearing up for an instant. Eyam. Foolow. Little Hucklow. Endless fields crisscrossed by dry-stone walls, distant hills a jagged shadow across the base of the sky.

All day long, his mind had been drifting back to the way Carla had lost her temper. The initial concern she'd shown over Ryan's arrival in the police car had quickly changed to irritation, and then outrage. The look she'd sent him before marching off to the bedroom! Jason hoped he never attracted a look like that. Not that he would; he'd treat her with the respect she deserved. Not that he'd be weak or anything. For instance, with telling her the friendship with that Simone needed to end. He'd be strong on certain things, but prepared to accept others. Within reason.

He remembered the way she'd pointed at Ryan's phone. Like it had caused their conflict. He touched the brakes of his bike as realisation hit: what if it was the cause? His messages to Ryan. Could they be what was bothering her? What else could they have been talking about? It had to be the messages. Jason smiled. All this time, he'd been terrified he'd only been making Carla and Ryan closer. But it wasn't true. Carla wasn't impressed with what Ryan was doing. In fact, she looked like it didn't make her pleased at all. He laughed out loud. I know what to do: send him more messages.

It was the headlights of an approaching Land Rover that made him realise the day was starting to fade. The next sign he reached said Butterton 3 miles. Where the hell was that? He stopped at the top of a farm track to check his phone. Just enough of a signal to bring up a map. Butterton was at the southern edge of the National Park, almost level with Stoke-on-Trent. Christ.

By the time he'd worked his way back to the Snake Pass, darkness had fallen. Coming back over the top, he slowed down: the shining sprawl of Manchester was spread out below him. Hundreds. Thousands. Tens of thousands of light sources. He gazed down and wondered if it would be possible to work out which was Carla's among the shimmering mass. Maybe a military satellite could do it. He couldn't. Not that it mattered. He'd be at the window of his apartment again in less than an hour.

CHAPTER 24

Jason double-checked the bathroom door was properly closed behind him before turning the light on. From the pockets of his leather jacket, he removed the items he'd bought at the big Tesco in the middle of Glossop: a phone charger, paracetamol for his headache, four cans of Red Bull, a few muesli bars and a big bag of peanuts.

There was, he noticed, a voicemail on his phone. Tabitha at Nail and Cable. He listened to her asking how it was all going with the measuring up. She'd popped by the building at two-thirty that afternoon and buzzed him on the intercom, but no one had answered. Her final comment was to remind him the keys had to be returned to her at the Deansgate office first thing Monday morning.

Snooping bitch, he thought, deleting her message.

He checked the time: nearly half-past eight. Surely Carla would be back from work by now? He hoped so much that she was. Perhaps she'd be having an evening meal. He liked the idea of watching her eat. Grabbing the bag of peanuts and a can of Red Bull, he turned the light off and then opened the door. They could have tea together, the two of them. He crawled across to the windows.

His heart sank. Ryan. Just seeing him in that flat caused Jason's pulse to flutter. You don't deserve to be there. He watched as the other man slowly scrolled through something on his iPad's screen. Jason had already set his phone to night display. He tapped on his secure work app and signed in to see what was happening with emergency calls. Two RTCs, a body in a flat in Pendleton, a house fire in Salford.

He checked the apartment again just as the door started to open. Jason's attention immediately shifted and, in the corner of his eye, he saw Ryan's head turn, too. Carla! She was home. At last. He felt his welcoming smile fade as she stepped into her home. You look so tired! You poor thing. He glanced at Ryan. Get up. Take her case and coat. Make her a drink.

But all the other man did was check his watch then swivel the laptop in her direction. Oaf.

She took a brief look then went to the kettle and turned it on. Jason glared at Ryan. You should be doing that. Selfish knob. The two of them carried on talking, but it wasn't friendly talk. No. Ryan seemed agitated: she seemed exhausted. Or bored. She practically collapsed on the sofa with her drink. The conversation stuttered to a halt. Ryan started twisting himself from side to side on the barstool.

Now, Jason thought. Let's see how they react to another message arriving. Right now. He turned to his phone. The list of incidents had updated; now at the top was the report of a casualty in Parsonage Gardens. A male, of about thirty, believed to have fallen from a height. There was an additional note: the person could have been disturbed while burgling a third-floor flat that overlooked the location. That flat was owned by a detective in the city's Counter Terrorism Unit. Happy days, Jason thought. That will result in the cavalry being called out. He fed the location into what3words and sent the code to Ryan.

#

Ryan listened as the gallery owner's voicemail played out.

'Ivan Sussman. Speak now or forever hold your peace.'

'Hi, Ivan. It's me, Ryan Lamb. Er... I was just wondering: did you mention my hospital visit to anyone? Only, something odd happened after I'd visited that woman earlier today. Call me, can you? Thanks.'

He put the phone aside and regarded the laptop's screen. The story was already in the Entertainment section of the Manchester Evening Chronicle's site.

Local photographer turns hero. Charlotte Fairburn, Entertainment Correspondent.

She had a little photograph beside her name. It was her, the woman who'd stopped him in the hospital's foyer. The whole thing had been planned. He scrolled down to the picture she'd taken of him.

At the time, he thought she'd manoeuvred him so the massive rubber plant formed a backdrop. But he'd been wrong: directly behind him was the sign listing all the various departments and wards, including the one where Renata Witas was staying.

The end of the article finished with a poor copy of, surprise, surprise, *Vulpine Plunderer*. Except the picture editor had flipped the shot, so the fox was on the man's left, not his right. The mistake needled Ryan. Below that were details of the coming exhibition, including ticket bookings alongside the gallery's phone number and email address. Must have been Ivan.

He heard a key in the lock and looked up from the screen. Carla shuffled into the apartment looking ready to collapse.

'Hey there,' she said, dumping her case beside the door.

He checked the time. Eight-fifty-two. 'The shoot finished, then?'

'Yup. All done.' She flung her jacket on to the sofa and continued towards the kettle. 'I left as the party was getting started.' She flicked its switch and glanced at the laptop's screen. 'What's that?'

'Have a look.' He slid it across and sat back on the barstool. Bluish light bathed her face as she worked her way up. She paused at his image before carrying on to the headline. 'Hero? When did you visit the hospital?'

He explained what had happened. 'So, I'm thinking it was Ivan. I rang the woman from Victim Support and she said it absolutely wasn't her. Who else could it have been?'

She pushed the device back and shrugged. 'Suppose so. Free publicity for your exhibition.'

'Yeah, but...' He could feel his kneecaps touching the drawer where the memory stick was hidden. 'The way she describes me. I sound like such a weirdo. Roaming the city in the small hours, searching out disasters and taking pictures of them. And the bit about insomnia; that was a throwaway comment to a blogger about how I sometimes can't sleep. She makes me sound like a vampire!'

Carla dropped a chamomile teabag into a mug and poured in boiling water. 'It's not that bad, Ryan. It gives you a persona. A brand. That's what it's all about.'

'What, like the EM leisure range? Fuck that.'

She flopped down on the sofa and tipped her head back. 'You know what I mean.'

He began to pick at his lower lip with a forefinger and thumb.

'What?' she asked, one eye open. 'You're doing that thing.'

He dropped his hand. 'What if the police see this? Surely, they'll start to wonder if what I said was...you know, if I told them the truth.'

'Which is why I said you needed to ring them. I take it you didn't get round to that, then?'

'I was about to. Then Annabelle said my meeting with Ivan needed to move forward. After that...'

She sat in silence, both eyes now closed.

'What?' he asked.

'I didn't say a thing.'

'You didn't need to. The disapproval is coming off you in clouds.'

'You're the one stressing over this. You've got that detective's number. Ring him.'

'What if the police want to speak with you?'

'Why would they do that?'

'I said the reason I was on Pinnington Street was to look at properties in that estate agent's window – because you fancied moving to the area.'

She let her head fall to the side and opened her eyes. They shone with anger. 'Don't drag me into your mess, OK?'

'I'm only saying.'

'Well, don't.' She closed her eyes again. 'They won't contact me.'

He shut the laptop and crossed his arms. The ensuing silence was finally broken by his phone emitting a buzz. Instantly, he checked the screen. 'Bloody hell! It's him again.'

Her back straightened. 'What's he saying?'

'Nothing. The usual: a what3words location.'

'Don't go.' She stood, her tea forgotten. 'Ryan, please don't go.'

He looked towards the window. The lure of massed lights beyond the glass. The screen dragged his eyes back. 'There's no time with this one.'

'So what? This isn't right. I don't like it.'

'Why don't I just see where it is?'

'Ryan, no. I'm serious.'

'But it could be... I don't know, the main concourse of Piccadilly Station.' He couldn't get the empty space for his exhibition out of his mind. One more decent shot. Just one. 'Somewhere completely harmless. A woman in labour or something.'

Carla's head was shaking. 'When has it ever been something completely harmless? Think about it; they've been getting steadily darker and darker.'

'Let's see.' He opened the app and entered the location.

'I can't believe you just did that.'

'What?' He could see her in the periphery of his vision. Hands on hips. 'There you go: Parsonage Gardens. That nice little square tucked in behind Kendals.'

She picked her tea up and started walking towards the bedroom. 'You know what? I need to sleep. Do what you want: I don't fucking care.'

The door slammed shut, and he glanced about the empty living area while swivelling himself slowly from side to side once again. Quite a hissy fit, he said to himself. Proper dramatic exit. But it was late, and she'd said herself she was really tired.

He got off the stool and walked quietly over to the main window. Opened it a crack and listened. A couple of sirens mixed in with the general hubbub. The oily aroma from a takeaway's extractor fan. Nothing unusual. He closed it again and took up his previous position at the breakfast bar. His phone was like a magnet for his eyes. He held out for a few seconds then picked it up and studied the message once more. There was a number, but it was so annoying: he'd tried replying to it a few times, even tried ringing it. Nothing. Not even a voicemail for leaving a message.

He reopened the *Manchester Evening Chronicle's* website. Their live feed was pretty good, especially for crime. He couldn't see anything about Parsonage Gardens. He pictured the modest expanse of grass. It was favoured by workers located in the expensive office buildings that encircled it. A pleasant area for eating sandwiches. Deansgate – one of the city's busiest roads – was just a stone's throw from it. No way it could be anything like last night, surely?

He knocked gently on the bedroom door. 'La-la?'

No reply.

He knocked a touch more loudly.

'Do what you want, Ryan. You obviously don't care what I think.'

He opened the door a crack. She was sitting on the bed, phone in one hand, tea in the other. 'What if I just wander over there, but without my camera? Just to check things out.'

Her gaze didn't lift from the screen. 'Whatever.'

'Don't be like that.'

'Like what?'

'Passive-aggressive.'

'Passive-aggressive?'

'What are you acting like, if it's not that?'

Her laugh contained absolutely no cheer. 'You need to bloody well develop a bit of emotional intuition.'

'Meaning?'

'This isn't passive-aggression, Ryan.' She looked over her shoulder at him. 'I don't think you should be doing anything with those messages apart from deleting them. And blocking that number. But you need to make up your own mind on this. I'm not going to stop you replying to them. Now, shut the door so I can get some sleep.'

CHAPTER 25

'You're wrong, mate. Sarah! Tell him he's wrong. I made the last round yesterday. Just after five.' DI Graham Roebuck looked across at his partner, brows raised in expectation. 'Did I not?'

DC Sarah Potter's eyes narrowed. 'I do believe he did, Adam.'

'Yes!' Roebuck leaned back in his seat and triumphantly lifted his mug. Big letters on the side said: Grumpy Old Fart's. A birthday present from his son.

DS Adam Robinson turned to the officer sitting opposite him. 'Independent verification required. I sure as hell don't remember drinking any brew yesterday that was made by him. Danny?'

'You did,' Roebuck quietly crowed. 'You so did.'

'Danny?' Robinson repeated.

His partner grimaced. 'He did. Crap, mind. But it still counted as a drink. Just.'

'When you're ready, cheers.' Roebuck still had his mug raised.

'Bollocks,' Robinson said, hauling himself to his feet. 'Sarah? Coffee?'

She slid her cup to the edge of the desk. 'Ta.'

Robinson glanced at his partner, who nodded. He reached across, took his cup and circled behind Graham Roebuck. 'What'll it be, Chief?'

'Any of your funny ones?'

'You mean rooibus?'

'That's it. I quite like them.'

'If no bugger's robbed them all from our cupboard.'

The danger of setting up an incident room in one of the city's many police stations; you never knew how bad the culture of borrowing might be until you left stuff in the communal kitchen.

Hand now empty, Roebuck lowered it to continue typing at his computer. 'Sarah, did we get anywhere with the CCTV from the Estate Agents?' After the patrol car had driven Ryan Lamb away, he'd immediately doubled back to the office on the opposite side of the road from the Pop-In. He couldn't see any camera in the darkened interior, but still – you never knew. And something about Lamb wasn't quite right.

'The manager emailed this morning. No joy.'

Roebuck's lips pushed out in disappointment. 'Oh well.' There were over twenty tabs open on his screen. Mostly profiles from the PNC of local faces he thought might be good for the armed robbery. Of those, seven were currently inside. Two were no longer in Manchester. That left about a dozen to check.

The evening before, he'd checked the log for stolen white Golfs; the type captured in the phone footage Ryan had shot. Two had been taken in the previous forty-eight hours. One from Burnage, one from Timperley. Roebuck was fairly certain the burned-out remains of one would soon be reported. Probably sitting on a bit of waste ground somewhere close to Salford. If nothing came in, he'd do a recce later of a few dumping grounds he was familiar with.

'Your man from the late-night store,' Adam Robinson called from behind him.

Roebuck twisted in his seat. The detective was brandishing a copy of the Manchester Evening Chronicle's Sunday edition.

'This him?' The paper was dropped on his desk. Adam had folded it open on a page that was dominated by a single story.

Local photographer turns hero.

Roebuck leaned forward. There he was, the bloke who'd witnessed the two robbers leaving the shop. 'He's a photographer?'

'Not just a photographer,' Robinson said. 'A street photographer who specialises in Urban Trauma. Read what it says about the exhibition he's got coming up. I'll fetch the drinks.'

Sarah appeared at Roebuck's side. 'What's he doing at the MRI?'

'Not sure, yet,' Roebuck murmured, starting to read the story. A minute later, he sat back. 'Fuck me, he forgot to mention any of this.'

Sarah had perched on the edge of his desk. 'Go on.'

'He takes photographs of, like Adam said, urban trauma. Grim stuff: RTAs, crashed scooters, arson attacks, God-knows what else.'

Sarah looked perplexed. 'How does that work?'

'According to this, he just wanders the city at night.'

'On foot?'

'Suppose so.'

'For real?'

'Apparently.'

A frown was on Sarah's face. 'And what? Sprints after the sound of any siren? Like some sort of Olympic ambulance chaser?'

'It's him, then?' Adam asked, returning with the drinks.

'Cheers.' Graham took his mug and placed it beside the paper. 'Yes, it's him. So, two things strike me here. What are the chances of him passing a convenience store as it's being robbed?'

He looked about for his colleagues' reactions. Adam directed his thumb towards the floor. Danny had a dubious expression on his face.

'Well, is he wandering the city every night?' Sarah asked. 'It's not totally ridiculous, if he is.'

Roebuck nodded. 'And second, he's got an exhibition opening tomorrow and here he is, doing in a photoshoot at the hospital where the victims of that robbery ended up.'

Adam's head shook. 'Stinks to me.'

The door opened and DC Simon White stepped into the room. 'Boss, guess who I saw last night?'

Roebuck sat back. 'If this is your late-night internet viewing, I'm not sure I want to hear.'

The younger officer gave a quick grin. 'Hilarious. I went to the incident in Parsonage Gardens. Attempted burglary of an officer's flat. Someone in the CTU.'

'Oh yeah, I saw the call go out for it.'

'Not much anyone could do – but I'll get to that in a minute. Thing is, there was someone at the scene, watching. Three guesses.'

'Please, Simon,' Roebuck sighed. 'Don't keep us in suspense.'

'Ryan Lamb. Skulking about, looking very interested in events.'

Graham glanced at the newspaper photo once again. 'I think we need another word with Mr Lamb. Adam, mind doing the honours?'

#

Ryan turned over in bed and stared up at the ceiling. He could remember Carla coming out of the bathroom. That lovely wash of warm air, heavy with the aroma of her shower gel and shampoo. The click and clink of her make-up bottles, the sound of a metal lid being unscrewed.

Rustle of clothes and squirts of perfume. But rather than get up and chat with her over breakfast, he must have fallen back to sleep.

He checked his phone. Nearly nine. Just over twenty-four hours before the opening of his exhibition. The incident from the previous night had been weird. Carla had been right when she'd said the messages were tipping him off about darker and darker stuff. He raised himself on to an elbow and ran through the scene.

The first thing that struck him as he'd turned off Deansgate was the weird screaming. Just a quick one that abruptly cut off. A few seconds of silence, then it repeated. He'd counted five of them before he entered the gardens themselves. Second thing that was weird: the number of police cars at the scene. Some marked, others not. Three on the far side, four dotted around where he stood. Something at the edge of the grass had officers clustered around it. Something squat, not much more than waist high. It started to make the screaming noise.

Ryan had slipped between a couple of benches and stepped on to the grass for a better look. It was a person, head lolling forward as if asleep. He seemed to suddenly wake up, and another scream came out before the head fell forward again. The officers seemed transfixed. Ryan heard someone ask how long until paramedics arrived. He edged closer, intrigued by the spectacle. The victim seemed to be wearing shorts and, below them, flesh-coloured socks that were thick and wrinkly. His legs weren't right. Too stubby. A voice called down from a balcony some seven metres above. A uniformed officer. Finally, Ryan understood. The victim wasn't wearing pink socks: it was skin bunched up like a pair of accordions. He must have tried jumping. Were the bones of his lower legs jammed deep into the turf, or had they been driven up into his thighs? The person shrieked before passing out yet again.

'Get back, can you, sir? We'll need space for the ambulance.'

A young officer was shooing him away from the scene. Ryan turned round and made for the shadows.

The bedroom felt cool after the warmth of the bed. Shame, he thought, I missed Carla. It would have been good to have told her about it. Seen what she made of things. Phone in hand, he wandered into the living area. As usual, she'd put all her breakfast stuff away. It meant he immediately spotted the envelope propped against the kettle. White paper against black plastic.

He placed his phone on the breakfast bar. She'd probably left a reminder about the money he owed for last month's bills, he thought, putting it next to his phone. He added water to the kettle and flicked the switch. The red light on the top came on. She was right, of course. Even running the tap and boiling the kettle cost a few pence. There was a price to bloody everything.

He sat on one of the bar stools and scratched at his side for a second or two before pulling the envelope's flap open.

Ryan,

I've been awake half the night thinking about how to write this.

Over the past few weeks, you've changed.

It's brilliant about your photography and the energy it's given you.

But not all that energy is positive.

Last night didn't just leave me upset – I was scared by it, too.

I was scared that's how it will be from now on. I asked you not to open that message, not to go out, but you didn't listen. Worse than that, you didn't <u>care</u>.

His eyes lingered on the way she'd underlined the word 'care'. Even as part of his mind raced to form a denial, a different bit of his brain was slowing. He glimpsed himself the previous evening. Oh Jesus, he thought. I can see what she's talking about. How could I have been such a dick? He wanted to close his eyes. She even said it was up to me to decide, and I just didn't listen. He went back to the note.

That's what worries me most. You don't care what I think anymore.

I believe it's best you move out.

He felt himself flinch. No. The piece of paper almost slid from his fingers. Move out. She couldn't be serious. No way could she be bloody serious! He was reaching for his phone before he knew what he was doing. Move out? Come on, Carla, for fuck's sake...

Her answer phone clicked in before a single ring. Phone was off.

'Carla, what the hell? Listen, I can see I've not been... not been the, you know, the best. My behaviour, I mean. My behaviour hasn't been –' The words were like chewed up biscuit. He gave up trying to get them out. 'Just call me,' he sighed. 'Can you, Carla? OK, bye.'

He put his phone aside, then realised he hadn't even read the last of her note.

I really don't know if this is the end for us. All I know is I need time and space alone. Also, I think you do as well.

I've got a day over at MediaCity on a TV shoot, so I won't be answering my phone. Please don't try ringing me.

This isn't a spur of the moment thing. I've thought this through, believe me.

I don't expect to get home until later tonight. But if you still care what I want, don't be waiting for me, please.

Let's both have a few days to work out how we feel and speak then.

Carla x

Now his eyes snagged on the x. Normally, it would be a row of three big ones. Now, just one little one. But it was still a kiss. So that meant she still did care, didn't she? Or was it just a polite kiss, like you'd put at the end of –

He slapped his palm against the granite surface. Christ, I'm analysing a bloody x. She wants me out. Simple as that. And she's deliberately written the note so I don't have a choice. Stay here and show that I don't care what she says or clear off and I have the chance of us speaking...when? He went back to the last line. A few days.

My exhibition will be over by then. She'll miss being at it. Miss my little speech where I thank her for supporting me. He bowed his head in disbelief. How could she be doing this? Now, of all times?

Another thought hit home, and he checked the message that had come in from Annabelle the previous evening. It had been to rearrange the interrupted meeting with Ivan. He'd accepted the proposed time, which was for ten o'clock that morning.

Halfway to the bedroom, his phone started ringing. He whirled round. Carla? She'd probably got his message. Maybe having second thoughts? He rushed back to the breakfast bar where the handset lay.

Rather than Carla's name, the screen was displaying two words: number withheld. Sales call? Nerves got the better of him; maybe there was a poor signal in the studio where she was. Perhaps she was using a landline in the director's office, or something.

'Hello?' he asked hopefully.

'Is that Ryan speaking?'

It was a male voice. Official sounding. 'Yes, it is.'

'Ryan, my name's Detective Sergeant Robinson. I work with Detective Inspector Roebuck here at the Major

Incident Team. He'd like you to come by the station.'

'The station?' The pit of his stomach plummeted.

'Yes. He's available at ten fifteen. Let me tell you how to find us.'

'Hang on, ten fifteen, did you say?'

'Correct.'

'Well...' He wondered if he should ask if he had any choice in the matter. Or would that make him seem more guilty? 'This is about the armed robbery?'

'There are a few details he'd like to clear up with you.'

Ryan looked to the window, thinking of his ten o'clock with Ivan. 'That time isn't really the best...'

'It shouldn't take long.'

He wondered what would happen if he refused to go. Would they just arrest him? 'Ten fifteen, you say?'

'Yes. The incident room is at the police station on Belvedere Road in Salford. If you need to get a train, nearest station is Salford Crescent. Come into the main reception and ask for DI Roebuck.'

'Right... the main reception and ask –' it sounded like the call was no longer connected. 'Hello?' He held the phone away from his face to see the screen. The officer had already hung up.

CHAPTER 26

It was more than luck that brought Jason awake. To him, it was proof of the instinctive bond that had developed between them. The fact that he opened his eyes and she was there, sitting in the dimly lit flat, busily writing.

The sky was still dark and he checked the time. Ten to six in the morning. He'd slept for hours. Was Ryan even back? He spotted the bloke's coat draped over the back of the sofa. No idea when he got in.

Carla was now folding the letter over and sealing it in an envelope. She propped it against the kettle. It had to be for Ryan. An ultimatum? Worse? Jason could only hope. Poor Carla. She looked close to tears as she slipped out of the flat with her make-up case.

Ryan didn't appear from the bedroom for another three hours.

By then, Jason had retreated to the little mezzanine floor and laid the carpet over himself. Like a bird watcher or something, he thought. With all the lights off, he was confident that only someone who was really suspicious would be able to spot him from the other building. And so what? It was his flat. He could be here, relaxing. From his higher vantage point, Ryan was only just in view. As the other man read the letter, Jason saw his face turn more and more pale. It was bad! The news was bad. Really bad. He was transfixed as Ryan snatched up his phone and spoke into it for a few seconds. Then he laid it aside, looking ill. For the first time, Jason let himself believe that this was it. Carla had finally cast him away. Rejected him. If it's true, Jason thought, what more proof do I need? She knows, in her heart, she knows. It's time for us to be together. That's why she's sweeping Ryan aside.

To make room in her life for me.

When Ryan started putting on his coat, Jason did, too. He followed the other man to Victoria Station, where he got on a train to Blackpool North. The seaside? Why the seaside? But he got off just a few stops later at Salford Crescent. He turned right out of the station and made his way to a police station. Jason hung back as the other man wandered uncertainly up to the front doors. This was interesting. Something to do with the incident in the convenience store, perhaps?

#

Ryan looked around the reception area of the police station on Belvedere Road. The desk was off to the side. 'Yeah, hello. I'm here to see Detective Roebuck. Detective Inspector, I mean. It's a ten-fifteen meeting.'

The uniformed officer behind the Perspex screen tapped at her keyboard while scrutinising a monitor. She frowned. 'DI Roebuck, you say?'

'Yes.'

She moved the mouse about. 'Roebuck... Roebuck... oh yes. You are?'

'Ryan Lamb.'

She reached for her phone. 'Hello, is DI Roebuck there? I have a Ryan Lamb at reception. OK, thanks.' She replaced the receiver and tipped her head to the side. 'Take a seat.'

'Right, thanks.'

The area had that unmistakable feel of a waiting room. Shiny floor with several rows of thick plastic chairs bolted to it. Notice boards with various posters. A quiet resignation hanging in the air. He noticed a few of the halogen lights in the ceiling weren't working as he took a corner seat as far as possible from the other people.

Earlier, Annabelle had sounded a bit irritated when he'd rung to say he couldn't see Ivan at ten. Well, fuck you, he wanted to say. There's a very good chance it's because he tipped off a newspaper reporter about my visit to the hospital. But, of course, he'd stayed quiet as she searched for another slot.

'He's taking his mother out to lunch, but I know he's free directly before that. Quarter past twelve would work.'

Ryan had done a quick mental calculation. The officer who'd rung said it was only to clear up a few things. Surely it would all be done by noon? 'Quarter past twelve would be great. Sorry to mess him around.'

'Right. See you then.'

There was a monotonous beeping sound coming from behind the Perspex screen where the uniformed officer was working. She seemed totally oblivious to it. He sat back in the seat and checked his phone. Nothing from Carla. He so wanted to try her number again, make sure she properly understood what she'd done. Instead, he took a quick look about. Closest to him was a woman in her early twenties with that weird dip-dyed hair. Black on top, bright blue at the lower extremities. Looked bloody awful. She was rotating a white A4 envelope round and round on her pudgy knees.

Further along was an older man, whose bulbous nose and flabby cheeks were a bit too rosy. He kept reaching to the side pocket of his bulky coat and checking whatever was inside.

Ryan stopped himself from trying to guess why they were there. Instead, he re-examined the ceiling lights, looking to see if the ones that weren't working formed any kind of pattern. Wondering if it could make a good shot. Trying not to think about Carla.

'Ryan.'

He turned his head; a lady in normal clothes was beckoning. He recognised her as the officer who had turned up at the convenience store with DI Roebuck. How many detectives were on his team? She was holding the door on the far side of the reception desk half open.

'This way, please.'

He got to his feet and hurried over. 'Thanks.'

Once she'd ushered him through, the door swung back. A solid click as the lock re-engaged. 'You live in the Northern Quarter, don't you?' she asked, sweeping past him.

'Ancoats, actually.'

'Did you get the train?'

'Walked.'

'Really? Bit of a trek, wasn't it?'

She seemed a lot friendlier than the detective who rang earlier, he thought, setting off after her. 'It's OK, I like to walk if I can. You see more of the city that way.'

'So I gather.' She started trotting up some stairs.

What, he thought, did she mean by that?

'We have taken over a room on the first floor. Did the officer on reception take long to find the number?'

'She did, actually.'

'Temporary incident rooms normally do. We're not based here permanently; just while this investigation is ongoing.' She stopped half-way along the corridor. 'This is us. After you.'

He'd been expecting a bustling office like on the TV programs. But it was just a small room with a table and three chairs. No Detective Inspector Roebuck. He checked the walls, expecting a mirror to be set into one of them. Just plain white. The ceiling had a camera, though.

He looked at her. 'Is this like, a formal interview?'

She smiled. 'Not unless you want it to be. Just

somewhere to chat. The main room is a bit noisy. By the way, I'm Detective Constable Sarah Potter. Can I get you a tea or a coffee?'

'No thanks.'

'Water?'

'No, I'm good, cheers.'

'OK,' she pointed to the single chair on the far side of the table. 'You take that one. I'm sure DI Roebuck will be through shortly.'

'Thanks.'

The door closed, and he tried not to look up at the camera as he crossed the room. The chair juddered on the cheap carpet tiles as he slid it out. He sat down and placed his hands in his lap. He was acutely aware of the little lens above him. They'll be there, won't they? All squashed into a side room, studying me, waiting for anything suspicious. Don't be so paranoid. This isn't like something off the telly. The thing probably isn't even turned on. He glanced at the door. It was properly shut. Am I locked in?

Even though he suspected this was all a tactic to unsettle him, he could feel nervousness spreading through him. Like fungus infecting a leaf. He realised he was picking at his lower lip. Needing something to do with his hands, he took out his phone. Had Carla been in touch? Nope. After checking his Instagram, he began flicking through screens. It occurred to him the phone could get impounded, or whatever the word was. If that happened, they'd find the bloody messages with the what3words codes. Shit. He swiftly tucked it back in his pocket while keeping his eyes averted from the camera.

Another few minutes dragged by before the door suddenly opened. DI Roebuck stepped into the room, holding a manila file. The female detective followed in behind.

'Ryan, good of you to pop in.' He was at the table in two paces, right hand thrust out.

Ryan reached across and felt his fingers momentarily crushed.

'You just met my colleague, DC Potter.' Roebuck plonked himself down and tapped his forefingers on the table. 'OK, why don't you tell me a bit about yourself?'

Ryan glanced at Potter as she lowered herself with a lot more grace into her chair. 'How do you mean?'

'You know, hobbies and interests,' Roebuck replied, stretching his legs out. 'Where you studied, what you do for a living. Small talk stuff.'

'Well, I'm twenty-five-years old and I did a degree at The University of Salford.'

'In what?'

'Photography.'

'Yeah? Enjoy it, did you?'

He nodded. 'It's not the sort of course that leads to earning mega-bucks, but that isn't why I did it.'

Roebuck gave his colleague a knowing glance. 'I can relate to that.'

She grinned briefly in response before turning to Ryan. 'But you work now, don't you?'

'Only part-time. There's a photographic agency in town. Q2. I'm just in there for catalogue work, but they have studios for proper fashion shoots, too.'

'Part-time?' she asked. 'Don't do yourself down. Shouldn't you be saying you're freelance? Sounds far more impressive.'

'Freelance?' He shook his head. 'I think you need more than a zero-hours contract with one employer to claim that. But thanks anyway.'

She shrugged. 'Fashion shoots? Anything I'll have heard of?'

'There was one going on this week for EM.'

She looked at him blankly.

'He played in the Premiership a while back. Has his own range of leisurewear. It's all plastered with his initials...' He saw Roebuck stifle a yawn. 'They've done quite a lot with football clubs over the years. Each season's new strip.'

'City's or United's?' she asked, as Roebuck casually opened his folder.

Ryan was about to reply when he saw what was uppermost in it. That day's copy of the Manchester Evening Chronicle. His words dried up. It was open on the story about him. Roebuck slid it to the side and glanced up. 'Sorry, did you lose your thread there?'

He didn't know what to say.

'DC Potter asked you, City's or United's?'

'Er... both. They do both.'

'Very good.' Roebuck started flicking through the first few print outs that had been beneath the newspaper.

Silence built. Ryan shifted in his seat. Do I say something? He's obviously read the article. He glanced at Potter to see her gazing at him expectantly. His eyes shifted back to Roebuck. The man's head was still down. What's he doing? Seeing how long I keep my mouth shut? He was about to try and explain, when Roebuck lifted a sheet.

'I appreciate, Ryan, you only got a brief glimpse of the men who left the convenience store on Pinnington Street on Friday night. But – just on the off chance – any of these stand out?'

Row after row of men's faces. About five in each one. Roebuck placed the sheet right beside Ryan's image. In his photo, he was smiling. The men on these sheets just stared. He scanned the shaved skulls, body-builder necks, tattoos, crooked noses and scars. One or two were sneering at the camera, missing teeth exposed. 'I... I couldn't say, sorry. They both were wearing balaclavas.' He waved a hand in apology.

'Mmm, worth a try.' Roebuck removed the sheet. 'It's uncertain Stanisłow Witas will survive the attack.'

Ryan felt his eyes widening. 'But I thought he was... they said surgeons were...'

'They were. Unfortunately, there's been complications. An armed robbery is serious enough, but if this turns into a murder investigation... that becomes a whole new ball game.' He paused for a moment. 'Lots more budget, lots more staff. And if we find anyone has been less than honest with us, that person risks a whole load of misery.'

He put the sheet of photos back in the folder and closed it. The newspaper lay to the side, untouched.

'Actually,' he continued, 'I didn't expect you to point the finger at any of that lot. They're all Salford lads, but every one of them is currently inside. Sarah and me; we put most them away. These are the sorts of people who rob shops and slash up the staff. Stick a broken beer glass in some random pub-goer's face. Bust into houses with baseball bats; use them on the owner's legs even after he's handed over the car keys. Savages. How would you find it, Ryan, locked up with them? More importantly, what do you think they'd make of you?'

Ryan sucked a lungful of air in through his nose. When the breath came back out, he couldn't stop a shiver from passing through his shoulders.

Roebuck tapped the newspaper. 'All the stuff here. It slipped your mind when we spoke?'

'I didn't think it was relevant.'

'What didn't you think was relevant?'

'You know, that I'm a photographer.'

'You mean a street photographer?' He sent a smirking oh-la-la look to his colleague. 'Not a zero-hours contractor doing catalogues? A photographer?'

'Well, I take shots, yes.'

'Enough to have your own exhibition coming up, according to that article.'

He stayed quiet.

'And these shots are of what?'

'All sorts.'

'Speak up, Ryan, What was that?'

He lifted his chin. 'All sorts, really. Things I spot when

walking about in the city centre.'

'Ah, yes.' He turned the paper round and read in a dramatic whisper. 'Unflinching in nature, the images captured by Ryan Lamb on his midnight ramblings force the viewer to witness the struggles – often brutal – that play out in the heart of the city.' He nodded, as if impressed. 'Midnight ramblings. That's clever, that is. You know the song, Midnight Rambler, Ryan?'

'Yes.'

'You do?'

'It's by the Rolling Stones, I think.'

'It is. Do you know what it's about?'

'No.' He bit back on an apology.

'The song's about a serial killer known as the Boston Strangler. He murdered thirteen women in the early sixties. Look up the lyrics when you get the chance. It talks about this person who creeps round the city, jumping garden walls, sneaking into kitchens. Going about his business before the light of the morning. Should I be worried about your nocturnal habits, Ryan?'

'What? No! I take pictures, that's all.'

Roebuck placed both elbows on the table, eyes locked on Ryan's. 'So how come you just happen to be on hand to get images of all this stuff?'

Ryan had to look away. It was like being stared at by an angry baboon. 'I'm out most nights.'

'Where you out last night?'

He sensed a trap. 'Er... I was, yes.'

'And?'

'I came across a scene in Parsonage Gardens. But I didn't have my camera.'

Potter tipped her head to the side. 'So, do you just listen for the sounds of sirens? Head to where they are?'

'Quite often, yes.'

'There were no sirens outside that late-night store as the two blokes were violently robbing it,' Roebuck stated.

Christ, Ryan thought. He knows I'm not telling the

truth. 'I'd gone over there to look at the properties in that estate agents.'

'Internet images no good? You prefer walking across town late at night to squint through a window, rather than just clicking on a website?'

'I'd also planned to walk past any that looked promising. Get a feel for the streets they're on.'

Roebuck sat back, a look of disbelief on his face.

Ryan glanced at Potter. She was revealing nothing. He looked down at his lap, had to interlink his fingers beneath the table to stop them shaking.

'Did you have your camera with you that night?' Potter asked quietly.

'No, I wasn't –'

'On a midnight ramble,' Roebuck cut in. 'That coat you were wearing. The Napa-thingamajig, it was very big and baggy. Nothing hidden beneath that, no?'

'No.'

'We're hauling in CCTV, Ryan. You're sure about that?'

He nodded.

'Right, let's stay on the wandering photographer thing,' Roebuck continued. 'I'm offering you another chance to be honest about it. Because I'll be honest with you, Ryan. I've got major problems with it.'

Ryan kept looking at his lap. He wished he'd asked for a glass of water. At least he'd have had something to do in these awful silences.

'No?' Roebuck asked. 'Very well. Let's press on. You've also been at the MRI. Visiting the owner of the shop that was being robbed just as, again by chance, you showed up.'

'I was asked to visit her. By someone who works for victim support. A woman. I have her number, if you want it.'

'Yes, but not now. And the reporter for The Chronicle? Did victim support call her, too?'

'I don't know.'

'Who called her, then?'

Ryan pictured Ivan shooing him out of his gallery with a twenty-pound note. 'I don't know. Not me.'

'Good timing, though. Right before your exhibition starts.'

Ryan gave a little shake of his head.

Roebuck was on it in an instant. 'What?'

'Nothing.'

'No, go on. You obviously have some sort of problem with what I just said.'

Another silence.

'Ryan?' DC Potter asked gently. 'This exhibition you're having. How much money do those things make? For the photographer, I mean.'

He raised his eyes for a moment. She was looking concerned. 'I don't know. It's commission only. However much gets sold by the gallery.'

'Well, what does it cost to buy a print? You're not selling off your originals, I presume?'

'Depends. Between eighty and a few hundred.'

'Nice,' Roebuck answered. 'A few dozen of each print, maybe?'

Ryan wanted to laugh but didn't dare. 'Maybe eight to ten.'

'So, let's get this straight,' Roebuck said in a measured way. 'You wander round Manchester at night, stumbling over incidents like road traffic accidents, burglaries, arson attacks. Armed robberies. All by chance. You take photos of those incidents and, with this exhibition, you stand to make quite a tidy amount.'

Ryan lifted a hand and rubbed at the side of his face. 'I know it looks dodgy. I know it does. But...it's what I do. I spend hours wandering around. Really. If you knew how often I get home with nothing. Or the amount of shots I take that are no good. It's like anything. You put the time and effort in and hope things work out.' He checked their faces.

Roebuck was leaning back in his chair with his

eyebrows half raised. Potter's head was cocked partly to the side, as if eager to catch whatever he said next.

'I always wanted to be a photographer,' he found himself saying. 'But not of this kind of thing.'

'What kind of thing?' Potter asked quietly.

He pointed a finger at the paper. 'Urban trauma, to use the title.'

'OK,' she said. 'What did you want to be taking photos of?'

'The sort of dramas you find in nature. Animals.' He couldn't believe he'd actually said it. The thing he'd never admitted out loud. Not even to Carla. He was back in the little garden of his childhood. Ten years old with his mum's Kodak EasyShare glued to his hands. Mucking about, as usual, shadowing anything that moved. The cornflakes he'd laid out had attracted a squirrel. It had crept its way down the fence and was filling his viewfinder when a neighbour's cat launched itself from some unseen spot.

As the shutter clicked all he could see was hackles and claws: those of the cat raking at grass, the squirrel's clawing the air. He'd lifted his head in shock. The end of a fluffy grey tail was vanishing over the top of the fence, the cat was at the base, whirling in the wrong direction before slinking away across the lawn.

He could still see his dad's reaction when he'd stepped into the garage and held out the shot; it was the only time the man had seemed impressed about anything he'd done. The way he put the dumbbells aside that he had been lifting to silently study the image. A soft whistle as he looked closer. Those precious three words. *Not bad, that.*

Roebuck's guffaw broke the silence. 'Jesus! A frustrated David Attenborough?' He nudged Potter with an elbow. 'Did you get that? Wildlife?'

Ryan stared at the man. How the veins in his neck were standing out. The muscle tensing at the corner of his jaw. Just like dad's. The person who had never shown him any affection. Never hugged him or took him anywhere. The man who, one day, simply deserted his mum for someone else. Resentment like bile at the back of his throat. Still smiling, Roebuck turned to look at Ryan once more. Ryan kept staring. Some of the merry sparkle in Roebuck's eyes faded.

The detective cleared his throat. 'So... let's go back to this business with following sirens. You're on foot. These incidents – they're not all in the city centre, like you said earlier. The car crash for a start, that was the Mancunian Way. Are you a fast runner?'

Ryan checked his watch. 'I have an appointment. The person who rang me said this wouldn't take long. But it is.'

Roebuck sat back. There was now an appraising look on his face. 'We won't be much longer, Ryan.' The bravado in his voice had mostly gone.

To his surprise, Ryan felt his head shake. 'No, I need to be off. I can go, can't I?'

Roebuck lifted a hand towards the door. 'Be my guest.'

Ryan looked from him to DC Potter. She didn't look like she was about to stop him.

'But this isn't over,' Roebuck announced. 'Far from it. When we need to speak with you again, you might not have a choice in the matter.'

Ryan got to his feet. 'Whatever.'

He had got down the stairs and was half-way along the corridor when he heard DC Potter call out behind him. 'Ryan? I'll need to buzz you out.'

He slowed his step without looking back. 'Cheers.'

She drew alongside him and he could see her looking at him in the periphery of his vision. 'I realise DI Roebuck can be overbearing. He's under a lot of –'

'That's a nice way of putting it.'

'Sorry?'

'That wasn't overbearing. That was bullying.'

'Well, I wouldn't say –'

'I've known men like him. He's a bully.' They were now

at the door out to reception. He waited in front of it, jaw set tight.

After a second, she tapped in a few numbers. 'Well, thanks for coming in today.'

He pushed the door open and looked back at her. 'He mentioned a son to me, Roebuck did. You know what? I feel sorry for the lad.'

CHAPTER 27

Jason checked his watch. It had been half an hour since Ryan had gone into the police station. He was sure it was starting to look suspicious, him hanging around on the street outside it. He produced his phone and checked Carla's Instagram feed. She was doing another job out at MediaCity. Something else for the TV. He didn't want to think about the misunderstanding that had occurred on the set of *Unsung Heroes*. Looking back on it, he could now see what had really been going on. The attention had simply embarrassed Carla. Not so much from him, but all the other people working there. If the self-important idiot in the white shirt hadn't got security involved, Carla would have been happy to come over. More than happy. They could have talked and, maybe, gone for a walk together along one of the nearby quays. Fed the swans and held hands. He could have given her the pendant, too. But that idiot who thought he owned the place had put pressure on her. Probably said they weren't allowed to talk with members of the audience. Pointed out it wasn't even her break and, no, she couldn't take it early. He wouldn't even grant her that! Maybe he fancied Carla and wanted to prevent her from speaking to anyone else.

He continued walking along the A6 then turned left at Trinity Way. A few minutes' later, he was on Pinnington Street. The shop had a handwritten sign stuck to the glass inside the front door. He could just make out the words.

Sorry. Opening later today.

The walk back to Loom Street didn't take long. Once in the apartment, he ate a few muesli bars and drank two more cans of Red Bull in the bathroom. He still felt thirsty, so filled the empties up at the sink. Carla's apartment was deserted. He retreated to his spot on the mezzanine floor to keep watch.

#

Once out of the police station, Ryan had to pause for a few seconds. His pulse wasn't slowing down. Emotions veered from elation one moment to apprehension the next. And tagging a ride with both was a sharp sense of bitterness at how Roebuck had mocked him. Laughed at how he'd wanted to capture images from the natural world. Ryan winced at the memory of his admission. Why did I even tell them that? It must have been a weird effect of being in that room. Nervousness. A need to admit to something. He remembered the way the female detective had looked at him. The kindness in her eyes and softness in her voice. He wanted to yell in frustration. They played me. Good cop, bad cop. And I fell for it. Dickhead!

He started striding back towards the city centre, keen to put some distance between himself and the scene of his humiliation. An urge to grin suddenly swamped his sense of despair. It had felt so good informing Roebuck he was off, that he wasn't putting up with his shit a moment longer. The detective's face! The man's words had faltered. The way he'd gestured weakly at the door. Yes, Ryan told himself. Just for a second, the power had been with me in there. And it felt good. But then trepidation robbed him of his cheer. What had Roebuck said as he'd walked out? This isn't over. They might not be able to say exactly how I'm lying, but they can sense it all the same. And if Stanisłow Witas dies, and it turns into a full-blown murder investigation. Jesus.

He produced his phone. At least they didn't take that off me. For now. Just seeing the word 'Mum' on his contacts list made him feel a tiny bit calmer.

'Ryan! What a treat. You OK, love?'

His eyes smarted with approaching tears. When he tried to speak, the words came out cracked and he had to clear his throat. Fuck's sake, Ryan. 'Yeah, I'm good, Mum. What are you up to?'

A moment's pause. Stupid question, he said to himself. What did he think she was up to? It was late morning; she'd have finished her first cleaning job and would be on the way to her second. Almost sixty and still working every weekend. But what choice did she have after the bastard who'd married her walked out?

'Waiting for the bus. Nice weather, isn't it?'

'Yeah,' he said, glancing up and registering the ragged blue patches above him. 'Mum, can I ask a favour?'

'I'm sure you can. What is it?'

'Can I have my old room back for a bit?'

'Oh no – you and Carla haven't...?'

'We've had a fall out, that's all. It's best we spend a bit of time apart.'

'Oh Ryan.'

'Don't worry, Mum, it's not... you know... forever.'

'Course you can, love. When were you thinking?'

'Well – tonight?'

'To –' He could hear the shock in her voice. 'That'll be lovely. Will you be wanting some tea?'

He hadn't thought that far ahead. Didn't want to put his Mum out by making her cook for him. But the thought of sitting down at the kitchen table... he could see those little salt and pepper pots. And the bottle of ketchup. Glass, not one of those plastic squeezy ones. 'No, you're all right. I can grab something on the way.'

'Don't be doing that! Much easier for me to do double.'

'Well... what had you planned?'

'I don't know. Cheese and onion pie with home-made chips?'

He felt the fight go out of him. Cheese and onion pie: a childhood favourite. Had she chosen it deliberately? Of course she had. 'Sounds great, thanks Mum.'

The university buildings were now behind him. There was a considerable drop beyond the waist-high railings on his left. Below, the River Irwell looped so sharply, the sluggish brown water almost fully enclosed a piece of scrubby heath. He looked down in astonishment. A deer was silently making its way along the overgrown riverbank. A deer in the middle of Salford. Must have followed the river for miles. He wished he had his camera: the animal was beneath branches festooned with ripped carrier bags and other ragged pieces of plastic. The contrast between the animal's pristine coat and the mud-stained litter was striking. It lifted its huge brown eyes, seemed to register the figure against the sky above and, with a slight bunching of its hind quarters, bounded beneath a fan of branches and out of sight.

He wondered again whether to call Carla. Just to say he'd be gone by the evening. Maybe she'd want to talk. He lifted his phone, then the image of her screen from two nights ago appeared in his mind's eye.

I hope he took it OK? Simone XXX

Hope I took what OK? A thought struck him like a knee in the nuts. Was something going on between Simone and Carla? More than friendship? Was that the real reason behind her kicking him out? He thought of the amount of time Carla spent with the other woman. Girls' nights out. How often had Carla got back in the early hours of the morning, wrecked after a session with Simone? She'd even stayed over once or twice. At the place Simone owned on the edge of Heaton Mersey Common.

He rubbed at the back of his head. No, don't be stupid, Ryan. You're stressed to fuck. Seeing shadows where there are none. He looked back down at the riverbank. Had there really been a deer down there? He couldn't see any hoof prints in the mud. But what did the message on Carla's phone mean? She wasn't telling him something. And whatever it was, Simone knew all about it, too.

#

'Ryan! Come, come!' Ivan was beckoning rapidly with one hand. 'So good you could make it at last!'

Ryan stepped fully into the gallery with an apologetic smile. 'Something came up and I –'

'It's fine. I'm pulling your leg. Has Annabelle told you about ticket sales?'

He glanced questioningly at the glacial-faced assistant. 'No...'

Ivan clapped his hands. 'Up by another thirty percent. I've ordered extra prints. You, dear boy, have a lot of signing to do. Here, it's all in here.' He led Ryan across to the side room where a trestle-table had been set up. Stacked at one end was a pile of Ryan's images. 'Thank God we hadn't done the numbering already. So, there's another twenty-five of *Vulpine Plunderer*. A limited edition of seventy-five. That's a good number. For everything else, I've added another ten. We'll give you scrivener's palsy yet, you'll see!'

Ryan surveyed the table. A chair was at the mid-point.

Ivan waved him on. 'It's a little production line; I pass you a print, you sign it, Annabelle slides it out the way. It won't take long. We'll add the numbering later – just in case we need to increase print runs again.'

Ryan was trying to remember how the payment structure worked. Didn't his share increase if they exceeded a certain number of sales?

'Now,' Ivan said, 'would you like a drink before getting started?'

Ryan glanced over his shoulder. Annabelle was standing in the main gallery. 'A coffee would be great, thanks.' He waited until she was round the corner, then turned to Ivan. 'Did you tell someone at the Manchester Evening Chronicle about my hospital visit?'

Ivan cocked his head. 'Hospital visit?'

'Yesterday, when I went to see the woman from that armed robbery.'

'Oh, you meant the newspaper feature! I spotted that, yes.' He arched an eyebrow. 'That wasn't you, then?'

'Me?' Ryan touched his own chest. 'Why would I...?'

'There's no such thing as bad publicity, Ryan. A cliché, but one that is true. And there was me thinking you'd been a crafty little tinker. Driving up ticket sales with a well-placed bit of media coverage.' He gave Ryan a little smirk as he circled the table.

'I was late getting here because the police called me in.'

'Called you in? How do you mean, called you in?'

'After they saw that story in the paper, they wanted to ask me a load of questions.'

Ivan's head was bowed as he checked over the pile of prints. 'Really? What sort of questions?'

'Just... wanting to know about me.' Ryan felt a sudden need to take care with what he said. 'And my photographs.'

As Annabelle appeared with his drink, Ivan raised a palm. 'Far from it being my business, Ryan. But I can see why they might have been... intrigued, if that's the right word.' His eyes touched Ryan's. 'But it's hardly my business.'

Right, thought Ryan. So we're not standing in your gallery and I'm not signing a load of extra prints you've trotted out at lightning speed. None of this is your business.

Ivan patted the chair. 'Now, you make yourself

comfortable. Unfortunately, I have a prior engagement for lunch but – Annabelle? – you can be a darling and order in sandwiches if Ryan's not finished before I go.'

CHAPTER 28

'You certainly touched a nerve there, laughing at his ambitions for being a wildlife photographer,' DC Sarah Potter said she settled behind her desk.

Roebuck ran a finger across his forehead, a regretful look on his face. 'Yeah, I overdid it in there. Scared him off. Sorry.'

She nodded. 'He was really touchy. When I showed him out, he accused you of being a bully.'

Roebuck snorted. 'A bully? He's in for questioning about an armed fucking robbery. This generation of bloody snowflakes. Had his sensibilities dented by the nasty mean detective? Jesus.'

He waited for Potter to respond, but she kept quiet. His mind went to a recent heated exchange with his wife. She'd asked him to go easy on their teenage son. To stop badgering him about taking up a sport. Roebuck wasn't fussed exactly which sport. Preferably in a team, but anything to get him out of his bedroom and away from his sodding computer. He'd shot back that Archie would have no problem handling prison if he ever was convicted; he willingly locked himself away for most of each day. She'd not been happy with his comment.

'I'd love to know where his information is coming from,' Potter said. 'Because it's coming from somewhere.'

Roebuck looked up, glad the conversation had moved on from his overbearing interview style. 'Shifty, wasn't he? When we asked him about that.'

Potter tapped her pen against her pad. 'Especially when you throw in last night's incident in Parsonage Gardens.'

'The way I see it, we have several options – and all of them involve someone on the inside,' Roebuck replied. 'First, we have the city centre CCTV control room. The camera operators there are civilian, but they've all got the surveillance license thing. Plus, they'll have been fully vetted.' He peered round his monitor. 'What's that thing you've got, Jenny? For accessing the systems?'

'BS7858?'

'That's it.'

'But not all the incidents have occurred within the network's coverage,' Potter countered.

'Doesn't really matter,' Roebuck said. 'The control room is tuned into the emergency services' channels. They get to hear about anything as it's being radioed in.'

'Really?' Potter sounded surprised. 'I didn't realise they had that level of access. My bet was a call handler.'

'You mean where calls to the emergency services are answered?' Roebuck asked. 'That's certainly another possible. But it's going to be a bastard of a job cross-referencing shift patterns with incidents our man has miraculously shown up at.'

'How about someone who's tapped into the network illegally?' Robinson asked.

'Not with Airwaves,' Roebuck responded, referring to the digital radio network that had replaced the old system a few years back. 'Everything's encrypted. Gone are the days of some geek with a CB radio sitting up in the attic eavesdropping on what's happening round the city.'

'There's another option,' Potter announced.

The DI sat back. 'Go on.'

'It's one of us.'

'A serving officer?'

She lowered her voice so Jenny, who was typing away at the end of the room, couldn't hear. 'Possibly. Or someone working with the emergency services. Fire. Ambulance. They'll all have support workers who get to hear what's going on, won't they?'

Roebuck closed his eyes for a second. 'Christ. That opens things right up. Let's park that one until we've exhausted other options, don't you think?'

She nodded. 'Your call, boss.'

'And let's not get distracted from the armed robbery. By the way, Stanisłow will be able to talk with us later today.'

'Nice touch, by the way,' Potter said. 'Telling Ryan Lamb it was likely to become a murder investigation.'

He mirrored her smile. 'Put the shits up him, didn't it?'

'How is Mr Witas?'

'Well, victim support – the one that Ryan mentioned – told me he's had over one-hundred-and-forty stitches. The little ones plastic surgeons use. His face is a mess.'

At the adjacent desk, Robinson stretched his arms out. 'And you think it's the same two that did it?'

Roebuck considered the evidence so far. Two males with Salford accents. One carrying a machete. Camera in the shop disabled with a hammer. Cash taken from the till, along with as many bottles of spirits and cigarettes they could fit in a green hold-all. It was a familiar pattern. In fact, the only major difference to the other four robberies that had recently occurred was the escalation in violence. 'I do,' he stated. 'But now they're enjoying themselves. It'll be interesting to hear what Mr Witas has to say.' He checked his watch. 'In another three hours, we can find out.'

Simone's eyes tracked Carla's reflection in the brightly lit mirror. 'Really? You kicked him out?'

Carla moved behind the chair her friend was sitting in, pausing to twist a ringlet of lush dark hair around the straighteners in her hand. 'I didn't kick him out. Just asked him to leave for a few days.' She checked the mirror, caught Simone's shocked expression. 'He's being such a... such a fucking idiot. This whole photography thing has taken him over. I told him – last night – I told him do not go out. I pleaded. Did he listen?' She shook her head as she released the strand of hair. It was no different. 'Bloody things,' she murmured, giving the straighteners a quick shake. 'They aren't working.'

Simone wrinkled her nose. 'Put a clip in. No one's going to notice.'

Carla turned away to rummage in her case. 'You know when I called you the other day about that person who showed up at the studio where I'd been filming?'

Simone twisted round in her seat. 'What about him? Have you seen him again?'

'No,' Carla replied, still looking into her case. 'Not that I could say what he really looked like. I mean, not accurately.'

'What, then?'

'So, you said about if I'd got any strange messages. Emails.'

'And have you?'

'You mean besides the usual dick pics and requests to send nudes?' She glanced back at Simone with a weary smile.

'Carla?' Her friend's face was serious.

'A message caught my eye. It came through my website's enquiry screen.'

'What did it say?'

Carla slid her phone out of her back pocket. 'It's probably nothing. I mean, it's just a message. Not even crude. More…I don't know. Here, see what you think.'

Simone took the device and scrutinised the screen. 'You are beautiful,' she murmured. 'All my love, Gabriel.' She looked up at Carla. 'OK, that's a bit weird. Any others like that?'

Carla took the device from Simone's hand. 'No. Not that I've noticed. Though I usually delete spammy stuff like that without looking. Just odd there's no link or anything. That's why I noticed it. And the address, it's just numbers and letters.'

'Don't delete it.'

'Why not?'

'You never know…it might be useful. Like, if it's from that freak who showed up. It's what you're thinking, right?'

'Suppose.'

'Did he say his name was Gabriel? At the studio?'

'I don't remember, to be honest. But fair enough, I'll save it.' She returned the phone to her pocket and reached into her make-up case.

Simone tutted to herself. 'Kicking him out? Carla, that's like going straight to Defcon1.'

'Def what?' Carla asked, pinning the stray strand of hair back.

'Like, red alert. No warnings, nothing.'

'Ha! Well, he's had plenty of warnings, don't you worry. And if he cared even the teeniest bit about what I feel, he'd have picked up on them. But he doesn't care what I think.' She adjusted one of the chopsticks jutting out from the mass of hair bunched at the back of Simone's head.

'Where will he go?'

'His mum's. I'm sure. Only for a few days – and then we'll speak.'

'And is it really?' Simone asked. 'A few days?'

Carla's bottom lip suddenly trembled. She pursed her lips.

'Oh, sweetie,' Simone said, reaching back with a hand.

She clasped Simone's outstretched fingers. 'I don't want things to finish. I just want him to act like I'm actually in the room with him. To stop just thinking about himself.'

'Once this exhibition is out of the way, he will be.'

'But what if he isn't? What if this is just the start of – you know – a new Ryan?'

'I can't see that. He's not the fame-hungry type.'

'You should see how often he checks his Instagram followers. It's becoming an obsession.'

'Hey, I'm on a flight at six tomorrow morning to New York. Why don't you stay at my place while I'm gone? Just so you're not pacing around in your empty apartment.'

Carla gave a quick smile. 'That's really kind of you, but I couldn't.'

'Why not? It would get you out of the city centre. You'd have the garden. Gorgeous views across to the woods. It will be a chance to clear your head.'

Carla pictured her friend's beautiful little cottage tucked away at the end of a cul-de-sac that overlooked Heaton Mersey Common. 'Maybe if I didn't have so much work already booked in.'

'Well, the offer's there. Maggy next door has a spare key.'

'Thanks.'

Simone gave Carla's fingers another little squeeze. 'I have to ask: you're sure this isn't you avoiding having the conversation with him? About the weirdo?'

A voice called from the doorway. 'Let's have you, ladies!'

Carla stood back to check her friend's face, somehow avoiding all eye contact. She whipped a brush out and circled it over Simone's cheekbone.

'Carla?'

She blinked. 'No! It isn't: he just never gives me the chance. It's only ever, "my photographs this, my photographs that". And now the thing with the police.'

The same voice called again. 'OK, let's go!'

When Simone stood, her Okobo platforms meant she

towered over Carla. Smoothing her kimono, she said from the side of her mouth, 'Because I don't think that little freak has gone away. Trust me on that.'

CHAPTER 29

Ryan almost knocked on the door of the flat before letting himself in. Don't be stupid, he said to himself. She's at work. The place is empty. As he pushed the door open, he realised his fingers still ached from writing his signature out so many times. What had Ivan called it? Scrivener's palsy.

After Ivan had left, Annabelle had been even more quiet than usual. He'd wondered if she was feeling guilty about the newspaper story. For all he knew, she'd made the call. Because if the tip-off hadn't come from the gallery, who'd made it?

The living area was exactly as he'd left it that morning. He let his gaze linger on the sofa, the rubber plant, the magazines scattered across the low table in front of the telly. Half of those were his. *Outdoor Photography Magazine. Juxtapoz. Offscreen.* A few *Taschen* publications. The wide-screen telly was his, too. Not that it would fit into his old bedroom back home. Shit, how depressing? Much as he loved his mum, he didn't want to be moving back in with her at twenty-five years old. He had to push the thought aside. Tell himself it was only temporary. They'd patch things up, him and Carla. Come out the other side stronger.

Once he'd arranged the contents of his little shopping bag on the breakfast bar, he went through to the bedroom and started placing items of clothing in the big hold-all they'd bought for their trip to Turkey last summer. Flight tags were still on the straps. Memories of a rooftop restaurant and the smell of barbecuing lamb as an amber sun slowly merged with a molten sea. Sipping ice cold beers. Laughing at his astonishment at spotting a live tortoise ambling along the track that led to the beach. He'd assumed it was an escaped pet, before realising they lived wild in the area. Were as common as squirrels in England. What had gone wrong with their relationship since then? He knew the answer: the messages turning up on his phone.

He packed toiletries into a wash bag and chucked it on top of his clothes. Back in the living area, he summoned an Uber. There was a driver five minutes away. He wondered what else to take. Camera, obviously. Plus, his lenses. Once they were in, he found himself starting to gather his magazines, then stopped. A few days, he told himself again. You'll be back in a few days. He couldn't get his mind to work properly. He'd need his MacBook and charger. Plus the one for his phone. And the memory stick from the kitchen drawer! Really, he should delete all the photos from the convenience store. He would never use them. The fact he'd even taken the things made him cringe. His mouth felt dry, and he headed to the fridge.

The cluster of snaps stuck to its door caught his attention. The two of them on a walk at Fletcher Moss. Sharing a pizza at Crazy Pedro's at God-knew-what-time of night. Probably early morning. His eyes stopped at the photo of Carla and Simone sitting at a table with a couple of cocktails. It was like seeing the photo for the first time. The way they were leaning in towards each other, shoulders almost touching. Has this been staring me in the face all along?

He recalled something else and crouched at the alcove where Carla kept her cookery books. There it was: *Bosh! Simple Recipes. Amazing Food. All Plants.* He slid it out and opened the cover.

To my gorgeous English rose. Stay healthy! Stay happy! Simone x

He replaced it and straightened up. Could I be right? Had something developed between the two of them?

His phone pinged. The Uber was waiting outside. He took a can of Pepsi from the fridge and had a last quick look round. MacBook and chargers! Jesus, Ryan, get it together. He added them to the holdall then made his way out of the flat, slamming the door behind him.

#

Ryan finally reappeared at two forty-six. Jason immediately lay down and pulled a length of carpet over himself, peeped out from below it. Long time at the police station, he thought, watching Ryan just standing in the middle of the room.

After a while, he arranged the contents of a shopping bag on the breakfast bar. Some of those little pudding things Carla had been eating the other night. And what looked like a card. He watched as Ryan trudged across to the bedroom, emerging a few minutes later with a large hold-all. The thing didn't weigh much, not from the way he slung it on the sofa. Had to be just clothes inside. Is he packing his stuff? Moving out? Jason's heart started to thud. It couldn't be true. Not with his exhibition the very next day, surely?

The other man seemed in a daze. He wandered across to the kitchenette and paused to look at some photos on the fridge door. He crouched down to read something in a large book. What's he doing? Next, he checked his phone.

Moving more quickly now, he took a can of Pepsi from the fridge and then scooted around the flat, sweeping up a couple of chargers. They went into the bag and he started for the door.

Jason threw off the carpet and raced down the stairs. In the lobby, he noticed an Uber was parked outside the doors of Jethro Mill. By the time the other man came out, Jason had undone his bike lock and had his helmet and gloves on. He followed the white Honda out of Ancoats and along the A665. When it turned left onto the A57, he laughed. You're going to Reddish! Back to your mum's! Carla has kicked you out. She's done it. She's got you out of her life because she wants me, not you. Not you! He could have accelerated up to the taxi and banged on the passenger window with his fist. Not you, you pathetic little shit! Me! She loves me!

As the Uber pulled up on Melrose Crescent, Jason dropped his speed right down. In front of him, Ryan got out of the car and started up the garden path of number 15. Number 15! Back home to his mum. He let the engine rip and the bike had almost hit sixty before he finally hit the brakes.

#

Here I am again, Ryan thought, walking up the short path to his old front door. Somewhere on the road behind him, an idiot revved the engine of his bike unnecessarily loudly. The machine and rider raced off towards the end of the road. Arsehole. He turned back to the house. It needed a fresh coat of paint; cracks were opening up in it. Flakes coming off around the letter box. Still screwed into the brickwork was the little placard that used to so embarrass him as a teenager. *Brambles.* It was number fifteen, Melrose Crescent, Reddish. A cramped little semi just inside the M60. Not some cottage in the woods. For the second time that day, it felt odd to be opening a front door. He called out while it was slightly ajar. 'Mum? Only me!'

She appeared in the kitchen doorway, an apron round her waist. Same one she'd had for as long as he could remember. Same pale blue cardigan. Same hair style. Hair a brighter shade of chestnut, though. Too bright. Maybe she'd experimented with a different dye. Misjudged its strength.

'Hi, Mum,' he said, plonking the hold-all down. 'You look well.'

She deflected the compliment with a slight turn of her head. 'Come on through. Cup of tea?'

'Go on, then. Cheers.' Before starting towards the kitchen, he glanced up the narrow staircase. Imagining his room up there. How tiny it was going to seem. 'So,' he announced loudly, careful to inject some cheer into his voice. 'You been back long?'

'About half-an-hour. I went by Asda.'

To buy stuff for my tea, he thought guiltily. He stepped into the miniscule kitchen. 'Listen, Mum – I'll pay you for while I'm here.'

'Don't be silly,' she said. Her back was to him as she took a couple of mugs from the cupboard. She was looking older. Less steady on her feet.

'Well, I am,' he replied. 'This exhibition at the art gallery I'm having – it could be quite a decent pay day.'

'That would be wonderful, but I don't expect anything for while you're here.'

He sat at the table. With Carla not going to the opening night, he needed to bring someone along. Could he take his mum? Why not? 'Do you fancy coming with me? You've never been to anything like that before.'

'Me?' She rotated stiffly, one hand staying on the counter for balance. 'I don't think so. What would I wear for a start?'

'Wear whatever you want, Mum. It's not posh or anything.'

She put the cups on the table. 'No. I'd feel all out of place. Will Carla not be going, then?'

He felt dismay at how quickly she'd worked out the reason for his offer. 'I don't think so, no.'

She lowered herself into the other chair. 'Oh, Ryan. What's going on?'

He tried to smile. 'It's just... she wants us to have some breathing space. It's been a bit hectic these last few weeks. Especially with the exhibition. I suppose we've been neglecting each other.'

'How will you moving out help with that?'

He shrugged. 'Give us time to think. Work out what's what.'

She reached across and placed her hand on his. 'You still love each other?'

He nodded. 'Yes, Mum. I think we do. I do.'

'Well, that's all that matters. Things will work out.' She withdrew her hand. 'You drink your tea.'

He made an effort to smile again as he reached for the cup. She'd selected him the one with the little pun. *You're tea-rrific.*

CHAPTER 30

DI Roebuck eased the door open. Stanisłow Witas had already been told they'd arrived to ask him some questions. He was sitting up in bed with a remote control in his bandaged hand. Swiftly, he pressed a button, resulting in the television mounted at the end of a grey plastic arm falling silent. He swung it away from the bed. 'Please,' he gestured at two chairs, 'sit.'

Roebuck nodded. 'Thanks for seeing us, Mr Witas. This is DS Potter and I am DI Roebuck. We're handling the investigation into who attacked you.'

'Yes, please.' He gestured at the chairs again, keen to ensure his guests were comfortable. 'Thank you for coming.'

Roebuck moved towards the farthest chair, glad of the opportunity to shift his gaze from Stanisłow's face. The man looked like he was part-way through being made up to play Frankenstein. The hair at the front of his head had been shaved off, but not the top and sides. An ugly red welt began at the centre point of the newly exposed skin, ran down his forehead to touch the end of his right eyebrow. A thicket of incredibly fine black threads sprouted from the angry flesh. Roebuck tried to remember how many stitches the plastic surgeon had put in. Well over a hundred, that was for sure. Stubble coated the lower part of his face and the skin below his eyes was an ugly purple. Roebuck couldn't tell if that was due to bruising. He took his notebook out of his jacket and composed his face before looking up once more. The man was watching with an expectant, almost hungry expression. 'First, Stanisłow, how are you feeling?'

'Yes, I am OK. My head is still sore. Sometimes I have – like a camera taking photos. Bright. But this will pass, the doctor said.'

'And your hands?' Potter asked from the chair beside Roebuck.

Stanisłow smiled regretfully. 'This isn't so simple. I have damage to my tendons. This will be a long time for me.'

'We're sorry to hear that,' Roebuck said.

'You will catch these men who did this? They are bad people, very bad people. One punched my mother. She is seventy-six and they punch her in the face!' He had to look away, jaw clenched tight.

'We'll find them, sir. I promise you that,' Roebuck replied. 'And I hope you might be able to help us.'

Stanisłow's head swung back round. 'Yes, I will help you.'

'That's great. Now, can you tell me what happened?'

They both took notes as he described how he'd been restocking at the front of the shop. A display stand of sweets. Two men had come through the doors very fast. One of them had ordered him to kneel. While that was taking place, the other one was smashing the camera above the door.

Roebuck flashed Potter a glance; the robbers knew the shop's layout. Which meant they'd been in before. How recently? Could they be on earlier CCTV footage? He nodded to Stanisłow to continue.

The other man went on to describe how neither he nor

his mum had been uncooperative. It was company policy; their training had been clear on that. But the one who'd gone behind the counter to empty the till had struck his mother. For no reason. None. When Stanisłow had tried to get up, the man standing before him started chopping down with his big knife. 'First here,' he said, lifting his bandaged hand. 'Next, my head. Then my memory stops.'

'That's fine,' Roebuck said. 'Absolutely fine. Did the two men say anything?'

He nodded. 'They're screaming to get down. To kneel. On your knees. Get down, these things.'

'Did they have any type of accent?'

'Same as most customers.'

'Salford?'

'Yes, Salford.'

The rest of Stanisłow's description pretty much tallied with Ryan Lamb's.

'And no one else was in the shop during the robbery?' Roebuck asked.

'No. No one.'

'How about before?'

'Yes, before. There was these teenage kids getting crisps and things. And a man who buys some cans of beer.'

Roebuck took out a photo of Ryan Lamb he'd copied from the Sussman Gallery's website. 'Did you see this person at any point during the evening?'

Stanislaw's eyes narrowed. 'No – but this is the man who helped Renata and me, I think?'

'That's right. And he wasn't in the shop before the robbery?'

'No.'

'Or perhaps the day before, or some time recently?'

'I do not think so.'

'OK.' Roebuck glanced at Potter. 'Shame they took out the CCTV so fast.'

'But you have the other camera, yes? The one from the side of the fridge?'

Roebuck's head turned. 'Other camera?'

'My mother – she told you?'

Roebuck felt a brief surge in his chest. Blood pulsed in his temples an instant later. 'No, she didn't.'

Stanisłow sent an accusatory look at the wall. As if his mother was in the next room. 'I have a little camera – for the sweets. The official one, it doesn't get the children who take the sweets.'

'When you say little,' DC Potter asked, 'what do you mean?'

'To go in small places like this.' He raised the forefinger and thumb of his un-bandaged hand. A matchbox-size space was between them.

'And it takes film?' Roebuck asked. 'There'll be footage?'

'Not films. Pictures. Like for in the garden when birds come. Something moves and it takes a picture.'

DC Potter looked at Roebuck. 'Motion sensor.'

'How many pictures does it store?' Roebuck asked. 'More than a few days' worth?'

'Yes, it has hundreds. Every month, I delete many. There is a little chip you take out.'

'And where is this camera?'

'The fridge with the cold drinks. It is against the wall and the front looks towards the sweets. I stick it on the side, in the little space there.'

#

Carla waited for a moment outside her apartment, ear turned towards the door. There weren't any sounds coming from inside. Come on, she said to herself. You know Ryan: he won't have wanted to cause a scene. He'll have gone. Her key turned in the lock and she pushed the door open. No lights were on. She ran her fingers across the panel of switches just inside the door and the deserted flat revealed itself.

So often recently, she'd come home to discover Ryan was out on one of his late-night jaunts, as she called them. But this felt different. She'd asked him to leave. Feelings of guilt mingled with a sense of relief. His absence suddenly made her realise how much his behaviour recently had been upsetting her. His constant fretting over the exhibition. What if he didn't sell any prints? Why hadn't he added any new Instagram followers on a particular day? Should he react to a blogger's faintly negative comment? When might the next tip-off arrive from the mystery sender of messages? His desire to make it as a photographer had got out of control. In fact, it was tipping into desperation.

She put her case down and made her way across to the kitchen area. Something was on the breakfast bar. She stopped. Damn it! Why had did he have to suddenly start being so considerate? The four-pack of chocolate desserts were sitting next to a little card. They were placed alongside the note she'd written to him. If it was an attempt to guilt-trip her, it had bloody well worked. He'd drawn a couple of musical notes on the front of the card. An echo of his pet-name for her.

To my La-la. Sorry for being an idiot. XXX

I should ring him, she immediately thought. Ordering him to leave like this was an overreaction. He knows how selfish his behaviour has been; why else leave a note like this?

She reached over and turned the kettle on. As it started to creak and tick, she took her phone out and brought up Ryan's number. She turned to the window and regarded her faint reflection as she pondered what to say. Unable to decide, she glanced at the note she'd left him.

I asked you not to open that message, not to go out, but you didn't listen. Worse than that, you didn't <u>care</u>. That's what worries me most. You don't care what I think anymore.

Did a peace offering of her favourite desserts really change all that? The exhibition was still going ahead the next day. Those bloody messages would keep popping up – and he'd keep reacting to them like a dog to a whistle.

Her eyes travelled down the note.

Let's both have a few days to work out how we feel and speak then.

Be strong, she said to herself. Don't start changing your mind just because you're feeling a twinge of guilt.

The kettle was now rumbling away, bubbling water reaching a crescendo. The switch clicked and silence resumed. She placed her phone on the breakfast bar. Music, she decided. That's what I need. She plucked the remote from its little bowl and turned the radio on. A vintage dance track was playing. Chaka Khan, was it? Strong vocals. Powerful. Carla swayed her hips as she selected a tea bag. Her mind was drifting to the next day. Having decided to keep away from Ryan's exhibition, she'd accepted an assistant's role for a shoot at Pomona Docks. The wide tree-lined boulevards would make a dramatic backdrop for the models.

She could picture Ryan moping about at his mum's. Probably sitting in the telly room with her, watching a gardening programme or something. She wondered whether to at least listen to the voicemail he'd left earlier that day. Even though she'd asked him not to ring her. Perhaps, she thought, he explains a bit more why he regrets acting like such a tit.

Sliding out a bar stool, she put her drink on the breakfast bar. Her make-up case caught her eye. The bloody straighteners! They needed new batteries. Turning up for a location job with straighteners that didn't work; how embarrassing would that have been?

She opened the case up and took them out. The base unscrewed and four Duracell batteries dropped into her palm. Ryan stored the dead ones somewhere, ready for recycling. Probably in the drawer with all the other gubbins. She slid it open. Yup: an old take-away carton. The lid made a cracking sound as she prized it off. The end of something plastic was peeping out at the bottom. Not a battery, whatever it was. She rummaged down with the tip of one finger. What was a memory stick doing in there? She recognised it as the one that usually lay beside his MacBook. Why move it to a carton of old batteries? He hadn't tried to hide it there, had he?

Her old laptop had a USB port. Within seconds, it was on, the memory stick jutting out from the side. The removable storage icon appeared on the screen. She clicked on it and examined the list of folders. All were labelled by dates. They were all several weeks old, except one. That had been created only two days ago. She thought for a second. The night he'd gone to the late-night store over in Salford. He'd said to her he had got no pictures from that night.

She opened the folder and studied the row of little images filling the screen. Oh, Ryan. You've been lying to me. She couldn't bear to open any of them; she could see enough as it was. A man facedown, blood pooled about his head. Packets of sweets and crisps scattered across the floor. A bright red drop running down a glass surface. It was... sick. Her boyfriend was a ghoul. He'd photographed someone as they lay injured and helpless.

She shut the folder down and yanked the stick out of her machine. Like the thing was dirty. Contagious. She didn't even want it in her hand. It went back among the old batteries. She wrapped her forearms round her stomach, feeling queasy. What has my boyfriend become?

CHAPTER 31

The lights in Carla's apartment didn't come on until eleven minutes past eight. She left her case by the door and, as she walked across to the breakfast bar, a look of sadness collapsed her face. Oh Carla. Don't be sad. You are doing so well. She stopped when she saw the gift Ryan had left. And when she opened the card, she looked like she might cry. Jason squeezed his fingertips against his temples, drilling her with his thoughts. He's lying! Whatever he's written, it's not true.

When she produced her phone, Jason focused every particle of his mind on her. Do not believe him. Do not believe him. She paused and her eyes had a faraway look in them as she gazed towards the window. She wasn't quite staring at him, but nearly was. He knew she sensed him somewhere close by. Looking over her. A guardian angel. Do not call him, Carla. If we're going to be together, us, the two of us, me and you, Carla, put the phone down. Put it down!

He didn't dare hope that the flow of his thoughts – their sheer strength – would be enough to change her mind, but her head began to drop, to bow under their weight. It was working! It was really working. The psychic bond between them was getting stronger all the time. She placed her phone to the side. Jason's hands dropped into his lap. It had taken every iota of his brain's power to persuade her. He let his breath seep slowly out. There, see? You feel better. He watched with a benign smile as she shifted her weight from foot to foot while making a cup of tea. Swaying her hips. Dancing with happiness. Good girl. Good girl. You did so well. Perhaps the time was right now? A message of his own to her, or even an actual call? It had been so long since they'd communicated with proper words. He toyed with his phone. No. What we have deserves more than a message or a phone call. I need to do this correctly. I need to present myself to you in a way you will respect and also be touched by. His fingers went to the guardian angel round his neck. Tomorrow morning. When she comes out of Jethro Mill tomorrow morning, I will be there waiting.

A fresh new day and the start of our future together.

He crawled across the concrete floor to the bathroom and shut himself inside. Really, he thought, I should shave. And get a new top. And underwear. How long have I been wearing this set of clothes? He wasn't sure. The image of Ryan with a hold-all of clothes popped into his head. Wouldn't it be fun to mess the bloke around a bit? Pull his strings and get him trekking across town for no reason? Right before his exhibition, remind him that everything – all his success – is down to me. That I am in charge. Where to send him? Jason brought up Google maps and surveyed the city. The business park in Harpurhey was a suitable shit hole. Poorly lit and pot-holed roads. The shutters on some of the abandoned units had been forced open. Crack heads and other drug users had wormed their way in. Parasites. A fitting place for Ryan to travel all the way out to. He sent the location code on its merry way.

#

Hold-all hanging from his shoulder, Ryan stood in the

centre of his old bedroom, eyes moving slowly about. She hadn't told him she'd repainted it after he'd moved out. Dark blue replaced by light purple. A new shade on the light. Sensible and old-fashioned: a smoked-glass bell shape. Maybe something she'd picked up in a charity shop.

He regarded the single bed. It now had a lilac duvet cover and matching pillows. He wondered what had happened to his old ones. Knowing mum, they were neatly folded in a cupboard somewhere. It was still the old frame, though. He looked at the shallow scratch marks where, sometime during his teens, he'd scraped off some childhood football stickers with a Stanley knife. Mum had gone ballistic. Partly at him, but more at her newly absent husband for leaving something so dangerous lying about.

He dropped his bag on the bed and sat down heavily beside it. His old wardrobe loomed over him. Next to that, three shelves lined with books. Some of his old hardback photography ones he'd insisted she keep. A few novels he'd also wanted to hang onto: *A Hitchhikers' Guide To The Galaxy*, a load of Terry Pratchetts. *Consider Phlebus* by Iain M. Banks. *Pandora's Star* by Peter Hamilton. There were some unfamiliar ones, too. Martina Cole, Ann Cleeves and Joy Ellis. Stuff his mum liked. He had an image of her bustling about in here, re-arranging things after he'd left. He had never really thought of her as a person entirely separate from him. What did he expect? That, as soon as he'd stepped out the front door to move in with Carla, she simply went into suspended animation, patiently waiting for his next return? Maybe that's what growing up was: appreciating your parents had a life completely disconnected from your own.

He got to his feet and opened the wardrobe, hoping it wouldn't now be stuffed with her old coats. But it was empty. Metal hangers gently clanged against each other. At the bottom were a few boxes. He immediately recognised the camouflage net he'd bought to create a hide for photographing local wildlife. It smelled fusty as he lifted it aside. Below it was his pair of camera traps. Wow! He knelt down for a closer look. These things, he thought, cost me about a year's worth of savings. Motion activated, night vision, 120° wide-angle lenses. Even Bluetooth for beaming images direct to your smart phone – not that he even owned a smart phone when he'd invested in them. A ripple of excitement made his spine tingle as he picked one up. He examined the camouflaged pattern on the thick plastic casing. What memories! A film of dust coated the lens and the strap for attaching it to a tree trunk was a little mouldy.

The box beside it contained several photo albums. He hauled it across the carpet, sat down with his back against the bed and lifted one out. Some shots he'd taken using mum's old Kodak. Seagulls lined up on the promenade railings on Llandudno's seafront. He remembered how the birds refused to look at the camera, their gimlet eyes always directed to a point just off to the side. Crafty. The hunched silhouette of a forlorn-looking heron motionless in some shallows. Where had that been? Reddish Vale Country Park, probably. Horses in a field, their lower legs shrouded by early-morning mist. Cobwebs strung with beads of dew backlit by a low sun. He smiled. Everyone had to take shots of glistening cobwebs, didn't they? Obligatory.

The next album had a label on the front with a single word written on it: Macro. Mum had got the short focus lens for him on his fifteenth birthday. Where she'd got the money from, he had no idea – his dad had vanished a few months before, taking all their savings and the car. He turned the first few pages. It was about the time Mrs Goodwin started letting him stay behind after school to use the biology lab. Endless close ups of stick insects. A stick insect perched on a laurel leaf. A stick insect perched on the tip of a pencil. A stick insect perched on the end of a ruler. Christ, Ryan, he thought. We get the idea; it's an insect that looks like a stick. Clue's in the name, pal.

Shots taken centimetres from a locust's head filled the next pages. Or was it a grasshopper? At least they were a bit more interesting, visually. Compound eyes with bands of red and brown running across them. Mottled patterns on their exoskeletons. He had a sudden memory of Mrs Goodwin pointing out to him the insect's smaller eyes: three tiny pinheads between the two main bulbous ones. Looking back at that time of his life, he realised the biology teacher had felt sorry for him. Maybe not sorry. Concerned? The slightly odd pupil who preferred taking photographs of creatures to playing with other kids. Not that he had many mates to choose from.

A series of beeps wrenched him back to the present. There was a familiar message on his screen: a three-word code. It was like a muscle-memory. An automatic reaction. He'd opened the app and retrieved the location almost without thinking. A unit on North Manchester Business Park over in Harpurhey. Even if he had a car, it would take half-an-hour to get there. But by train? Forget it. It was probably only an industrial fire, anyway. Maybe a break in. Not that he cared anymore.

He lifted the phone closer to his face. 'You're the reason I'm sitting here. It's your fault, you shady bastard. You shifty little shit.' It felt like when he'd told Roebuck he was leaving the room. He continued talking to the dead screen. 'Yeah, you heard me. I called you a shifty little shit. You don't like that? Too bad. And you know what else? I'm not doing this anymore. All this: it's over.'

He quickly typed out a message before he could change his mind.

Stop contacting me. I will not respond.

He hit send and sat back. That was it. Finished. He did not know if the person would even read his message, but that wasn't important. He'd put an end to it. And, more importantly, he could tell Carla that's what he'd done.

He was putting the phone aside when it beeped again.

There was a reply to his message. The person had actually replied! For the first-time ever, a response.

Problem?

Yes, Ryan thought. Yes, there is a bloody problem. He tapped at the screen: Plenty, actually. He waited for a few seconds.

Like what?

Ryan almost laughed. 'Like what? Total idiot.' He fired back a reply: Like the robbery on Pinnington Street. You told me about it while it was still happening.

Sometimes it will be like that.

Ryan had to read the words again. Who the hell was this person? It certainly didn't sound like a reclusive teenager with a radio set, he thought, typing once again: How did you know about it?

Not your concern.

Ryan hunched forward, fingers dabbing away: Ridiculous. How can it not be my concern?

The same three-word code appeared once more, with another message close behind. Hurry!

Ryan felt his face flush with anger, fingers moving rapidly across the screen: Piss off and don't contact me again.

He hit send with a sense of trepidation. I just told him to piss off! His phone beeped. The same three-word code.

Christ, he thought. Do you not listen? He typed again: What do you want from me?

A short wait, then: I will soon have all I want from you.

What the fuck did that mean? The sinister tone had Ryan's finger hovering above the phone. Another message arrived.

Is it thorny, the tangle you're in?

He frowned. Now the person was talking in riddles. He typed again: I don't understand.

Soon, you will.

Ryan turned his phone over. This was now freaking him out. *Soon, you will.* 'That's it,' he murmured. He went into the options, selected 'block caller' and tossed the phone onto the pillow. Job done. A moment later, he glanced uneasily at the hand set, wondering how the person would react when his next message bounced back.

CHAPTER 32

'So,' announced DI Roebuck, parking outside the Pop-in store. 'Got your fingers crossed?'

Lights were on inside. Back to business as usual, only with cover staff sent from the regional office in Rochdale. Just while Stanisłow and his mum were recovering.

'Could you do it?' DC Potter asked.

'What's that?' he replied.

'Go back to working in a place where you were slashed by a machete?'

Roebuck thought for a second. 'I'd certainly be nervous.'

'Nervous? I'd be a total wreck.'

'You do this job.'

'Bit different, though. The poor bastards in there are on their own.'

'True. Probably got no choice. Do a day job like this over here, or earn a fraction of the wage back in Eastern Europe.'

'Poland's not Eastern Europe, is it?'

'You know what I mean. Romania, Slovenia, Poland: those places. Tell you what, though – I'd happily take all of them and ship out the trash from this country. At least these people are prepared to work for a living. Not just sit around all day in their onesies, claiming foreigners have stolen all the jobs.'

'Detective Roebuck! Bit controversial.'

'Bloody true, though.'

She smiled. 'You know all these Turkish barbers springing up? I heard hardly any are actually run by people from Turkey. They're all Syrian.'

'Like the Indian restaurants: all the chefs are Iranian, apparently.'

'And where would you take the trash?'

'Yeah, that's trickier, isn't it? Used to be Australia, but they put a stop to that, damn it. Outer Mongolia? Plenty of room there.'

'Poor old Outer Mongolians.'

'True. Shall we see if it's still attached to the side of that fridge?'

'Definitely.'

The man behind the counter was white and in his early thirties. Neatly combed hair. When Roebuck had first started opening the door, his expression was wary. It soon relaxed when he saw the suit.

'Hello,' Roebuck announced, ID already in his hand. 'DI Roebuck and DC Potter. How are you this evening…' he checked the name tag on the man's green fleece, 'Damian?'

'Fine, thanks.'

Roebuck looked about. 'No more trouble, I hope?' The shop was free of customers. All evidence of the incident had vanished. Fresh bottles of spirits lined the shelves. Above the entrance, a new camera was looking down at him.

'Nope. I was told uniformed patrols would be checking by. Is this…?'

'Not directly, no. We're after the two people who carried out the robbery. Mr Witas – the man working when it took place – told us about a second camera. May I?'

The man's eyebrows lifted. 'Of course. How is he?'

'On the mend.' Roebuck crossed to the far side of the shop. The fridge was directly in line with the counter. Next to it, a set of shelves laden with bread stretched back into the shop. He homed in on the two-inch gap. Nothing tucked into there. Or inside it. Or on the top. 'Sarah, have I got this right?'

'Cool drinks cabinet,' she replied. 'Can't see another.'

Roebuck brushed his fingers down the casing, even though he knew nothing was there. He felt for any gap beneath it where the camera could have fallen. The base of the fridge connected snugly with the floor. Bloody hell.

'Damian, did you help clear up after the incident?' Potter asked.

'No,' he replied. 'A specialist team does that. Especially if there's blood involved. I just do the regular stuff.'

Roebuck turned round. 'Mr Witas said there was a little camera here. I think like you'd have mounted on a dashboard in your car.'

'Well, there's some of their stuff in the back. Personal possessions. But you're not meant to install anything of your own.'

Roebuck nodded. 'I won't say anything, if you won't. Can I take a look?'

'Sure, the counter isn't locked.' He pointed to the end section beside Roebuck. 'It lifts up.'

They made their way round to where Damian was standing in an open doorway. 'It's all in that storage container under the desk.'

The room was very narrow. Roebuck clocked the workstation squeezed in beside shelves piled high with stock. Another door in the far corner gave access to a tiny, but surprisingly clean, toilet. Mrs Witas, no doubt.

'Is this all you do?' Potter asked.

'Temporary cover, you mean?' Damian replied. 'Mostly.

There are shops all over the North West, right up to the border with Scotland. But it's not always robberies. Holiday and sickness, too.'

Roebuck sat in the office chair and lifted the container's lid. A couple of green fleeces. An anorak. A Tupperware container beside a collapsible umbrella.

'Don't you get nervous?' Potter asked. 'I know I would be.'

'Well, these areas aren't so bad. Footfall is better. It's the ones stuck out in the middle of nowhere that get to me.'

Roebuck lifted a book of Polish crossword puzzles aside. A loop of white cable was poking out beneath it. There it was. Single lens like a cyclops' eyes. He dug it out.

'The branch in Dove Holes,' Damian continued. 'That's been done over three times in one year. But normally, I just think of it as lightning. Where's the safest place to be after it strikes?'

'Not bloody Dove Holes,' Roebuck murmured, standing up.

CHAPTER 33

The faint sound of birdsong stirred Ryan from his sleep. It had been so long since he'd heard it. Such a pleasant sound. The comforting sound of childhood. Carefree. He was confused. The only thing you heard in the flat was the sound of cars going by. Maybe shouting in the street. He opened his eyes to a world of lilac and remembered where he was. In a too-narrow bed, in a too-narrow room. Back at my mum's. He turned over and lifted his phone from the bedside table. Shit! Almost ten. She was meant to wake me. Cursing himself for not setting an alarm, he threw the duvet off. The exhibition opened in just three hours' time. Before hurrying for the shower, he checked for any messages or missed calls. Nothing from Carla or anyone else.

There was a note waiting for him in the kitchen. It had been left beside a carton of eggs, a pack of bacon and a tin of beans.

Someone needed their sleep! I've got offices to do in Victoria Mill. Back at about three. There's bread in the fridge. Good luck today – you can tell me about it later. Mum.

He bowed his head. Forgot, he thought, that she never stopped working. She couldn't have come to the exhibition, even if she wanted. After a quick mental calculation, he decided that – if he only had a bacon sandwich – he could still make it to the Sussman Gallery by noon. That was the very latest Ivan said to be there for. To make sure everything was ready for when the doors opened at one.

Just over an hour later, his train ground to a stop. The bloody thing was over ten minutes late arriving at Levenshulme station. Now this. He could see Ardwick station on a different set of tracks away to his right. A motionless train on the platform there. He knew the two lines merged a few hundred metres in front for the final approach into Piccadilly. Idiot, he said to himself. Why did you get the train? You knew this happens all the time. He pulled his hood over his head and started jigging a knee up and down.

A short while later, the intercom crackled and buzzed. 'Apologies for the wait, ladies and gents. A bit of congestion in Piccadilly. Soon as a platform becomes free, we'll be on our way.'

He looked out the other window at Hyde Road. I could walk it to the station in under five minutes, he thought bitterly. His phone started to ring. An 0161 prefix. Manchester. He ignored it and, a minute later, got a voicemail alert.

'Ryan, it's DC Potter. We spoke the other day at the station in Salford? Would you mind popping back in?'

Oh, yeah. The nice polite one, he thought. Like I'm falling for that again.

'Some additional material about the robbery has come to light and we'd really appreciate your input. Contact me on this number soon as you can.'

He lowered his phone. Additional material? What did that mean? He hunched back over and started jiggling his knee up and down again. Somewhere further down the carriage, a toddler wailed.

#

The sound of men talking wrenched Jason awake. He immediately turned on his side and looked across to Carla's flat. Outside was bathed in daylight. He realised the carpet had slid off him during the night. The voices weren't out on the street; they were in the building. A drilling sound reverberated up from below. Someone started singing a song. Carla's flat was deserted, and Jason checked the time. Almost five past eight. How was that possible? He couldn't have slept through, surely? But he knew he had. Which meant Carla would have left for work over half-an-hour ago. No!

He jumped to his feet and trotted down the steps into the main part of the flat. Idiot, Jason. Bloody idiot. He'd missed the chance of presenting himself to her. Why, he wondered, didn't Carla wake me? She only had to picture me in her mind, and I'd have woken. Maybe she didn't want to disturb me. She was just being kind.

In the bathroom, he regarded the baseball cap he'd found discarded in the street the previous evening. Dark blue with the letters UCA on the front. Good move picking that up, he said to himself.

While dressing, he went over his exchange with Ryan the evening before. It was a bit late for the bloke to develop a spine now! Jason's smile slipped. It was annoying to have been blocked by him, though. Not that it really mattered: the messages had served their purpose. Carla had thrown him out. Now the way is clear for us to be together. In fact, he thought, I don't need to contact Ryan ever again. Why would I? He's a failure. A weak, pathetic man. Not even a man. He's more of a maggot than a man. A grub. A turd that a grub lives in. Yes! A bit of turd, that's what he is.

He stood in front of the bathroom mirror and checked his reflection. There were dark smudges beneath his eyes. They'd soon fade, he told himself. Once I get in the fresh air out at Salford Quays. A section of chain showed above the neck of the t-shirt. He reached up to his clavicle and felt the guardian angel beneath the thin cotton layer. Her face when she sees this! When she realises it's me. The person who's been sending her all those messages.

His phone rang. The bloody estate agent at Nail and Cable. He knew what she wanted. Once the new message icon appeared, he accessed his voicemail to listen.

Morning, Jason. It's Tabitha Ross. Just checking when you're returning those keys. I hope you managed everything you needed and I expect to see you shortly, bye.

Yeah, yeah, thought Jason as he deleted her message. The workmen looked mildly surprised when he came down the steps.

'This your bike?' The older of the three asked a little peevishly.

Jason nodded.

'You didn't think to use the secure parking?'

Jason halted halfway to the doors. 'Didn't know there was any.'

'The gates off Conran Street, just round the corner.'

'No one told me about that.'

'Well, can you move it? We're trying to finish up here. You've already left a tyre mark on the brand-new carpet.'

Jason contemplated telling the person he could shove his suggestion up his arse. But he was going to need the bike again at some point. He wondered if Carla liked bikes. They could go touring together! Not on the Fireblade, obviously. He'd need to get something the two of them could sit on. Maybe a Super Duke GT. He could go fast on that, really fast, and she'd have to wrap her arms tightly round his midriff as he powered – he realised the three were staring at him. 'Conran Street, did you say?'

The oldest one glanced at his workmates before nodding. 'Yes.'

'How do I get the gate open?'

'With the same fob you used for this door.'

Once the bike was safely stashed in the empty parking area, he made for the tram stop in Piccadilly Gardens. Would she have a break at any point? Half-an-hour when, maybe, she'd find a nice quiet bench to sit on? Or go for a stroll along the promenade beside the quay. That could be quite nice. They could stroll along together. Even hold hands, perhaps. Like a proper couple.

#

'Ryan, are you trying to give me heart failure?' Ivan had a red spot high on each cheek.

On the other side of the gallery, Annabelle floated him a stare that was at once disinterested and full of contempt.

'I'm really sorry. The bloody trains; we were stuck on the tracks for ages.'

'Trains!' Ivan exclaimed. 'You live a five-minute walk away!'

'No – I was at my mum's over in Reddish.'

'Well, it's twenty-past twelve. People will be arriving in thirty minutes. Next time, do me a favour and get a bloody taxi,' Ivan huffed. 'I'll happily pay.'

Annabelle had gone back to arranging cups and saucers on a table. A couple of staff from what Ryan guessed was the catering company were at the counter lifting the cling film off trays of canapes. There were several boxes on the floor with French writing on.

'Come through,' Ivan said. 'We can do a quick sound check. Another twenty or so tickets went last night. It could be quite a squeeze.'

'Sound check?' Ryan asked.

Ivan was unhooking a red rope that prevented access to the side room where Ryan's photographs were displayed. 'We don't let them in for a bit. Build a bit of tension.'

He followed the gallery owner through and immediately spotted a little dais with a microphone stand in the far corner. Two spotlights had been attached to the ceiling railings directly above the set up.

'It's your opening exhibition, Ryan. You have prepared a few words?'

Ryan felt his testicles start trying to claw their way up into his body.

#

Carla moved behind the arc lights. A light breeze was blowing down the quayside, rustling the leaves on the avenues of trees and rippling the water in the long lock. Outside shoots, she thought. Always dodgy. Especially in Manchester. She checked the sky. Lumps of cloud were building on the horizon, but nothing that suggested rain.

The model pirouetted for the photographer while angling her head from side to side. Wisps of hair were hanging across her forehead. A strand stuck to her glossy lipstick. Carla readied herself for the photographer to wave her forward and sort it out. But he went into a crouch, closing in like a crab, cooing words of encouragement. Fair enough, she thought. Going for an *au naturel* look.

She checked the barriers behind her. These things always attracted a few curious onlookers. A gaggle of teenagers who probably had got wind of things through a PR company tweet. A couple of mums with young kids. They looked like they'd paused while on the way to the Lowry outlet mall for some shopping and, maybe, the cinema. A lone male caught her eye. He was wearing a baseball cap low over his eyes. Something about him made her do a double take. Was he staring at her? He shifted slightly and now a slender tree trunk blocked her view.

'Carla?'

She looked to the trailer. Andrea was beckoning from the open door.

'Can I grab you a second?'

'Sure.' She reached for her case and, when she checked the smattering of people again, the man appeared to have gone.

#

When he got to Ontario Basin, where Carla's Instagram had said the shoot was taking place, he was irritated to see a load of metal fencing in his way. Not so high that he couldn't climb over, but that wasn't the point. There were several people arranging big lights along the section of walkway they'd taken over. He guessed Carla was in one of the two trailers. Not wanting her to spot him too soon, Jason made his way round to the far side of the narrow stretch of water. There was a load of young trees planted here, along with some raised borders that overflowed with bushy plants. He found a bench partially obscured from the photography set and took a seat.

It took almost two hours before he glimpsed her. She stepped out of the right-hand trailer and walked round the corner. Afraid, she was leaving, he almost jumped to his feet and ran round. But they hadn't even taken any photographs yet. Calm, he said to himself. Be calm. He took some deep breaths and focused on the sky. A few clouds were gathering. Big chunky ones. The first of the models appeared about twenty minutes later. Carla watched for a while from behind one of the lighting stands. He couldn't take his eyes off her. If she'd sensed his presence, she didn't show it. He decided not to send any thoughts her way: she needed to work. It wasn't fair to interrupt her. After a bit, she went back into the same trailer. Clothes were being loaded onto railings and wheeled into the back of a big lorry with a logo on the side that said *MissTrial*.

Jason decided to go back round; a few other people were now watching from behind the barriers, so it wasn't like he'd be the only one. They took some more photographs of the girls and the breeze picked up a bit. The clouds he'd spotted earlier had merged. She took up her same position, and he edged his way right up to the barriers for a better view. A security guard was sipping from a polystyrene cup. Next to Jason, a few teenagers were taking photos on their phones. When she finally glanced round, his mind froze. In his head, he couldn't even say hello. She looked away, then turned back to him. That same connection of their minds happened again. He felt so embarrassed. So tongue-tied and awkward. Before he knew what he was doing, he'd stepped behind a tree so she couldn't see him. How he hated his nervousness. It made him do such stupid things. He needed to reset, clear his mind, get in control of his stupid feelings. He walked quickly towards some nearby buildings. Remember, he said to himself, what you have is special. She won't mind if you aren't able to come out with smooth talk. In real life, people don't. That's just in films when they're following a script. When two real people are in love, sometimes, they don't even need to speak. Perhaps, when I present myself, I shouldn't say anything? Perhaps I should just hand the pendant to her? But he remembered what his dad used to say about faint words never winning a fair lady, even though it always used to make his mum scoff. Maybe if he just said something to her like, Hello again. Or, This is for you. Hello again, this is for you. That might be good. Hello again, I've got you this. Hello again, I've got you this. Do you like it? Too much? Hello again, I've got you this, I hope you like it. That was better. Hello again, I've got you this, I hope you like it.

#

Ryan could clearly hear Ivan's voice out in the gallery.

'Malcolm! So good to see you. How was the last week

of the show? I had a ticket for Tuesday before last and thought it stunning. Absolutely stunning.'

Ryan hunched lower over the little pad of paper balanced on his knees. The lid of the toilet was digging into his buttocks. He knew he couldn't stay locked in here much longer. Why did people have to arrive early? The posters and invites had all clearly said one o'clock. His few meagre lines of scrawl looked feeble and pathetic. Ivan had said to thank his photography tutor at Salford. Mention other photographers who inspired him. He was having trouble conjuring up a single name.

The sound of voices was building beyond the toilet door. Ivan's mellifluous bass rose above them. 'Julian, how dare you look so damned well. Have you been away?'

Ryan lifted his head. Had Julian Templeforth arrived?

'Ivan, you little rascal. Lovely to see you.'

'Let me introduce you to Malcolm Hobson. He directed *Sunflowers and Angel Dust* that was just showing at The Royal Exchange. Malcolm, this is Julian Templeforth.'

Ryan tried to concentrate on his lines. It was no good. He realised the biro was shaking in his hand. Actually shaking! He felt like turning round and throwing up into the toilet. Over at the sink, he splashed cold water against his face. He heard his name mentioned.

'Just applying the finishing touches to his make-up,' Ivan joked.

Polite laughter.

'No, he'll be with us soon. Now, can the gorgeous Annabelle offer you a drink?'

Ryan stared at his reflection. He remembered another phrase his dad liked to use. Death warmed up. That's what I look like. He blinked the thought away. This is the first step towards everything you've wanted. 'You've got this,' he whispered. 'You have.' He patted his face dry, twisted the lock and pulled the door open.

CHAPTER 34

'No joy?' DI Roebuck asked.

'Answer phone again,' DC Potter replied, replacing the receiver of her desk phone. 'He'll have known it was me. He'll recognise the number by now.'

Roebuck was standing before a board, scrutinising the collection of images pinned to it. The ones on the left-hand side all showed Ryan. First as he entered the Pop-In shop, then as he tentatively looked about. The quality was poor, but there was no mistaking it was him. His Napapijri coat was visible, as was the camera hanging over the top of it.

Next, he'd raised the camera to his face. Another of him well inside the premises, looking down at Stanisłow Witas lying on the floor. A couple more of him with the camera lifted again, taking photos of the counter area. Then him looking over it, before moving toward the shelves. The last one was him returning with bandages and other items.

Roebuck glanced at his watch. 'I know exactly where he is. Or where he'll be in about twenty minutes.'

Potter sent him a quizzical glance.

He pointed to the copy of the Manchester Evening

Chronicle on the edge of his desk. 'That article about him said his exhibition at the Sussman Gallery opens today at one o'clock. I'll drop by – just so he knows that he really should get in touch.'

Potter smiled. 'That'll be a nice surprise for him.'

Roebuck's attention turned to the batch of images he'd pinned to the centre of the board. Like the ones of Ryan, graininess meant fine detail was lost. Two men in dark clothing and balaclavas. The one about six feet tall was carrying a machete and a large bag. The one behind him was a few inches shorter. He was carrying a hammer.

Potter had arranged the images chronologically, in rows of three, from left to right. The first thing to happen was the figure smashed the camera above the door. The following images had Stanisłow Witas in the frame, hands raised in surrender. The one with the machete pointing down with his free hand. The one with the hammer stepping round the pair. To get behind the counter, he'd walked to within a few feet of the fridge where the camera had been mounted.

Roebuck tapped the image and turned to Potter. 'You're right, this is the best one. I'm so close to knowing who those little weasel eyes belong to.' He glanced back at his computer screen. No new messages. The technician in the photo unit had said to give him a couple of hours to clear up the most promising images.

Roebuck didn't linger on the lowermost rows: the images showing the taller of the two chopping down on Stanisłow's raised hand, then the top of his head.

The right-hand side of the board had a smattering of images that captured the arrival of the emergency services. Ryan Lamb once again was in the picture, this time heading out with a uniformed officer. The male and female ambulance drivers talking. More police coming through the door.

He went back to the main images. The pair in balaclavas definitely had an experienced partnership going.

There was no messing about. He was sure it was the same pair who'd carried out four other robberies.

A two-tone chime came from the direction of his computer. New email. He was in his seat and reaching for his mouse in a flash. Yes: from Sean Phillips, the guy in the photo unit. Subject line read: Images from robbery, Pinnington Street, Salford.

Roebuck clicked on the message. Three jpegs. Roebuck went straight to the one labelled 'closest to camera' and double-clicked. It was a much-improved version of the image he'd just tapped his finger on. 'Ha! Got you.'

Potter crouched down beside his chair. 'You recognise him?'

Roebuck was already opening a new window on the computer. 'Yup. Surprised you don't, too. It's Zack Patten. We put him away about four years ago. Let's see when the little shit-bag was let back out.'

#

Ryan looked fearfully at the press of bodies before him. Everyone was talking loudly, most with their back to him. He wasn't sure what to do. Get myself a drink? try to introduce myself to someone? To his relief, Ivan spotted him.

'Cometh the hour, cometh the man!' the gallery owner boomed. 'Ryan, come and meet Lucas Pelling. I know he's dying to ask you some questions.'

A few people were turning round. He met a few of their glances with what he hoped was a friendly smile. Someone leaned forward to make a comment.

'Wonderful work. Such energy.'

'Thanks.'

Ivan had an arm round a gaunt-faced man with a shock of long, white, straggly hair. 'Lucas Pelling: Ryan Lamb.'

The fingers of the man's skeletal right hand stayed clasped round his glass of red wine. When he spoke, Ryan saw he had very small teeth that the wine had stained slightly purple. 'Lovely shots, Ryan. Your portraits of the homeless people are redolent of Jamel Shabazz, I thought. The same startling honesty. Would you say he's an influence?'

As Ivan slipped away, Ryan nodded. 'I think he's amazing.'

'Isn't he? He's also interested in those who, you might say, have slipped through the cracks. Struggling with addictions.'

'Absolutely.'

'I believe he describes his camera as a compass. One that leads him. Do you feel the same way when roaming the city, camera in hand?'

'Well, I suppose so, yes.'

'It's a very good compass that you have. The immediacy of some of your photographs is remarkable. The way you thrust the viewer right in.'

'Would you class yourself as a photojournalist?' A voice asked from his right. It was a small lady with a shaved head and thick black glasses. 'Nancy Fraser. I work for the Lowry.' She extended a hand.

'Right, hi. Nice to meet you.' Ryan was thinking about the art centre's frequent photography exhibitions. They liked to make room for local photographers. 'Sorry, a photojournalist? No, not really.'

In the periphery of his vision, he could see that Pelling was no longer looking at his face. The man's eyes had dropped and were taking in every aspect of him. Shoes. Clothes. Posture, probably. He struggled to keep his thread. 'I suppose, if I had to, I'd say I'm a street photographer.'

'But,' she responded. 'A lot of what you capture has that dramatic element, wouldn't you say?'

'Well, yes. That's what really interests me.' He tried to choose words that would make him sound convincing. 'You know, the ramifications of an incident. Those shock waves that it sends out, I suppose.'

'So, aside from Shabazz, has any particular photographer influenced you?' Pelling asked.

'I really admire the way Richard Billingham makes his photographs. His work has a rawness I admire, definitely.'

Nancy inclined her head. 'I see that. Especially with the shots he's been taking recently of rough sleepers around Swansea. He shoots those images on digital, too, I think. Like you.'

'He does. In fact, he made a really good point about digital being better for those portraits. The way it renders modern surfaces so well. The Costa coffee cup being used for coins. The cellophane wrapping of a sandwich.'

Nancy was nodding enthusiastically.

She's impressed, Ryan thought. And I think Pelling is, too. Ryan contemplated whether to mention Billingham's love of nature and the man's prized childhood visits to Dudley Zoo. The way he brought that eye for capturing wildlife to his shots of human subjects. Would it be too presumptuous to mention that's how I aspire to work?

'So, who else?' Pelling asked. 'We've got Shabazz and Billingham.'

Ryan wondered what their reaction would be if he said his real photography hero was Jonathan Scott: the photographer who'd spent years chronicling the lives of big cats out in Africa.

'Ryan!'

Ivan again.

He smiled apologetically. 'Great talking to you both.'

They smiled back. He turned to Ivan, keenly aware that the two of them had already begun to confer quietly.

'This is a very dear friend of mine, Ryan. James O'Loughlin. He has the most wonderful art collection.'

Ivan had pre-warned him he'd be referring to his best customers – those who spent the most – as having collections. The man was heavily overweight, with a bulging bottom lip, as if it was being forced out by the inward pressure of his heavy cheeks. He was eyeing Ryan hungrily. 'Ivan tells me you have a remarkable talent. For one so early in his career. What I think that actually means is I need to get in quick before prices go up.' His eyes swivelled in Ivan's direction as he let out a wet chuckle. 'That so, Ivan?'

The gallery owner laughed innocently. 'Me? Speak in code? Never! James lives on a stunning estate out near Alderley Edge.'

'Estate? Ivan, you do exaggerate.'

Ryan noticed the man had a chunky Rolex on his wrist. 'That s lovely around there, isn't it?'

He wafted his fingers. 'It is. Who knows, maybe I can show you round one day? But don't let me hog you. You must mingle.' He retreated a step.

'Thanks.' Ryan glanced uneasily about. Ivan was already chatting with someone else. He felt horribly exposed. Giving O'Loughlin another quick smile, he said, 'I think I'll get...'

As he approached the drinks table, he felt a drip of sweat trickling down his side. Thank God, he thought, I wore a black shirt. No one can see my damp patches. One of the catering staff - a young woman who looked about eighteen - was filling glasses. She was also wearing a black shirt. 'Just an orange juice, please.'

'No problem.'

He had an urge to go behind the table and stand next to her. Serve drinks all afternoon. That would be so much less stressful than having to do this. She handed him a glass and he realised he was going to have to turn round. Here we go again. He shuffled through one-hundred-and-eighty degrees to find a man with short spiky hair and a tweed three-piece grinning at him impishly.

'Very generous of you,' he said, nodding to the bottles of Champagne and trays of canapes.

'Oh no,' Ryan replied, stepping aside so the man could help himself to a glass. 'The Sussman Gallery has provided all this.'

He took a sip. 'Kind of. But from where does the gallery get its income?'

Ryan frowned.

'Your sales,' the man whispered, clinking his glass against Ryan's. 'Cheers.' He surveyed the room with a slightly pained expression. 'You know how Hemingway described this sort of event? Like a bottle full of tapeworms trying to feed on each other.'

CHAPTER 35

Carla was in the trailer working on a model's eyeshadow when word came from outside. The bank of cloud had moved closer, so there'd be a two-hour break until the light breeze had cleared it.

'Early lunch it is, then,' Andrea said, stepping away from the model she was working on. 'Fancy grabbing something up the road?'

'Thanks for the offer,' Carla replied. 'But I need to pop into town. A job last week paid me by cheque, can you believe?'

'That's just a royal pain in the arse,' Andrea said, removing the silky shroud from the shoulders of the girl sitting in the chair.

A security guard let Carla through the barriers and she made her way quickly towards the nearby tram stop. She could hear the whine and screech of one approaching from away to her left. Emerging from the gap between two buildings, she saw it crawling round the corner from the direction of Media City. Jogging the last thirty metres, she reached the platform as it slid to a stop.

#

Jason was making his way back across when he saw her slip through a gap in the barriers. He wanted to call out to her, but didn't dare. Instead, he tried shouting her name in his mind. Carla! But she didn't look back. She was walking quickly. Then he heard the clank and whine of a tram and started to run.

By the time he made it to the platform, the carriages had come to a stop and the doors were opening. It was all so rushed. People jostling at the doors. And then her phone rang and so speaking to her was totally out of the question. All he could do was get on and take a seat directly behind her. She was busy talking to whoever had rung her. He stared at her hair, the way it hung down. So perfect. He spotted a single strand had come loose. Half of it was on the back of her jacket, half on the seat rest.

It's not like I'm stealing or anything, he thought, reaching up and drawing it clear. It was so fine, he couldn't see it once his hand was back in shadow. If he held it up to the window, he'd be able to see it then, he was sure. He twisted it round his forefinger, felt the microscopic pressure of it. A bit of Carla digging into his skin. Garrotting his finger. He hadn't thought about garrotting. That would be a good way to kill his brother, too. Maybe with a length of washing line, drawn so tight his tongue was forced out of his mouth. She was using her chatty voice, talking about the job. But then her tone changed and she partly turned to the window. He dipped his head and closed his eyes so he could focus on her voice. Just her voice.

#

'How's it going, babe? What time did you just say? Nearly six? Have you just finished, then?' Carla listened to her friend describing how a cold snap had hit New York and the temperature had dropped to a degree below freezing.

'Anyway,' Simone continued. 'Not the reason for my

call to bore you with weather. How are things with you, sweetie?'

Carla went through some basic details about the shoot, even though she knew that wasn't what her friend wanted to know.

'Putting work aside,' Simone eventually interjected, 'how are you feeling?'

'Oh, so so. Keeping busy.'

'And are you still keeping radio silence with Ryan?'

Carla shifted in her seat, angling herself towards the window. She couldn't stand it when people unpicked their private lives in earshot of all the other passengers. 'So far, yes,' she said quietly.

'Has he tried calling you?'

'I don't know. I don't think so. Just that voicemail he left from before, which I still can't face listening to.'

'And are you still thinking the same way about him?'

The pictures on the memory stick flashed up in Carla's mind. It wasn't the Ryan she knew, to have done something like that.

'Carla, did you hear me?'

'Yes,' she murmured. 'I did.'

'And?'

She heard the echo of those texts arriving. The bloody what3words codes that appeared uninvited, any time, day or night. 'I think somewhere out there is a pathetic little specimen who cowers behind his computer screen. And I will not let him ruin our lives.'

'Who are you talking about?'

'This freak who's been messaging Ryan. Messing with his head. Playing some kind of sick game, for all I know. He's the reason we're in this situation and I won't let it carry on.'

#

Jason looked up. It felt like cold air was blasting out from invisible vents. You're...you're talking about me, Carla? He stared in shock at the back of her head. Don't. Please don't call me a freak, Carla. He used all his mental power to lodge the thought in her head. But she kept on, anyway. Ignoring him.

#

'Carla Bell!' Simone said, delightedly. 'Fighting talk. I like it.'

She sat up a little straighter. 'That what I'm going to tell him when –'

'Who?'

'Ryan. He blocks the messages or we're finished. Simple as that.'

'OK. A clean choice. That works. And the other thing? The person who showed up at the TV studios?'

Carla looked out the window. They'd now crossed the Manchester Ship Canal and the city centre was spread out before them. The tram was slowing down for the Cornbrook stop. 'I'm not sure, Simone. I'm really not.'

#

When she said the name Simone, Jason felt his lips tighten. Oh no, not her. You're better than that person, my darling. Can't you see? Can't you see she's not good for you?

She was whispering now and the train had begun to slow. He struggled to hear her words. '... what you think... random bloke... I was... knows?'

Jason bowed his head again, desperate to make out her words. People were standing up, shoes scraping. He looked around. They were at Cornbrook. The bleeping of the bloody doors! Now she was leaning her head against the window. The tram was speeding up again, noise of the engine levelling out. Her words became audible once more.

'Do I still love Ryan?' she asked.

Jason didn't dare breathe.

'Yes, I still love him.'

#

'What aren't you sure about?'

'Saying anything,' she whispered. 'I know what you think. But, seriously? Maybe I snogged some random bloke. Maybe. Or I was a bit flirty. Who knows?' A few people were readying themselves to get off, and she leaned forward, glad of the surrounding commotion. 'Does Ryan really need to find that out?'

'It's your chance to press the reset the button, Carla.'

The tram came to a stop. Carla sighed as people got off and others climbed on. 'I suppose so.'

'Suppose so? You're not sounding a hundred percent on this. Listen, you're giving him a condition, but you won't apply some of that to yourself?'

The doors began to beep and Carla leaned her head against the glass. 'It's not that –'

'From where I'm sitting, it looks like it is. Do you still love him, Carla?'

The tram was moving again, hum of the electric engine picking up. 'Do I still love Ryan?'

'Correct.'

She nodded. 'Yes, I still love him.'

'And you want to be with him? Build a future together?'

'Yes, of course. I don't want to be alone in that flat. Really, I'd like us to sell it. Buy somewhere together. Somewhere a bit more like your place. All those things.'

'And he wants that too, right?'

'I think so. That's what he says, yes.'

'Listen, sweetie, I'm about to lose reception. We're entering a tunnel. Just wait. I'll be back soon. Don't hang up!'

'OK.' She kept the handset to her ear, watching their progress towards the city centre. Her friend was right. In fact, she'd cut through the crap and got to what mattered. They did love each other. They should stay together. The tram was now passing the Manchester Convention Centre with its curved roof. Next, it crawled along the side of the Midland Hotel before emerging into the newly developed plaza before the city's main library. They came to a halt at the St Peter's Square stop.

#

He sat back. That's not what I just heard. It wasn't. He shook his head. Am I asleep, is that it? He let go of the strand of Carla's hair and dug his fingernails into the soft skin of his inner wrist. Scratched hard enough to break the skin and wake himself up. But this wasn't a dream. This was real.

She continued to speak. 'Yes, of course. I don't want to be alone in that flat. Really, I'd like us to sell it. Buy somewhere together. Somewhere a bit more like your place. All those things.' She sighed and moved the phone from her ear.

Jason felt himself blinking. His mouth was now dry. Why would she say those things? Outside, the hedges and trees were moving more quickly. Fuzzing into each other. He remembered the time his brother had persuaded him to try a joint. The world felt like that now. Unstable. He closed his eyes. The engine was whining. It had to be Simone. Yes, that fucking bitch Simone. She was polluting Carla's mind, making her say things she didn't really believe. He wanted to rip the handset from Carla's grip and fling it out the window. When he opened his eyes, the outside was becoming less blurry. Were they slowing? He still felt dizzy. Like he might faint. Simone. When I have my way, that damned woman will never speak to you again.

#

Simone came back on the line. 'You still there, Carla?'

'Still here.' She got to her feet, vaguely aware of a male figure who'd been sitting directly behind her rising, too. 'Just getting off the tram.'

'OK, as I was saying, you can only move forward with Ryan if –'

'You don't need to say, Simone. I know.'

'What do you mean?'

'I can only sort things out with Ryan if I tell him.'

'Right!'

'I mean, like you said, I'm not the one in the wrong here.'

'Absolutely! So, you tell Ryan, and you say that, whoever the person is, he somehow thinks there's something between you both.'

'Excuse me,' Carla squeezed between some people standing by the door. 'That's the thing! I don't even remember doing anything! Like, maybe we flirted? Maybe. But certainly nothing more. I don't get how he could –'

'I do,' Simone interrupted. 'He's deluded.'

'Yes,' Carla agreed enthusiastically, stepping on to the platform. 'He obviously has nothing in his life. He's pathetic. I could tell that the moment he popped up in the studio audience that time.' She weaved her way between the other passengers, who were crowding the platform as the tram eased away. Another was waiting to pull in directly behind it. 'Part of me wants to see him again. Just to tell him – face-to-face – to get the fuck out of my life. I don't even hate him, Simone. I just think he's sad. A pathetic sad –'

#

He realised that, as Carla got up, the tram had come to a halt. Once again, he was losing bits of what she was saying. He stood up, too, and had to grip the handrail for a moment. She was almost at the doors. People were in his way and he had to grip a boy by the shoulders and shove him aside. The doors beeped and he only just got out in time. He moved in close behind her and started listening. But his mind didn't want to. The things she was saying. To be that cruel. That nasty about him. As she squeezed between the people lining the platform, he yanked the chain from his neck. What was coming out of her mouth, it was bile. Black sour bile. He reached out and slipped the chain and pendant into her jacket pocket. Have this. Not that you deserve it. But still she kept on. Kept talking. Kept cutting him and slicing him and gouging him with her words. He wanted her to stop. To shut up. He had to make her shut up.

#

She felt a shoulder in her back and was about to turn her head. Tell the man – and it had to have been a man; it always was – to be more bloody careful. But the pressure didn't let up. She took an involuntary step forward. Now the edge of the platform was just beyond the toes of her trainers. She tried to brace her legs but a hand, she clearly felt the pressure of someone's palm, shoved her.

'Hey!' She tried to drop to the ground, but it was too late. One foot went clean over the edge. She reached back to clutch at the person's arm, but was already tumbling. Someone screamed. A whole chorus of screams. Shrill and deafening. She felt the impact of landing on hard concrete, a cold rail against her cheek. It wasn't screaming she could hear. It was the tram's brakes. She opened her eyes: a massive metal wheel was skidding towards her face.

CHAPTER 36

Ryan wasn't sure what to say. A bottle of tapeworms? He looked uneasily at the room. Everyone seemed in motion. Bodies slipping past one another, hands squeezing arms, brief embraces, sucker-like lips extending toward cheeks. He could see teeth being bared. Eyes swivelling above too-wide smiles. Conversations were bubbling everywhere, but no one was really paying attention. Everyone too busy casting hungry glances about the room.

The person beside him said quietly, 'Time I made myself scarce.'

Ryan turned his head. 'Sorry?'

'The man himself approaches.'

Ryan checked the direction of his glance. Ivan was making his way over.

'I'll call you. When things are less... manic,' the man said.

Ryan frowned. 'Who are you?'

'Nick Quigly. Good luck with the event.' He placed his glass on the table and melted into the throng.

'Ryan, I think it's almost time.' Ivan said from behind him.

'Right, yes,' Ryan replied.

'What was that person saying to you?'

'Who?'

'The man who was just standing right here.'

Ryan didn't like the suspicious look on Ivan's face. 'Nothing much. He just said the champagne is very nice. Why?'

Ivan's eyes were now sweeping the room. The man had vanished. 'No matter.'

Quigly, Ryan thought. Am I meant to have heard of the name? The man acted like it, but not in an arrogant way.

'And how are you feeling, Ryan?' Ivan asked more quietly. 'Keeping those nerves in check?'

He let out a weak laugh. 'Just about. I haven't exactly got a whole speech prepared.'

'You'll be fine,' Ivan responded. 'They won't be expecting more than a few thank yous. Just give me a look and I'll take over and whip up a frenzy.' He leaned his head closer. 'It's my job, after all.'

'Right, I'll do that.' He lifted his glass to drain the last of his drink. Over the rim, he had a quick check for his old photography tutor, Harry Cooper. No sign of him. He spotted a man wearing a baseball cap. Standing slightly apart from everyone else. He seemed a little out of breath and was staring in Ryan's direction. He was wearing a black leather jacket, but it wasn't fashionable. The sort you'd wear for riding a motorbike. Chunky pads on the shoulders. Seeming to realise that Ryan had spotted him, he stepped behind a small group of people. By doing so, he revealed someone else.

It was like Ryan was suddenly peering down a tube; the new person's face filled his vision. Oh Jesus, no. DI Roebuck. Positioned just inside the door. The detective cocked his head, raised a forefinger to his chest, then pointed it at Ryan. We need to speak, he mouthed.

'Friend of yours?' Ivan asked.

'What?' Ryan felt like the orange juice had been spiked. He wanted to sit down. 'Just... someone.'

Ivan narrowed his eyes. 'Clearly.'

Ryan put his empty glass next to Quigly's.

'Very well,' Ivan said, 'let's –' He felt in his pocket for his phone. 'Sorry, Ryan, just give me a moment.'

Ryan took the opportunity to look back towards the door. Roebuck was still there. Still watching. Ryan half expected a couple of uniformed officers to appear. Make their way over and drag him out, the press photographer snapping away. He tried to think about what he was going to say on the podium. The only name he could recall was Mrs Goodwin's, his GCSE biology teacher. Thank you, Mrs Goodwin, for letting me photograph stick insects in your classroom. You, more than anyone, were encouraging and kind and –

'Ryan?' Ivan had a bemused expression on his face. 'This message. It says it's for you. Some kind of joke?'

'What does it say?'

'It says: "Message for Ryan. One for his exhibition?"' He held the phone out with a slightly alarmed expression. 'Who even is that?'

The image on the screen was slightly blurred, as if the person who'd taken it hadn't been standing still. Was it of Carla? Ryan had to pluck the phone from Ivan's hand to look more closely. It was. She was on the ground, lying between two metal rails, mouth open in a scream. She'd lifted one hand in a feeble attempt to ward off the bumper of a tram that had already swallowed her lower legs.

CHRIS SIMMS

PART 3

CHAPTER 37

Ryan shoved the phone back at Ivan and reached for his own. The noise in the room was too loud. He had to place a finger in his other ear to shut some of it out. Staring down at his feet, he heard Carla's voicemail kicking in. 'She's not answering.' He looked up at the gallery owner. 'She's not answering!'

'OK,' Ivan said. 'Who's not answering?'

'Carla! My girlfriend, Carla. That's...' He pointed to Ivan's phone as it beeped again. The gallery owner stared at Ryan for a second before checking the screen. 'Another message. Just says, "St Peters Square".'

He immediately started for the doors. Ivan's voice rose behind him. 'Ryan, wait a moment...' Roebuck was off to the side, back turned, talking on his phone. After the din of voices in the gallery, the street seemed like a cemetery. He ran to the end of the narrow road, turned right and was on Market Street in seconds. He paused while trying to work out the fastest way to St Peter's Square. Shoppers crowded the pavements. A man in a pale blue gilet holding a clipboard stepped up to him. 'Hi, sir, how do you feel about Polar –'

Ryan jinked past him. A tram was stationary on the

tracks leading from Piccadilly Station. He realised there were sirens. Lots of sirens. Jesus, the noise was echoing up the canyon-like confines of Mosley Street. Its far end led into the plaza of St Peter's Square. Five hundred metres of arrow-straight road. Sprinting down it, Ryan passed another motionless tram, annoyed faces peering down from its windows. Blue lights were flashing in the distance. He kept going, breath raw in his throat by the time he got to the other end. A police car was blocking the tram tracks, officers in yellow tabards positioned beside the vehicle. People were standing on benches and the steps of the cenotaph for a better view. Ryan went on tiptoes, saw another tram at a standstill, this one at the platform's edge. Men in hard hats and orange boiler suits were standing in front of it. An ambulance was backing up along the tracks. Voice floated at him from all directions.

'Went under, a woman it was.'

'Why would you try to run across, just as –'

'Did she, heck! The lass fell. From the platform edge.'

'Did the tram, you know, was she...'

Ryan stepped up to the nearest police officer. 'Please, it's my girlfriend who's in that ambulance. Carla Bell, she's the one –'

'She's not in there, sir.'

'But I know it was her who –'

'The young lady who was on the tracks? She was taken away about ten minutes ago.'

'Where? Where did they take her? She's not answering her phone.'

The officer looked to his colleague. 'Andy. The casualty. Where did they go?'

The colleague gestured towards his head. 'Salford, it would have been.'

Ryan knew Salford was the regional unit for serious head injuries. Oh my God. 'Is she OK?'

'All I heard was it could have been a lot worse. Sorry.'

The ambulance was now clear of the platform. Ryan

couldn't see any blood or anything on the front of the tram. He backed away from the patrol car and tried Carla's phone again. Voicemail.

'Carla, it's me. I'm coming to find you, OK? I'm on my way. I think... well, I don't know what's happening. I need to speak to you. He sent me a photo, Carla. Of you. Christ – I think it's the same person. The one who's been sending the codes. Call me if you get this, OK? I'll be there soon.'

#

Detective Inspector Roebuck saw Ryan run past the window of the Sussman Gallery. 'I'll call you back.' He turned round. The fat lump of the gallery owner had his mouth open. People were staring at the door or whispering to one another.

He had to squeeze round a bloke in a biker's jacket and baseball cap. Terrible case of body odour. Really nasty. The gallery owner was now examining his phone. 'Excuse me?' Roebuck asked. 'Where was Mr Lamb going?'

The gallery owner had fixed a smile on his face before lifting his collection of chins. 'Sorry?' He turned to the room. 'A temporary hitch, my good people. Please carry on, there'll be more drinks and canapés coming round, so as you were. As you were!'

Roebuck watched the man waddling off in the direction of the refreshments table, where he lifted a tray of drinks. This was interesting. A temporary hitch? If that was true, Ryan wouldn't have gone far. He slipped out the door. Less than a three-minute drive got him to the apartment on Loom Street. He parked half on the pavement and tried Ryan's number again. No reply, surprise, surprise. He and his girlfriend had a flat on the first floor of Jethro Mill. He approached the entrance and buzzed the button marked sixteen. No one replied. Hands in pockets, he ambled back to his vehicle.

A short wait later, he noticed a bit of movement at the

entrance to another building at the junction of Loom Street and Conran Street. A man was at the main doors having what looked like a heated discussion with two workmen. Roebuck's eyes narrowed. Baseball cap and black leather jacket. Same guy as at the Sussman Gallery? The one who stank. Could be.

The person walked quickly round the corner and entered the building through a door on Conran Street. Roebuck was climbing out of his vehicle when he heard the meaty noise of an engine beginning to rev. A motorbike nosed through the door, the rider now wearing a helmet. Definitely the same leather jacket. The rider barely checked the pavement was clear before driving his bike across it and accelerating on to the street. He swung the machine away from Roebuck and the detective scrabbled for his phone. He snapped off a picture as the bike powered past a cyclist wearing a Deliveroo backpack. Next second, it was round the corner. Gone. Roebuck checked the image. The cyclist's right leg was obscuring most of the bike's registration plate. Roebuck expanded the image. First two letters were JK. And what was a 3 or part of an 8. Might be enough for a search on the DVLA's database.

CHAPTER 38

The taxi driver nodded to the side, eyes on Ryan in his rear-view mirror. 'Here you go, mate.'

He shifted forward on the back seat as they turned off Stott Lane. Ahead of them, the words Emergency Department ran across the silver-coloured overhang of a large building.

'It's queuing for the drop-off,' the driver commented, taking the right-hand fork of the approach road. 'I'll go this way and you can get in on foot. Quicker.'

Ryan unclipped his seatbelt; a ten-pound note ready in his hand. 'Cheers.'

He noted a row of ambulances parked up in a series of bays to his right as he jogged towards the main doors. Another lobby, this one not as airy as the MRI's. A colour-coded map was directly in front. He searched the list of departments for anything to do with head injuries. There! Acute Neurology Unit. Humphrey Building. A brown part of the map, towards the far side of the floor plan. Almost five minutes ticked by before he found his way to a door that didn't need a code. A nurse in the corridor beyond explained he'd come to the wrong place: he needed the Emergency Assessment Unit in the Hope Building. Back to where he started and another search of the board. When he finally found a reception desk, almost fifteen minutes had passed since he'd jumped out of the taxi.

'Hello, my partner was brought in, probably about half an hour ago. I'm trying to find out how she –'

'What's her name, sir?'

'Bell. Carla Bell.'

'Let's take a look.' He studied his screen for a few seconds. 'And she was brought to this unit?'

'Yes, a police officer at the scene said so.'

'I'm not seeing her on our admissions list.'

'They took her in an ambulance, and I asked –'

'An ambulance?'

'Yes. She went under a tram at St Peter's Square.'

'I'll check Accident and Emergency. That would have been her point of arrival. Sometimes the system doesn't get updated as quickly as we'd like. Especially if it's busy.'

Ryan watched the man's eyes moving slowly from one side of his screen to the other. His head shook. 'How long ago was this? I'm not seeing a Carla Bell. That's B E and double L?'

'Yes. I don't know exactly. By the time I got to where it happened, she'd already gone. They said she'd been brought here.'

'The accident took place in St Peter's Square, you said?'

'Yes.'

'Mmm. Normally, they'd be directed to the MRI. Far closer. Let me make a call, sir. I'm sure we'll work this out. Would you like to take a seat?'

'Right. OK.' He turned away from the counter. Another bloody waiting area. There were some empty seats off to his right. Almost twenty minutes crawled by before the receptionist beckoned him over.

'Hello, sir. I've got to the bottom of this and you needn't worry. She was taken to the MRI, where she's been checked out. Nothing more than a twisted ankle, some abrasions to her lower legs and a minor cut to the head.'

'Really?' Ryan relaxed his grip on the counter's edge. 'But at the scene, the police officer said –'

'Maybe they were misdirected. The only reason for bringing her here would be if she'd sustained a serious head injury, and that doesn't appear to be the case. Head wounds bleed heavily, so perhaps the officer saw that and...'

Ryan felt like laughing. 'So the tram didn't –' He could still see the image on Ivan's phone. 'Just a twisted ankle?'

'And some minor scrapes. The system shows she's already been discharged. Must be quieter over there than it is here.'

'Thank you. Thank you so much. That's such a relief, thank you.' He hurried back to the lobby area and through the doors. His phone started a muffled ring, and he pulled it from his pocket. Ivan. No thanks. There was also a missed call from Roebuck. Piss off, thought Ryan, I'm finding my girlfriend first.

#

Carla had the keys to her flat in her hand when a voice spoke behind her. 'Carla Bell?'

She looked back to see a thick-set man with peppery-grey hair. Something intense about his eyes. He was holding up a Greater Manchester Police badge. 'Yes.'

'My name's Detective Inspector Roebuck. Can I help you with the door? Can't be easy with those crutches.'

They took the lift to the first floor, and he also opened the door to her flat for her. Once inside, he immediately directed her to the sofa. She watched as the detective pulled the coffee table closer to her, then positioned a cushion on it. Roebuck was the name Ryan had mentioned to her. The detective handling the armed robbery at that late-night store. Where Ryan had taken those awful photos of the injured man. Gratefully, she placed her bandaged foot on the cushion and sank back into the sofa. 'I thought, when you appeared behind me, impressive.

They're here to ask about what happened in St Peter's Square. That's fast.'

'No, but I'm sure whoever's been assigned to it won't be long,' Roebuck replied, sitting at the far end of the sofa. 'What makes you think it might have been deliberate?'

'I don't know. Because it went on for so long? At first, yes, I was about to have words. People often bump you. Men, usually. But this wasn't like that. It was more of a push because it just didn't stop.'

'How long did you feel pressure being applied for?'

'It's hard to say. It felt like ages. But maybe two seconds? Three?'

'How close were you to the platform edge?'

'A step or two. I was certainly well back from the yellow line.'

'And did you see anyone behind you?'

'No. I started to try and look, but then I realised I was right on the edge. Then I was tipping forward and the next thing, I'm lying there and the...' Her words dwindled to nothing.

'That's a terrible thing. If there is something to suggest it wasn't a simple accident, it will be on CCTV, Carla. Both on the platform and in the tram driver's cab. Thank God he applied the brakes as quickly as he did.'

She took a deep breath. 'Yes. Thank God.'

'I know the investigating officer will ask, so you may as well be thinking about it now: can you think of anyone who might have done this?'

Carla looked at her foot. 'No, well, I'm not sure. Not really.'

'Not really? That sounds like a maybe.'

She glanced at him. 'I got this random text. About me being special. I don't know who sent it.'

'I suggest you write everything down. Including what you told me about on the tram platform.' His eyes swept round the room, lingering for a moment on the door to the bedroom. 'Have you seen Ryan recently? I've been trying to get hold of him.'

He was looking right at her now. Carla had to check the plaster high on her forehead, hand acting as a temporary shield from his gaze. 'Ryan? He doesn't actually live here anymore.' She tried not to think about his missed calls stacking up on her phone. 'What's it about?'

'When did he move out?'

'Yesterday, actually.'

'Yesterday? The day before his big exhibition at the swish gallery?'

She dropped her hand. 'Timings could have been better, yes.'

'Where is he now?'

'At his mum's, I think.'

'Where's that?'

'Over in Reddish?'

'Do you have an address or number?'

She wasn't sure why she decided not to tell him. Just something a bit overbearing about the bloke. The sort who enjoyed their power. 'No. Sorry. It's on a curvy road. Something Crescent, maybe?'

He didn't look very impressed. 'Not to worry.'

The tram platform in St Peter's Square was suddenly in her head again. 'You know, one time I was down in London, I was on the Underground and the doors were shutting as I rushed down the steps and out onto the platform. I just kept running. I don't know why. I mean, there's another tube train every few minutes, isn't there? I shoved my hand in to stop the doors closing, but the rubber seal just clamped around my wrist so I couldn't pull my hand back out. The train set off. Slowly at first, but quickly getting faster. I'm jogging, then I'm running, banging on the window, shouting stop and the tunnel entrance is getting closer and the people in the carriage who are standing just the other side of the glass – inches away – are watching, like it's a TV program or something.

Just watching. I'll never forget their faces. I'm almost being dragged off my feet when someone finally jumped up and hit the emergency stop button. The train lurches to a halt and the doors all released and do you know what? I just turned round and ran away. Back up the stairs and out on to the street. I was so, kind of embarrassed. But also scared and shocked, I suppose. The way no one was doing anything – I don't know. I just had to get away. So, just because no one stayed at that platform, it doesn't mean it couldn't have been an accident, right? If someone did genuinely lose their balance and fall against me, they might have been scared, too, don't you think? At what ended up happening?'

'Absolutely.' Roebuck got to his feet. 'So you'll be alright here, on your own?'

'Yes, fine.'

'OK.' He glanced about the apartment again. 'Lovely place, you've got.'

'Thanks.'

His gaze travelled to the large windows and the building opposite. 'By the way, do you know anyone who owns a sports motorbike?'

'I don't even know what a sports motorbike is.'

'One of those racing models.'

'No. Sorry.'

'OK. Not to worry. I'll let myself out. And please, ask Ryan to call me as a matter of urgency.'

#

Ryan's taxi turned on to Loom Street. He sat forward on the backseat and had just told the driver he could pull over when he saw Roebuck coming out the entrance of Jethro Mill. 'Actually, keep going.'

'This is Loom Street.'

'Yeah, I know. But keep going.'

'Keep going?'

There were passing him now. He was talking on his phone. 'Yes! Carry on.'

'To where?'

Ryan twisted round to look out of the rear window. Still talking on his phone, the detective was now opening the door of a blue Audi half-parked on the pavement. The bastard was waiting for him outside the flat now! Fuck.

'To where? You want I just drive around?'

'No. Can you take me to Reddish? Melrose Crescent. I'll give you the post code for your sat nav.'

Once they were on Great Ancoats Street, he tried calling Carla another time. Still voicemail. Come on, he thought, you can't keep doing this to me. As soon as he cut the call, his phone started to ring. Ivan. Bloody hell. 'Hi, Ivan.'

'Where the hell are you?'

The anger in his voice caught Ryan by surprise. 'I'm really sorry –'

'You should be. What happened? People gave up waiting. A few placed orders, at least, but not anywhere near the numbers I envisaged. You realise I've incurred substantial costs? I called you repeatedly, and you didn't even have the courtesy to –'

'Can I speak?' Ryan asked, anger making his face feel hot.

'What?'

'You know, get a word in?'

'Get a word in? Certainly. But, as far as I'm concerned, the exhibition is dead in the water. So you better make it good.'

Make it good? Tactless prick. 'Well, is my girlfriend going under a tram good enough? I mean, you saw the picture. It was sent to your fucking phone. You know, sorry for not ringing you back, but I've been a tiny bit busy. And hospitals, well, hospitals have all these stupid rules about phone use. So selfish of them. What can I say?'

Ivan took a moment to speak. 'The news report I saw

said she only sustained minor injuries. Is that correct?'

'As far as I know, yes. She's been discharged from A and E. I haven't been able to see her yet.'

'And this photo on my phone... I don't understand. How could someone take a photograph... I just don't understand? Who sent it? And why to me?'

'I... I'm trying to work all that out.'

'Well, it sounds more than bizarre to me. We need to discuss the exhibition. There are all the prints to factor in, the expense of them. Where are you now?'

'You mean, am I coming in?'

'That would be a good outcome, yes.'

Ryan registered the hint of sarcasm in the gallery owner's voice. 'Ivan, did you take in any of what I just said? Someone tried to kill Carla, they –'

'Whoah! You said she went under a tram. She didn't fall?'

'I don't know. What did the message say with that photo?'

'Give me a second to bring it...here. "Message for Ryan. One for his exhibition?" And the other one just said, "St Peters Square".'

'Can you send me those two messages?'

'Of course.'

'Thanks. I'll call you, OK? I just need to speak with Carla –'

'When will you call?'

'Tomorrow, probably.'

'I'll speak to you tomorrow, then. In the meantime, Annabelle and I will clear the side room.'

So the exhibition was over. Whatever. 'Fine.'

'See you tomorrow, Ryan.'

'Bye.'

'Goodbye for now.'

Ryan pressed red, unable to believe how quickly the man's jovial manner had vanished once his business and reputation were taking a hit. What a complete dick.

CHAPTER 39

Detective Inspector Roebuck had a dark look on his face as he neared his desk. 'Sarah? Scores on the doors with Zack Patten, please.'

The sharpness of his tone caused his colleague to briefly glance up. 'Being that he's NFA, I'm struggling so far. Adam called up a contact who reckons Patten's been staying in a squat over in Openshaw –'

Roebuck held up a silencing finger and looked across to DS Robinson. 'Who's this contact?'

The other detective tapped the side of his nose. 'My snitch, not yours.'

Roebuck looked ready to punch something. 'You see me laughing? Their name.'

Robinson sat back, light-hearted smile now gone. 'Seriously boss, I can't say.'

Roebuck glared at his colleague a second longer. 'Is this person sound?'

'Most of the time, yes.'

Roebuck turned back to Potter. 'Carry on.'

'If he's not there,' she continued, 'this contact says he's also been spending a lot of time at an address in Beswick. Ackroyd Street.'

'What sort of address?'

'Private residence. Bit of a party house, apparently. Probable drug dealing. That's what he's heard.'

'You have a number for this house?'

'Yup. Fifty-one. According to the electoral roll, a Jason Kirby lives there.'

'What have we got on him?'

'The bloke's clean. He doesn't have a record. No arrests, anyway. He's received two warnings for making unwanted contact with women, but neither incident even led to a caution. And there's certainly no record of anything relating to robbery or violence.'

'Really? We need to know more about him. I'll leave that with you.'

'OK.'

Roebuck took his phone out as he sat down. 'Ryan fucking Lamb is really getting on my tits.'

'You called in at the art gallery, then?'

'I did.'

'Was he not there?'

'Of course he was bloody there. It was the opening of his exhibition. But he didn't stay long. Minutes before the show is about to start, he runs off. I saw him sprint past the window, moving like a bloody giraffe on steroids.'

'Going where?'

'If I knew that... I took a bet and went across to the apartment on Loom Street. The girlfriend eventually showed up. She's lying for him, I know that much. In between wittering on about her falling off the bloody platform at St Peter's Square. Anyway, she claims he hasn't been in contact, but that was bullshit. Which reminds me.' He stood and called across to the civilian support worker in the corner. 'Jenny, do me a favour, would you? I need a DVLA check on a partial motorbike reg'. It's urgent.' He read out to her what he had and sat back down. 'Right: either we trawl around trying to find Zack Patten or we focus on Ryan Lamb. My money's on Lamb. He's key to this, I just know it.'

Potter fiddled with her pen. 'I'm not so sure. We've got Patten at the robbery in Salford. Surely with our hands on him, we can –'

'That's the issue, though, isn't it? The bloke is no fixed address. If we go into this squat and miss him, word's out. He'll slither off somewhere. And say we strike lucky and do lift him. He's not stupid. Everything we ask will get a no comment. He knows the game. But Ryan Lamb? Give me ten minutes with him and we'll have all the names we need. Addresses. Locations of stolen goods. He'll spill the lot, trust me.'

Potter's gaze was still on her pen. 'He's given us the run-around, Lamb, I understand that. But are you sure you're not letting that get to you a bit?'

'What do you mean?'

She checked his expression. His eyebrows were dipped in an aggressive scowl. 'Just – you know – that you're not taking it as a personal thing?'

'Definitely not,' he said in a clipped voice. 'It's our best approach.'

Potter nodded. 'OK. So where might Lamb be?'

'Our little Larry the lost Lamb?' Roebuck grinned. 'I've got a fairly good idea. Back with his mummy. She lives in Reddish, according to the girlfriend. Possibly on a crescent.' He reached for his keyboard.

#

Jason Kirby drew to a stop on the narrow flyover that spanned the M60. Once the Fireblade's stand was safely engaged, he climbed off the machine and removed his helmet.

What did Carla want? He thought of her moving about in her flat. The happiest he'd seen her was when she'd been eating that dessert at the breakfast bar. The type Jason had bought her as a making-up present. He took his phone out and fired off a message. To her mobile, this time. Not her website.

Below him, the hum of passing traffic lifted and ebbed, but never ceased. He returned his phone to his pocket. Breathing in the fume-tinged air, he studied the procession racing past below him. What if, in reality, it was the same set of vehicles? All of them just revolving round and round the ring road in a never-ending circle, like the band of dust and boulders that orbited Saturn. He quite liked it when his mind started working like this. Throwing up possibilities that bent reality. Finding cracks in the everyday landscape of life. When he'd had to see the doctor, she said to treat it like a warning sign. Of things not being quite right in his head. Pop a pill time, he'd called it. He didn't want to go back to that. It occurred to him that he could just stand where he was, elbows resting on the guardrail and wait for the same little white motorhome, the same lorry with the German writing, the same red people carrier to eventually reappear. Prove him right.

The phone's ring interrupted his line of thought. Danny's number on the screen. This was it, surely? Good old Danny has sorted things out at work. 'Hi Danny.'

'Jason, hello. Out and about again? Is that the seaside I can hear?'

Jason couldn't be bothered to put him right. He didn't have the energy. 'Yup.'

'Nice. I love driving over to the coast, watch the waves. Listen, Jason, I wish I had better news. Apparently, there's a new guy with hold of the reins at GMP's traffic unit. I'm not sure if he's keen to make an impression, or he's just a knob-head. Either way, he's not prepared to play ball. Thirty-six miles an hour? He would have let it slide. That's ten percent over the limit and three-miles-an-hour leeway. But you were clocked at thirty-seven. One mile-an-hour difference, but he won't budge. What can I say? It's not the end of the world.'

It is, Jason thought. It bloody is.

'You still there?' Danny asked.

'Yes.'

'OK. I'm meeting Archer later and we'll work out the best way forward. But I've already said, you're a valued member of the MRU. It might just mean working ambulances for a while. When they're short-staffed. That and getting seriously good at entering CPI data!'

Jason let his eyes skim the roofs of the vehicles below. A bike shot into view in the outside lane, speed so high it made the centre-lane traffic look slow. It wasn't fair. No one was catching him, were they?

'Jason, I'll see you Tuesday, OK? And please don't be too down on yourself. It's a minor setback, that's all. Understood? Jason?'

'Yes, I'm here.'

'Say it then. This is just a minor setback. I'm waiting.'

Danny pressed the red button and then hurled his phone towards the sky. It span in a slow arc, landing in the middle lane where the back of the casing went spinning off. A split second later, a lorry ran over the main part of the handset. When the rear tyres cleared it, only tiny fragments remained. 'I'm not a fucking child, Danny,' he murmured. Though actually, he thought, that's how I've behaved. The sight of Carla lying on the tracks intruded into his mind. Oh, God, why? Why did I do it? He had to force back the tears. It wasn't her saying those things. It wasn't. Simone was feeding her lines, pressuring her into making those nasty comments. I never liked her. Never! Really, it's a good thing I heard their conversation. At least I now know Simone for the enemy she is. The bitch wanted a battle, did she? He began pacing back and forth beside the railings. Bring it on, you fucking tart. You frizzy-haired fucking slag. You don't know who you're messing with. He noticed the extra-weight in his jacket and slid the Stanley knife out. It had been beside the off cuts of carpet back at Sunlight House. He was now glad he'd taken it. The blade was wickedly sharp. If it could go clean through carpet and underlay, what would it do to skin? He mimed switching it back and forth across the bitch's face. Seeing ribbons of black flesh falling away. Slicing off those fat lips. 'How does that feel? Not so fucking mouthy now, are you? Try doing your meddling now. Haha! Career tip, little Miss Smart-arse Model. You like people looking at you? Try the fucking circus.'

#

Carla was still sitting on the sofa when her phone gave a beep. She couldn't face checking who it was. Not yet. The conversation with the detective kept rattling about in her head. He'd kind of agreed when she'd told him about that time in London. Whoever had bumped into her could have been so appalled, they'd run away. Just like she'd done when the tube doors sprang open. The sensation of fingers clamping across the base of her spine came back. It wasn't someone stumbling into me. She needed music. Something to distract her. The bloody remote was beside the four pack of chocolate desserts. Forgot to put them in the fridge. Can I, she wondered, be arsed to get up? Could have a dessert when I'm over there. Could have all four. And end up fat. Her ankle was a throbbing drum beat at the base of her leg. She turned to her phone instead. Maybe it's the police.

I can buy you puddings in little purple pots if that's what you want! Gabriel.

The silence of the room was like a woollen blanket. She became aware of a high-pitched humming sound. When she swallowed, it stopped. Slowly, she turned her head. Four chocolate desserts on the breakfast bar. Oh Christ. Her eyes lifted to the windows and she focused on the buildings opposite. Workmen had been going in and out of that one facing her apartment for weeks. How many weeks? The top floor had several lights on - there were people in there now. She couldn't stop her legs from shivering. The pain in her ankle had evaporated. Not wanting to, she examined her phone again. Gabriel. Him again. Was it someone from an assignment? Something to do with work? Gabriel. For the first time, the name seemed vaguely familiar. Where else have I seen it? Was it spam? Among the endless junk messages that came through on her website? Miracle cures for tinnitus. Shark tank investment tips from America. Wi-Fi boosters. USmile teeth whitener. Network news. Health Tech. Bizarre ones, too. Some just saying 'Hi' with a link. Nonsensical ones made up of random strings of words. Like the rantings of a precinct preacher. Was that where she'd seen the name?

She checked the breakfast bar again. Purple pots. Whoever it is has my phone number and work email. And they know where I live. Her mind touched on the tram platform, and she closed her eyes. No. No fucking way. No. No. No. I need to speak to someone. Check I'm not going crazy here. Mum? Simone? Ryan? Mum didn't need to know this. Not yet, anyway. Simone: it could be anytime day or night wherever she was now. Ryan? She knew it made sense. How many messages had this Gabriel been leaving? She went to her voicemail. Best to hear what Ryan has to say first.

For some of the calls, he didn't leave a message. A few were him just begging her to ring. It got to the messages left that day, first at 12.58. Must have been just after the tram thing, she thought.

His voice was high and wavery. The same as the time when he thought someone had stolen his precious Canon. She stared across the room at the unlit TV screen as his message played out. Jesus. The same person? A picture of me? The one who's been sending the codes? The thought of the rows of windows across the street were making her feel sick. He's been watching us. He knows both our phone numbers. He's been going on my website. He knows my favourite pudding! Is he watching me now?

She struggled to her feet, groped for a crutch. I'm not staying here. Not on my own. No way. I'm going to mum's. She hobbled across to the bedroom, hesitated for a moment and then flung the door open. Empty. Of course it's empty! She could see into the tiny bathroom. No one's here, she assured herself. You've got to keep a clear head. Think. What do you need? Work clothes, toiletries, phone charger. Tomorrow was just a day in the studio at Q2. Oh, shit. She realised her make-up case was still over at Salford Quays. Andrea would keep it safe. There'd been a man, beyond the barrier. Baseball cap. Nothing unusual to get a lone bloke perving at the models. Had he been staring at me? Think, Carla! Spare work case. The one with old your old shit from college. That would have to do. OK. She lined items up on the bed. Poor mum, what will she say when I turn up?

Another thought sprang up: what if he knows where my mum lives? Oh, Christ. I can't go there. Which left only one other option. She nodded: somewhere he has no chance of knowing about. Because I've not been there in bloody ages. Simone's place, tucked away on the edge of Heaton Mersey Common.

CHAPTER 40

Jason touched the key fob against the sensor at the side door of Sunlight House for a third time. The lock mechanism on the metal gate wasn't clicking open. What the fuck? He raised the visor of his crash helmet and studied the pebble-shaped piece of plastic. Breathed on its underside and rubbed it against the thigh of his jeans. Lifted it to the sensor again. Nothing. That woman at the office. Tabitha. She must have done something to the system. Bitch. He wheeled his bike round to the main entrance and chained it up. If the same guys were in the foyer, it was going to be tricky getting them to let him in. He was wondering what he could say when the door started sliding open. A new bloke, wearing paint-spattered overalls, an unlit cigarette hanging from his mouth.

'Nice one!' Jason announced cheerily, stepping past him. 'Bloody key fob's kaput. I'm on the first floor.' He jangled the Nail and Cable keys. The other man wasn't looking convinced.

'Hang on. Which flat?'

Jason kept going towards the stairs. 'Number five. I'm only picking up some wallpaper samples. I can let myself out.'

As soon as he saw across to Carla's flat, he knew it had been abandoned. The lights were off and the bedroom door was ajar. A couple of items of clothing were visible on the bed. He stood at the window as regret needled him. I shouldn't have sent that message about the puddings. The four little pots were still on the breakfast bar. It had been silly. A peevish thing to have done. Yes, the sort of thing that occurred between couples, but I don't want our relationship to be like that. From now, we shall only be loving and kind to each other, Carla, I promise.

He walked slowly away from the window. I know what I have to do. It won't take long on my bike, getting down to Chester. I'll be at your mum's very soon. He pictured himself knocking on the front door of that lovely little cottage. He liked Maggy. When she saw the bond between him and her daughter, she would be touched. Perhaps regretful to no longer have anyone like that in her life? He'd take her flowers. First impressions and all that. He wondered which ones she'd like. Roses, probably. Yes, I'll get her roses. Pink or perhaps white.

#

'Come in here and talk to me, Ryan, for God's sake!'

He came to a halt partway up the stairs. His mum was standing in the hallway, looking up at him through the banisters. Outside, he could hear the taxi pulling away. 'I was just going to –'

'Stop hiding in your bloody bedroom. You're not a teenager anymore. Come to the kitchen and tell me what the hell is going on.'

He backed down the steps and followed her in. She was sitting at the table with that look on her face. The one for when he'd screwed up. Like the time he'd left his schoolbag on the bus and, in a panic, said some older boys had stolen it from him in the park. She'd called the police and two officers had driven him round the surrounding streets for almost half an hour.

'Any of that lot? Outside the Spa?'

'No.'

'You're sure?'

'I think so.'

'What were these two lads wearing again?'

'I didn't really see that well. Dark coats and trousers. Black shoes, I think.'

'And black hair, you said earlier. Some of them are wearing dark clothing. That one at the side has black hair. How can you be sure, from over here, it's not any of them?'

They'd both twisted round in their seats to look at him. All he could do was shrug.

'I don't know, Steve, you reckon it's worth bringing them all in for questioning? They certainly fit the lad's description.'

'No – honestly.' His voice had gone high. 'It isn't any of them. They're... none of them are tall enough.'

Of course, they knew he was making it up. Even at thirteen, he could tell they weren't really searching for two older boys. He was being shown what can happen if you lie, and then stick to it. The consequences that quickly snowball.

When they'd dropped him back home, they barely bothered looking at him. He could sense their disapproval. His mum had tersely thanked them and closed the door. The next thing she said was that school had rung; the bus company had been in contact. A schoolbag had been found on a downstairs seat. The surname Lamb was on a few of the books inside it.

'What happened at the exhibition?' she asked. 'From the look of you, it didn't go well.'

He stared down into his lap.

'Ryan?'

'I left before it even started.'

When he looked up, she was regarding him with concern. 'Why?'

For a second, he just wanted a hug. 'I've lost her, Mum. I've been so stupid. I got caught up in the exhibition and needing to get enough shots for it to happen, and this person – I don't even know who – started sending me messages about incidents, but one...one was for a robbery that he predicted, basically, and now I think he's targeted Carla.'

'Carla? Why Carla?'

'She's had some kind of... something happened and she fell from the platform in St Peter's Square. Oh, Mum, I don't know what to do. She's refusing to take my calls.'

'Slow down, Ryan. Take a breath or two. Now, start again. Slowly this time.'

By the time he'd finished telling her everything – the messages, the incident in the convenience store, the involvement of Roebuck, the escalating fallouts with Carla – two empty mugs were on the table between them. She hadn't chosen the *You're tea-rrific* one for him this time.

'What a terrible mess,' she said in a muted voice.

Just the act of saying it out loud to someone else had felt so good. The only thing he'd held back about were the photos he'd taken in the convenience store. The ones on the memory stick. Now he felt exhausted. Like it was the early hours of the morning and he really needed to sleep.

'I'm going to tell you two things, Ryan. OK?'

He nodded.

'However this all turns out, I still love you. You know that, don't you?'

'Thanks, Mum.'

'I know things were difficult for us. I wish I could have been there for you more. Your years at school, those problems with the other boys picking on you.'

'You were working, Mum. You had to work to keep this place. I get that.'

'Still, I regret it and that's that. But I want you to know something else. Your dad didn't run off with another woman.'

Ryan felt the floor beneath him tilt. The back of the seat pressed into his spine. 'He didn't? Then what...?'

'Your father was – still is, I imagine – weak. I know what you're thinking; that he was always going to the gym. That he was so muscle-bound. But I'm not talking about physical strength. I mean here.' She tapped her breastbone. 'And up here.' She tapped her temple. 'He was selfish and immature, and he'd lie and then lie again. The reason we were so broke is that he gambled. He lost our savings and lied about it. He would go out drinking and lie. He sold our car and lied. He set up so many businesses – laying driveways was one you might remember – take people's money and run. Eventually, I'd had enough. I told him I had evidence of his fraud and I'd go to the police with it all if he didn't leave. And you know what? He was so pathetic, so feeble, that's what he did.' She waved a hand. 'He just walked out, leaving me with thousands of pounds of debt on this place.'

Ryan turned his head, looked down the corridor towards the front door. 'But...is he even in Canada?'

'Last I heard, Swansea. Living with someone down there. I can give you the address, if you want. No idea if he's still there, though.'

'How come he didn't contact me?' He realised he was brushing a hand back and forth across the table. 'Swansea? It's not even that far.'

'Your life is better without him in it, Ryan. Get in touch if you want, but he'll be a disappointment. He'll let you down. As soon as he thinks he can, he'll ask to borrow money. But you're an adult. It's your choice.'

Ryan let his hand drop from the table onto his thigh. 'Jesus.'

'The reason I've told you this now, Ryan, is because you need to decide about Carla. Never mind this business with the art gallery, the messages, the police: all that can sort itself out. Carla. Do you love her?'

'Yes,' he whispered without hesitation.

'So now you need to be strong. You need to show her how much she means to you.' She gestured to the ceiling. 'No more retreating. Hiding up there in your childhood room. Talk to her, Ryan. Win her back.'

'She won't even return my calls! Every time –'

'Forget the bloody phone! All your social media... routes. Speak to her. Face-to-face. Look into her eyes. Let her look into your eyes.'

He sat up in his chair. 'You're right. You are.'

'Are you sure she's even at the apartment in town?'

'Actually, I'm not. I mean, the detective was waiting outside. I think he'd tried buzzing the door.'

'She'd been injured. You think she might – just might – have listened to your messages?'

'Yes.'

'So she's going to be pretty scared, too. If I had to guess, she'll be at her mum's. I doubt she even went home after leaving hospital. Knowing Maggy, she'll have driven up from Chester to collect her.'

'God, you're right. That's where she'll be. I'll get the train –'

'Take my car.'

'Really?'

'Take my car, Ryan. Get yourself down to Chester and tell her how much she means to you. If it's coming from here,' she tapped her sternum again, 'she'll know. She'll listen. Believe me, she will.'

#

Carla plonked her bag down on the upstairs landing. She'd sent a message to Simone from the taxi on the way over, saying about the tram incident and that she needed to use her house. Opposite her was Simone's room. Crash in there? It felt a little weird. There was a tiny spare room beside the bathroom. Up in the attic, she remembered, there was a futon. Phone signal was stronger up in the top of the house, too. She'd need to call Ryan eventually. She left the crutch by her bag and half-crawled up the steep chairs to check. Simone's exercise equipment was spread out all over the place. Abdominal roller, yoga mat, Bosu ball. She cleared it all to the edge, beside a little rack of brightly coloured dumbbells.

She stood on the low bed and opened the skylight up. Opposite, a dense slope of trees led down to the grassy area of the common. A couple of people were chatting as their dogs tore round the grass. Such a lovely little spot. She eased the futon frame out and pulled the foam mattress across it. This would do just fine. Sleeping beneath a giant Velux window was a bonus, too. It reminded her of camping. She lay down on the bare mattress and stared up at the patch of sky. It was darkening. Time, she decided, to ring Ryan. Tell him what had been going on. She felt the breast pocket of her jacket.

No phone.

Instant jolt as she recalled using it in the back of the taxi to call Simone. Please, don't let it be there. She thrust her hands into the side pockets. The fingers of her left hand immediately felt its thin casing. Her right fingers had become entwined in something light and threadlike. She lifted both hands. Her phone in one, a broken neck chain in the other. Gold. She hated gold: gave her a rash. There was a pendant hanging from it. A little figure. With wings. A male figure, hands pressed together in prayer. An angel. She threw it to the floor and checked the message on her phone. Gabriel. This was too fucking weird. Gabriel was the name of an angel, wasn't it? She crawled off the bed and slid her way down the stairs. Sitting on the landing carpet, she took her laptop from her bag and went to the junk folder. The reams of shit that were sent. Her eyes snagged on an especially short subject line. 'My love.' She clicked on it. 'Never forget how special you are. Gabriel.'

Oh my God.

She typed 'Gabriel' into the junk folder's search field and pressed return. So many messages came up. This had been going on for days. Weeks. They must have crossed paths at some point. But when? Blurry memories of nights out with Simone. She cringed at some of the stuff they got up to. Not that she'd ever been properly unfaithful, she told herself. Just flirting. Sometimes a kiss. How many blokes had they toyed with for a bit of fun? She turned her mind to work. The messages were coming through the website of her business. She went to so many places, met so many different people. There weren't that many men she'd done make-up for, but plenty who worked behind the scenes in photographic agencies and TV studios. TV studios. That time on set. Filming *Unsung Heroes*. The oddball who'd got the floor manager to pass on a message to her. Who the hell did he say he was? A mystery knight? Knight in shining armour? Not that, but something similar. Something creepy.

The ring of her phone made her whole body jerk. Her eyes crept towards the device like it was a scorpion about to strike. Simone. Thank fuck for that. 'Hey you.'

'Carla, are you there? At my house?'

'Yeah, I'm here. Sitting outside your room. I'm trying to work out who this fucker is. Simone, he's been sending emails to my work address for weeks. I've just found them all in my junk folder –'

'Carla?'

'Yeah, I can hear you. It's a bit crackly. God, Simone, he's right in my life. There's a pendant – I found a pendant in my jacket pocket just now and I'm pretty certain it's the same person who turned up at the set of –'

'Carla?'

'Yeah, I can hear you. I'm pretty certain he was at –'

'Carla, I'm not getting everything you're saying, but I know who he is.'

Carla froze, mouth half-open.

'Carla?'

'Yes.' Her voice sounded very small. 'You know who it is?'

'I've just seen him. On the internet. I remember who it is.'

CHAPTER 41

DI Roebuck slung his jacket onto an empty desk. It slid right across it and fell on the floor. 'Fuck's sake.'

DC Potter peered round her monitor. 'No joy?'

Roebuck yanked his chair back and sat down heavily. 'Oh, she was at home. But I'm not driving to Chester – which is where his mum says he's gone.'

'You believed her?'

He screwed his mouth up. 'Yeah, I did. Ryan had been there, but he'd told her that Carla was really upset. She'd had some kind of accident in town, so he was driving down to be with her.'

'The accident being her fall from the tram platform?'

'She didn't say. I don't know if Ryan was being deliberately vague with her, or what. Anyway, what's been going on here? Where's Jenny? Did she get me that motorbike registration?'

'Not yet. But I think you're going to like this.'

He sat back. 'Go on.'

'Turns out Jason Kirby, who lives at the address Zack Patten has been spending a lot of time at, is a paramedic.'

Roebuck's face was blank. 'So?'

'We've been trying to figure out how Ryan Lamb has

been showing up at so many –'

'He's Ryan Lamb's source! Oh, that's beautiful, Sarah.'

She lifted a piece of paper. 'This is his line manager's number at the North West Ambulance Service. Danny Hayes.'

'Is he in work at the moment?'

'Awaiting our call.'

Roebuck looked to the side meeting room. 'Let's get him on loudspeaker.'

The burr of Haye's extension ringing rose from the pyramid-shaped speaker in the centre of the table. 'Danny Hayes speaking.'

'Mr Hayes, it's DI Roebuck from Greater Manchester Police. I gather my colleague, DC Potter, has been in contact?'

'Yes, I got a message to expect a call.'

'Great. She's alongside me here. We've got you on speakerphone. I'll let her take over since she did the bulk of the legwork on this.'

Potter cleared her throat. 'Mr Hayes, hello, it's Sarah speaking.'

'Danny, please.'

'OK, thanks Danny. Are you in earshot of anyone, Danny?'

'No, I'm in my office.'

'Right, I need to stress this is all confidential, Danny. We're calling in relation to one of your ambulance personnel. Jason Kirby.'

'Jason? He's not ambulance, he's MRU.'

'Sorry, what's that?'

'Motorbike Response Unit.'

Roebuck immediately sat forward. 'Motorbike?' He turned to Sarah. 'The bike I saw in Ancoats.'

She nodded. 'Where is Mr Kirby at the moment?'

'Well, that's a slightly sticky situation. He's not due in until tomorrow.'

'Why is that a sticky situation?'

'I thought this may have been why you were calling. He got caught speeding the other week. It's going through at the moment. Three points on his licence, which means we're having to –'

'On his work bike?' Sarah asked.

'No – he was off duty.'

'Do you know what sort of bike he rides?'

'Yes. In fact, if you hang on, I have a copy of his Notice of Intended Prosecution here. We've been liaising with your traffic department, trying to get it downgraded to –'

Roebuck butted in. 'What's the registration?'

'It is…' Danny read it out and Roebuck clicked his fingers in triumph. 'Starts with a JK, and has the number eight. Knew it. And the make?'

'A Honda Fireblade. Cracking bike. 1000 CC engine.'

'What's Jason like as a character?' Sarah asked.

'Jason? Not the most gregarious member of the team. Keeps himself to himself. He rarely sits on base when on shift, which suits me fine. Prefers to stay mobile in the area – a boon when it comes to deploying jobs.'

'And as a paramedic?'

'One of my best. Utterly dependable. If anything, a bit too invested in the job.'

Sarah was readying herself to ask another question when Roebuck cut across her. 'Danny, how does it work with the comms system? You're the same as us, Airwaves?'

'Correct.'

'So what does Jason have when he's doing a shift?' Roebuck tapped Sarah's pad, indicating that she should start taking notes.

'A handset and usually a MDT – Mobile Data Terminal – which has an iPad-sized screen displaying all incoming calls. That includes the category, address, sat nav location and brief details, when practical.'

'How easy would it be to track down where Jason was when a specific incident occurred while he was on duty?'

'Not a problem. If he was despatched to it, very easy. Each handset has an ISSI number. There'll be a record of each ISSI and its GPS location when an incident was despatched. Plus, of course, the bikes all have GPS trackers. So there'll be those records, too.'

Roebuck silently pumped a fist.

'I'm not sure if this is relevant to why you're calling, but I spoke to Jason earlier. He's very upset about this speeding ticket. It means we're having to take him off driving duties, you see. I think it's hit him pretty hard. He hasn't returned my subsequent call, yet.'

'That's interesting, thanks,' Roebuck answered. 'Can you send us a photo of Jason? From his personnel file?'

'Can do.'

'Danny?' Sarah asked. 'Are you aware of Jason having any financial difficulties?'

'Financial? No.'

'He isn't someone who likes to gamble? Perhaps has borrowed money from colleagues in the past?'

'He lives mortgage free, I know that much. Inherited the house from his parents. Single, no kids. I don't think he's short of cash.'

Sarah consulted her notes. 'This is 51 Ackroyd Street, in Beswick?'

'Yes – same as on the Notice of Intended Prosecution I have here.'

'You say he's single? He lives alone?'

'As far as I'm aware. I'm not sure what this is about, but I like the bloke. For what it's worth. Social skills aren't the best, but we're not in the job for that, are we?'

#

Carla hunched forward. 'I don't get it. You've seen him? Where?'

'Can you get online?' Simone asked.

'Yes – my laptop's right here.'

'After you left me that message, I checked the news

over there. Manchester Evening Chronicle's site. I wanted to see what you said about the tram. Not being sure if it was accidental. I spotted a headline linking to the culture section. *Midnight Rambler does a runner.* It was the opening of Ryan's show, wasn't it? Midnight Rambler is the name they gave him.'

Carla nodded. 'What did it say?'

'Well – it's not that. I mean, it is. He ran out of the gallery just as the show was about to officially open.'

Carla pieced it together in her head: she'd fallen under the tram shortly before Ryan's big moment. He did it for me. To find me.

'It's the pictures, Carla. The ones from inside the gallery. You there yet?'

'Hang on.' She typed the newspaper's address in, saw the headline in the sidebar and clicked. 'What am I looking for?'

'Sixth picture down. The one with the gallery owner giving a speech.'

Carla scrolled to it. There was Ivan, little hands raised. Cheeks flushed crimson. 'I see it.'

'Go to his left. Zoom in on the guy with a baseball cap. UCA on the front of it. Standing a bit away from everyone else.'

'Oh, fuck. Simone, he was at the shoot this morning! The shoot at Salford Quays.'

'Honey, don't you remember his face?'

She squinted at the screen. The guy wasn't ugly. Not by any means. Square jaw, maybe something wonky with his upper lip. His eyes were in shadow, but she could still make out they were a bit starey. 'Should I?'

'It's the guy from when that taxi we were in had a bump! Oxford Road. We were trashed. You weren't wearing a seatbelt. He checked you over for whiplash, or whatever, even though there was no need.'

'The paramedic! The bloke on the motorb –' She swallowed. 'Oh my God, I called him my guardian angel.

That's it! Gabriel. He's been signing his messages Gabriel. And at the TV studio, that's what he called himself. Guardian Angel. Oh Christ, Simone, I might throw up.'

'You know you kissed him?'

'Don't!'

'You did, honey. I was over the road. You gave him a peck on the cheek.'

She hung her head. 'We had this entire conversation, didn't we? Me and him.'

'I think so. I remember thinking he was making a big deal of it all. And shining the pen in your eyes? That went on way too long.'

'I thought he was just being really thorough.'

'And another thing. That form you helped him fill in. The report. It had all your details on it, remember? Mobile phone, address, date of birth, everything.'

Carla couldn't even remember what she'd done with her copy. Maybe back at the flat somewhere.

'And Carla? You need to ring your mum. That form had her name and number on it, too.'

CHAPTER 42

He rapped his knuckles against Maggy's front door. Come on, come on, answer it, will you? Stepping away from the cottage, he examined the first-floor windows. No sign of her up there. No sign of either of them. He stepped forward and knocked again. Don't leave me out here, please. Movement at the window to his side. Domino! Up on the windowsill, tail flicking about. Maggy had to be at home. He was about to knock again when he heard footsteps beyond the door. Thank Christ for that. The key turned and the door opened about half-way. She looked totally surprised to see him, bless her. 'Yes, can I help?'

'Maggy, if I may call you Maggy, you don't know me. But I've brought you these.' He held out the bouquet of Carnations from the petrol station down the road. They didn't have roses, which was a shame.

'I'm sorry: who are you?' Her eyes dropped momentarily to his mouth.

Go on, have your little look. 'My name's Jason and I think Carla might be expecting me. Here.'

She glanced down at the flowers but didn't take them. 'Carla? She's not here. Jason, you say? Jason who?'

He tried to smile. 'If you just say it's her guardian angel, then she'll know.'

'As I said, I'm afraid she's not here. How do you know my daughter, exactly?'

'We met a while ago.' He shifted his weight, trying to see past her into the house. 'Carla! Carla, it's me!' To his horror, she started to close the door on him. He had to jam his hand against it. The one holding the flowers. Several stems snapped. Blooms fell to the step. 'Maggy, please don't do that.'

'Will you let go of my door! Get your hand off it!'

He kept enough pressure up to stop it from closing and called into the gap. 'Carla – you know me as Gabriel. I'm not really Gabriel. That's not my name. I know you've been waiting for me, so I've come. I'm here!'

A phone began to ring from within the house. 'I've told you already, she isn't here! I'll call the police if you don't leave.'

'Carla! Tell your mum; she doesn't understand about us. Carla, please! Carla!' He felt a hand clamp down on his shoulder.

'Get off Mrs Bell's property. Now!' A voice ordered behind him.

He twisted his head. The old colonel-type from next door. Why did he have to poke his nose in? He turned back to the house, roared this time. 'Carla!'

'That's enough!'

A sharp impact on the top of his head. Enough to fill the air with a swarm of bright dots. He looked over his shoulder. The old man had a walking stick raised and was bringing it down again. Jason just grabbed hold of it with his left hand before it connected with his head. Behind him, the door slammed shut and they grappled on the step for a second. He didn't mean to take the Stanley knife from his jacket, but suddenly it was in his free hand, there, right in front of him, passing down the side of the old man's face and neck, opening up a red line in the wrinkly skin, the flaps of it coming apart, blood welling up and, where it had gone down his neck, spraying out quite strongly. Like a bottle of half-flat lemonade being opened. The old man didn't seem to know his skin was hanging open. He was snarling, making a fist with his right hand, so Jason swiped across the knuckles and then back along the wrist. The blade was sharp! Could use it in a surgical theatre, this. He glimpsed white bone and the old man was now stepping backwards, looking at the blood cascading from his fingers in total confusion.

'Oh my God, what have you done? Bernard!'

Maggy had opened the door a crack and this time Jason kicked it. Hard. The corner connected with her head and her eyes rolled up as she fell against the hallway wall. He ran past her into the front room, glimpsing a streak of black as the cat fled. 'Carla! Where are you, Carla!' Kitchen: empty. Side room: empty. His sight bumped and bounced as he ran up the stairs, checking under beds, pulling wardrobe doors open. The rings of the shower curtain made a skittering noise as he yanked it aside. Where could she be? Back down to the hallway. The cupboard under the stairs! 'Carla, you can come out. It's me.' Just a bloody vacuum inside. Maggy was lying beside the open front door. Had she been telling the truth? He stepped over her and out onto the front step. The nosey bastard had crawled across most of the front lawn towards his house, but was now on his side, grass dark and wet beneath his slack face. Jason stood for a moment, hands hanging by his sides. Why is everyone trying to keep us apart? Trying to stop us from being together. It wasn't fair. He looked across to his bike. And now he faced even more trouble, because if Carla wasn't here, he could think of only one other place she might be. The worst of all. The place that belonged to the one who's been trying to poison her against me from the start: Simone.

#

'Thanks, Mum,' Ryan said, coming down the stairs. 'I don't think I'd have been able to handle him again. Not now.'

'Just get going,' she replied, handing him the keys to her car. 'I watched him drive round the corner. Go on, before he comes back!'

He started towards the door as his phone rang. He checked the screen. It's her! Calling me, at last. 'Carla, oh my God, where are you?'

'Ryan, I know who it is! The person who's been sending you the tips – he's also been messaging me. He knows about our apartment, my job, where my mum lives. He was at your exhibition, Ryan. In the audience at your exhibition.'

'Hang on.' Ryan doubled back into the kitchen. 'Did you get my message? About the tram stop in St Peter's Square?'

'Yes – but only just. Which photo are you talking about?'

'I blocked him from my phone and so he sent it to Ivan. Carla, it was of you. When you were on the tracks. Your legs were under the front of that tram. I was so scared, Carla. I thought you might have been –'

'It was him, then,' she whispered. 'He did it. We need to call the police – tell that detective everything.'

'We will. We will. Where are you, Carla?'

'Simone's. She's in America. It's the only place I could think of that'll be safe.'

'All right. That's good. I'm coming over, OK?'

'Hurry, will you? It's getting dark and this is... just hurry.'

'I will. We'll work this out together. And Carla?'

'Yes?'

'I love you. And it's going to be OK, I promise.'

'Hurry, Ryan. Please.'

'On my way.' He was almost out the front door when he paused, turned round, darted up the stairs and stepped into his old bedroom. The wardrobe wobbled as he yanked the doors open, dragged out the nearest box and started delving his hand between the old photo albums.

#

'So, everyone's clear on their role?' Roebuck asked the four officers assembled before the white board. Behind them DC Potter stood with her arms crossed. Heads nodded, faces serious. 'And keep a copy of his photo handy. There might well be others in the property. Word is, it's being used as a venue for all sorts.'

The six of them were filing across the main office when Jenny, the CSW, called over. 'DI Roebuck? A couple of things you need to know about.'

He flashed her an irritated look. 'Can they wait? We're about to –'

'It's relevant to the operation. We put a flag on his bike's registration. The Honda Fireblade.'

'Hang on guys,' Roebuck murmured, diverting towards her. 'What's up?'

The CSW pointed to her screen. 'This is showing up, literally in the last couple of minutes. Incident down in Chester. Home invasion and serious assault. Elderly man might not make it. A younger male turned up at the address, slashed his neck and assaulted the female homeowner. Left the scene on a Honda Fireblade that matches our guy's registration.'

'Really? Who lived at the house?'

'A Margaret Bell.'

'Bell?' Roebuck hurried back to his desk and checked his file. 'Thought so. Carla's surname. It'll be her mum: has to be. What else?'

'That incident was called in by a member of the public at seven minutes past six. Then, twelve minutes ago, an ANPR camera on the M56 picked up the same bike heading towards Manchester. Estimated speed of over one-hundred and-ten miles an hour.'

'And that was twelve minutes ago?'

'Correct.'

'He'll be in the city centre by now. You said someone was slashed?'

'With a blade of some sort.'

'We know he carries a machete for the convenience store robberies. I want a patrol car at Carla Bell's address. Now.'

A question came from the waiting group. 'What are we doing, sir?'

'Still heading for his house, but it looks like we'll be spectators on this one. He's got a weapon; I'm requesting an armed response unit be scrambled. Let's go.'

DC Potter waved a hand towards Jenny. 'Can you go into the Police Intelligence System? Have a look for anything on Jason Kirby. Juvenile offences, stuff that's fallen off the system. He can't have gone from nothing to this overnight. There has to be something on him, somewhere.'

#

The front door of 51 Ackroyd Street was crashed in less than twenty minutes later. DI Roebuck and his team watched from a vantage point further up the street as specialist firearms officers bundled into the property. While the team had been preparing to go in, Jenny had been back in touch. Latest from Chester was Margaret Bell had a fractured cheekbone and concussion; she was being kept in hospital overnight for observation. The elderly male had gone into cardiac arrest en route to hospital and been pronounced dead on arrival. It was now a murder enquiry.

They could hear his shouts before their man was practically carried out through the front door by two of the entry team. Roebuck strode out from behind an unmarked police car to meet the group at the front gate.

The officer who had hold of one tattooed arm gave Roebuck a sarcastic smile as he forced the elbow upwards.

The cursing and swearing stopped. 'Excuse his head covering. Poor little fellow's a little shy, I think.'

Roebuck regarded the flimsy cloth of the spit-hood. A circular section was flexing in and out with each person's breath. 'Well, well, Mr Kirby, been busy, haven't you?'

'Fuck you, you fucking pig-cunt.'

'Charming.' He glanced at the lead officer. 'All clear?'

'Clear.'

'No one else inside?'

'Just him.'

'Anything I should know about?'

'Have a look in the kitchen. You'll find a hold-all with a dirty great machete in it, plus a hammer and a load of cigarette cartons.'

'That so?' He wondered where the Fireblade was stashed. No sign of it at the front of the house.

'And an upstairs room was padlocked from the outside. We took that off and had a peek. You'll find what's in there quite interesting.'

'OK, thanks for that, boys.'

'Where do you want him?'

'Can you take him to the station at Salford? We've got an incident room set up there.' He turned to the handcuffed man. 'Jason Kirby, I'm Detective Inspector Roebuck. And it's my pleasure to be placing you under arrest.'

CHAPTER 43

Ryan briefly pressed the ringer on the front door of Simone's house.

'Who's there?' asked Carla from the other side.

'Me.'

He heard the rattle of a chain, then a bolt slide back. The door opened a few inches. She looked exhausted with worry. 'Carla.'

The door swung back enough for him to slip through. She immediately closed it and worked the bolt back into place. 'Where've you been? You said you were coming straight here.'

'Yeah, I needed to sort something.'

She turned round and hobbled towards the sofa.

'Is your ankle OK?'

'Just sore. And the size of a melon.' All the curtains were drawn, even though it wasn't fully dark yet. Perching on the sofa, she nodded at her open laptop. 'I've pieced it all together, Ryan. I think, well, I know...' She closed her eyes and wiped at the tears spilling down her cheeks. 'I'm really sorry.'

He crossed the room and tried to put his arms around her, but she raised a hand to fend him off.

'Don't,' she sniffed. 'It's my fault. I caused all this.'

He backed off and lowered himself onto the armrest of the adjacent chair. 'That's bollocks, Carla. This person is fucking crazy. I'll show you the messages he sent before I blocked him. He's not right in the head.'

'I know that. I said he's also been messaging me. I met him, Ryan. He treated me that time the taxi I was in collided with a van.'

'He treated you? What, in an ambulance?'

'At the roadside. He turned up on a motorbike – he's one of those. Simone said he was weird with me then. I don't know. I was drunk – feeling all silly grateful. I gave him a little kiss, Ryan. Just to say thanks. I'm so sorry.'

Ryan looked away. 'What sort of a kiss?' he asked nervously.

'Just on his cheek! I told him how amazing he was. That's when it started.'

'A peck on the cheek? So what? That's no reason –'

'I now realise he started making contact after that. Just crap to my website. Cryptic little messages. I didn't even read most of them; just assumed it was spam. Then he turned up at a job at MediaCity, in the audience. He asked to see me at the end. Said he was my guardian angel.'

'When was this?'

'About a month ago? I didn't have a clue who he was. You know – just some random weirdo. Security escorted him out. That's when it changed: that's when you started getting sent the codes. I think he was using you to get at me.'

Ryan slid off the armrest and into the seat proper. 'Fuck,' he whispered, staring ahead. 'But how did he know we're even together? That I do photography?'

'OK – he has all my details from the accident report form I had to fill out. From when he treated me. I mean everything. Even next-of-kin.'

'He knows who your mum is?'

'Yes. She's not answering, but I left a message. Said not

to answer the door to – what was that?' She looked towards the rear window. 'Did you...?'

The sound came again. A screeching cry that slowly fell away. She looked at Ryan with terrified eyes.

He lifted both hands. 'An owl, Carla. It's an owl.'

'Owls go twit-twoo, don't they? That was not –'

'Tawny owls do that. Barn owls make that scream thing. Trust me – I was into all that with my photography, remember?'

She glanced at the back window again. 'Maybe this isn't such a good place. Right on the edge of a park. Beside a wood.'

'Come on – you were saying about the incident form.'

'I don't know, but I think he's been watching our apartment. It wouldn't be so difficult to latch on to you. I probably even did an Instagram post about my boyfriend's exhibition. Once he knew about that...'

'Jesus. It fits. The messages he sent me.' He took his phone out and a frown came over his face. 'Have you got a signal?'

'It's shit here. You need to be upstairs.'

He sighed in annoyance. 'So, this is from last night. He said, "I will soon have all I want from you." That was after he sent me another code.'

'What does that mean?'

'Don't know. Then he says, "Is it thorny, the tangle –' He stopped talking.

'Ryan, what's the matter?' She glanced nervously at the back window. 'What is it?'

Ryan was still staring at his phone. 'My...my mum's house. It's number fifteen, but she calls it "Brambles".' He met her eyes. 'But you'd only know that from the little placard by the front porch.'

Carla put her head in her hands. 'This is freaking me the fuck out! How much does this person... We need to call the police. Right now.'

Ryan was nodding. 'I'll ring 999.'

'No! Call that detective.'
'Roebuck?'
'Yes. What's the problem with that?'
'I can't stand the bloke.'
'At least he has an idea of what's going on.'
'Yeah, you're right. Can you make it up the stairs?'
'It's fine. As long as I crawl.'

He led the way, phone held before his face.

'Simone's room,' Carla announced behind him. 'On the right. Signal's better in there.'

He had to step over what he realised was Carla's old make up case. Once at Simone's bedroom, his display teetered on three bars. He brought up the most recent of Roebuck's many calls and went to the ring back option.

#

'Fuck, this is seriously twisted,' DC Potter said quietly, eyes drifting over the montage of images stuck to Jason's bedroom wall.

'Like Hannibal Lector's cell,' Roebuck replied. 'How many has he got of her?'

'Ninety, a hundred?'

'And it all relates perfectly to the earlier stuff, doesn't it?' Roebuck said, thinking about the call he'd just taken from Jenny back at the office. She'd accessed the intelligence file on Kirby – stuff from his teenage years that hadn't resulted in any formal action – and discovered a very unsettling incident from when he'd been sixteen. While on a camp that involved male and female Explorer Scouts, Jason had developed what was described as an infatuation with one of the girls: Rebecca Pritchard. She hadn't welcomed the attention and had made a complaint to her leader. Jason had been called up before a panel of staff, reprimanded, and told to keep his distance. But on a later hike across the Kinder plateau, cloud had descended and she'd become detached from her group. In the following search, Jason was the one who'd found her. But she'd panicked and tried to run away from him. Unfortunately, she had been by the Kinder Downfall – a thirty-metre cliff. She'd fallen to her death. Scratches on her wrist were judged to have been made by human fingernails. Jason had been formally interviewed but claimed the injury must have happened when he'd tried to stop her from falling. Nothing could be proven, and it never went to court.

Sarah was treading gingerly towards the computer. 'I dread to think what's going to be on this. Stuff of nightmares, I imagine.'

'Look at those near the skirting board! That's Ryan Lamb. He's scribbled the bloke's eyes out. There – look – he's drawn a knife sticking out of his neck.' His phone started to buzz and he pulled it from his pocket. 'Speak of the devil,' he said to Sarah before taking the call. 'Ryan – so kind of you to call me.'

'Detective Inspector Roebuck?'

'It is I.'

'Sorry – the line isn't so good. Detective Roebuck?'

'Yes.'

'We need to come and see you.'

'And who might we be?'

'Carla and me. I think we might be in danger. Proper danger. There's this person who –'

'Is Carla with you?'

'Yes.'

'And where's that?'

'We're at her friend's house. On the edge of Heaton Mersey Common.'

'Very good. So, what's with the ghosting business?'

'Sorry?'

'Isn't that what you lot call it? When you simply ignore someone's messages?'

'Oh – yeah.'

'Do you always disregard phone calls from members of the police? How many messages have I left you, Ryan?'

'Sorry about that. I kept meaning to ring you but, as I said, we've been stalked. Well, Carla has been. We don't know his name, but we do know he's a paramedic –'

'I have him in custody.'

'What was that? You broke up again.'

'He. Is. In. Custody.'

'You've arrested him?'

Roebuck heard Ryan speaking away from the phone. 'I'll still need to speak with you both, but we've got a bit more to do here. Can you put Carla on the line? I need to have a word.'

'I can't believe it. Do you know the stuff he's been –'

'I do. Is Carla there, please?'

'She just ducked into the toilet. When I told her you'd got him. I think she's being sick?'

'Oh. Is she OK?'

'Stress. Or relief. I don't know: both?'

'Get her to call me as soon as she comes out.'

'Of course. Thanks, Mr... Detective Roebuck.'

'My pleasure.' He ended the call and floated a sigh in Sarah's direction. 'Jesus Christ, why do they turn every comment into a question?' He put on a whiney voice. '"I think she's being sick?" Don't fucking ask me! You're the one who's with her. Bloody snowflakes.'

'A bit harsh.'

Roebuck shrugged. 'But fair. Let's get back to the station. See what this Kirby character is prepared to tell us.'

CHAPTER 44

Ryan let his back slide down the wall until he was sitting on the carpet. He lifted his phone and kissed the edge of its casing. They'd got him. They'd bloody got him! 'You OK, Carla?'

'Two minutes!'

The skin of his throat stretched and tightened as he tilted his head back, eyes shut in relief. Thank God. From the bathroom came the flush of the toilet, then the sound of a tap running. He listened to the noise, imagining himself beside a trickling brook somewhere nice. Maybe the Peak District. Fuck it, the Alps. They should go. Wander in meadows. Drink lovely wine and eat cheese. Gorge themselves. It seemed like so long since they'd done anything like that.

As the gurgle of water died away, he thought he heard the sound of a motorbike. That weird revving bikers sometimes did as they came to a stop. The door opened. Carla had some colour back in her cheeks and her hair was damp where she'd run wet fingers through it.

'Can you believe they got him?' he asked, putting his phone aside and looking up at her with a crooked smile.

She dropped to her knees. He could smell toothpaste

as she curled her arms around his neck, pressed his face to her breast.

'It's over,' he said, relishing the contact. Feeling her warmth. He slid an arm around her waist and they stayed like that, neither saying a word.

'I found that memory stick,' she eventually said. 'In with the old batteries.'

He sagged against her.

'He set you up,' she said, kissing his hair. 'It was part of his plan.'

'Even so. I fucking hate myself. I took them before trying to help those people.'

'Shush. This isn't about what you did and didn't do. It's about that... that horrific... I don't even know how to describe him. Fucking monster.'

He leaned his head back to make eye contact. 'But I want you to know I'm ashamed of the photos. All of them. If I could destroy each and every print in the Sussman Gallery, I would. They're not what I'm about. *Vulpine Plunderer*, when I think about it, for me, the drunk guy is a prop. It's the fox that makes the shot for me. It's always been animals, Carla. I realise that now.'

'What's going to happen with Ivan Sussman?'

'To be honest? I don't really give a shit. None of that stuff is me. Especially not the shots I got because of the tips.'

She smiled. 'I am so bloody relieved to hear you say that.'

They gazed at each other for a few seconds.

'I was scared I was losing you, Carla,' he whispered.

'The same.'

'You know, I couldn't live without you, don't you?'

She smiled down at him. 'Me too. You know, there's a futon up in the attic bedroom? It's beneath a skylight. Very romantic.'

He shuffled himself into a kneeling position. How long

is it since we last had sex? 'That sounds like the best place to be on earth.'

She was starting to unbutton her blouse when his phone gave a double buzz. He immediately looked down at it.

'Ryan,' she whispered. 'Whoever it is can wait.'

He reached out a hand. 'That's not a message. It's...' He swiped across to a little icon of a camera lens and tapped it. An image immediately took over the screen. The infrared rendered everything in shades of grey and green. Everything except the two black discs where the person's eyes should have been. A mass of bushes was behind him. Faint tree silhouettes loomed large. He was in a crouched position, one hand on the lawn.

'What is that?' Carla asked.

Ryan was climbing to his feet. 'I set up two camera traps. One at the front, one at the back.' He waggled his phone. 'Bluetoothed to this.'

She shook her head. 'But that's him. It's him! Are you saying –'

'Just stay here! Let me check.' He bounded down the stairs, glancing at his screen when he reached the bottom. Back garden. Had to be. He raced to the rear of the cottage, found himself in a narrow little kitchen with a door at the far end. He rushed across the tiled floor and immediately checked it for locks. Bolted at the top and bottom. There was a small window to the side, a little red and white chequered curtain drawn across it. He slid the material aside to see another man's face looking in.

#

When the curtain was pulled back, I didn't expect to see him. Not Ryan. He wasn't meant to be here. He wasn't part of our lives anymore. The idiot's mouth opened in a gasp and his face moved away from the glass. That's when I saw her. She was in the kitchen doorway, and she looked so frightened. So very frightened.

Even though she appeared barely strong enough to stand, she started to shriek over and over. Get away. Get away. Leave us alone. Just leave us alone. Ryan span round and ran at her, grabbed her by the shoulders and started forcing her backwards. She tried to resist him, started shouting out again. I hate you. I fucking hate you.

'What are you doing to her?' I bellowed as loud as I could. 'Don't you touch her!'

He shoved her round the corner and I couldn't see her anymore. My Carla. The Stanley knife was in my hand and I turned it round, used its stubby end to smash the glass. I could still hear her voice. No, no, no, she was crying. Please no. I reached through, bits of glass going into my skin as I tried to find a latch for the door. No good. When I brought my forearm back out, there were a lot of cuts. Deep enough for sutures. I tried kicking at it a few times, but it didn't move. Inside, he was hurting her. I knew he was hurting her. I brought my face to the smashed window and shouted through it. 'Don't you touch her! I'm coming, Carla! Carla, I'm here!'

#

I saw a phone beside the TV. A landline! Simone had a landline. Carla was just standing on the spot, shouting the word 'no' over and over. The receiver felt ridiculously chunky as I picked it up. 'Lock the front door! Both bolts!' The thing wasn't making a sound. Wasn't it meant to make a sound? I tried pressing the green button a few times. Then 999. From the kitchen came the sound of a window being smashed. 'Can't get the fucker to –'

'He's cut the line,' Carla sobbed next to me. 'We need to get upstairs. Phone from there.'

His voice boomed out from the kitchen again. He sounded savage. Demented. Saying he was coming. Every time he shouted her name, she flinched.

'Let's go!' I helped her towards the stairs. 'Come on. Up, up, up!'

I left her at the top and ran into Simone's bedroom. Downstairs had gone quiet. Roebuck's phone rang twice before going to voicemail. You are fucking kidding me. 'He's here! The person who's been doing this is here!' I went back to the doorway. Carla was sitting on the stairs to the attic, hugging her knees. 'What's the address?'

'Two. Pinfold Lane.'

'Two, Pinfold Lane, Heaton Mersey.' I cut the call and peered down the stairs. Still no sounds. Had he, maybe, gone?

#

DI Roebuck and DC Potter trotted down the stairs to the custody suite. 'Where's my boy?' Roebuck asked, scanning the panel of TV screens that displayed a view of each cell.

'Number three,' the custody sergeant replied. 'He's refusing to say a thing. I mean, not a word. Wouldn't confirm his name, age, address: nothing.'

'Changed his tune from when we arrested him, then,' Roebuck responded. 'Wouldn't stop with the spitting and abuse.' He studied the interior of cell three. Kirby had taken the thin plastic mattress off the bunk and placed it on the floor. He was stretched out, hands behind his head, eyes closed. Certainly didn't look like a stranger to all this. It seemed incredible he didn't have a single conviction to his name.

'Those tattoos on his arms,' Potter said uneasily. 'They look like prison tats, to me. Weird.'

Roebuck nodded. 'Know what you mean.'

She took out a print of the photo from his Ambulance Service file. 'He looks younger in this. Less rough, too.' She stared at the screen. 'Maybe he's been using a lot of drugs recently?'

Roebuck shrugged. 'Maybe.'

'Good luck with any interview,' the custody sergeant muttered. 'I think you might not even be getting the obligatory "no comment" from this one.'

'Doesn't really matter what he does or doesn't say,' Roebuck stated. 'The amount of evidence we've got on him? He is royally fucked.'

Back up in the office, Roebuck plucked his phone from the desk. 'Oops. Missed call from Ryan's number. That was probably Carla Bell.'

CHAPTER 45

There were two wicker chairs on the patio area. They hardly weighed a thing. In the corner were plant pots. Three in a neat little group. I picked up the largest one and heaved it at the living room window. The glass shattered and the curtains folded around so it disappeared from view. There was a massive thud as it hit the carpet beyond. I used one of the chairs to smash away the rest of the glass from the edges of the frame, then climbed up onto the windowsill. More stabs of pain. Shards of glass clinging to my palms, sticking out from my knees. I swept the curtains aside and jumped down. Soil was all over the floor, the plant pot beside an armchair. I brushed my hands back and forth along the top of a sofa, leaving a lot of red smears. Where was she? Where had he taken her? I went to the front door. The bolt was drawn across. They were still in here somewhere. 'Carla! Try and make a sound, Carla! Let me know where you are! Ryan, if you hurt her, I will carve your fucking face off. You hear?'

Kitchen was empty. I walked back into the main living area and looked up the narrow flight of stairs.

#

When we heard a big window downstairs being smashed in, Carla leaned the side of her head against the wall. 'Are they coming?'

I pointed upwards and whispered. 'The attic.'

She shook her head. 'We'll be trapped.'

'We can climb out onto the roof! You said there's a skylight. Come on.' I helped her round, and she started crawling up. Her make-up case was on the floor. Hard plastic with metal edges at each corner. It might have to do as a weapon. I grabbed it and, once on the bottom step, twisted round and swung the door shut. The key was like one you'd use for a doll's house. The door itself was hardly thicker than cardboard. I locked it anyway and crept to the top.

Carla was standing on a futon, struggling with the handle of the window. 'I can't do this.'

'Here, let me.' I placed the case on the floor and she moved aside as I swung the window up until the hinge clicked. We had a gap of about seventy-five centimetres to try and get through.

His voice rose up to us. He was in the house. Asking Carla to make a sound. Shouting stuff at me. I got my head and shoulders out into the cool evening air. A stream of traffic was moving along the Kingsway just a few hundred metres away. The tiles leading down to the roof edge were steep. Really steep. Angling my head, I tried to work things out. If I climbed through first, and lay down at the side of the window, then reached back through, I could help Carla out. We could then close the window. We couldn't lock it, but I could lean on the lower edge and stop him from opening it. That could work. I ducked my head back inside. 'I'll go first, OK? Once I'm out –'

Her head shook. 'I can't get up there. Not with this ankle. He wants me. You get out. I'll wait for him here.'

'No fucking way. We can both get out.'

Banging sounds were now coming from the floor below. He was turning the bedrooms over, trying to find out where we were hiding. Carla reached up and pressed her hands to the sides of my face. 'I'm his obsession,' she whispered. 'You've heard what he's been saying. He thinks he loves me. He thinks you're stopping us – me and him – from being together. In his mind, that's what's real. I'll go with him. He's not going to hurt me.'

'He tried to push you under a tram.'

'That was him losing control. Because he heard me talking about you. Trust me. I know this will work.'

'You don't know what he's planning. It could be anything.'

'Listen, you need to get out. I'll handle him. Go!'

I looked uncertainly at the small rectangle of dark sky above me. 'This is –'

'Go,' she pleaded. 'You haven't got long.'

I levered my elbows to either side of the window's opening and started swinging my legs about, scrabbling for a foothold. Carla's hands closed round one of my shins and I pressed down against it. The tiles felt very smooth beneath my palms and I looked down the slope to where they abruptly ended. How high was the drop if I lost my grip and slid down? The wail of a siren came from the Kingsway. I could see the pulse of blue lights speeding along it. Too late. You're too fucking late. 'You need to push me higher,' I said over my shoulder.

'I can't.'

'Carla! Is that you? Carla! Carla!' There was a rattle as he tried the attic door.

Suddenly, I felt a pulling at my legs. I slid back into the room and half-fell onto the futon. Carla was looking down at me, eyes wide.

'What are you doing?' I asked.

'Carla! Are you up there? Can you hear me?'

'Lie down,' she hissed. 'Lay your head over the edge of the mattress.'

She was yanking her make-up box open, pulling out brushes, a pair of scissors, little plastic trays. Her fingers settled on a small bottle of blackish liquid. A label on the side said, Stage Blood – Supreme Dark. 'I'll say I knocked you out.'

This was crazy. I got on my hands and knees. 'Carla?'

She pressed the nozzle into my hair and squeezed. Cold liquid seeped across my scalp. A drip emerged to tickle at my eyebrow. 'This is good,' she nodded. 'Lie down. Close your eyes.' As soon as my head was over the mattress edge, she yelled out. 'Just leave me alone!'

'Carla! It's OK, Carla!' It sounded like he was trying to tear the door off its hinges.

She looked about, picked up a bowl of dried flowers and smashed it against the wall.

The impacts on the door picked up speed. Wood started to splinter. She draped a throw over her make-up case and hopped across to the top step. 'Gabriel? Gabriel! Quickly, we need to go.' The stairs began to swallow her as she eased herself down them. Outside, the sound of sirens became audible again, much louder now.

'Carla! Are you OK? Did he hurt you?'

'No. Quickly, before he comes around!'

'What did you do?'

'Hit him. Over the head. Come on, let's go!'

'I want to see him.'

'There's no time!' The top of her head reappeared. 'Gabriel, please – let's go!'

'I want to see him.'

She had retreated to the top step. A look of panic was thrown in my direction. 'There,' she said, gesturing loosely towards me. 'OK?'

Heart now battering my chest, I lowered my eyelids. My view of the world narrowed to a hazy glimmer. I could just make things out as, bit by bit, he came into view. Blood had streaked his forehead and both cheeks. Drips were falling steadily from his fingertips. He stared directly at me for several seconds. Apart from the sound of approaching sirens, the only noise was his jagged breathing and the tap-tap-tappity-tap of blood landing on the carpet.

'What did you hit him with?'

'A bowl. There – those pieces on the carpet! Gabriel, take me away from this. I want you to take me away now. Please.'

His head swung slowly from side to side. Could he tell? Was he able to see my eyes weren't properly shut? 'Not yet. He was hurting you, Carla. I'll never let him do that again.' Something was in his right hand. There was a metallic clicking sound. A triangular blade extended from his grip.

'Oh my God,' Carla said. 'Leave him. Just leave him!'

He took an unsteady step towards me. 'I'll be quick. I know how this is done.'

#

The stench coming off him. I almost retched. As he started shuffling towards Ryan, I readied myself to plead with him again. The words wouldn't even form in my head. I suddenly felt exhausted. It was useless. He would never stop. This fucking…this fucking maniac was going to rip our lives apart. Worse, he was going to kill Ryan. Simple as that. Then maybe me. My legs started to tremble. I so wanted to curl up into a ball. Squeeze my eyes closed. If I did, might I wake up? Back in my bed at mum's? That's where I could be, couldn't I? If I wished it to happen hard enough.

#

Should I let him get closer to me and then kick out with both legs? Or sit up now and try to reason with him? He was adjusting his grip on, what I could see now, was a Stanley knife. Just as I was about to open my eyes properly and beg him to leave us alone, Carla's hand lifted above her head. She brought it down on the back of his neck. His mouth opened wide, but no sound came out. He turned. Carla had clapped both hands over her mouth. The handle of her scissors – the ones from her makeup case – were sticking out above the collar of his leather jacket.

'Carla, what did you do?' Tentatively, he felt along his shoulder with the fingers of his left hand. They came to a stop on the pair of little metal ovals. 'Carla?'

'You're a demon!' she screamed suddenly. 'I fucking hate you!'

Slowly, he pulled the scissors out. 'You... you were lying?' His voice had the whine of a lost schoolboy as he briefly examined the blood-stained blades before letting them fall to the floor. 'You were lying?' His voice had dropped. 'You lied?' Words now a snarl. 'You lied!'

I saw the hand holding the Stanley knife start to twitch back and forth at his side. Carla pressed herself against the far wall, squeezing her eyes shut. 'Just fuck off,' she whispered.

He was moaning now. A keening noise coming from deep in his throat.

I sat up and looked to my left. A rack of dumbbells. Like the ones my dad used to have in the garage. But these were pink, and smaller. I got to my feet. The one at the end nearest to me had the words '8 kg' printed on the side. My fingers curled round the handle and I lifted it clear. All the times dad used to challenge me to arm curls, sneering at how few I could manage. But I could lift this one just fine. I focused on the back of his head. Do it, Ryan. Just fucking do it. The end of the dumbbell connected with his skull, but not properly and I couldn't stop my hand from continuing its swing. The hard plastic crunched into the shin of my left leg. Pain, like lightning, travelling up to my hip. He took a stumbling step forward and one of his legs folded. I dropped the dumbbell and it rolled to the top of the stairs and then bounced its way down. He had a palm flat against the floor, making a tripod of both legs and one arm, struggling to get upright. To grab another dumbbell meant putting my weight on my left leg. I tried, but found myself pitching to the side, shoulder connecting with the edge of the futon. Glancing back, I saw him looming over me, swaying slightly, eyes bulging as the knife lifted. Carla sank to the floor behind him and her hand started sweeping across the carpet. I scrambled towards the rack of weights, knowing he just had to manage one step and that blade would be going into me. I registered a rapid patting sound, followed by a groan. The stab of his knife didn't come. Carla was on her knees, plunging the blades of the scissors in and out of his thigh. He tottered back towards the top of the stairs and only the banister stopped him from tumbling down. A river of blood was already making its way down his trousers. He stared at it in confusion as my fingers latched round the next dumbbell.

He regarded Carla, who was still on her knees brandishing the scissors back and forth.

'Just…just,' she sobbed, 'fucking die, will you?'

He seemed to flinch at her words and that low whine started up again, growing louder, turning into a suppressed scream. Eyes locked on Carla, he lifted his knife hand.

I forced my leg to take a step in his direction. 'Hey!'

His head started to turn, eyes not following fast enough. This time the end of the dumbbell hit him square in the forehead. The sound it made: I was ten again, in a French supermarket; a huge melon toppling from a display and hitting the hard floor. His head snapped back round. He was facing Carla once more and he dropped to his knees. He stayed like that for a moment, as if in prayer. As if in prayer to Carla, who was now shuffling away from him towards the wall. Twin lines of blood snaked from his nostrils and across his lips as he keeled forwards onto his face, knife bouncing from his fingers across the blood-spattered carpet.

Carla struggled to her feet and we stared down at him in silence, waiting to see what he would do next. His shoulders raised and lowered a few times as if he was readying himself to get back to his feet. I lifted the dumbbell, so it was directly above the back of his head.

The moment he moved, I would cave it in. But his breathing slowed. He made a few wet coughing sounds, and his arms and legs began to tremble and twitch. A long, slow breath seeped out and, finally, he lay still.

I placed the dumbbell on the floor and reached my hand towards Carla, helped her step across his body. Then we were half-stumbling, half-sliding down the stairs towards the sound of sirens.

EPILOGUE

The sunlight making its way through the row of cream-coloured blinds filled the apartment with a peaceful glow.

'You OK?' Ryan asked.

Carla nodded.

'Sure? I don't need this cushion.'

'One's fine, Ry. Honestly.' She regarded her foot where it lay across the cushion on the coffee table. 'Look.' She rotated lifted her heel and rotated the foot three-hundred-and-sixty degrees. 'Doesn't hurt.'

He sat back on the sofa beside her. 'Still a bit swollen, though. Your ankle.'

'The physio said it would be for a while. It's only trapped fluid.' She leaned into him 'Funny, it's what Roebuck did for me. When he turned up.'

'What did he do?' Ryan's voice had tightened a notch.

'Put a cushion out for me.' She placed a hand on his leg. Felt the tension in his muscles. 'He's not that bad. Couldn't have been more apologetic.'

'You mean, without actually saying sorry?'

She sighed. 'Let's not go there again. So, Quigly. You were saying…'

Ryan retrieved his phone. 'This is his website. He only represents a few photographers, but they are, like, really, really well known. And all so different.'

'Let's have a look at the gallery, then.'

Ryan clicked on it. A row of images popped up of the man who'd approached him in the Sussman Gallery. In each one, he was standing alongside someone whose smile looked utterly genuine. 'He picks and chooses his clients, Carla. That's how good his reputation is. Check this quote. It's from Peter Fridaman, who I have been following for bloody years. "Without Nick, I've no idea where I'd be. He's a bloody legend."'

'And he's picked you,' Carla stated.

The buzzer went and her head immediately turned. 'That'll be her!' she said, face breaking into a smile.

Ryan got to his feet and walked over to the console. Simone's afro filled most of the screen. 'Come on up!'

She was at their door seconds later. 'Ryan.' Her arms lifted and she pulled him in close. 'How are you?'

'You know...pretty good, actually.'

She held him tight for a few more seconds. 'And...?'

He stepped aside. 'On the sofa.'

Simone strode into the apartment, saw Carla and broke into a run. 'Have I been dying to see you!' She practically vaulted the armrest, and the two of them grabbed hold of each other.

'Tea, Simone?' Ryan asked, smiling at the sight of them.

She peeled her cheek away from Carla's. 'Tea? I want to know how soon we can all go clubbing!'

Carla giggled. 'Have a brew, for God's sake!'

Simone waved a hand in defeat. 'OK, then. So,' she glanced round the apartment, eyes settling momentarily on the lowered blinds. 'How is it all? Really, how is it?'

Carla's smile was tinged with sadness. 'It's OK, considering. We're both seeing this counsellor who is amazing. I've got this thing about windows, though. Don't think that one's going away in a hurry.'

Simone clutched her hand. 'I couldn't believe it. Just…beyond belief.'

'You saw it though, Simone. The danger. You saw it.'

Simone rolled her eyes. 'Goes with the job, babe. We get told what to look out for. And your mum, how's she?'

'Not bad, I suppose. She's moving into sheltered housing. It's been on the cards for a while. What happened? It just decided it for her. And Domino's going with her, which is good.'

Simone nodded in understanding. 'Well, you two have got this place looking so nice. The blinds and those new lamps. It's all very serene.'

'We're not staying,' Carla replied. 'There's a buyer. We're off.'

'Sorry?'

'We've sold it,' Carla said, looking amused at Simone's shocked expression. 'We're getting out of Manchester. Heading to the coast.'

Simone's eyes moved to Ryan, then back to Carla. 'Which coast? Where?'

'Anglesey,' Ryan said. 'We've got this bungalow. You can actually see the ocean.'

'Nothing overlooking us,' Carla added. 'And wait until you see the sunsets.'

Simone's hands lifted. 'Slow up. Please. Where even is this place?'

'Anglesey?' Ryan put the cups down and sank into the armchair. 'Couple of hours away. It's an island off the coast of Wales. A bridge goes over. Photographer's paradise.'

Simone turned to Carla. 'And what will you do?'

'I've got a job at this exclusive spa. Trearddur Bay. It's very posh. You will love it, Simone. Weekend breaks. There's a spare room.' She wiggled her toes. 'And I contacted this theatre in Bangor, which isn't far. They were very interested in my qualifications.'

'I...I don't know what to say. It sounds lovely. But...it's rural, right?' She looked at Ryan. 'What will you...you know...photograph?'

'Oh, loads of stuff. Seals, dolphins, birds by the thousand. Red squirrels. Puffins.'

'Wildlife? Real wildlife? Not,' she gestured to the window, 'the human sort that's out there?'

He shook his head. 'I've got this agent taking me on. It's the nature stuff he wants me for.'

'That's a relief.' She glanced briefly at Carla. 'It never really struck me as your thing.'

'What's that?' Ryan asked.

'You know,' Simone said cautiously, 'wandering the streets late at night.'

'The Midnight Rambler?' Ryan managed a grin. 'That is definitely over.'

THE END

KILLING THE BEASTS – FIRST NOVEL IN THE DI JOHN SPICER SERIES

The Commonwealth Games have come to Manchester and the city is buzzing.

Caught up in the commercial feeding frenzy is Tom Benwell, an advertising executive. But the pressure is getting to Tom - too many deals to make and lies to tell. Meanwhile his friend, DI Jon Spicer, is on the fast track, showing a love for the job that borders on obsession, according to his girlfriend, Alice.

Then, in the aftermath of the Games, a string of brutal murders shatters the city's newfound spirit. Spicer gets the case. Each victim has been murdered in the same bizarre and grotesque manner, yet the lack of motive leaves the police utterly baffled.

With the race on to catch the killer, both men find themselves caught up in a nightmare where the most innocent action can cost the highest price.

KILLING THE BEASTS

PROLOGUE

Leaning forward on the sofa, she gratefully accepted the stick of gum, unwrapped it and then folded it into her mouth. 'Thanks,' she said breathlessly, looking expectantly at her visitor and eagerly chewing.

'My pleasure,' came the reply from the smartly dressed man sitting opposite her. They continued looking at each other for a moment longer. 'Now, if you could just get . . .'

'Oh God, yes, sorry! It's upstairs.' She jumped to her feet. 'I'm all excited. Sorry.'

He smiled. 'No problem.'

She almost skipped across the room, then ran up the stairs. While she was gone the man stood up, walked over to her living room window and checked the street outside. By the time she returned he was sitting down once again.

'Here,' she said, handing him a small booklet.

'Great.' He looked up at her with a slightly embarrassed expression. 'Do you mind if I have a cup of tea before we get started?'

'Oh!' She jumped up again, her dressing gown falling slightly open to reveal a flash of upper thigh. 'I'm so rude. Sorry. Milk? Sugar?'

'Milk and two sugars, thanks.'

Flustered, she paced quickly down the short corridor to the kitchen, bare feet slapping against the lino as she crossed the room. She plucked two mugs from the dirty crockery piled up in the sink and quickly washed them out. As she waited for the kettle to boil she jigged from foot to foot, occasionally taking a deep breath and running her hands through her spiky blonde hair.

A few minutes later she walked back in, a red flush now evident on her throat and cheeks. 'Here you go.' She placed a mug decorated with a cartoon snail on the low table in front of the man's knees. Now furiously chewing on the gum, she went to sit down again but, on impulse, veered towards the hi-fi system in the corner and turned up the music.

'God, I feel like I could dance,' she said urgently, blowing her breath out and running her fingers through her hair once again. 'Is it hot in here? Are you hot?'

The man looked around the room as if heat was a visible thing. 'No,' he replied with a little shake of his head.

'I feel hot,' she said, placing her mug on the table, then waving one hand a little too energetically at her cheek and pulling distractedly at the neck of her dressing gown. The man kept his head lowered, pretending to search for a pen in his jacket pocket.

The girl went to sit down, stumbling against the leg of the coffee table. 'Whoops!' she said with a strange giggle, though panic was beginning to show in her eyes. 'I . . . I'm dizzy.'

The room had begun to shift in and out of focus and her breath wouldn't come properly. She leaned forward and tried to steady herself by putting one hand on the arm of the sofa.

The man watched impassively.

Now visibly distressed, she attempted a half turn to sit down, but her coordination was going and she missed the sofa, crashing onto the carpet. As she lay on her back, her eyes rolled up into her head and then closed completely.

The man calmly got to his feet and put his briefcase on the table. After entering the combination for the lock, he opened it up and removed a long pair of stainless-steel pincers from inside.

CHAPTER 1

30 October 2002

Jon Spicer was driving back to the station when he heard the Community Support Officer's call for help on his police radio. The CSO said he was outside a house in which a corpse had just been discovered. He said the dead girl's mother was still inside, refusing to leave her daughter's body. He went on to explain to the operator that his patrol partner was in the kitchen, trying to comfort her. His voice was high and panicky.

When the address in Berrybridge Road was read out Jon realized he was just a few streets away. Telling the operator he would attend the scene, Jon turned off the main road, cut down a side street and pulled up outside the house.

As he got out of his car and straightened his tie, the sight of a very young and nervous-looking officer confronted him. The officer was trying to reason with an irate woman, who stood with one hand rocking a buggy, stout legs planted firmly apart. As the officer repeated that she wasn't allowed past, the red-faced toddler in the buggy leaned back, shut its eyes and started to bawl.

'You can't stop me getting in my own sodding house,' the woman said, holding another chocolate button in front of the angry infant's face. 'The kid wants his lunch – you can hear, can't you?' In an attempt to keep the cold autumnal breeze off him, she began tucking the tattered blanket around his legs. 'It's all right, Liam.'

Crafty little shit, thought Jon Spicer, noticing how he immediately stopped crying when the button appeared. If his eyes were shut in genuine distress, he wouldn't have known the button was there. Jon had accepted long ago that deviousness was as much a part of human make-up as kindness or joy. What always amazed him was how early people appeared to learn the process of manipulation.

'Sorry madam, we won't be much longer.' Jon intervened, a placatory tone in his voice. Hoping that, if he and Alice had the baby they were trying for, it didn't turn out like that one, he guided the CSO out of earshot. 'Hello. My name's Jon Spicer.'

The young officer glanced at Jon's warrant card, saw his rank, and replied, 'CSO Whyte and I'm glad to see you, sir.'

'You said on the radio that you heard wailing noises from inside the house. Then what?'

He took out his notebook as if in court. 'Yes, that was at 9.55 a.m. We proceeded up the driveway to the front door, which we found to be ajar. On receiving no response from the person in distress within the property, we proceeded inside and found a middle-aged woman sitting on the floor of the living room hugging a deceased woman of around twenty. My patrol partner, CSO Payne, entered the room and crouched down to check for a pulse. At that point she noticed thick white matter at the back of the deceased woman's mouth.' He looked up and breaking from his notes, said, 'It was hanging open you see, though I didn't catch sight of it myself. When we separated the mother from the body, the dead girl's head lay back on the carpet and I couldn't see in.'

Jon nodded. 'So you called for assistance. And no one has been in there except you and your patrol partner?'

'Yes, that's correct, sir.'

'And this woman has confirmed the deceased is her daughter and that her daughter lives in the house?'

'Yes.'

'And no one else lives there?'

'That's correct.'

'OK, good work. Well done.'

A smile broke out momentarily across the young man's face. Then, remembering the gravity of the situation, he reorganized his features into an expression of appropriate seriousness.

The toddler started its bawling once again. His mum gave in and shoved the entire packet of chocolate buttons into his hands. The crying immediately stopped and Jon thought: another victory to the little people. 'So, we've just got to keep Lucifer and his mum, Mrs Beelzebub, at bay for a bit longer,' he murmured, turning back to the woman.

'OK, madam. I'm afraid, because you share a driveway with your neighbour's house – and she's died in what could be suspicious circumstances – I'm having to declare the driveway and front gardens a designated crime scene. Have you a friend you could stay with just while we search this area in front of the house?'

'Pissing hell,' said the woman, pulling a mobile from the pocket of her padded jacket and dialling a number. 'Janine? It's me, Sue. That little blonde ravehead next door won't be keeping me awake with any more loud music. She's turned up dead and the police won't let me up the driveway and into my own frigging house. Can I come round for a cuppa and to give our Liam his lunch? Cheers.'

'Thanks very much, madam,' Jon said, making a mental

note of the ravehead description. 'If I can have your number we'll call as soon as access is possible.'

He jotted it down and she trundled moodily off up the road, the buggy's wheels picking up bits of sodden brown leaves littering the street.

'Right,' said Jon, looking at the house. 'Have you checked the rest of the property?'

'No,' said CSO Whyte, looking alarmed that he'd failed in his duty.

'That's fine,' said Jon. But, having been caught by surprise on a recent murder investigation when the offender had still been hiding in the upstairs of the house, Jon was taking no chances. 'What's your patrol partner's name again?'

'CSO Margaret Payne. She's comforting the girl's mother in the kitchen.'

Jon trod carefully across the patchy lawn, eyes on the driveway for any suspicious objects. When he reached the front doorstep he called over his shoulder, 'CSO Whyte, only people with direct permission from me are allowed past, understood?'

'Yes sir,' he replied, checking down the street as if there was a danger of being charged by a curious crowd.

Pushing from his mind the information he had been given by the officer, Jon turned his attention to the front door. He saw that there were no signs of a forced entry. He stepped into the hallway, keeping his feet as close to the skirting board as possible. Immediately he was struck by an odd smell – sharp and slightly fruity. For some reason he was reminded of DIY superstores. As he made his way along the hall he examined the carpet for anything unusual. Reaching the doorway to the front room, he glanced in. The body of a young white female with bleached spiky hair lay partially on its side by the coffee table. Her pale pink dressing gown was crumpled up around her legs and had partly fallen open at the front, revealing her left breast. He didn't know if it was the lack of obvious injuries, but she didn't look like she was dead. Unconscious, perhaps, but not dead.

He carried on into the kitchen where CSO Payne was sitting, holding the mother's hand across the table. Aware that a six-foot-four stranger with a beaten-up face suddenly stepping into the room could prove unsettling for both women, Jon gently coughed before quietly announcing, 'Hello, my name is Jon Spicer. I'm a detective with Greater Manchester Police.'

The woman lowered a damp handkerchief and looked up at him. Her face had that emptiness which shock and grief instils, but her eyes were alert. He felt them flickering over his face, settling for a second on the lump in the bridge of his nose, which had been broken in a rugby match.

'Could I ask your name, please?' he continued.

'Diane Mather,' she whispered, reaching out and taking a sip of tea from a mug with a snail on it.

'OK, Diane,' said Jon, walking round the table and checking the back door. A bolt was slid across the top and a key was in the lock. 'Has anyone touched this door?' he asked them both.

CSO Payne answered no and he looked at Diane, who also shook her head.

'And have you been in any other parts of the house apart from the hallway, here and the front room?'

'No.' Now she was watching him a little more closely.

Jon walked from the kitchen. Carefully he climbed the stairs, pausing when his head was level with the landing to check where the doors were. The first led into a little bathroom: no one behind the shower curtain. The next was the spare room, only just big enough for a clothes horse that was adorned with vest tops, socks and knickers. The final room was the main bedroom, fairly tidy except for the middle drawer of the chest in the corner. It hung half open, and a few photo albums and booklets lay haphazardly on the corner of the bed, as if dumped there in a hurry. Jon checked under the bed and in the wardrobe. Satisfied no one else was in the house, he walked over to the bedside table and looked in the ashtray. Amongst the Marlboro Light cigarette butts were a few crumpled bits of foil, dried brown crusts on one side. A plastic tube lay next to the small alarm clock.

Jon shook his head. From his earliest days as a uniformed officer, he had watched as more and more drugs crept into Manchester. Now, along with the alcohol riots on Friday and Saturday nights, they were dealing with the devastating effects that crack, heroin, speed and God knew what else were having on people's lives.

At the window he looked down to the road below and saw the CSOs' supervisor had arrived. He went back down the stairs and headed outside.

'Sergeant Evans,' the older man said, shaking Jon's hand over the police tape now cordoning off the driveway and front garden.

'DI Spicer, MISU. I was just passing when I heard the radio call.'

The sergeant nodded. 'So, we have a body inside?'

'Yup,' Jon replied. 'Apparently her throat is blocked with a load of white stuff.' Jon looked at CSO Whyte. 'Could it not have been saliva? An allergic reaction or something?'

The officer looked at him as if he had asked a rhetorical question and was about to supply the answer.

Sergeant Evans then dropped a question into the silence. 'When CSO Payne checked for a pulse, did she say how cold the body felt?'

CSO Whyte thought for a second. 'No. She was trying to get the mother away from the body when she spotted the white stuff . . .' Abruptly, he stopped talking.

'What?' Jon prompted.

The officer stumbled slightly with his words. 'She didn't actually check for a pulse. But the mum – she kept on saying, "She's dead. She's dead." So we just sort of assumed—'

'Jesus Christ,' said Jon. He went to his car, grabbed a pair of latex gloves from inside and hurried back into the house. In the hallway he spotted a pile of women's magazines by the telephone. One by one he laid them across the living room floor, creating a series of stepping stones that enabled him to get to the girl without treading on the carpet.

As he got closer to her, he noticed that the strange smell was getting stronger. As he'd noted before, the dressing gown was crumpled, but he couldn't tell whether she had been assaulted, dragged there, or the disturbance to her clothing was from where her mother had been hugging her.

He crouched down and checked for a pulse. The skin was cold to the touch. He let out a sigh, then examined the rest of her more closely.

No defence wounds to her forearms or hands, no obvious sign of any injury at all. He leaned in for a closer look at her fingers. Apart from being bluish in colour, the nails were fine – no debris under them or damage caused by a struggle.

Next he looked at her face. Her eyes were shut, a few small red dots around them. Mouth slightly open, lips also a faint blue. No blood, saliva or vomit on her lips. No bruising to her throat. Getting up he made his way back across the magazines and into the kitchen. 'CSO Payne,' he said, pointing to her utility belt, 'could I borrow your torch, please?'

In the front room he switched it on and directed the beam into the girl's mouth. Peering in, he saw the back of her throat was completely clogged with something white and viscous. The substance had completely blocked her airways. Death by suffocation? Some sort of lung purge or bizarre vomit?

He bent forward so his head was just above the carpet.

Holding the torch to one side he swept the beam backwards and forwards across the floor, looking to see if the light picked out any tiny fragments lying on the carpet. Nothing apart from fragments of cigarette ash and an old chewing gum wrapper. Standing up, he noted the bin in the corner was full of crushed cans, empty cigarette packets, bits of cigarette paper and other pieces of rubbish. Next to it were a couple of empty three-litre cider bottles.

Back in the kitchen he sat down and quietly asked the mother, 'Do you know what time it was when you discovered your daughter?'

'About quarter to ten,' she replied shakily, stubbing a cigarette out in the full ashtray.

'And you found her in the front room?'

She nodded once.

'On the floor?'

'Yes, lying on her back with her arms out by her sides.'

'How did you get into the house?'

'I have a key. We were going shopping together in town.'

'Was the door locked when you arrived?'

Another nod.

Keeping eye contact, Jon continued. 'OK, Mrs Mather, it's best you go now and let us take over. Margaret here will accompany you down to the station. We'll need to take a statement. Is that OK with you?'

'Yes.' Then she whispered beseechingly, 'What happened to my little girl?'

'We'll find out, Mrs Mather. We'll find out,' Jon said, a note of firmness now in his voice.

As they stood, CSO Payne asked, 'Can we call anyone to meet you at the station?'

She shook her head and Jon wondered if it was an unwillingness to share with anyone else what had happened to her daughter.

He led the way back towards the front door, CSO Payne with her arm round the mother's shoulders. He paused in the doorway to the living room, subtly trying to discourage any further contact. 'We'll be as fast as we can, Mrs Mather. You'll have your daughter back as quickly as possible.' No mention of the coming autopsy, the gutting of her corpse, the sifting-through of her stomach contents.

At the front step he instructed CSO Payne to keep to the grass. Once the two women were back on the street he called out to the young policewoman, 'Oh, your torch. I've left it in the kitchen.'

She walked back across the grass and into the house. Jon was waiting for her. 'Did you touch anything in here?' he asked, handing it back to her.

'I don't think so. We got the mum out of the front room as quickly as we could. I brought her in here and made her a cup of tea . . .' She pointed to the draining board at the side of the sink.

Jon saw that she wasn't pointing at the sink full of dirty cups and glasses. 'Where did you find the mug?'

'Just there, sir, washed up on the draining board. Next to that other one.'

'Washed up? You mean still wet?'

'Yes, I dried it with the tea towel.'

Jon ran his fingers through his cropped brown hair in a gesture of disappointment. 'Go on.'

Aware that she was now being questioned, the officer went on more carefully. 'She smoked three or four cigarettes. Stubbed them out in the ashtray on the table.'

'Yeah, they were Lambert & Butler.' Jon looked into the ashtray and said almost to himself, 'The daughter smoked Marlboro Lights, I think. There's Silk Cut and Benson & Hedges in there, too.' The urge to light up suddenly hit him. He turned away from the ashtray and its stale smell that should have been so unpleasant. 'OK, get her to the station; we'll need her fingerprints, a DNA swab and samples from her clothes. Her fibres will be all over the body.'

'So it's definitely suspicious then, sir?' She sounded

thrilled. 'I thought she might have had a heart attack or something.'

'Don't get too excited – you're in for a bollocking from your sergeant out there. You forgot to check for a pulse. But yeah, I'd say it looks dodgy. The neighbour described her as a ravehead and there are signs of her smoking heroin in the bedroom. And whatever that stuff is blocking her throat, it doesn't look or smell like puke to me.'

As soon as he was alone, Jon went back into the kitchen. Balanced on top of the soiled glasses and cups in the sink was a bowl and spoon, fragments of bran flakes clinging to the surfaces. If the cups and glasses were left over from the night before, and the bowl was from breakfast, why were there just two freshly washed-up cups on the draining board? Had someone else been here that morning? Someone she had offered to make a drink for?

He pulled his phone out and called his base. 'Detective Chief Inspector McCloughlin, please. It's Detective Inspector Spicer.'

After a few moments his senior officer came on the line. 'DI Spicer, I hear you were the first plain clothes officer at the scene of a suspicious death. What have you got?'

'Young female, appears to have choked to death on something. We'll need a post-mortem to ascertain what. My guess is that, if we have a killer, he came in and went out by the front door. It appears the person was let in, so she probably knew them. There's certainly no sign of forced entry or any kind of struggle.'

'So you don't think the case will turn into a runner?'

'I doubt it. My guess is it will be the usual – a friend or family member. I think it should be fairly clear-cut.'

'Right, how do you want to play it?'

'Well, until we've established cause of death, there's no point panicking and calling the whole circus out. We need to photograph her and get a pathologist down to pronounce her, so we can get the body to Tameside

General for an autopsy. The scene is preserved here, so I'll call in a crime scene manager to make sure it stays that way. Then, if cause of death turns out to be suspicious, we can start worrying about calling in a SOCO and the full forensics rigmarole.'

'Sounds like a good way of playing it. Which other cases are you working on?'

'My main one is the gang hooking car keys through people's letter boxes.'

'Operation Fisherman?' asked McCloughlin. 'How many officers are assigned to it?'

'Seven, including me.'

There was a pause as McCloughlin mentally divided up manpower and caseloads.

Jon knew his senior officer was deciding whether to move him to the murder investigation. Before he could decide, Jon said, 'I'd really like to remain on Operation Fisherman, if only in a minor role, while this murder investigation is ongoing.'

'Your partner's still off with his back problem, isn't he?'

'Yeah,' Jon replied.

'Listen. It's time you led a murder investigation yourself. This one seems like it should be quite straightforward. I think it'll be a good one for you to cut your teeth on.'

'You're making me Senior Investigating Officer?'

'You've got it. Just keep me up to speed on everything.'

'And Operation Fisherman?'

'They can do without you while you get this one wrapped up.'

A mixture of excitement and disappointment ran through him. The gang stealing high-performance cars had taken up so much of his time over the last few months, but now he had his own murder case. 'Will do, boss,' Jon replied.

Next he called his base. 'Hello, Detective Inspector Jon Spicer here. We need a pathologist, a photographer and a

CSM at Fifteen Berrybridge Road, Hyde. Who's available for scene management?'

'Nikki Kingston is on duty,' said the duty officer.

Jon immediately smiled – the case had just become a whole lot more attractive. 'Send her down, please,' said Jon, flipping his phone shut and popping a stick of chewing gum in his mouth.

The pathologist and photographer arrived less than fifteen minutes later. While they were still clambering into their white suits, Nikki's car pulled up. She climbed out and went straight round to the boot, opened it up and put on a large red and black jacket that looked like it had been designed for scaling Everest in. As she walked over, the bulky garment only emphasized how petite she was and Jon found himself wanting to scoop her up and hug her.

Looking Jon up and down she said, 'You not freezing your nuts off in that suit?'

Jon grinned. 'Good to see you, Nikki.'

She was already looking at the house. 'So come on then: scores on the doors, please.'

'OK, the two CSOs over there are passing the house on a foot patrol when they hear a commotion inside. They go in to find what turns out to be the victim's mother in the front room hugging the body. One officer retires immediately to call for supervision; the other officer manages to get the mum away from the daughter and into the kitchen. I arrive, check over the rest of the property . . .'

Nikki interrupted. 'So you've been round the rest of the house?'

Jon nodded.

'OK,' said Nikki. 'I'll probably need a scraping from your suit for fibre analysis at some point.'

'No problem,' Jon replied. 'On realizing the body hadn't been checked for a pulse, I re-entered the house and, using a load of magazines for footplates, got to the body. Obviously she was dead.'

Nikki raised her eyebrows. 'Magazines for footplates? Nice bit of improvisation.'

Jon smiled briefly. 'One other thing. There's a cup on the draining board next to the sink and another on the kitchen table with a kiddy-style picture of a snail on it. They're worth bagging up as potential evidence – someone was drinking out of them recently. Problem is the CSO made a brew for the mum in the one with the snail on the side.'

Nikki shook her head. 'We'll be lucky to get anything off that.'

At that moment the ambulance pulled up, so Jon moved his car to allow it to reverse into the mouth of the driveway.

The pathologist and photographer approached the house, pausing on the front doorstep to put on white overshoes, caps and face masks. Laying rubber footplates out before him, the pathologist led the way inside. Almost immediately the front room was filled by white flashes as the photographer went about his work. Ten minutes later the pathologist reappeared in the doorway and beckoned the ambulance men in with the stretcher. Stepping carefully on the footplates, they disappeared into the property.

Nikki and Jon moved round the side of the vehicle, out of sight of the small crowd of onlookers who had now gathered.

'How's giving up going, then?' asked Nikki, still looking towards the house.

He thrust his hands into his pockets as if to stop them scrabbling around for a cigarette. 'Doesn't get much easier. I haven't had one since before the Commonwealth Games, though.'

'That's bloody good. How long is that – three months or so?'

'Yeah, about that. Did you find it a nightmare for this long?'

'Did? Still do. Though on fewer and fewer occasions. Pubs are the place to avoid for me. That and meetings about the divorce with my solicitor.'

'Your ex is still acting the prick, then?'

'Oh yes, he's really honing that skill of his nowadays.'

Jon's lips tightened in sympathy and he said, 'Well, just thank God no kids are involved, I suppose.'

Nikki let out an incredulous laugh. 'There's no way that's ever going to happen. I've seen too many friends go on Prozac immediately after they give birth. Motherhood? No bloody thank you. Anyway.' She clapped her hands together softly to end that part of the conversation. 'You're still using chewing gum. Is that to fight your cigarette cravings or to make sure your breath smells sweet for me?' Impishly, she glanced up at him.

Enjoying the game, Jon caught her eye then looked skywards, only to see Alice's face in the clouds above him. Quickly he looked down and said with a smile, 'In your dreams, Nikki – you know I'm way out of your league.'

'Cheeky bastard.' She laughed, and went to jab him in the ribs.

Jon caught her fist just as the ambulance men reappeared with the body, the pathologist following along behind. Clicking instantly back into professional mode, Nikki pulled her hand free and walked back round the ambulance. Once the body was safely inside, she got the ambulance men to sign their names in the log book for people who had entered the crime scene. Meanwhile Jon had stepped over to the pathologist. 'Any ideas?'

He pulled off his face mask and started removing the white shoe covers. 'Well, I'd say death occurred due to suffocation. All the signs are there: bluish lips, ears and nails, petechiae – burst capillaries around the eyes and on the eyeballs themselves.'

'And the white stuff blocking her airway?'

'It's not any sort of secretion I've seen. I'd say she's had the stuff pumped down her throat somehow, but until

I've seen in her lungs and stomach, I can't say for sure.'

'Can you start the autopsy?'

'Yes, that's fine. Of course, I'll hand over to the home office pathologist as soon as I can confirm it wasn't natural causes.'

'OK – can one of you call me as soon as you know?' said Jon, handing him a card.

He turned to Nikki. 'I need to get away and interview the mum. Can we completely seal the house until the autopsy result is confirmed? If it's suspicious you can arrange for forensics to come over.'

In a voice kept low so none of the onlookers could hear, she said, 'Tighter than a camel's arse in a sandstorm.'

Jon winked in reply and walked over to his car.

#

After a bit of persuasion Mrs Mather had accepted the fact that her fingerprints, a swab from the inside of her cheek for DNA testing and combings from her clothes for fibre analysis were needed. After that, she answered Jon's questions about her daughter, Polly.

Twenty-two years old, single, keen on music and clubbing, worked in the Virgin Megastore on Market Street. As was often the case with people hovering at the edge of an industry, she had ambitions for a more central role. In Polly's case she was lead vocalist of a band, The Soup.

The beer cans and full ashtrays in Polly's front room were the result of the band having been round at her house the night before. Because he had recently been her daughter's boyfriend, Mrs Mather had a phone number for the band's bass player, Phil Wainwright. She asserted that the split had been amicable – the result of Polly wanting to travel round the world while he wanted to concentrate on gigging and trying to find a record deal.

Shortly after Jon had arranged for a patrol car to take her home, his mobile went. It was the home office pathologist. The autopsy had been handed over to him because there were only small amounts of the white substance in the oesophagus and trachea, and none in the lungs or stomach. This meant it had definitely been introduced from the outside, probably while she was still alive. What was confusing the pathologist was how it could have got there. He explained to Jon that for the cough reflex not to function, a person would have to be in a coma or under very heavy sedation. In his opinion this was the case – the substance had formed a neat plug at the back of the girl's throat with almost no evidence of her choking and spluttering. Therefore, with the victim unconscious at the time of the substance being introduced, a third party had to be involved.

'So we'll need a toxicology report then?'

'Yes. If she was subdued with a hospital anaesthetic – propofol or maybe sodium thiopentone – it should be present in her blood in the form of metabolites, but I haven't found any marks so far to suggest she's been injected. Of course, in order to find evidence of narcotics, a full toxicology analysis will be needed. We haven't got the necessary facilities here.'

'Right – can you prepare a blood sample for me? I'll get it sent down to the forensic science lab at Chepstow.'

Next he called DCI McCloughlin. 'Boss? It looks like murder.'

'OK, open an incident room. Ring round and see which stations have any rooms available and I'll start getting a team together for you.'

'Will do.'

After finding a room at the divisional headquarters in Ashton, Jon decided to give Phil Wainwright a ring. As soon as the phone was answered Jon could hear loud talking and music in the background. A second later a gruff voice said, 'Hello?' It was spoken loudly, as if the person was anticipating not being able to hear very well.

'Is that Phil Wainwright?'

'Yeah! Who's this?'

'Detective Inspector Jon Spicer, Greater Manchester Police.'

'Oh, hang on.' The voice disappeared and Jon could hear only background noise until a door shutting caused it to suddenly grow fainter. 'Sorry, you caught me behind the bar. This is about Polly?'

Emotion made the last syllable wobble and Jon thought, he knows already. 'Yes.'

'I thought it would be. Her mum rang me an hour or so ago. You're going to question me, aren't you?'

'Not formally, no. But I need to talk with everyone who was at her house last night. Where are you now, Phil?'

'Peveril of the Peak. I'm a barman here.'

'Nice boozer. Any chance of chatting to you?'

'Well, the evening rush hasn't started yet, if you can get over here.'

'I'll see you in a bit.'

It was dusk as he crossed over the junction for the M60 ring road, a steady stream of cars gliding by beneath him. Following the signs for Aldwinians Rugby Club, he entered Droylsden. The perfectly straight road stretched far off into the distance, regularly interspersed by traffic lights shining red, amber or green. Flanking each side of the road was an endless terrace of the chunky red-brick houses with grey lintels that made up so much of Manchester's Victorian estates.

Abruptly the built-up area came to an end and he emerged into the open space of Sportcity, Manchester City Football Club's new stadium dominating the facilities around it. Then he was past and the road dipped, only to start rising upwards to dark mills that loomed forlorn and empty, brickwork crumbling and broken windows gaping in silent howls. Reaching the crest of the slope he could see beyond them to where the lights of the city centre twinkled, Portland Tower and the CIS building clearly visible. Jon felt an itch of adrenaline as he looked at the city and contemplated all that was happening in its depths.

Dating from the mid-1800s and one of Manchester city centre's proper pubs, Peveril of the Peak was a strangely shaped wedge of a building. Clad in green glazed bricks and tucked away on a little triangular concrete island, it was closed in on all sides by towering office buildings and apartment blocks. Jon parked by some recently completed flats and slipped through the side door of the pub. The bar was in the centre, various rooms leading off to the sides. He looked round the smoke-filled interior, surprised by the lack of people: his mobile phone had made it sound like the place was packed. Instead just a few students and real ale types were dotted about. Jon glanced over the three bar staff, eyes settling on a youngish man with about four days' stubble. He was dragging nervously on a cigarette and wearing a T-shirt from a Radiohead concert.

'Phil Wainwright?'

'Yeah,' he replied, grinding the cigarette out with a bit too much urgency. 'Fancy a drink? The Summer Lightning is a great pint.' His finger pointed to the tap marked 'Guest Beer'.

'Tempting, but no thanks,' said Jon. 'Is there a quiet room we could . . .?'

Phil lifted up a section of the wooden counter and stepped into the customers' side of the pub. 'This room's empty.'

They sat down on some ancient and battered chairs, the upholstery rubbed smooth through years of use. He pulled another cigarette out of a packet of Silk Cut and offered one to Jon.

Another show of hospitality. Another attempt to break down the occasion's formality. Slightly irritated, Jon waved it away and took out his notebook.

'So, how are you feeling?'

Flicking a lighter, Phil dragged hard on the cigarette. 'Pretty numb, actually.' Smoke crept from his lips by the second word.

Jon's eyes strayed to the tip of the lit cigarette and he reached into his pocket for a fresh stick of gum. 'Giving up,' he explained, unwrapping it and regretting the fact he had allowed Phil an angle into him as a person, not a police officer. Before the insight could be seized upon, Jon continued. 'Now, you were round at Polly's last night? What time did everyone leave?'

'Just before midnight.'

Noting this down, Jon continued, 'And was anyone else there apart from the members of your band?'

'No, just us.'

'Did anyone stay the night?'

'No, we all left together. Ade walked back with Deggs – they share a flat. I went about halfway and turned off to go to my own place.'

'How did Polly seem to you last night?'

'Fine.' He paused and frowned. 'Although she's been up to something lately. She's had the odd call on her mobile that she's been really shifty about.'

Jon kept quiet to tease another comment out of him.

'Walking off to have conversations – it was really annoying. I assumed she had started seeing someone else.'

The silence began to stretch out as Phil examined the tip of his cigarette, so Jon said, 'She was due to be going out today with her mum to do a bit of shopping.'

'Yeah, she was looking forward to it. In fact, she hoofed us all out before midnight so she wouldn't be too rough this morning.'

'Did she mention that she was expecting any visitors before her mum?'

'No.'

'OK, what are Ade's and Deggs' full names?'

'Adrian Reeves and Simon Deggerton.'

'Telephone numbers and address?'

Phil pulled out a mobile and started pressing buttons. As he did so Jon suddenly dropped in, 'Why did you and

Polly split up?' watching closely for the reaction.

Phil's finger hovered for a moment over a button as he lost his train of thought. 'Erm, we'd just drifted apart. God, that sounds a cliché, but we had. She was saving up to go backpacking round the world. I wasn't into it.'

'That's bad news I presume – to lose your lead vocalist?'

He looked up, a slightly wounded expression on his face. 'Yeah, but what could we do? It was her decision. You want those numbers?'

Jon noted them down and then drove back to Ashton police station. He removed his box from the car boot and headed up to the incident room on the top floor of the building – the usual soulless set-up of empty desks, blank monitors and silent phones. Putting the box on a corner desk, he got out his paper management system, desk tidy, stapler, hole punch and calculator, then sat back in his chair and blew out a long breath.

The place would be a hive of activity first thing the next morning: office manager, receiver, allocator, indexer, typist, all arranging their stuff on the desks; plants and other personal effects appearing, the outside enquiry team milling around, waiting to be briefed. And him, in charge of it all.

He booted up the computer, entered his name and password, then went on to HOLMES – the Home Office Large Major Enquiry System. The computer package was based on strictly designated roles and procedures in order that every large enquiry progressed in an ordered manner. It was established directly in the wake of the chaotic hunt for the Yorkshire Ripper, when it was discovered that he had been questioned on various occasions, but the paper reports had never been crossmatched.

Jon studied the search indexes, deciding whether to concentrate on any to steer the investigation in a particular direction. With the information he had at this stage, he decided the usual ones would suffice – family, friends, house by house enquiries and victim profile. He then created an additional one marked 'Narcotics/ sedatives'.

On impulse he went on to the Police National Computer's database and typed in all three band members' names.

Nothing showed up for Adrian Reeves or Simon Deggerton, but after he typed in Phil Wainwright the computer pinged up a result: two cautions for possession of cannabis, the second one accompanied by an order to attend a drugs rehabilitation course.

#

It was almost nine thirty by the time he got home. The front door clicked shut behind him, provoking the usual Pavlovian reaction from the kitchen. Paws scrabbled excitedly on the lino floor and an instant later the crumpled face of his boxer dog appeared round the corner, eyebrows hopefully raised.

Jon slapped his hands against his thighs and crouched down. 'Come here, you stupid boy!'

The dog let out a snort of delight through its squashed nose and bounded towards the front door. Jon caught it by its front legs and twisted it onto the faded carpet. Grabbing it by its jowls, he planted a big kiss on its grinning mouth, then released the animal and stood up. Instantly it regained its feet, stumpy tail wagging so violently its entire back half shook.

By now Alice was standing in the doorway to the telly room, arms folded and a smile on her face. 'Nice to see you getting your priorities right,' she said, nodding down at the dog. 'You're late back – you've missed rugby training again.'

Jon let his shoulders drop. 'New case,' he said, walking towards his partner and bending forward to kiss her.

'Not after you've just snogged that ugly hound,' she said, raising her arms and shying away from his puckered lips. 'Go and wash your mouth out first.'

'Did you hear that, Punch?' he asked the dog, feigning outrage. 'You're ugly and Daddy gets no kiss!'

From the corner of his eye he saw that she had lowered her arms. Suddenly he dipped to the side, then straightened his legs so his face burrowed upward to her throat.

Instinctively she pressed her chin down to her sternum to protect her windpipe. Giggling through clenched teeth, she said in a contracted voice, 'Get off!' A foot snaked round the back of his right ankle.

Not fully aware whether it was a play-fight or not, Punch had started up a half-anxious, half-delighted barking. Jon felt Alice's forearm forcing its way across his chest, and realized she was manoeuvring towards one of her tae kwon do throws. He broke the embrace, stepping away from her and laughing breathlessly. 'I'll have none of your martial arts high jinks in my house.'

Her feet now planted firmly apart, Alice flexed her knees and held up the back of one hand to Jon. The tips of her fingers flexed inwards once and she whispered with Hollywood menace, 'Come and try it, motherfucker.'

His eyes flicked over her combat stance and he took another step back, realizing that he'd think twice about taking on someone like that in a real life situation. 'Later,' he smiled, then looked towards the kitchen door and sniffed, signalling that the fooling around was over. 'Something smells good.'

'Shepherd's pie,' Alice answered, relaxing her posture. 'With salad in the fridge.'

'Ah, nice one, Ali,' Jon answered with genuine appreciation. 'Do you mind if I go for a quick r—u—n first?' Having missed rugby training, he was twitching for some exercise.

'Course not; I ate mine hours ago.'

Jon looked down at the dog. 'Fancy a run?'

At the word 'run' the dog let out a moan of delight and padded towards the front door, eyes fixed on his lead hanging from the coat peg.

'How was your day?' he asked as he began climbing the stairs. 'Tell me as I'm getting changed.'

'I was late for work again. The stupid train into Piccadilly was cancelled.' She followed him up to the spare room, stepping over the weights stacked on the floor and sitting down on the gym bench in the corner. Jon was standing at an open wicker unit, pulling his running gear from the assorted items of sports kit piled up on its shelves. Quickly he removed his shoes and socks, hung up his suit and returned his tie to a coat hanger that had another half-dozen threaded through it.

As he began unbuttoning his shirt, Alice said, while innocently examining the nails on one hand, 'Actually Melvyn introduced a new beauty regime to the salon today.'

Clocking her tone, Jon replied guardedly, 'Go on, what's he up to now?'

He dropped his boxer shorts to the floor and bent forward to pick up the neoprene cycling shorts he wore under his cut-off tracksuit bottoms when running. He glanced up and caught her looking meaningfully at his arse.

'It's waxing for men. "Backs, cracks and sacks", Melvyn's calling it.'

Jon digested the information for a second, then looked at her. 'You're not ripping the hair off other men's bollocks?'

She gave him a provocative little grin.

'Oh, sweet mother of God, tell me it isn't true,' he groaned, holding his head in his hands and pretending to cry. 'If this gets out I'm a dead man.' He looked at her again for confirmation that she was having him on.

Alice held his glance for a second longer, then suddenly smiled. 'Why, got a problem with that?'

'Backs I can understand. Cracks maybe at a push – but sacks? Oh, Jesus.'

'Don't worry. It's going to be Melvyn's special

treatment; he's already drooling at the prospect.' She grimaced. 'Can you imagine it? First booking on a Monday morning, pulling some bloke's knackers to the side and . . .' She yanked sharply at the air while making a ripping noise at the back of her throat.

'Don't.' Jon winced. 'It's making me feel ill. What is the world coming to? Backs, cracks and bloody sacks.' He shook his head in disbelief.

'You'd be surprised at the demand for it. And not just gay guys, as you're probably imagining. Besides, you've never objected to me doing other women's bikini lines.'

'Well, that's different, isn't it?' answered Jon, voice suddenly brighter. 'Why, any recent ones to tell me about?'

'Sad,' she replied, as Jon pulled on a running top with reflective panels at the front and back. Downstairs, he clicked the lead on his dog's collar.

'Punch, if you ever catch her creeping up behind you with a waxy strip in her hands, run for the bloody hills.'

He could still hear her laughing as he slammed the door shut.

The cold night air hit him as he ran along Shawbrook Road to Heaton Moor Golf Course. After cutting on to the grass, he kept to the perimeter, making his way round to the playing fields of Heaton School where he could do some sprints up and down the dark and empty football pitches. Rounding the corner of the school buildings, he saw a group of young lads sitting on a low brick wall, the scent of spliff hanging in the air. Having chosen to ignore them, Jon was jogging past when one of them let out a low wolf whistle. A burst of raucous laughter broke out. Jon carried on and another cocky voice said, 'I hate fucking boxer dogs.'

Jon slowed up, turned round and jogged back, Punch's claws tick-tacking on the concrete as they approached. Jon surveyed them for a second, then narrowed his eyes and lowered his voice to a whisper. 'My dog don't like people laughing. He gets the crazy idea you're laughing at him.

Now, if you apologise like I know you're going to, I might convince him that you really didn't mean it.'

From the blank silence he knew they didn't have a clue what he was on about – and certainly no idea which film he was quoting from. 'I thought you lot looked too thick to be anywhere near a school.'

Now aware he was having a go at them, they looked uncertainly at each other, wondering who would be first to speak. Jon switched to bullshit mode. 'I'm doing two circuits of these fields. Next time I pass this point I'll have my warrant card on me. If you're still here, I'll lift you.'

'You a policeman?' one asked, eyes now wide.

'That's right. And I've got better things to be doing with my free time than nicking little twats like you. But I will, if you make me.'

They started getting to their feet, joint now hidden up a coat sleeve. Without another word, Jon turned away and resumed his run.

Back home, he showered and pulled on an old rugby shirt and tracksuit bottoms. After retrieving his supper from the oven, he sat down on the sofa. Punch was already stretched out in front of the gas fire, one brown eye tracking Jon's every move.

'What's this?' he asked, looking at the telly.

'I don't know,' Alice answered sleepily, moving across the sofa to rest her head on his leg. Holding the plate below his chin to stop any bits falling into her hair, he began shovelling great forkfuls of food into his mouth.

After a few seconds he felt her jaw moving as she began to chew. He glanced at the table. Next to a jar of folic acid pills was an open packet of nicotine gum. 'You fighting an urge?' he asked quietly.

'Mmmmm,' she replied without moving. 'It came on just after you went out. First one since lunch, though.'

'That's great; well done babe,' he answered, thinking how close he'd come to sneaking a cigarette earlier that day. 'By the way, this new case I'm on . . . it's a murder investigation and McCloughlin's made me SIO.'

Alice sat up. 'That's brilliant! Why didn't you tell me before?'

Jon scratched his head. 'I was mulling it over, I suppose.'

'Why? Surely you think it's good news?'

He gave a half smile. 'It is and it isn't. It means I'm being taken off the car thief case.'

'Jon!' said Alice, holding both palms up as if weighing two objects. 'A gang of scrotes nicking cars.' She lowered one hand a couple of inches. 'And SIO on a murder case.' She dropped her other hand so it banged against the sofa. 'Come on.'

Jon nodded. 'I know.'

She settled back into the crook of his arm, head against his chest. 'That's the problem with you. You get your teeth into something and you can't let it go. What's this new case, then?'

Jon leaned over the arm of the sofa and placed the empty plate on the floor. He noticed a strand of saliva set off on a vertical journey from Punch's lower lip and make it to the carpet without breaking. 'A young woman, twenty-two, lived over in Hyde. Someone choked her to death.'

'That's so sad,' Alice murmured. Jon knew she'd be curious to learn more, but she understood that he hated bringing the details of his cases into their home. 'By the way, I heard a bit of gossip in the salon today. That guy you used to play rugby with for Stockport. Married a blonde girl called Charlotte.'

'Tom Benwell?'

'That's him. Have you seen him recently?'

'No. I had two tickets for us to see the rugby sevens at the Commonwealth Games, but he didn't show up. I ended up giving it to a Kiwi then had to sit next to him and watch as his team demolished everyone.'

'That was three months ago, Jon,' said Alice, cutting in

as he was about to start giving a blow-by-blow account of each match.

'Yeah, you're right.' He realized how time had flown by. 'But I tried ringing his mobile a few times. There was never any answer and eventually the line went dead. He must have changed networks.'

'Well, one of the ladies who comes in to get her legs waxed trains at the same gym as that little bimbo he married. She thought Charlotte had walked out on him. Something about him losing his job.'

'Really?'

'Apparently he turned up at the gym searching for her one time. She said he looked a complete wreck.'

'Fuck,' said Jon, feeling guilty. 'We went for a beer once and he told me how he was getting out of the rat race. Said he was selling up and moving to Cornwall, starting a beach cafe or something. I just assumed he'd done it and would ring me when he got the chance.'

'I think you should at least go round and see him, especially after what happened a few years ago.'

'What?' said Jon.

'What?' repeated Alice, rolling her eyes. 'When he got ill, remember? Missed half the season at Stockport?'

Jon frowned. 'That was just some stress thing, wasn't it?'

Alice shook her head. 'Men. What is it with your inability to discuss health problems? According to the gossiping girlfriends at the rugby club, he had a complete breakdown – ended up on the psychiatric wing at Stepping Hill Hospital for two months.'

'Really? He never told me it was that bad.'

'Did you ever ask him?'

'No.'

'Exactly,' said Alice, point made.

Jon sat staring at the TV screen, but uneasiness was now nagging at the back of his mind. He unwrapped his arm from Alice's shoulders.

'What are you doing?' she asked.

'Calling him.'

He got up and retrieved his mobile from the hall. He dialled Tom's mobile, but got the same continuous tone as the last time he'd tried. Scrolling to his phonebook's next entry, he rang Tom's home number. The line was also dead. 'Sounds like both numbers have been disconnected. When did that customer say she'd seen him?'

'About a month ago, I think.'

Worried now, Jon shoved the mobile into his trouser pocket and began pacing back and forth. Punch raised his eyebrows to watch him. 'I'll pop round to his house. It's only five minutes in the car,' Jon announced, looking at Alice for confirmation.

She glanced at the clock on the video. 'At ten forty?'

'I won't start hammering at his door. Just check the house over, see if it's up for sale or if any lights are on.'

#

Jon pulled out of his side street. Soon he crossed Kingsway, a main road leading into the city centre, and headed towards Didsbury. A few turns later and he was on Moorfield Road. He pulled up outside number sixteen and looked at the house. It was dark and deserted, every light turned off.

He got out of the car and glanced around for an estate agent's sign telling him the property was up for sale. Nothing. Walking up the driveway, he noted the absence of any vehicle, then crouched down at the front door. As he lifted the flap of the letter box up, he prepared himself for the buzz of flies and stench of rotting flesh. Pitch blackness greeted him, the temperature inside the house no warmer than the night air outside.

He walked across the lawn to the front window. The main curtains weren't drawn and a chink in the net curtains allowed a strip of light from the street into the room beyond. He saw bare floorboards and no sign of any furniture.

After plunging his hands into his pockets, he walked back down the drive. With each step the sense of being watched grew stronger. At the end of the drive he swivelled round, eyes going straight to the first-floor windows. For an instant he thought something pale shifted behind a dark pane of glass. But focusing on the window, all he could see was dim light from the street lamps reflected there.

Turning the mobile over and over in his pocket, Jon's mind went back to the start of the summer.

Find out more at www.chrissimms.info

Printed in Great Britain
by Amazon